Welcome to the Low Life 2

By Natavia

SOUL Publications

Welcome to the Low Life 2

SOUL Publications

*****Warning*****

This novel contains: broken English, strong language, sex, violence, and vulgar situations, which may be offensive to some readers.

SOUL Publications

Beretta

Present day, August 2017...

I was lying on the floor, gasping for air, while my wife was telling me how much she loved me. I had a feeling something bad was going to happen to me. A nigga had been living foul for many years. Before our wedding anniversary dinner, I put on a bulletproof vest. Matter of fact, for the past few weeks, I had been wearing one. Mara couldn't wear one because she was pregnant with our daughter. Honestly, I didn't think a nigga was crazy enough to touch my wife. Blood was coming from the wound on the back of my head. When the shots rang out, I shielded Mara and bust my head on the table. My vision was blurry but I saw two masked niggas standing over my wife's bloody body. Tears of regret and everything I had done to her in my past flooded my mind. All she wanted from me was a loyal nigga and I couldn't give her that. Shorty was rocking with me from when I was corner hustling to moving major weight. I thought once I reached a few million, I could stop, but the shit made me grind harder and neglect my wife. My eyes zeroed in on her stomach. Pain tugged at my heart because it was our fourth child.

"Mara," I whispered as the two masked men argued.

SOUL Publications

"Beretta, I can't hold on. I'm so sorry but I can't," she cried.

I couldn't move the way I wanted to. My head felt like it weighed a ton.

I was hallucinating, had to be because I was seeing bodies of niggas I had killed over the years. They were smiling at me because it was my turn to go. I saw a familiar face. It was my nigga, Ammo. My mind was definitely playing tricks on me.

"Yoooo, come on, Beretta. You can't go out like this, nigga. The strongest survive, remember that? Listen, bruh. Those niggas gotta pay for what they did to you and Mara. Even if you don't make it out alive, they gotta pay. It ain't your time to join me. You've come too far to get caught slippin," Ammo said before he disappeared.

I saw a gun lying next to me on the floor. It wasn't far from me but if I wasn't fast enough, they'd catch me and merk me. I didn't give a fuck about dying, but I had to make sure Mara and my daughter survived. The two masked men began tussling around and a shot rang off. I slowly reached for the gun; blood was dripping into my eyes, blinding me. When I grabbed the cold steel, I aimed at one of the masked men. I had to concentrate because if I missed, that would be the end of me and Mara. One of the nigga's mask came off, exposing his face.

What the fuck! Noooooo, my nigga, I thought.

Without hesitation, I pulled the trigger. A bullet pierced through the masked man's head and he dropped to the ground. The other nigga was ready to shoot at me, but I fired. The bullet sent him crashing through the glass table. I slowly got up and crawled to Mara.

"Baby, wake up! Come on, Mara! Get up!" I sobbed as blood dripped from her mouth.

"Save the baby," she cried.

A shot rang out and flew over my head. When I turned around, he was pointing the gun at me.

"My nigga, you really lost your fuckin' mind! My fuckin' wife?" I asked.

"I loved her! When you cheated on her, she cried on my shoulder! I couldn't wait to get older to merk your bitch ass anyway," he said.

"Nigga, you did all of this for a woman you'll never have?" I replied.

"Oh, I had her, muthafucka. I banged dat pussy out a few times. You ain't know about dat, did you? I appreciate you for puttin' me on and all dat other shit you did for me, but your time is up. You wanna know what's crazy? I wanted to be like you when I was a lil' nigga, but dat shit changed once I realized I could be betta than you," he gritted.

SOUL Publications

Welcome to the Low Life 2

"Let Mara get some help, bruh. Take whateva you want. I'll give you the code to anything you want. Just get some help for my wife," I said and he smirked.

"Naw, nigga. That bitch can die witchu," he said.

I had a quick flashback of the past and realized how fucked up I was to mess up a good thing. I loved my wife but I fell in love with the streets even more. We had a wild relationship. We fought, broke up, and I even stepped out a few times. Now here she was dying in my arms and all I wanted to do was take it back but I couldn't.

"I bet you thinkin' about how much you love her now, huh?" he laughed. The muthafucka wasn't lying. I was thinking about everything, especially our first child, Zyira. I remember those chapters of my life like it was yesterday...

SOUL Publications

Part 4:

The Streets Don't Love Nobody

Six years ago, ...

SOUL Publications

Beretta

I woke up with my head pounding, and the sunlight shining through the window didn't make it any better. Kemara was sleeping on my chest as last night came back to me. Shorty admitted to fucking that bitch-ass nigga, Tyshawn. She woke up when she felt me moving and rubbed the sleep from her eyes.

"Babe, we need to talk," she said.

I stumbled out of bed and headed towards the bathroom. The door was half-way off the hinge. Kemara followed me inside.

"Yo, can I fuckin' piss in peace? The fuck you followin' me for?" I asked.

"We need to talk about last night. You got drunk and started wildin' out," she said.

"I'm gonna start shootin' if you don't get the fuck outta my face. Matter of fact, get the fuck outta my crib. Go be with dat broke ass nigga you opened your legs for," I gritted. After I was finished, I shook my dick so piss wouldn't drip on the toilet seat. Kemara was still staring at me. What did shorty want me to say? All she did was lie and hide shit.

"You fucked Takeda and I took you back!" Kemara yelled at me.

"Shorty, check this out. I'on give a fuck about what I did in the past! I was man enough to tell you everything. Bitch, you lied to me about dat nigga wit' a straight face. Naw, I ain't feelin' you right now," I said. I flushed the toilet then took off my clothes so I could shower. She had tears in her eyes and the shit was pissing me off.

"Go ahead and cry. Fuck you and those tears on da' real," I said and she wiped her eyes.

"I'm pregnant," she blurted out.

"I guess you think that's gonna change my mind about yah hoe ass," I said. She left the bathroom and came back with a sonogram and a few papers. She handed them to me and I snatched them out of her hand.

"You ain't gotta like me right now but we are in this together. I'm not goin' anywhere. We created this baby and you hurt me, too. I may not show it, but I cried many damn nights because YOU couldn't keep your dick in your pants. So, if you want to talk about someone bein' a hoe, let's talk then, nigga, 'cause I got all day to read your filth," she said before she walked out the bathroom.

"This better be my seed. On God, I swear this better be my seed!" I called out to her.

While I was in the shower, I heard the vacuum. One thing about Mara, she wasn't a lazy female. She cooked, cleaned, and kept a nigga sexually satisfied. I was lucky to wife shorty up but her fucking another nigga was eating me up badly. I ain't gonna lie, the shit was hurting my stomach. The liquor I drank the night before came up when I stepped out of the shower. I leaned over the toilet and threw up everything I had in my stomach. Afterwards, I brushed my teeth and washed my face. Mara was making up the bed when I came out of the bathroom.

"You need to stop drinkin'," she said.

"Not now, Mara. I got a headache," I replied. She grabbed the lotion off the dresser and massaged my back. I leaned into her and she kissed the side of my face. We were still young and had a ways to go, but I already knew there wasn't another shorty out there for me.

"What are you doin' today?" she asked.

"Barbershop, then take care of a few things," I replied.

"I'm goin' with you," she said. She climbed off the bed and went into the bathroom to take a shower. Mara's cell phone rang and I snatched it off the dresser. I wasn't playing when I said she wasn't fucking with Poppa on that tip anymore. He was fresh outta jail and probably needed some money. He was going to drag Mara back into that life again and I wasn't having it. I'll merk the nigga before he had my shorty out there robbing niggas. She was carrying my seed, too, so that was a big fucking no.

SOUL Publications

"Yoooo," I answered the phone.

"Gooooooodddd morn'ting!" Silk sang into the phone.

"Aye, nigga! Don't get excited talkin' to me," I replied and he smacked his teeth.

"Anyways, where is my baby mama?" he asked.

"Ask me dat shit when I come through the hood today," I replied and he hung up on me.

"I'm gonna fuck Silk's bitch-ass up, too, if he keeps playin' wit' me," I called out to Mara.

"You can't pay Silk no mind. He's always playin'," she laughed.

"Yeah, it was cool until dat nigga ended up with a baby mama," I replied.

Minutes later, Kemara came out of the bathroom with a towel wrapped around her. I couldn't keep my eyes off her ass because it was hanging out the bottom of the towel. When she walked past me, I pulled it off and she tried to cover herself.

"Damn, it's like that?" I asked.

"No, but I'm bloated. I feel heavy this mornin'," she said. I pulled her onto my lap and wrapped my arms around her.

"Knocked up, fat and all, I still love you," I said and she blushed.

"Do you love me enough to give me some?" she asked.

"Some what?" I asked.

"Dick," she replied with a straight face.

I leaned back on the bed so she could straddle me. I should've known shorty was knocked up because her pussy was wetter than before and I didn't think it could get any better. Kemara rode my dick until I busted inside of her three times. What can I say? A nigga was pussy-whipped.

Piper

Two days later...

"You mean to tell me you really cut Poppa off?" I asked Kemara while we were doing a little shopping.

"I mean, he's my brother and I love him to death, but we both know his energy isn't what I need. I gotta focus on my nigga and this baby I'm carryin'. Oh, and let's not forget school. I finally have peace in my life. That old shit is dead to me now. If Poppa proves to me that he's changed, I'll reconsider, then him and Beretta will just have to get along," she said.

"My bitch finally came around," I replied and she smiled.

"Love, Piper. I'm in love," she beamed.

"I wish I had that," I admitted and she looked at me.

"Wait, what about Glock?" she asked.

"Our love ain't on dat level. I also don't think I can wait for him while he does that bid," I admitted.

SOUL Publications

"Technically, you're not his shorty, so you can get you a lil' sumthin on the side. You have been doin' you for a minute, so what's the problem now?" Mara asked.

"I want a relationship. Movies, dinner, late-night movie night in bed. Shit that Glock didn't give me because he was busy fuckin' other females or runnin' the streets. Hell, even Silk has a damn baby mama even though he claims he's done wit' her, but he still loves dat bitch. All of my friends have someone and sometimes I get bored. On the real, Mara, I wish my mother wasn't a crackhead. I think about her death every day," I replied.

"Awww, Piper, you know I'm always here. You can come and stay the night with me when you get bored," she said and I rolled my eyes.

"Who in da hell wants to spend the night over Beretta's house?" I asked and she laughed. My cell phone rang and I knew it was Glock. While Mara was looking through the clothes rack, I walked away to get a little privacy. His voice came through as soon as I accepted his call.

"What's up, shorty?" he asked.

"Nothin', just doin' a little shoppin' with Mara," I replied.

"Damn, tell her I said, 'congrats.' I heard my nigga knocked her up," Glock said.

Welcome to the Low Life 2

"Okay, I will, how have you been holdin' up? Is everything straight? Do you need me to do anything?" I asked.

"No, I'm good. Listen, Piper, I got some shit to tell you. I know you been wondering why I haven't been callin' much but dat's 'cause I sorta got myself into sumthin. Remember when Bridget was spreading rumors a few years back about me knockin' her up?" he said. I began to sweat profusely as I clutched my cell phone. I knew Glock like the back of my hand, so I had a feeling he was up to something. There were rumors circulating about Glock knocking up a white girl. He said it wasn't true so I ignored it.

"What about it?" I asked.

"Mannn, Piper, I swear I didn't want to tell you this but she dropped a bomb on me when she came to visit me today," he said.

"Wait da fuck a minute! How come dat bitch is allowed to visit you? I thought you couldn't have any visitors because you got into a fight. That's what was in the letter you sent me!" I yelled into the phone. The people in the store were looking at me like I was crazy.

"Yo, Pipe, calm da fuck down and let me explain. This shit is hard," he said.

"Nigga, hurry the fuck up and explain before I bang on your ass," I replied. "Bang" was another term we used for hanging up on someone.

Welcome to the Low Life 2

"We have a daughter together. I found out last year she was mine. I smashed her two more times and now she's talking about I knocked her up again. I don't stay on the phone long because I call my daughter and talk to her before I call you," he said.

"I'm so happy I got that abortion," I replied.

"WHAT!" he yelled into the phone.

"Nigga, you heard me. Since you hidin' kids and shit, you ain't gotta worry about me anymore. Why would you lie about sumthin like that? And she's pregnant again? I can't deal with this right now," I said.

"Yo, Pipe! You killed my seed and didn't tell me you were pregnant? Bitch, you foul for dat one!" he yelled into the phone.

"Just go on ahead and be wit' your family because that's exactly what da fuck you have, a damn family! It had to take for you to get locked up to tell me. I just lost my damn mother and now I gotta deal with this shit! Don't call me anymore because I'm done!" I said and hung up. Kemara paid for her clothes and rushed over to me.

"What happened? Girl, people lookin' at you like you're crazy," she said.

"Glock called me to tell me he knocked up some white girl again," I replied.

"Wait, Glock fuck wit' white girls? His hood ass?" she asked.

"Well, his mama is white. I heard the rumor before but he said it wasn't true. He's finally admittin' that he has a daughter by her and one on the way. I would've been left him alone if I knew he was knockin' bitches up. Glock is still lyin' to me; he's makin' it seem as if he only fucked her a few times. That bitch is permanent in his life. Glock isn't goin' to just fuck a girl raw. It has to be some feelings involved. I know dat muthafucka too well," I said.

"Damn, niggas ain't shit," Mara mumbled.

"The whole damn GMBAM is ain't-shit niggas," I replied.

"Move on," she said.

"I'm about to get to this money. Fuck these lames," I replied.

We did a little more shopping before we left the mall. I dropped Mara off at home and kept going. She told me I could come in since Beretta wasn't home but I didn't want to. All I wanted to do was go home and get in bed. Ammo's car was parked in front of my house when I pulled into my driveway. I snatched my bags off my seat and got out of my car. I unlocked the door and he was sitting on my couch, eating a steak sub.

"Where is Thickems?" I asked.

"Upstairs in the shower. The fuck wrong wit' you?" he asked.

"First of all, you have your shoes on and I just had the carpet shampooed a few days ago. Second of all, your fat ass is eatin' on white suede furniture. I'm just not feelin' you right now and I bet your hoe ass knew Glock had a bitch. Matter of fact, get the hell outta my house. I see why Swan can't stand y'all asses!" I yelled at him.

"DEBRAE! COME GET THIS BROAD!" Ammo called out to Thickems. Thickems came downstairs in pajamas and a towel wrapped around her head.

"What is goin' on?" she asked.

"Glock has two kids and his niggas smilin' all up in my face, callin' me their sister and shit," I fussed.

"Yo, I didn't know dat nigga had a baby mama," Ammo said.

"Oh, really, nigga?" Thickems asked him.

"You supposed to be on my side. Fuck is you questionin' me fah?" Ammo asked Thickems.

"You ain't my nigga," Thickems replied.

"Keep tellin' ya self dat bullshit. I am your nigga and will always be your nigga. Fuck is you runnin' yah mouth for?" Ammo asked her.

"Y'all ain't shit," Thickems said.

"You ain't shit, neither, shorty. Let's not forget you was just shakin' your ass down at the strip club a few months ago. I know you was fuckin' and suckin' those niggas down there," Ammo said to Thickems.

"And you were eatin' my pussy in the back room, so I guess that means you are just as nasty, muthafucka," Thickems fired back. Thickems and Ammo began arguing and I headed into the kitchen to pour myself a glass of Henny and Coke. My cell phone rang and it was Pistol calling me.

"WHAT!" I answered the phone.

"Glock wanted me to hit you up to see if you were straight. Listen, shorty, that's my right-hand man and whatever beef y'all got ain't my beef. I didn't wanna call you but that nigga got a lot on his plate and he wanted to make sure you were aight," Pistol said.

"Tell Glock to do his bid and leave me da hell alone. You don't have to call me or check up on me anymore. I'm done! And tell him I mean dat shit from the bottom of my heart. That bitch is more than a baby mama, so let's stop playin' games wit' folks' hearts," I replied.

"I understand that but, shorty, sometimes niggas get caught up. That doesn't mean he ain't rockin' wit' you," he said and I rolled my eyes.

"Make sure you tell him what I said," I replied and hung up.

Ammo was gone when I walked back into the living room. Thickems was sitting on the couch with her arms crossed.

"I can't stand Ammo's ass," Thickems lied.

"You love that fool," I said.

"I do but he deceived me. I didn't know he had all of that going on. He only told me some of it. Swan is a stalker and its takin' everything in me to not beat her ass. If I wasn't pregnant, Lord knows I'd drag her down the street and stomp a hole in her neck. I hate that bitch. She should be mad at Ammo, not me. Girlllll, she still calls him to tell him how much she loves him. One night, she called him while she was masturbating. That bitch is just insane," Thickems said.

"I'm telling you it be those good girls. Niggas always want those type of girls and can't do shit wit' 'em," I replied.

"On the real, you need to find a good guy and ride it out wit' him. Glock is just puppy love and most times we grow out of them shits," she said and I agreed.

Then again, fuck love. I'm about to stack this paper, I thought.

SOUL Publications

Poppa

Knock! Knock!

I knocked on Tyshawn's apartment door and he opened it seconds later. It took the nigga two days to get in touch with me. I had to text him from a pre-paid phone to let him know it was me. He wasn't answering when I tried to hit him up from the phone in the motel I was staying at.

"My nigga!" he said and gave me a dap hug. I walked into the half-empty apartment and he closed the door behind me.

"You just moved in?" I asked.

"Yeah, a few weeks ago. Make ya' self at home, nigga," he said. He sat across from me on the couch and began bagging the little work he had sprawled out on the coffee table.

"You got big, nigga," he chuckled.

"Jail shit, bruh. Did you talk to Mara?" I asked him.

"Naw, shorty don't fuck with me like dat. No offense, but she let me smash one time and was done with me after that. Her and dat nigga back on good terms I heard," Tyshawn said.

"Mannnn, I hit Mara up as soon as I came home and this nigga talkin' about he'll merk her if he finds out she's back to settin' niggas up. He basically told me that Mara wasn't rockin' with me anymore. I called dat bitch phone and she got her number changed on me," I said.

"Yo, don't nobody like that lil' nigga, bruh. Him and his team is gettin' hella money and other niggas who ain't down with him is goin' broke. He gotta go or at least take one of his niggas out," he said.

"I got the perfect idea. You know that nigga Mike that own the strip club?" I asked and he nodded his head.

"That's my brother," I said.

"Get the fuck outta here. That clown-ass nigga that be rapin' bitches? I heard he tried to rape Piper and Pistol fucked him up," he said.

"Yo, fuck that broad. I say we knock off GMBAM and make it look like Mike's beef since he can't stand those niggas anyway. But, first, I gotta get my name on the deed to the strip club. I'm takin' over," I replied.

"How are you goin' to do that, nigga?" he asked.

"I was locked up with a nigga named Rich. He's about to come home in a week so and he's tryna be down with me, ya feel me? Anyways, I told dat nigga to merk Sid when I give him the say so. See, Sid thinks I'm going to help Mike take down GMBAM. I'm not helping Mike do shit. He thinks I gotta better chance because my sister fuck with Beretta, but she ain't rockin' with me anymore so that shit is dead," I said.

"Whatever you down wit', just let me know. I bumped into the nigga a week ago at the club. He was lookin' at me like he knew I fucked his girl," Tyshawn chuckled.

"I gotta hit up Nika's dumb ass. Wit' me outta jail, I know Mara ain't gonna pay her anymore," I replied.

"Mara paid her upfront for a whole year, so you're straight," Tyshawn said. He rolled up a blunt and passed it to me. Someone knocked on the door and I looked at Tyshawn.

"You expectin' company?" I asked.

"Yeah, just some lil' bitch I'm fuckin'," he said. He got up to get the door. Ammo's shorty, Swan, walked in decked out in diamonds and a fur coat that hugged her frame. I always thought Swan was bad but shorty was too stuck up for my liking.

How did this nigga bag her? Tyshawn is broke, I thought.

"When did you come home?" Swan asked me. She dropped her purse on the table then took off her coat. Underneath her coat, she only had on a sleeveless see-through top with a lace bra. I ain't gonna lie, my dick was harder than a brick. I haven't had any good pussy in almost four years.

SOUL Publications

"You trust her?" I asked Tyshawn.

"What do you mean? Of course, he trusts me. Question is if he should trust you. Everyone knows you're a grimy nigga," Swan spat.

"Aye, shorty, that's my nigga," Tyshawn said.

"Umph, anyways, hurry up with him. I'm going to be waiting for you in the room," she said. She gave Tyshawn a deep kiss before she walked down the hall to his bedroom.

"Yoooo, when did this shit happen?" I asked.

"Remember that night my nigga, Shag, threw me that lil' party? Anyways, I was on my way to the bathroom and shorty was coming out of the women's bathroom. I pulled her to the side and she gave me her number. I have been smashing shorty since. I knocked her up, too," he said.

"Yoooo, word? Ammo knows about this?" I asked.

"That nigga got a girl. He fucks with some stripper bitch that be wit' Piper," he said.

"Aight, nigga. I'll get up wit' you lata. Go on and handle your business," I said. I slapped hands with him before I left out of his apartment. I opened the door to my Chevy Impala I bought the day before. I had to be careful how I spent my money because forty-five g's could go fast. I had fifty-three g's but I bought some new gear and a whip to get around in. My cell phone rang when I pulled out into traffic; it was Mike hitting me up.

"Yoooo," I answered.

"You got any info yet? The clock is ticking," he said.

"Nigga, I only been home for like three fuckin' days! You ain't gotta clock me, bruh!" I spat.

"Nigga, I'm goin' to clock you because you work for me! It's because of me your punk ass is out of the cage. Don't bit the hand that feeds you, lil' nigga. Beretta betta' be dead by the end of the month," he said and hung up.

Minutes later, when I arrived at the motel, Jasmine, the receptionist was walking out the door to the lobby. I got out of my car and called her over to me.

"What's up, shorty? Are you off yet?" I asked when she walked over to me.

"Yeah, I'm off. What's up with you?" she replied.

"Shit, I was wondering if you were tryna chill for a little bit. I can take you home lata," I said.

"Okay," she replied.

Jasmine looked better than she did when I ran into her a few days ago. Her hair was in braids and not that nappy-ass weave she had in her hair. Shorty had sex appeal and a cute face. I slid my key into the door of my room and held it open so she could walk in.

"Where do you live?" she asked.

"Nowhere right now. You know I just got outta jail," I replied.

"I know but I thought maybe you had a girl to go home to or sumthin," she said.

Jasmine was young and dumb; she sorta reminded me of Mara. She had the same thirsty look in her eyes Mara had when she was sixteen. All I had to do was throw money out there to Jasmine and she would do anything for it.

"Naw, shorty. I ain't got a girl at the moment but I'm tryna see what's up wit' you," I replied. She sat on the bed and crossed her thick legs. I sat next to her and wrapped my arm around her shoulder. Her phone rang inside her purse. She reached in to answer it.

"Hey, Tiko, I have a ride home from work, so you don't have to pick me up," she said into the phone before she hung up.

"That was my brother," she said. Quite frankly, I didn't give a fuck who it was, I just needed some pussy.

"I got some Henny in the fridge. You want some?" I asked.

"Okay," she replied.

I went into the small fridge in the corner of the room and grabbed the Henny. I poured some into a plastic cup. She was playing a game on her cell phone when I turned around to see if she was watching me. I used the Henny bottle to crush the ecstasy pill up then dumped it into her drink. After stirring it up with my finger, I gave it to her.

"I love Henny," she said.

"Yeah, me, too," I replied.

While she was sipping, I was rolling up a blunt. Hopefully the kush was going to make her roll kick in faster.

"Do you go to school or sumthin?" I asked.

"Not really a school but I take CNA classes. I'm tired of workin' at this dirty ass motel. The owner is an old Jewish pervert," she said.

"Oh yeah?" I asked.

"Yes," she replied.

"What if I can help you make more money? Would you accept it?" I asked.

"It depends," she replied.

"Naw, lil' shorty. It ain't no 'it depends' when you tryin' to make dat bread. It's either you want the shit or not. How much you get paid every two weeks? Three hundred dollars?" I asked.

"Four hundred," she replied.

SOUL Publications

Welcome to the Low Life 2

"Shorty, I can put you on to ten thou' a month and that's da minimum," I said.

"What do I have to do?" she nervously asked.

"Find a nigga dat will break bread on you then leave the rest up to me. Listen, shorty, you got a nice lil' body and a cute face but I can turn you into a bad bitch," I said.

"So, you want me to be a set-up chick?" she asked.

"Yeah, that's how most bitches in the hood gettin' it. You can still go to school and all dat, but you don't need this shitty-ass job," I replied. After I hit the blunt, I passed it to her. While she was smoking, I went to pour myself a drink. The way her eyes began to look, I could tell she was beginning to feel the effects of the pill.

"I feellllll sooooo gooooodd," she said after she passed the blunt back to me. She laid back on the bed and I laid on top of her.

"What are you doin'?" she giggled.

"You feel dat?" I asked as I pressed my hard dick into her.

"What do you wanna do with dat?" she asked and bit her bottom lip.

"What do you think?" I asked.

She sat up on the bed and took off her sweater. Jasmine's nipples and navel were pierced. She unclasped her bra and had the sexiest titties I'd ever seen. They were round, full and perky. She stood up to pull her pants off and the thong she had on was too small and gave her a camel toe but I wasn't complaining. Pre-cum was already ejaculating from my dick. Jasmine was fresh meat and she was attractive so I was definitely going to keep her around. When she stepped out of her thong, she was already wet. I could see her pussy juice saturated in her nicely-trimmed pussy hairs. I hurriedly got undressed and she went to grab a condom out of her purse. Condoms wasn't my thing but I had knocked up a few bitches already so I wasn't taking a chance.

"I don't know, Poppa. You're a little too big," she said, eyeing my dick.

"You're a big girl, aren't you?" I asked while putting the condom on. Instead of responding, she straddled me. I knew she was easy when I approached her.

"DAMN!" I groaned when she eased her wet and tight pussy down my dick. Her walls were sucking me in like a vacuum cleaner. Jasmine gripped my shoulders as she rode me. Her meaty ass cheeks slapped against my nuts as her pussy dripped down my dick. I gripped her hips to slow her down but the pill, liquor and weed had her gone. Shorty was fucking the drool out of my mouth.

"FUCK ME BACK!" she screamed and slapped my chest.

"I'M READY TO BUST, BITCH! HOL' ON!" I yelled, trying to match her pace. The headboard slammed against the wall and she began squirting on my dick.

"ARRGGHHHHHH!" I groaned as I blasted off into the condom. Jasmine climbed off and bent over so I could hit it from the back. Her fat cat was dripping down her inner thighs and her thick essence was bubbly like champagne. I snatched the condom off and went into her purse to get another one. Soon as I put it on my dick, I eased between her walls. She clutched the sheets then threw her ass back at me.

"OHHHH, BABY!" she moaned. Sweat dripped down my chest as I banged shorty's back out. I wrapped my hand around the back of her neck and pushed her face down into the mattress. With her ass tooted up in the air, I could hit shit that hadn't been hit before. Jasmine was moaning my name and pulling at the sheets while I repeatedly hit her spot. Her legs trembled and her pussy burst like a pressure cooker.

"UMMMMMMMMMM!" I moaned when the strokes got deeper and her pussy tightened around me. When she told me she was cumming again, I went faster. I didn't have any plans on pulling out any time soon.

The next day...

Me and Jasmine slept until the next afternoon. The sound of her cell phone ringing woke me up. She reached over me and grabbed her phone off the nightstand. It was a nigga and he sounded mad about something.

"I stayed over a friend's house! What is your fuckin' problem? I'm grown I keep tellin' you. Stop clockin' my moves, Tiko! I'll be home shortly, so tell Mama stop worrying," she said and hung up.

"My brother is a damn pest!" Jasmine said.

"Who is your brother?" I asked.

"Tiko but they call him, Sniper, because he's down with GMBAM," she said. I remember a nigga named Sniper that hung around Beretta. He was quiet and barely talked. The nigga was just weird. He wasn't from our hood, though, but you would've thought he was since he was always around the way.

"I don't know him," I lied.

"He thinks he's my father or sumthin. The shit is gettin' out of hand," she said.

"How about we get a crib together," I said.

"Already?" she asked curiously.

"Yeah, I can pay the bills but you have to put it in your name. Besides, we will be workin' together. I can sleep in a separate room, ya' feel me?" I asked.

"You don't have to do that. I'll just be glad to get away from Sniper. He doesn't like the niggas I have talked to. He claimed they were too hood and I needed some square-ass nigga. Our father is livin' life with his other family and I'm cool with dat. I don't need another father," she said.

SOUL Publications

Bitch, be thankful! Mara was the same way but she didn't listen to shit I told her and now she's shacking up with a nigga I want dead, I thought.

"We can start lookin' today," I replied.

Jasmine didn't know it, but everything I was getting was going in her name. All I had to do was make sure she was straight in exchange for her loyalty. Soon, she'd be telling me everything she knew about GMBAM.

"Whatever you do, don't tell nobody we stay together. I mean dat shit," I warned her.

"I won't tell a soul," she smiled. She went underneath the sheets and placed my dick inside her mouth. I stared at the ceiling fan thinking about how everything was finally working in my favor.

SOUL Publications

Kemara

"**W**atch where the fuck you're going!" I yelled at a student. He bumped into me while I was walking out of school and my text books fell out of my hand. Frustrated, I snatched my books off the ground.

"Kemara, is that you?" I heard from behind me. When I turned around, Emma was smiling at me. I hadn't seen her since we graduated. She was in my homeroom class in high school. Emma wanted to hang out with me at one point, but I didn't feel comfortable at the time. She came from the suburbs and I came from the hood. Not saying she was one of those judgmental folks, but I didn't want to find out.

"Hey, Emma. Girl, I almost didn't recognize you," I said. She used to wear glasses and her hair was always in a ponytail. Her style had changed. She was wearing a cute jacket with skinny jeans and Chanel riding boots. She was no longer wearing those big glasses she used to wear.

"Let's just say I discovered a lot of things after I left home. My mom would kill me if she saw how tight my jeans are. You look amazing. I always thought you were pretty but now you are breathtakingly beautiful. Too bad we didn't get to hang out," she said.

"High school was the worst years of my life. I didn't want to hang out with anybody, but it wasn't anything against you. What are you doing now? Wanna grab a bite to eat?" I asked.

"Sure, let me tell my boyfriend. Matter of fact, you should meet him," she said.

"Ummm, I don't know. I really don't like meeting people," I replied.

"It's the only way he'll feel safe with me going out to dinner with you. He hates when I hang out with people he doesn't know," she said.

"Okay," I replied.

We walked through the parking lot and there was a white Mercedes G-Wagon truck parked in two parking spaces. In front of the truck was a tall guy with a close cut and a full beard. He was dark-skinned and had hazel eyes. I always thought the combination was unique. I saw a tattoo on his hand and it read, *MMN*. He was part of a gang. Being around Beretta taught me a lot about gang tattoos. No wonder Emma's swag was different since high school. She was dating a hood nigga.

"Quanta, this is my friend from high school, Kemara. Kemara, this is my boyfriend, Quanta," Emma said.

"What's up?" he asked and gave me a head nod.

"Hey," I replied.

SOUL Publications

"We are gonna grab sumthin to eat. Is that cool with you?" Emma asked.

"Damn, you made me drive all the way out here from Lanham just to tell me this bullshit? Aight, hit me up later and don't forget," he said. He kissed her lips before he got inside his truck.

"My nigga would've had a whole fit," I laughed.

"Oh, trust me, he's going to have one later," she replied.

Emma rode with me to a small restaurant around the corner. My stomach was rumbling as I thought about eating a big crab cake sandwich with coleslaw and fries. Once we arrived, we waited for fifteen minutes before we were seated.

"What are you majoring in?" Emma asked.

"Business and you?" I replied.

"Accounting," she said.

"That's great," I replied.

"My parents wanted me to get into law but considering the circumstances, I chose not to. I met Quanta down in Ocean City after we graduated high school. Let's just say him and the law is on opposite sides. It was a sacrifice but I'm happy with it," she said.

"So, good girls really do like bad guys," I said and she laughed.

"That man was feeling my dorky glasses and whack-ass ponytail, so I knew the love was real. He actually fussed about my contacts and weave. Tell me about your boyfriend?" she said.

"We've been together for seven months and already are expecting our first child. Shit happened so fast," I replied.

"Wow, congrats! Is he excited about it?" she asked.

"He doesn't show emotions like that but I'm excited about it," I replied.

"Yeah, I totally understand. Quanta is the same way. He can't give me his all because he's so heavy in the streets that he brings it into our relationship. Sometimes, I have to beg him to show his true feelings. Some days, I want to leave him alone but I know I can't because I love him too much," Emma said.

"I totally feel you on that one," I replied.

"That's why I don't go home as much. I love my parents, but I love Quanta, too. They will never accept him and I don't want to pretend like he isn't a part of my life just to please them. It was the hardest decision I made," she said.

"You cut your family off?" I asked.

"No, I didn't cut them off. I talk to them every day but I cannot allow them to run my life. Until they can accept my choice in education and my love life, I gotta do what's best for me," she said. Emma made me think of my situation with Poppa. I had to do what was best for me until he could accept my choices in life. The waitress came over to take our orders with an attitude.

"Hi, what do you want to drink?" she asked Emma.

"A Pepsi with light ice, please," Emma said politely.

"We don't have Pepsi products. So, what do you wanna drink?" she asked.

"I'll take a Coke then, please," Emma said.

"And what do you want?" the waitress asked me.

"Your manager and hurry the fuck up before I cause a scene," I replied and she stormed off.

"Wow, she's a mean bitch," Emma laughed.

A few minutes later, the manager came over to our table and Emma told her how rude the waitress was to us. We ended up eating free meals and I even ordered one to go for Beretta.

"We have to exchange numbers," Emma said.

SOUL Publications

"Of course, dinner was fun. I would've ran into you sooner if campus wasn't so big," I replied and she giggled.

"I know, right. You'll see different people almost every day. I'm glad I ran into you because you're the only female I can talk to. I don't have any friends—at all. I tried building a relationship with Quanta's sister but she doesn't like me. She hates the fact that I lived different than them. I don't get that," she said.

"You're not meant to get it but us hood folks do. She probably doesn't dislike you, she's just protecting her brother. It's insecurities some people develop when living in poor conditions. I had them for a while. I was more comfortable with bein' around people who lived like me," I replied.

"So, that's why you didn't wanna go to the movies with me in high school?" she asked.

"Yeah, and the fact they would've stolen your mother's car if you came through to pick me up," I said and laughed.

"I can respect your honesty," she said as she got inside my truck. I dropped Emma off at her car on campus before I headed back to Annapolis. It had been a while since I saw Silk, so I decided to visit him.

****

Knock. Knock.

"Who is it?" Silk asked.

"Mara!" I yelled out. He opened the door butterball naked with baby oil on his body.

"Girllll, I was just in here meditating," he said as I stepped inside his apartment. There were candles lit around his living room and the pillow he was sitting on had a big greasy stain on it. I assumed the stain came from his oily ass.

"Put some damn clothes on," I said.

"And hide all of this fine silk?" he asked as he plopped down on the pillow.

"I think I came at a bad time," I said.

"Oh, bitch, hush. A big dick ain't never hurt nobody. Isn't that how Beretta knocked you up? Tuh, that should've been my baby," Silk said.

"Boy, shut the fuck up and tell me what's wrong wit' you," I spat and he smacked his teeth.

"Fushia wants me to meet her parents. I don't know what to wear. Should I wear my off-the-shoulder blouse or a button-up shirt? Kitten heels or Timbs? Bitch, I'm confused right now. That hoe had no business fuckin' me anyway. She keeps tellin' me I'm too fine to be gay. Dat lil' sexy hoe is tryna change me. I should've fucked her in the ass," he said.

SOUL Publications

"I'll help you find something to wear. When are you supposed to be meeting them?" I asked.

"In an hour. They are having family dinner at her house," he said.

"So, you mean to tell me you haven't met her parents after all this time?" I asked.

"We have been comin' up with excuses. They are church folk so I have been stayin' away. That bald spotted, spider-cricket head bitch bought me all these man clothes and tennis shoes," he said. I was ready to respond but there was a knock on the door.

"Who is it? Damn it," Silk yelled out.

"Beretta!"

"Can you please put some pants on before that nigga kills us up in here," I said and Silk rolled his eyes.

"OOOOHHHHH, SHORTY! DAMN THIS PUSSY GOOD!" Silk yelled out in a manly voice. Beretta banged on the door and a picture on the wall fell on the floor.

"Open da fuckin' door, nigga!" Beretta yelled out. Silk got up and ran down the hall to his bedroom. I opened the door and Beretta had a scowl on his face.

"Silk was just acting silly," I said.

"Oh, so you come to the hood and not hit me up? Yo, why is there candles lit everywhere? And I smell baby oil. What's good, shorty? You got sumthin you wanna tell me?" he asked.

"You know damn well Silk is my girlfriend," I said. Silk came down the hallway dressed in a pair of jeans, a blouse and Timbs.

"The fuck! You turned this nigga out, Mara?" Beretta asked.

"I wish you'd shut the hell up. I'm helpin' him with his outfit," I replied.

"What's good, fam?" Silk asked Beretta with bass in his voice. Beretta pulled out his gun and Silk began to scream like a woman.

"He still got some bitch in him. What time you gonna be home? It's gettin' late, shorty," Beretta said, putting his gun back in his pants.

"In a few, you can wait for me," I replied. Beretta sat at Silk's kitchen table to roll up his blunt.

"I don't know. Maybe you should take the eyeliner off," I suggested and Silk smacked his teeth.

"I'm not goin'," Silk said.

"Beretta, help me out here."

SOUL Publications

"For what? Tell him to wear a dress or some shit. I'on know why you askin' for my help. Can you hurry up, though? I wanna go home to eat, shit, shower then get some pussy," Beretta said.

"Where is your car?" I asked.

"I was ridin' around with Pistol today," Beretta replied and I rolled my eyes at him. Silk left the living room and came back minutes later wearing a suit with kitten heels.

"Yooooo, is this nigga serious?" Beretta chuckled.

"Ummm, Silk, honey. Fushia's daddy will baptize you if you walk into the house like that for dinner," I said. Beretta stood up and walked over to Silk.

"Straighten your back, nigga. Stop walkin' like you got titties or sumthin. And when you walk, lean to the side a lil' bit but not too much. Show me what you got," Beretta said. Silk straightened his back out and walked across the living room with a little hood bop that came naturally for Beretta.

"Aight, now take those puppy heels off," Beretta said.

"Kitten heels, baby," I laughed.

"Don't be correctin' me on this sweet shit. I'm only helpin' because I need to get the fuck home," he replied. Silk took off his heels and did the walk again.

"That's a little betta. Now go change your clothes and wash that shit off your face, bruh. Get your shit Mara so we can go. I need to use the toilet," Beretta complained.

"Use Silk's bathroom," he said.

"My nuts ain't touchin' dat nigga's toilet seat. If I use someone else's shit, your mouth gonna be open," he said.

"Go ahead and use Denesha's bathroom so I can knock your teeth down your throat," I replied.

"My fuckin' point. Hurry your fat ass up," he spat. He grabbed his gun and phones off the table before he walked back outside. When I went into Silk's bedroom, he was stepping into a pair of denim jeans. He wiped the eyeliner off his face then put on a sweater with a pair of Timbs.

"Zammnnnn, daddy," I teased and he rolled his eyes.

"Whateva, bitch. Did Beretta's fine ass leave yet? I like to piss him off so he can give me chills. Girlll, I squirted a little bit when he pulled that gun out on me," he said.

"Don't get on my bad side, nigga," I warned him.

"Sharing is caring," he joked. He grabbed his peacoat out the closet along with his purse. I snatched the purse from him then threw it back in the closet.

"Stick to the script, Silk. You're straight and masculine tonight. Just mimic Beretta or sumthin. You got this, and if it ain't enough for Fushia, let me know so I can shoot her ass," I said.

"Girl, you ain't shootin' nobody," he replied.

"Yeah, whateva. Call me lata and let me know how everything goes," I said. I grabbed my purse out the living before I left Silk's apartment. When I walked to my truck, I spotted Denesha and she was in Beretta's face. Beretta was talking to Pistol, Machete, and Ammo but she was trying to be seen. After I unlocked the door to my truck, I put my purse in the back seat. Denesha's click was sitting on the steps in front of her building so she was trying to put on a show for them. I told that bitch once before not to play with me. As soon as I was close enough, I pushed her into the fence.

"Bitch, you gotta problem or sumthin? Are you tryna disrespect me?" I asked. She got in my face but Beretta stood between us.

"Yo' ain't you knocked up?" Beretta asked me with agitation in his voice.

"Anyways, Beretta. I'll see you lata," Denesha said and walked off.

"My nigga was chillin'," Pistol said to me.

"Bring his ass home then since you wanna speak up for him," I replied to Pistol. Beretta followed me to my truck, asking me why I was tripping on him. He opened up the driver's door and I gave him the key.

"What you mad for? I ain't do shit. I was rappin' to my niggas and Denesha came over to me but I was ignorin' shorty. Yo, you be wilin' for no reason," he said.

"Denesha was bein' disrespectful but since you don't see any wrong in it, let me ask you this. How would you have acted if you saw a nigga I fucked in my face?" I asked.

"I'll dead his ass but I ain't gonna embarrass you in front of yah friends unless you were entertaining dat nigga," he said.

"You always embarrass me," I replied and he chuckled.

"That's 'cause I love you. I love you more than you love me so I can do shit like that," he said and it sent chills down my spine. He grabbed my hand and kissed the back of it.

"But don't expect this mushy shit tomorrow. I'm only bein' nice 'cause I'm tryna taste dat pussy tonight. You know what yah tight jeans do to me," he said. He placed my hand on his erection and I snatched away from him.

"You always kill the moment," I replied.

"I'm fuckin' wit' you. But on da real, I want you to ride with me tomorrow mornin' before you go to class so we can get passports. I'm tryna take my shorty across da world," he said. Tears filled my eyes and they began coming down like water. I was crying so hard Beretta had to pull over on the side of the road.

Welcome to the Low Life 2

"What's the matta? Damn it, Mara. Yo, you crazy as shit," he said and pulled me into him.

"I don't deserve this," I replied.

"Da fuck is you talkin' bout?" he asked.

"I have been a mean person to you and it hurts," I replied. There was actually more to it. Every time Beretta showed me a sentimental side, guilt set in because of the things I did and knew. Sometimes I wanted him to be mean to me so I wouldn't think about it, but all I could see was us back at the hotel room four years ago when I was supposed to set him up to get killed. It bothered me so much I got sick to my stomach. I opened the door and threw up everything I ate for dinner. For some reason, I kept envisioning his blood on my hands. Letting the past go was easier said than done. I couldn't let it go because it was haunting me in my sleep and in my thoughts. I wanted to ask for his forgiveness but how could I if he didn't know what I needed it for?

He gave me a napkin after I finished throwing up. I sat back in the seat and he rubbed my stomach.

"You ate a crab cake, didn't you?" he asked.

"Yeah and coleslaw," I replied.

"You get sick every time you eat coleslaw. Stop eatin' dat shit," he said.

"Okay," I replied.

I'm going to tell him, but what if I lose him? Oh Lord, I can't lose him, I thought. I was more afraid of losing Beretta than my past. I needed him like I needed air in my lungs. There was no way in hell I could lose him for something that happened a while ago. I knew his thought process, he would think I was still trying to set him up. Once his mind was made up, there wasn't anything anyone could do about it.

Piper

I walked into a strip club called, Fat Cat with Mara and Thickems. They rode with me to audition. The club was twice the size of Mikey's and the strippers weren't as hood. The music was mellow and boring and the majority of the crowd was dressed casually.

"You can turn this place out," Thickems said to me as she looked around.

"I'm going to own this muthafucka' by the time I get done," I replied. The owner, Delonte, came downstairs and he was looking nice and clean-cut. He looked to be in his mid-to-late thirties. He was wearing black jeans, a sweater, and a pair of black leather Timbs. He was baldheaded and had a nice beard. I sent a few of my pictures to his email after Thickems gave me one of his flyers with his information on it. He knew exactly who I was when he walked over to me.

"You're even sexier in person. Are your friends dancing for the audition tonight?" he asked.

"No, they just came to watch," I replied.

"Would you ladies like anything to drink?" he asked.

"No, we're fine," Thickems said.

"Follow me," Delonte said.

While we made small talk on our way upstairs, I couldn't help but notice the wedding band on his ring finger.

"Each girl has their own station. I'm gonna be real with you, I saw you dance at Mikey's plenty of times. I know what you can do so I'm not even trippin' about you showin' me yah kills, you feel me? All I need to know is when you can start," he smirked.

Damn, he's fine. I'm not into older men, married men at that! But Lord knows if he wasn't married, I'd put this pussy on his lips, I thought.

"When do you want me to start?" I asked.

"Tomorrow night. One of my niggas is havin' a party and I want to show you off. I'll make you very happy if you can do that for me," he said.

"What's the percentage?" I asked.

"All I want is thirty percent from you but that's between us," he said.

"I'll see you tomorrow," I replied.

Welcome to the Low Life 2

"You ain't gotta leave so soon. The kitchen is still open so you and your friends can chill out here. Don't worry about the tab, it's on the club," he said.

"Appreciate it, oh and can you please spice up the music?" I asked and he chuckled.

"Look here, shorty, a nigga is gettin' old. This gang-bang rap shit y'all listen to ain't my thang," he chuckled.

"But the crowd ain't hype. You need some Project Pat up in here. I know you know who that is, right?" I asked.

"Of course, I know. Question is, do the strippers know?" he laughed.

"Well, if they don't know, they will soon," I replied.

"I dig yah lil' style, sweetheart," he chuckled.

Delonte showed me around the three-level strip club. The upstairs was made like a penthouse suite. It had a Jacuzzi, a small stage, and a DJ booth.

"This is where the private parties go down at. It costs to get up here," he said.

"Wow. This is a big upgrade from Mikey's," I said.

"I had this built from the ground up, so the layout is the vision I had for it," he replied.

"I wanna be like you when I grow up," I joked.

"Oh, you can. You wouldn't believe half of the shit I have been through. Dedication will get you far. What do you plan on doing after this?" he asked.

"I don't know yet. All I want to do is stack my money and go from there. Who knows, I might get my own club," I replied.

"Just don't copy my layout," he joked and I playfully rolled my eyes. We headed back downstairs to the main level. Kemara and Thickems were sitting at a table in the back of the club eating Old Bay wings and crab dip.

"Ugh, pregnancy is so damn noticeable. Why are y'all dippin' wings into the crab dip?" I asked.

"Thickems got me eatin' it like this. Bitch, stop complaining and have some," Mara said. She shoved a wing into my mouth when I sat next to her. I was ready to curse her out but it was good.

"This is good. Give me some more," I replied.

"Delonte is fine, Piper. I saw how y'all were eyeing each other. Shidddd, an older nigga is just what you need right now," Thickems said.

"He's married," I replied.

"You'll meet a good nigga one day. Who knows, Glock might be a changed man when he comes home," Mara said and I rolled my eyes.

Welcome to the Low Life 2

"Fuck Glock with an infected pussy. I'm not feelin' his bitch ass right now. Two damn babies and I was so close to keepin' mine but sumthin told me not to do it," I replied.

"She wants to trade her Glock in for a Pistol," Thickems teased.

"I'm gettin' new bitches to hang wit'. I don't want Pistol's still livin' at home ass, neither," I said.

"First of all, you ain't gettin' new friends. Second of all, Pistol is far from broke so it ain't like he has to stay home. He's just a family man. I think it's kinda cute but you can't smash him anyway since he's Glock's homey," Mara said.

"You know what's crazy," I said.

"What's that?" Thickems asked.

"I don't think Glock ever loved me. I stripped in front of his friends and he didn't say shit about it 'til after he got locked up. At times, I wanted him to get jealous and tell me that he didn't want other niggas seein' my body. I was lookin' for dat shit," I replied.

"I feel you on that. Ammo gave me two choices: I stop strippin' or he blows the strip club up wit' me in it," Thickems laughed.

"I believe his fat ass, too," I said.

"Does he hit you?" Mara asked Thickems.

"Girl, fuck no! He choked me a few times, but that's because I was whippin' his ass with a broom and fryin' pan. Ammo be thuggin' out in these streets but he's really a teddy bear. I still love him, though, I'm just not ready to get back into a serious relationship with him. I like the space we have," Thickems said.

My phone rang and it was Pistol calling me. I ignored his call because he was calling for Glock. We sat at the club for a few hours before we left. Kemara went straight home and Thickems rode home with me. When I got in the house, I laid across the couch and dozed off. The drinks I had hit me hard.

****

The next day, I went to the mall to get a few things for the party at the strip club later. I was inside an erotic store where they sold whips, sex toys, skimpy outfits, and stripper heels. While I was looking for my size in a cute fur thong set, I felt a pair of hands on my ass. I almost had a heart attack when I turned around. Poppa was staring at me with lust-filled eyes and it almost made me puke. He was too fine to be the way he was. Poppa was around six-foot-one and had thick wavy hair that he kept cut low. His lips were nice and full and the punk even had pretty teeth. Jail did his body good because he used to be skinny but he was all muscle.

"Talk that shit now, shorty," he said.

"Bitch, get your punk ass outta my face before I scream. I got sumthin in my purse that'll make your body twitch," I replied and he chuckled.

"Damn, it's like dat? I thought you loved me. I mean I did break yah lil' ass in. I don't want no beef wit' you. How is Mara doin?" he asked.

"Great and that's because you ain't around," I replied. Poppa pushed me into the dressing room and closed the door. He wrapped his hand around my neck and pressed his erection into my body.

"Don't you ever disrespect me again! I'll beat your ass like I used to if I have to," he gritted. He pulled out a gun from the back of his pants and held it to my head.

"I should make you suck my dick," he gritted as he kissed my lips.

"Get the fuck away from me, Poppa," I said. He stepped back and adjusted himself.

"You gonna need this dick one day," he said.

"That will be the day I watch you take your last breath. You are worthless alive," I replied. He opened the door and walked out of the fitting room.

"Babe, I was lookin' for you," a girl said to Poppa.

"Keep a leash on that muthafucka'. He was just tryin' to fuck me in the fittin' room," I said before I stormed out of the store.

"BITCH, STOP LYIN'!" Poppa yelled.

I began screaming and pointing at him. "HE HAS A GUN!" I yelled and took off running. A few people ran with me. Security called for backup and Poppa ran out of the mall with his girlfriend behind him. I slowed down to catch my breath when I got by the food court. It must've been a "shit on Piper day" because I saw Pistol giving a white pregnant girl some money while holding a little girl that looked exactly like Glock. It was Saturday and running into everybody in Annapolis at the mall was the norm because there was only one mall in the city. I straightened myself up before I made my way over to Glock's family.

"Awww, is this your goddaughter?" I asked Pistol.

"Cut the bull, Piper. You already know who this is," he whispered.

"Hi, my name is Piper. Glock has talked about you so much," I said to Bridget. It was my first time seeing her up-close. I thought she was going to be one of those white girls who acted ghetto but she was far from it. Her blonde hair stopped at her hips and she had pretty blue eyes. Bridget was very shapely even though she was on the slim side. For some reason, I was expecting a low-budget type of broad but Bridget was decked out in labels and had a diamond necklace that read "Glock" with a gun pendant hanging from it.

"Hi, it's nice to meet you. I finally get to meet Pistol's girlfriend. She's beautiful, Pistol," Bridget said.

"Ummmm, babe. Are you ready to go?" Pistol asked me.

"Wait the fuck a minute. Who told you I was Pistol's girlfriend?" I asked.

"Glock told me. I thought you two were messing around but he told me you were Pistol's girl and that's why you're always around. I was hearing your voice in the background whenever I called his phone," Bridget said.

"Shorty, you know they are having a sale in your favorite store," Pistol said. He put the little girl down and she clung to her mother's leg.

"You two get going. And thanks for the birthday money. Rashay, tell Uncle Olijah, thank you," Bridget said.

"Thank you," the little girl said to Pistol. Bridget grabbed her hand and walked away.

"Don't even think about showing your ass, Pipe. I know how you do and I'm not for dat bullshit," Pistol said. He walked out the food court and I followed him out the mall. I couldn't wait until we got to his truck.

"Glock played me like that?" I asked.

"Y'all was playin' each other. You knew he was fuckin' other bitches and you were fuckin' other niggas. What did you expect?" Pistol asked.

"And you played right along with it!" I yelled at him.

"Shorty, check this shit out. At the end of the day, that's my right-hand man. I'm not going to rat the nigga out, but I didn't know he told her that bullshit. What did you want me to say? Oh, naw, that nigga lyin' on me? That's my brother, mane. He would've told you everything if you answered the fuckin' phone. He was tryna tell you da truth about everything," he said.

"So, you're the only one who knew about his baby mama?" I asked.

"Yeah, I guess he wanted that part of his life untouched. I fucks witchu, and I shouldn't be sayin' this but because I'm in the middle of it, I have to say sumthin. Glock is about family. His baby mama and kids come first. Ain't no sense of arguin' about da shit. You either deal wit' it or don't. We can't always get what we want. It's life, baby girl," he said.

"Me and Glock were friends before anything. He could've told me the truth," I replied.

"He cares about you and that's why he tried to hide it. Bridget is tied down to da nigga, but you ain't. If anything, he betrayed her, so don't think you got played," he said and I smiled.

"You're right. She's the one who has to deal wit' an ain't-shit nigga," I replied.

"Aight, I'll see you around and be safe," he said. Pistol got into his truck and pulled off.

Welcome to the Low Life 2

All I can do is look and not touch. I'm not tryin' to be a hoe, but shit, it's tempting. Pistol is finer than a muthafucka, I thought. The mall started to clear out because word got out that an armed man was running loose. I hurriedly made it to my car and left the mall before they questioned me about it. All I wanted was for Glock to tell me the truth. Honestly, I couldn't find it in my heart to hate him because he did help me sort out a few things in the past. One thing was for sure, it was time for Mara to know about the shit Poppa did to me. I didn't feel safe with him being out of jail—nobody was safe. Poppa was always plotting and scheming, it never failed.

Beretta

"**B**ruh, do you hear me talkin' to you?" I asked Pistol. We were chilling at my condo in the city discussing a few moves. I wanted Mike and every nigga under him dead after he gave me the money he owed me.

"Yeah, nigga, I heard you," he said.

"I need yah attention, nigga. I'm thinkin' about an old-fashioned club sweep," I replied and he chuckled.

"I see dat old Beretta is back. Welcome home, bruh," Pistol chuckled. The old-fashioned sweep was walking up in the club and merking anybody who was down with Mike. Six of us could go in and get the job done in a few minutes before the cops came was how I saw it.

"Nigga, fuck is you talkin' about? I never left home," I said and slapped hands with him.

"Let me holla at you about sumthin," Pistol said. He was always on joke time so hearing him sounding serious had my full attention. I sat on the couch across from him.

"What's good, bruh?" I asked.

"Glock got me caught up in some bullshit. I mean dat's my right-hand man, but he told his baby mama Piper is my shorty. She was hot about dat shit earlier. Piper a bitch sometimes but she's cool people. I basically wanna tell da nigga I'm done wit' da bullshit. I'm out here takin' care of shorty, payin' her bills, and I get up when she needs sumthin. Bruh, I'm doin' shit for her dat he neva did. I told him I'll look out for her but this is too much. She got comfortable with it, too. She'll text me and ask me why I didn't hit her up if I don't call her," he said.

"Damn, nigga. Are you fuckin' her, too?" I asked.

"Be fa real, bruh," he said.

"I'on know what y'all niggas got goin' on but ain't none of y'all niggas takin' care of Mara like dat. I don't give a fuck if I'm dead and buried, nigga. Glock got you out here wifin' his shorty up and he don't even realize it. Dat nigga trippin," I replied.

"All dat nigga is doin' is tryin' to keep his spot for when he come home. He keeps gettin' into shit in jail. He got caught with a shank in his cell," Pistol said.

"Glock do be wilin'. Want me to holla him?" I asked.

"Naw, I'm good. I'll rap to da nigga the next time he calls me. I got this lil' shorty I have been chillin' wit', though," he said.

"Nigga, stop playin'," I replied.

"I'm serious, bruh. I mean, she's not on the wifey level but I think I can give her the personal cell number now, ya feel me?" he asked.

"Piper gonna fuck you up," I chuckled.

"Yeah, aight, nigga. You got jokes," he said. Ammo came out of the bathroom holding his stomach. Pistol covered his nose and I hurriedly opened the window.

"Nigga, what the fuck did you eat? A dead crackhead's pussy? Yo, take yah bitch-ass home. You know I haven't been breathing right since I got stabbed," I said to Ammo.

"Fuck you, yo. You stay talkin' shit," he said.

"Dat's why you ain't got no bitch now," I replied.

"But your shorty stays eyeing my print, though," he said.

"Nigga, that's a hernia," I replied and Pistol chuckled. Someone knocked on the door and I grabbed my gun off the table.

"That's Moesha. I told her to bring some liquor and pizza over here before she went home," Ammo said.

"Mannnn, you trippin'. I told you I didn't want nobody to know about my fuckin' crib, nigga!" I said.

"She's family, chill out!" he said. Ammo opened the door and Moesha walked in dressed like she was going to a club. I ain't gonna lie, shorty was looking right in her sweater dress. She walked over to me and kissed my cheek.

"Ain't nothin' but niggas up here, Moe. You gotta bounce," I said to her. She rolled her eyes at me and sat on the couch. Moesha was a cocky female. She had good pussy and a good job. I had a strong thing for her when I was a little nigga but it wasn't love. She was the first girl I fucked so she turned me out. I thought about how much I was betraying Mara every time I looked at Moesha's thick thighs.

"You can sit next me. Damn, nigga, I don't bite," Moesha said.

"Where is your nigga at? You moved back to Maryland?" Pistol asked.

"No, I didn't move back to Maryland. I just like visiting on the weekends, smart ass," she spat.

"Get yah sista, bruh, before I hurt her feelings," Pistol said to Ammo.

"Where Ebo at?" Ammo asked Moesha.

"We are on a break right now. Dat nigga can't stay away from those nasty-ass strippers. What's up with y'all niggas fallin' for strippers anyway?" Moesha asked Ammo.

"'Cause some of y'all high saddity broads think we owe y'all sumthin. Give me a broad dat knows about my struggles. I'm not sayin' all of y'all are like dat, but most of y'all be expecting too much because y'all got fancy ass jobs. Stop fuckin' street niggas if you want a husband type of nigga, ya' feel me?" Ammo asked.

SOUL Publications

"I like all kinds of bitches. Soon as a broad start clockin' my moves, I cut her off. I'on like dat police type of shit," Pistol replied.

"How do you feel about this, Beretta?" Moesha asked.

"About what?" I replied.

"Would you wife a stripper?" she asked.

"Naw, I'm too selfish for dat bullshit. My shorty will get merked for showin' off my pussy," I replied and she rolled her eyes at me.

"I heard Mara was a stripper, too," she said.

"Mara was just tryna piss me off. She knows betta. Besides, I knocked her up so she ain't doin' none of dat bullshit," I replied.

"Pussy-whipped ass nigga," Ammo chuckled.

"Says da nigga with two baby mamas," Pistol replied.

While they were talking shit to each other, Mara called my phone. I went to the bedroom so I could talk in private.

"What's good?" I asked.

"What time are you comin' home? I cooked dinner for you," she replied.

"I'm rappin' to my niggas right now. I'll be home in a bit so be ass-naked when I come in da crib. I'm gonna spread yah ass like peanut butter, girl." Mara burst out laughing into the phone.

"That sounds nasty," she giggled.

The door opened and it was Moesha. I knew it was going to be some shit because Mara was still on the phone.

"Where is your bathroom?" she asked.

"Down the fuckin' hall. Damn, shorty, you can't knock?" I replied.

"Don't get cute, Beretta. The shit I taught you is probably why these lil' bitches are actin' crazy now," she replied before walking out the bedroom.

"Who is that?" Mara yelled into the phone.

"Moesha, she stopped by to holla at Ammo. I'll be there in a few," I replied and she hung up. Pistol was gone when I went back into the living room and Ammo was on his way out the door.

"I gotta take Thickems some money. I'll holla at you lata," he said.

"Moesha is still here, nigga," I replied.

"Stop bein' paranoid. Tell her to go home when she comes out the bathroom," he said. He grabbed the box of pizza off the table before he left out my crib. Moesha came out the bathroom only wearing a bra and boy shorts. She walked over to me and wrapped her arms around my neck.

"I just want it one last time. Is that too much to ask? I know you want it, too, because your eyes betray you every time," she said. Moesha reached in to kiss me but I pulled away from her.

"Go home, Moe. I'm not tryna fuck you. Hurry up and put your clothes on before my shorty pop up over here. She already heard you," I replied.

"I'm not used to you rejecting me," she said.

"Get used to it because I'm not fuckin' you. Hurry da fuck up so I can go home and eat. You shouldn't be here anyway," I said. She stormed off down the hall to get her things. A few minutes later, she left out of the crib with the door slamming behind her.

Damn, Mara is gonna be trippin' on me when I walk in da crib, I thought.

****

It took me twenty minutes to get home. Mara was sitting on the couch in the living room reading a textbook when I walked into the crib.

"So, you did fuck Moesha," she said without looking up from her book.

"Yeah, when I was younger but I haven't touched dat broad in years. I know you ain't trippin' about dat bullshit," I replied. She closed her textbook then slammed it down on the coffee table.

"I don't like her. I heard what the bitch said," she seethed.

"You can't be gettin' mad at dumb shit while you're pregnant. I'm not fuckin' around," I said. She walked over to me and smelled my neck.

"How close were y'all or did you just happen to bump into her? I smelled her perfume as soon as you walked in. She hugged you or sumthin?" she asked. Instead of arguing with her, I just walked away. I didn't like to argue about nothing, especially if I didn't do shit. Mara followed me into the kitchen with a scowl on her face.

"Nigga, you must've smoked too much weed before you came home. You got amnesia or sumthin? I asked you why you smell like her," she said.

"She hugged me and kissed my face. What else you want me to say? I fucked her? I didn't touch her at all, so stop questionin' me," I replied.

"Umph," she said and walked out the kitchen.

Mara made fried fish, greens, baked macaroni and cheese with corn bread. I noticed the food wasn't touched, so I made her a plate, too. She was waiting on me to come home to eat with her. We argued a lot, but shorty was slowly changing me. I left the house to do what I had to do then went straight home to Mara. She was sitting in the living room when I took her the plate.

"I'm not hungry," she said.

"You still mad?" I asked.

"Yes, mad that I can't whip Moesha's ass. She's being disrespectful and on purpose," she said. While she was talking, I stuck a forkful of macaroni in her mouth. She ran to the bathroom once she swallowed the food. I followed her into the bathroom to check up on her.

"My stomach doesn't like macaroni anymore," Mara said while leaning over the toilet. I wet a rag for her and she wiped her face off.

"Go ahead and eat. I'm gonna take a shower then go to bed," she said. Mara was still mad about the Moesha situation. I couldn't blame her, though; me and her didn't like to let shit go. We were too much alike and it caused us to beef a lot but loved each other harder. After I ate and put the food away, I took a shower. Mara was sound asleep when I got out. I pulled her closer to me then placed my hand over her stomach. Truthfully, I think I was more excited about the baby than she was. It gave me something to look forward to in the future. I couldn't be a dope boy forever.

Poppa

Me and Tyshawn was chilling inside of Mikey's while a few bad-ass strippers entertained us. As much as I loved pussy, it was the furthest thing on my mind. A stripper named Caramel walked into our section. She sat on my lap and wrapped her arm around my neck.

"Are you tryna go to the back room?" she asked.

"Naw, I'm good. Where is Mike at? We been waitin' on dat nigga for an hour," I replied and she smacked her teeth.

"He's upstairs handling business. While he's doin' him, we should do us," she said.

"I said I'm straight. Go upstairs and tell dat nigga to hurry the fuck up!" I replied. She got off my lap and walked out our section.

"I think dat nigga is bluffing on you, bruh," Tyshawn said. Mike came down the stairs with a few niggas following behind him. He told the strippers to leave out the section so we could talk.

"About fuckin' time, nigga," I said.

"I'm gonna keep takin' my time as long as dat fuck-nigga keeps walkin' around," Mike spat.

"I came here to talk business. I think we should focus on takin Beretta's niggas out first," I replied.

"Nigga, do it look like we got time for dat?" Mike asked.

"Kill Beretta first and his whole gang is gonna start a street war. Niggas gonna bring it in here because everybody comes here. Your club wouldn't last a week if we killed dat nigga first. It ain't the move to make right now. It sounds good but the aftermath is gonna cause a lot of shit," I replied.

"The lil' nigga does have a point," Mike's homeboy Skibo said.

"Do what you gotta do. I just want those niggas gone," Mike said.

"The plan was to get rid of Beretta. It's gonna cost extra if you want me to help you take down the whole team," I replied.

"WHAT!" Mike yelled.

"You heard him, nigga. It's gonna cost you more unless you're willing to deal with the aftermath," Tyshawn said.

"All of this to kill one lil' bastard?" Mike asked in disbelief. The nigga was dumb if he thought we could just kill the leader of GMBAM and get away with it.

"What do you want?" Skibo asked.

"I want a small ownership of this club," I replied and Mike shook his head.

"Sid ain't goin' for dat!" Mike said.

"Let me holla at this nigga in private," I said to Tyshawn and Mike's small crew. I waited until everyone left the section before I ran down my plans.

"Is Sid's life important to you?" I asked.

"Nigga, what?" he replied.

"Come on, bruh. Don't tell me you care about dat punk-ass nigga," I chuckled.

"Sid still got clout in da streets," he said.

"And what does dat mean? Fuck him and his goons. What's da point of knockin' off Beretta if a muthafucka is still gettin' a cut off your money? This place wasn't shit up until a few years ago. You put work into this club, not dat nigga," I replied.

"He's untouchable in prison. I wanted him dead for a while but couldn't find a person bold enough to do it," Mike whispered.

SOUL Publications

"I gotta nigga named Rich who is in da same prison. He gets out in a few weeks. He got a family to feed, ya feel me? So, he ain't gonna do it for free," I replied.

"You make dat happen then we can talk business," Mike said. I slapped hands with him before I walked out the section. Tyshawn was outside smoking a Black & Mild when I walked out the club.

"He's down wit' it?" Tyshawn asked.

"Yeah," I chuckled.

"It was dat easy, huh?" Tyshawn chuckled.

"Nigga, I got a gift when it comes to talkin'," I replied. My phone rang and it was Nika. I had called her a few days ago and even sent her a text message but she was just now responding.

"What the fuck do you want?" Nika yelled into the phone when I answered.

"What do you think? I wanna see my daughter," I replied.

"You gotta be shittin' me. You wanna see her for what?" Nika asked.

"Because I want to! I'm tryna spend time with all my kids. We can meet halfway or sumthin," I replied.

"I don't think you are capable of being a positive role model in Hope's life. She's a special needs child and doesn't need shit from you but money for her care," Nika replied.

"I just wanna see her, damn. You ain't gotta be a fuckin' bitch about it. Nobody told you to fuck a young nigga anyway. Your slut ass can't put all of this on me. How does it feel givin' da pussy to a nigga that can be your son?" I asked.

"Say what you want, but you have an issue with my son. Therefore, you have an issue with me," she said.

"Shorty, ain't nobody trippin' over Beretta. Dat lil' issue is dead to me. I'm just tryna stack my money. How much do you want, Nika?" I asked. If I could get Nika on my good side, it could work out for me. She talked a good game but shorty was, and will always be, a money-hungry bitch. That's how she ended up with Hope in the first place. The line grew quiet on her end. I knew shorty was going to give in once money was involved.

"I live in New Jersey," she said.

"We can meet in Delaware tomorrow," I replied and she hung up on me.

"Damn, you got some shit witchu," Tyshawn said as we headed towards his whip.

"Whateva, nigga. I'm just tryna keep my enemies close. Nika will always be a hoodrat. I can buy her loyalty so she can be on my side. It ain't like she been a good mother to dat nigga anyway. I heard one of her old niggas had Beretta packaging up his work when he was a lil' nigga and Nika was cool wit' it," I replied.

Everything was slowly getting put into motion. Sid was going to get merked so Mike could give me part ownership. Mike thought I was riding with him but truthfully, I wanted him dead, too. The club was going to be all mine.

A half an hour later, Tyshawn dropped me off at the motel. I couldn't wait until my condo in Jasmine's name came through. Speaking of Jasmine, shorty was dick whipped already but she was tolerable for the time being. She was clingy and wanted to go everywhere with a nigga. She was sitting on the bed, talking on the phone, when I walked into the room.

"Damn, shorty. Don't you work downstairs?" I asked.

"Girl, let me call you back," she said into the phone before she hung up.

"Is it a problem? And, besides, I'm off. Where are you comin' from? It's late," she said. I walked into the bathroom and she followed me. Lolly was the same way, wouldn't let a nigga take a piss in peace.

"I was at the strip club," I replied.

"Why?" she asked.

"Why do most niggas go to da fuckin' strip club, Jasmine? I went to see some ass and titties," I replied.

SOUL Publications

"What's the matter with you?" she asked.

"Nothin' but you are bugging me right now. We just havin' fun with each other and you are about to fuck it up. Stop being so fuckin' clingy, bruh," I spat.

"Whateva, I'm gone," she replied. She grabbed her purse and jacket before she stormed out of the room. I took my clothes off and laid across the bed. I ain't going to lie, it felt weird being home and not being able to talk to Mara. Not once did she reach out to me and that's what hurt the most. She chose that muthafucka over her own flesh and blood. It was cool, though, because she was going to need me before I needed her. There were other dumb bitches out in the city who wouldn't mind doing what she did and could probably do it better. Kemara's biggest mistake was falling in love with a lick.

****

The drive to Delaware wasn't a long one. Nika was meeting me at Christiana Mall. I sat in my car and smoked a blunt waiting for her to pull up. She texted me and told me she was driving a white Mercedes truck. While I was waiting, my other baby mama called me. Sharonda was a bitch. I smashed just because she had a nice phat ass. Her face was trash and her hygiene wasn't all that. Shorty didn't stink but she didn't shave. She had a hairy pussy, legs, and underarms. She was a dread head but never had them re-twisted. My son by her was four years old. She had him a few weeks before I got locked up.

"What, Sharonda?" I asked.

"Lil' Kamar is sick and I thought you said you was gonna take us to the doctor's," she screamed into the phone.

"Catch the bus, bitch! I'm not nowhere near Annapolis!" I yelled back into the phone.

"You're a deadbeat!" she screamed.

"Deadbeat this dick and get the fuck off my line. I told you I'm not doin' shit for dat lil' nigga until I find out for sure he's mine. I'm brown-skinned and you're dark-skinned. How in da fuck is dat lil' nigga light skin with hazel eyes? Run me a blood test, shorty, but until then, I do what I feel like doin' and right now I don't feel like doin' shit for you," I replied.

I had two other kids, but they didn't look like me. Crazy how I didn't know about them until I started getting money and flossing on niggas. Sharonda didn't tell me she was pregnant until she saw me driving through the hood in a brand-new Expedition. My other baby mama moved out of Maryland and I hadn't heard from her since I got locked up.

"I'm puttin' you on child support," Sharonda said.

"Bitch, go shave and wash your hair. You don't do shit all day but eat onion pickles and smoke weed. Fuck outta here," I replied and hung up. A white Mercedes truck parked next to my whip. Nika rolled down the window. She had me stuck in a trance because of her natural beauty. She was one of the most beautiful women in the city. She cut her hair off and dyed it red. The hair-cut showed off her Asian features even more. Somebody was taking good care of her because I knew she wasn't working. Nika had diamonds dripping from her neck and ears. I got out of my car to get in the passenger seat of her truck. I looked in the back seat and the car seat was empty.

"Are you tryna play me?" I asked.

"Naw, Hope is in the mall with her nanny. I had to make sure you weren't with the shit. Now, run me my money, Poppa," she said. I went inside my pocket and pulled out a stack. I wasn't tripping considering I thought it was an investment. Nika counted the money before she placed it inside her purse. That's when I saw she was strapped.

"You ridin' around here with a gun in yah purse?" I asked.

"Only when I'm meetin' grimy niggas. You only gave me four thousand dollars," she said.

"And? I know Mara gave you some money already. You can manage off dat until I see Hope. Now, take me to her," I replied. She got out of the truck and I bit my bottom lip. Nika's ass was phatter. She was on the slim side when I smashed her but she must've gained baby weight. I got out of the truck and followed her inside the mall.

"I wish you'd stop starin' at me," Nika spat.

"Why you gotta be a bitch all of da time? I'm just admirin' my baby mama," I replied. Shorty gave me a dirty look, the type of look that wanted to kill a nigga.

"They are in the food court," Nika replied.

I followed Nika to a table where a woman was holding a little girl.

"I have it from here, Amona," Nika said to the nanny. Amona grabbed her purse and walked away from the table.

"Can I pick her up?" I asked Nika.

"Isn't that why you came here?" she replied.

Hope laid on my shoulder and closed her eyes after I picked her up.

"She's tired," Nika said, rubbing her back.

"She looks like Mara when she was a little girl. Beretta doesn't know about this?" I asked.

"No, he doesn't, and I want to keep it that way," Nika replied.

"He's gonna find out sooner or later. I guess you think I don't wanna see my daughter," I replied and she chuckled.

"You're up to sumthin and I hope damn well it doesn't involve my son. I'll hand you over on a silver platter if you are even thinking about bringing any harm to him," she said.

"I ain't worried about dat nigga. I'm on some other shit. I'm tryna get this paper," I replied. She took Hope from me and held her closely to her chest.

"I hope you pay your sister back for givin' me the money for Hope. You'll be a ain't-shit ass nigga if you don't," Nika said.

"I'll always be an ain't-shit nigga. Shit ain't gonna change. I'm only loyal to myself. I gotta bounce, but I appreciate you for bringin' Hope to see me," I replied. I kissed Hope's forehead and snuck a kiss on Nika's lips.

"Dirty-ass nigga," Nika said as she wiped off her lips.

"It doesn't matter. You let this dirty-ass nigga smash, though," I replied before I walked away.

When I got inside my whip, I called up my nigga Rich. Janet, the C.O. I was smashing when I was locked up, snuck a cell phone to Rich's cell. Janet thought I was going to be with her when I was released from prison. I told her I was moving in with her as soon as I finished spending time with my family. I was only kissing her ass until Rich was released from prison because I needed Janet to help get rid of Sid.

"Yooo," Rich answered.

"Remember what we talked about before I came home? Well, it's time, bruh," I said.

"Aight, bet. I'll take care of dat tonight. Don't fuck me over, bruh. My family gotta eat, ya' feel me?" he asked.

"I gotchu," I replied.

Rich was a ruthless nigga. He shanked a few dudes while we were in prison and never got caught. I needed someone like him on my team. He was down for anything as long as the price was right.

"One," he said before he hung up the phone.

Driving home to Annapolis gave me time to think. I wasn't regretting anything I was doing. It was a dog-eat-dog world and a nigga was starving.

Kemara

"**Y**ou might have to slap her one good time," Piper said while stuffing chips in her mouth. We were sitting around Piper's living room, eating snacks and watching TV. I couldn't keep myself from telling them about Moesha coming on to Beretta.

"If I smack her, I will have to smack my nigga, too. It would only be fair," I replied and Thickems laughed.

"Beretta loves you. He ain't doin' nothin'," Piper said.

"I know it's not him. I don't trust Moesha. That silly slut is rubbin' me the wrong way. All of a sudden, she's showin' face and I think it's because of Beretta's pockets. She had him before me so why the bitch been quiet up until now? I got pregnant at the wrong time because I feel like slicing that bitch's throat."

"Ugh, let's talk about sumthin else before I get mad," Piper said. A horn blew from outside and it was Ammo picking up Thickems. She grabbed her purse and jacket before she left out the house.

"I think they are back together. She's wit' dat nigga every day," Piper said.

Welcome to the Low Life 2

"They are tryin' to work it out," I replied.

"I've been meanin' to tell you sumthin but I didn't want to bring it up around Thickems. We can finally talk since we're alone," Piper said. I sat all the way up on the couch so she could have my full attention.

"I ran into Poppa at the mall a few days ago. He pushed me into the fittin' room and harassed me. That's not the first time he put his hands on me. A few years back, he whipped my ass really bad. I lied to you and told you it was someone else. I don't trust him being home," she said.

"Why didn't you tell me back then?" I asked.

"You couldn't even defend yourself when it came him so what would you have done for me? He had you wrapped around his finger. You looked past so many of his flaws and found an excuse for everything he did. I couldn't risk losin' my only friend, so I kept it to myself. Let's face it, it would've probably ruined our friendship," she admitted.

"That's a serious situation. I would've cut him off because you know how I feel about niggas beatin' on women. He was wrong for what he did to you and I damn sure wouldn't have taken his side. I'm ready to call his bitch-ass up right now," I said, reaching for my phone but she snatched it from me.

"Naw, don't call him. He's going to try and turn it around so you can get back on his good side. We don't need him in our lives because he's still the same grimy-ass nigga," Piper replied.

"I'm mad at you for not telling me. We are sisters and if a nigga hurt you, I'm supposed to know every detail. I swear I'm a ticking time bomb. If it ain't one thing, it's another," I said.

"I should've told you a long time ago but seein' him in the mall made me realize that I couldn't hold it in any longer. He was wit' some young girl that looked familiar. Who knows what he has her doin'," Piper said. The front door unlocked and it was Pistol walking in with Chinese food.

I rolled my eyes at him. "The fuck wrong wit' you?" Pistol asked.

"Your face," I joked.

"Yeah, whatever. I should dump your food on the floor," he said. Piper said she ordered Chinese food for us but I thought she was having it delivered. Pistol went into the kitchen to put the food on the counter. I shook my head at Piper because it was obvious what she was doing. She was taking advantage of Pistol's kindness and he was letting her.

"Girlllll, you need to stay away from Pistol. I can't believe you," I said.

"He was by a Chinese carry-out and he has to drive past here to go home, so why not? It's not that deep," she lied. There was a knock on the door and Piper looked at me.

SOUL Publications

"I don't know who that is," I said. She looked out the window and smacked her teeth.

"Some bitch is knockin' on the door," she said. She snatched the door open and a pretty light-skinned girl walked in. She was a little on the heavy side but was proportioned right with a big shapely ass.

"I'm sorry but can I use your bathroom? I tried to hold it but I couldn't. I'm Lezzi by the way," she said to Piper.

"Pistoolllllll!" I called out to him. He walked into the living room eating an egg roll.

"You left me in the truck so you could come in here and eat? I told you I had to go to the bathroom!" Lezzi yelled at Pistol.

"So, this is your girlfriend?" Piper asked Pistol. I smacked my teeth when he didn't answer right away. Pistol was acting like he got caught cheating.

"Yes, I'm his girlfriend. I wasn't expecting it to be just females in here," Lezzi said and mugged Pistol.

"They are like family, so chill out. Can she use your bathroom?" Pistol asked Piper.

"The toilet is broke," Piper snapped.

"The one in the hallway upstairs works," I spoke up.

"Thank you," Lezzi said and went upstairs. Piper rolled her eyes at me and I whispered we were even.

"Why y'all unhappy muthafuckas gotta be rude?" Pistol asked.

"Don't get jumped," I replied.

"We didn't know you had a shorty," Piper said.

"It ain't serious yet. Matter of fact, why does it even matter to you? Aren't you strippin' again?" Pistol asked with an attitude.

"Y'all sound like y'all fuckin' or sumthin," I chuckled.

"SHUT UP!" they said to me and I giggled.

"You already know I don't like strangers comin' to my house. Who told her she was welcome and she betta not be takin' a shit, neither," Piper said.

"This is my crib, shorty. I pay the bills in this muthafucka," Pistol replied back.

This is some dysfunctional shit goin' on. This is tooooo messy, I thought as I watched them argue. Lezzi came down the stairs and I could tell she was uncomfortable. Hell, I was uncomfortable, too.

"I'm ready to go and now!" Lezzi said to Pistol.

"I'll be out there," Pistol said. Lezzi walked out the house and slammed the door behind her. Piper was ready to go outside and check her about slamming the door but Pistol grabbed her arm.

"Chill out, damn," he said.

"I'm fine," Piper said.

"Aight, I'll get up wit' y'all lata. Oh, and don't hit my phone up until you know how to talk to people. I'm ready to start taxin' your dumb ass. I was supposed to take Lezzi to dinner and ended up bringin' y'all some food," Pistol said.

"You ain't bring me nothin'. That was all Piper," I laughed.

"Ah-kee-kee-kee. Shit, ain't funny wit' yah big forehead ass," Pistol replied.

"You betta go out there before Lezzi gets mad at you again," I replied.

"Don't hit me up, Piper, and I'm fa real, shorty," Pistol said and she waved him off. I couldn't wait to dig into her after he left.

"Wait a minute, bitch. Pistol has a house key?" I asked.

"Yeah, in case of an emergency," she said.

"What kind of emergency?" I laughed and she threw a pillow at me.

Welcome to the Low Life 2

"You wouldn't understand," she replied.

"And you think I keep secrets?" I asked and she rolled her eyes.

"I think I like him," she admitted.

"You know I'm all for your happiness but this can ruin Glock and Pistol's friendship. Pistol is a loyal dude, so it will mess up his character," I replied.

"You can't put candy in front of a child and expect them to not touch it. Glock's simple-minded ass told his baby mother that I was Pistol's girl, and let's not forget, Glock wanted Pistol to look after me. What did he think was gonna happen? Trust me, I don't want them to beef but I can't deny the sudden attraction I have for dat nigga. Glock needs to understand he played a part in this, too, damn it. Plus, I'm just a little pissed off at Glock right now, so my attraction to Pistol might go away. I wish I would've known he had all of this shit going on. It makes me feel like I meant nothin' to him at all," she replied.

"How about you start datin' again? I'm sure it will all go away," I replied.

"I don't wanna date anyone right now. Pistol is spoilin' me," she said and we burst out laughing.

"Guard your heart," I replied.

"Or maybe we can hook up. I always thought you had a thing for me anyway," she joked.

SOUL Publications

"Bitcchhhh, I doubt if you can dig in these guts and make me cry. Carry on, chile," I replied. Beretta called me and I answered on the first ring.

"Whatchu want?" I asked.

"Don't fuck with me, shorty. Where you at? I thought you wanted to go to da movies," he said.

"I'm over Piper's house," I replied.

"Tell her ass you gotta nigga so you ain't got time for her anymore. I'm horny and I'm tryna dig up in your stuff while you watch the movie. Plus, she startin' shit wit' my niggas and I'on want you in dat," Beretta said.

"I'll be home in a few," I replied.

"I'm ready to come and scoop you since I'm in the area. I'll get one of my niggas to bring your truck home lata," he said.

"Okay," I said, smiling. Piper was looking at me with her arms crossed when I hung up the phone.

"I know his ass said sumthin smart," she said.

"He thinks you're startin' shit between Glock and Pistol," I replied and she smacked her teeth.

"I'm not worried about Beretta's crazy ass. It ain't like he's a saint. Hell, none of them are," she replied.

SOUL Publications

Welcome to the Low Life 2

"Nobody is a saint, period. You just gotta be careful how you move, but whatever makes you happy makes me happy. If you and Pistol do take it there, I hope one of y'all tell Glock before he hears it from the streets," I said.

"Hopefully it doesn't get to dat point," she said.

I slipped my boots on and grabbed my purse when I saw the lights to Beretta's Mercedes through the window.

"I'll call you tomorrow," I said.

"So, you're not mad at me?" Piper asked.

"I was for a second but I understand exactly how you felt. Besides, I ain't gotta like you right now but I will always love my sister," I replied. Piper slid off the couch into a split and bounced her ass.

"Yesssssss, bitchhhhhhh," Piper said.

"You popped a pill?" I asked.

"Ugh, a half of one. I need to leave them alone," she said.

"Yeah, you do!" I replied before I walked out the door.

A hint of weed mixed with cologne hit my face when I opened the door to Beretta's whip.

"Wait, don't get in yet. Turn around so I can see how tight those jeans are. That's not how you left out da house earlier," he said.

"Piper bought these for me. You like 'em?" I asked, modeling for him.

"Bend over a lil' bit," he said and I turned around.

"Damn, shorty. I did all of dat," he replied.

"You stay feelin' ya self," I laughed.

When I got in and closed the door, he leaned in and kissed me. I slipped my tongue into his mouth to deepen the kiss. He grabbed my breasts and massaged them, making my nipples erect. He pulled away from me and pulled off to the dark end of the street. He leaned his seat back after he parked the car. I lustfully watched him as he unzipped his pants to pull out the big dick I was addicted to.

"Climb yah sexy ass up here," he said.

His slanted eyes were bloodshot red because he was high. The weed always brought out his Asian features he inherited from Nika. In a matter of seconds, I was naked from the waist down. My ass honked the horn when I tried to get comfortable on his lap. He gripped my meaty cheeks and pushed his dick at my opening. A moan escaped my lips when the wideness of his tip stretched me. He moaned my name against my lips as he kissed me and gripped my ass. The wetness that exploded from my pussy reminded me of a levee breaking. The car slightly rocked as I rode him. When he pushed further up into me, he hit my spot, making me cum. He held me closer to him and fucked me back just as hard as I was fucking him. He lifted my shirt then my bra to suck on my erect nipples.

"FUCK! DAMN, BABY!" Beretta groaned against my ear. He got harder and his strokes got deeper. I passionately bit his lip when I came again. He was right behind me; my weave was almost snatched out of my head and he bit my nipple. He moaned loudly as he jerked, spilling his seeds into me.

"I'm weak," he said.

"Me, too. Now I don't even want to go to the movies," I replied.

"Let's go home then. You got me out here fuckin' in da whip like we sneakin' with each other. Stop wearin' those tight-ass jeans. A nigga like me will fuck you in the front row of a church. You might have to get on birth control after you have the baby because I ain't never pulling out, fuck it," Beretta said and I playfully smacked his arm.

"I low-key wouldn't mind giving you a bunch of babies," I said while he fixed himself.

"See what good dick can do? I turned my savage chick into a lovin' and carin' woman," he bragged.

"Nigga, it's called growing up. That dick ain't all that!" I replied and he pulled off.

SOUL Publications

"Yeah, aight," he said. He grabbed my hand and kissed the back of it. Beretta opened my eyes to a lot of things but I wasn't complaining. His life was ruthless, but he wanted mine to be different. Instead of dragging me down with him and making me his gutta bitch, he wanted me to be better than him.

"You're the stability in my life, you know that? At first, I was out here not givin' a fuck how I moved. Didn't even care if a nigga took me out but I look forward to living now because of you and my seed. That's real nigga shit though from the bottom of my heart. Remember I told you this if sumthin happens to me," he said.

"Stop sayin' that shit," I replied and snatched away from him.

"We gotta talk about this. You don't have a nine-to-five educated nigga. I'm preparing you to be strong for our family if I ever get caught slippin', but I guarantee I won't be doin' this forever," he said.

The ride home was a quiet one. I was twenty years old, pregnant, and simply just tired of the fast life. Beretta went into the kitchen to find something to eat when we got home. I headed straight to the shower. It was getting late and I had to wake up for school the next day.

****

SOUL Publications

Welcome to the Low Life 2

"I have been looking all over for you," Emma said when she saw me coming out of class.

"I only have two classes on Fridays so I don't hang around much. Are you hungry?" I asked.

"No, but I need to show you something," she said and grabbed my hand. She pulled me into the girl's bathroom and showed me her cell phone. It was a picture of her boyfriend lying on a female's chest.

"I couldn't concentrate all day! This muthafucka is cheating on me. I went against my family and my friends—everyone! I don't know what to do. Please tell me what you think I should do." Emma's hands trembled.

"You might get locked up if I tell you what to do. What did he say about it?" I asked.

"He didn't come home last night because he's scared of confrontation. I think I know where he's at, but can you please ride with me? You can just stay in the car and pull off if anything goes down. I just need someone there in case something bad happens to me," she said.

"I'll go but whatever you do, please don't get yourself into anything," I replied and she hugged me.

"Thank you so much. Now, let's hurry up. I have a feeling he's still at her condo," she said as we walked out of the bathroom.

"Who is she?" I asked.

"His sister's best friend," Emma replied.

****

Twenty-seven minutes later, Emma pulled up to a newly-built neighborhood in Laurel, Maryland.

"There goes his truck!" Emma shouted.

"Okay, you know he's here so maybe we should leave," I replied. Hell, I could've been home taking a nap or watching TV. I rode with her cause she begged me, but I wasn't stalking a nigga that didn't belong to me. Emma was cool but me and her didn't put years into a friendship for me to be on a mission with her. Emma pulled out her cell phone and called her boyfriend. A woman answered his phone.

"Put Quanta on the phone!" Emma shouted into the phone.

"Bitch, he's in the shower!" the woman shouted back and hung up on Emma.

"She sent me a picture of them last night and now she's doing this! What did I do to her?" Emma asked.

"She's trying to punk you because she knows she can. Secondly, your nigga is letting her because he doesn't think you'll do anything about it. Call that phone back and tell that bitch to put your man on the phone or else you're going to knock on the door and drag her out. Let her know you got five bitches in the car with you waiting to beat her ass," I said and she looked at me like I was crazy.

"What?" I asked.

"What if she calls the police?" Emma asked.

"Trust me, your man ain't gonna let her call the police. Niggas hate the police," I replied. Emma called the phone back and the girl answered again.

"Bitch, didn't I tell you he's the shower?" she asked Emma.

"Put him on the phone before we knock on your door and drag your ass outside! Bitch, look out the window! I'm right here so tell that nigga he better come the fuck out if he doesn't want his car sittin' on flats!" Emma said.

"QUANNNTTAAAA! Your crazy bitch is outside of my house! You better go and see what that hoe wants before I go out there and tag her ass," the girl said. She hung up on Emma and four minutes later, her boyfriend came outside. Emma jumped out of the car and ran to him. I covered my mouth when she popped him in the face. Honestly, I wasn't expecting her to do that but she was screaming and crying as she hit him. She was stronger than me because I would've got real nasty with it. Beretta was going to pay the price if he ever cheated on me again and I put that on my unborn child.

"Get the fuck off of me!" her boyfriend yelled and pushed her. She tripped and fell on her face. I got out of the car and ran to her.

SOUL Publications

"Nigga, you crazy!" I yelled at him. He reached out to help Emma up with regret in his eyes but she snatched away from him.

"I'm done, Quanta," Emma said, fixing her hair.

"Done? All because I slipped up one time?" he asked her.

An Impala pulled up to the building while they were arguing. The passenger door opened and a young girl stepped out holding a box. My heart raced when Poppa got out the driver's side door. Our eyes locked and he smiled at me.

"Damn, Mara. Your brother been gone for almost four years and you ain't gonna show a nigga love?" he asked.

"Fuck you," I gritted and he grilled me.

"What did you just say to me? Fuck me? Bitch, you must've forgotten who took care of your dirty fat ass a few years ago. But because you ridin' that nigga's dick you want to act tough?" he said.

"And you must've forgotten about the bitch I keep tucked in my purse! Nigga, I'm not that little girl anymore. You keep talkin' 'bout you took care of me but I paid my dues. I helped you get money and I looked out for your daughter. So, we're even. Hell, you should be payin' me because I overpaid, the way I see it," I replied.

"I'll slap the taste outta your mouth. Don't think I won't because I will," he said, walking up on me.

"You like fightin' women because you're a bitch. Touch me if you want to, my nigga is only a dial tone away. I know what you did to Piper, too, so go ahead and put your hands on me. Anything goes when it's self-defense," I replied.

"Are you threatenin' me?" Poppa asked.

"Are you threatenin' me?" I replied. He pushed me onto the ground and Emma ran over to us.

"She's pregnant, moron!" Emma yelled at Poppa.

"Shorty, get over here and beat this bitch's ass!" Poppa called out to his girlfriend. Quanta pulled Emma back and got in Poppa's face.

"Naw, nigga. You ain't fuckin' with this one. Tell your bitch to step back," Quanta said. Poppa grilled him before he grabbed his girlfriend by the arm and pulled her down the sidewalk to a building. Emma helped me up and I brushed off my clothes.

"Who is that?" Emma asked.

"My brother. Are you ready to go?" I asked.

"Yeah, let's bounce. I have to pack when I get home," she said.

"Packing what? So, that's it? You don't wanna hear shit I gotta say?" Quanta asked her.

"Naw, not today. Go on back to the same bitch that has been playing on my phone for the past few weeks. You lied to me about this happening one time. This has been happening for a while now but this time you got caught. Fuck you, Quanta!" Emma said, and gave him the finger. Once we got into her car, she sped out of the parking lot.

"Have you followed your man here before?" I asked Emma.

"Remember I told you his sister doesn't like me? Well, she's been trying to hook her friend and Quanta up for a while. One day, Quanta picked his sister up from that address and her friend came outside to speak to Quanta. Something didn't seem right, but he kept saying she was like a sister to him. I guess she's fed up with being the side-chick because now she wants me to know," Emma said.

"You just need your space," I replied.

"I'm moving back in with my parents," Emma said sadly. I felt bad for her because she was a sweet person but sometimes being too nice will break you down. She took me back to my truck on campus.

"Are you sure you're okay?" I asked.

"No, but I'll live. Thank you for coming with me," she said.

"I'll see you on campus Monday," I replied. I grabbed my purse and got out of her car.

What a fucking day! I thought as I unlocked the door to my truck. While driving home, I thought about Poppa. He thought I still owed him because he helped me out when we were younger. Poppa was practically robbing me after every lick we hit. He kept most of the money and didn't do anything to get it. He was giving me chump change when I knew I deserved more. At one point, I looked up to him but I was beginning to see the hateful bitch he turned into. Poppa was digging his own grave.

Beretta

An hour later...

"What's up, Ma? What made you stop by, and who is this? You know I don't like people showin' up at my crib," I said. Nika stopped by unannounced with another female and Hope. I wasn't trippin' because I missed my little sister, but I had shit to do and was on my way out the door when she pulled up.

"This is Amona, she's Hope's babysitter. I had to come to Annapolis to take care of business and I wanted to stop over before I headed home," she replied. I took Hope from Nika's arms and she laid on my chest. The Amona chick was checking me out and shorty wasn't trying to hide it.

"Wow, Nika. The pictures you have of him don't do him any justice. I didn't know he was this tall. Nice house by the way," Amona said, looking around. Nika went into my kitchen and I followed her.

"Why did you bring shorty here? You know Kemara is pregnant and be trippin' about shit," I said.

"You made her insecure, not me. I came here because I have to ask a favor of you. Now, before you fly off the hinge, just hear me out," she said.

"What is it?" I asked.

"I need thirty thousand dollars. I'm opening up a restaurant and it needs repairs," she said.

"The fuck, Nika. You can't cook. What are you gonna do? Sell burnt hot dogs and Capri suns?" I asked and she rolled her eyes at me.

"I don't have to cook to own a restaurant. Amona can cook and so can her sisters. I can hire them. I'm too old to go back to school and find a job, plus I have to take care of Hope. I need steady income," she said.

"Let me think about this," I replied and she kissed my cheek. The front door opened and I heard heels clicking down the hall. It was Kemara coming home from school. I looked at the time and she was late getting home. I wasn't trying to clock shorty but I didn't want her running the streets.

"Who is that bitch in my livin' room, Beretta?" Kemara asked when she came into the kitchen.

"Hope's babysitter," Nika replied. Kemara took Hope out of my arms then kissed my lips.

"Why you gettin' home so late?" I asked.

"Some shit happened today but I will tell you about it later," she replied.

"How is school coming along?" Nika asked Mara.

"Great," Mara replied.

"Well, I gotta get going before I get stuck in traffic. Oh, and the building I was telling you about is not too far from your house. You can check it out if you want to and let me know if you change your mind," Nika said. She took Hope away from Kemara and left out of the house with her babysitter.

"Yo, Nika is always needin' sumthin but when I was laid up from gettin' stabbed, she couldn't stick around to see if a nigga was straight," I told Mara.

"What does she need?" Mara asked.

"Thirty g's," I replied.

"For Hope?" she asked.

"Naw, some restaurant. Nika's ass just bored and ain't got shit else to do but have muthafuckas take care of her. I give her money for Hope every month like I'm on child support. She's trippin' but enough about her, what happened today?" I asked.

"I ran into Poppa and we had some words," she said and my nostrils flared.

"And what dat bitch-ass nigga say?" I asked.

SOUL Publications

"The same as always. He thinks I'm not loyal because I can't fuck with him like that. He whipped Piper's ass a few years ago and she's just telling me. I still remember how her face looked. She was bedridden for a week and her eyes were swollen shut," Kemara said.

"Where did you see dat nigga at?" I asked.

"A neighborhood in Laurel. My friend from school wanted me to ride with her to see about her boyfriend and Poppa was in the same neighborhood. I'm exhausted really," she said then limped out of the kitchen.

"What happened to you?" I asked.

"Walking down the stairs in school and I tripped. I'm fine, it's just a little sprain," she said.

"Dat nigga put his hands on you?" I asked and she got quiet.

"No, I fell down a few steps and landed wrong. I need to stop wearing heels, that's all," she replied.

"Aight, I gotta leave out but I'll be back in a few hours. I gotta holla at my niggas about sumthin," I said.

"Okay, be safe and call me," she replied and limped out the kitchen. I grabbed my car keys off the counter and left out of the crib.

****

SOUL Publications

We were chilling at a little bar on the other side of town. It was me, Pistol, Sniper, Machete, and a few other GMBAM niggas. The owner of the bar was affiliated with GMBAM so every weekend he let us use the back of the club to discuss business. I looked at the time on my Rolex and Ammo was running late.

"Yo, where is Ammo at? Dat nigga ain't answering the phone," I said to Pistol.

"He said he had to meet up with Swan or sumthin. He might be diggin' in shorty's guts," Pistol said. I called Ammo again but it went to voicemail. I'd known him for a while now and he was always on time. I had a feeling something was bound to happen. Everyone around me at the table was talking shit, smoking and drinking.

"Meeting is over. Find Ammo," I said aloud.

"What, nigga? We just got here and you know he got two baby mamas now. Nigga just busy," Sniper said.

"I said, meetin' is over, lil' nigga and go find Ammo. Why are y'all niggas still sittin' at da fuckin' table?" I asked.

"Aight, damn. You trippin' but I'll go through Newtowne. Y'all niggas can go to his favorite spots," Sniper said to the crew. Everyone at the table left and it was just me and Pistol still sitting.

"Yo, you straight?" Pistol asked.

"Hustler's intuition, bruh. Look, I'm ready to bounce and see what's up with this nigga," I replied.

"I'm comin' witchu," Pistol said. He grabbed his gun off the table and placed it behind his jeans. The owner, Ray, walked over to us as we were leaving out.

"Why is everybody leaving? Everything straight?" Ray asked me.

"Yeah, everything is cool," I replied.

"We'll be back," Pistol said before we left out of the bar.

"What if he's just fuckin', though?" Pistol asked, getting into my whip.

"Nigga, you know Ammo, too. He'll pull out in the middle of nuttin' if money is involved. The streets are too quiet," I replied and he shook his head.

"You're one paranoid muthafucka'. The streets are quiet because everyone is eatin'," Pistol said.

"Or niggas plottin'. I don't care if I'm right or wrong. I'm gonna always follow my gut instinct and right now sumthin is tellin' me shit ain't right around us. You think all these niggas really fuck with us?" I asked.

"Naw, fam. You got some A-1 niggas on your team. Niggas who have been down with GMBAM since you started it and switched the game up," he said.

The problem is nobody knew how paranoid I really was because of all the fucked-up shit I did to niggas in the past. Eventually, it was going to come back on me but that was a part of the life I lived—karma.

"Yo, let's just bounce and find this nigga," I said and started the car up. I drove out of the parking lot and headed to Annapolis. I was itching to go back to being that heartless nigga again. It had been a minute since I merked a nigga.

SOUL Publications

Poppa

"**W**here are you going? We just moved in and you need to help me unpack," Jasmine said while I got dressed in all black. Shorty was really driving me insane, and on top of that, that shit with Mara a few hours ago still had me heated. Mara was going to have that nigga's seed and I couldn't deal with that shit. I was hoping their little relationship ran its course, but that nigga was definitely in the picture for good.

"Yo, I'm going to handle some shit. Stay off my back!" I yelled at Jasmine.

"You ain't gonna keep talkin' to me like this, punk!" she yelled back. I drew my fist back and slammed it in the middle of her face. She tripped over a box and landed on her back with blood dripping from her nose.

"You still want to talk shit? From now on, don't question me or else I'll kill you. Do you understand me?" I asked.

"I can't believe you just hit me!" she yelled.

"Bitch, I'll do it again if you keep runnin' off at da mouth. Unpack all of this shit and it better be done by the time I get home," I said. She was still sitting on the floor crying. I put my gun to her head and yanked her off the floor by her hair.

"Toughen up! In this life, you gotta know how to take a hit. You're a grown woman, right?" I asked and she nodded her head.

"Well, act like it! You shouldn't have let me into your life. Don't have any regrets now because I own you. I'm gonna slit your throat if you speak a word about this to anybody. Oh, and stop answering your bitch-ass brother's calls," I gritted. She snatched away from me and I mushed her head into the wall.

"Clean all this shit up!" I barked and she jumped. Jasmine ran to the bathroom and locked the door.

"Stupid bitch," I mumbled to myself as I left out of the door. Tyshawn called me and said he had something for me but he couldn't tell me over the phone. He sent me the address to the place he wanted me to meet him at.

****

When I pulled up to the address Tyshawn gave me, it was a vacant row house on the outskirts of Baltimore city. I spotted a few cat-sized rats running across the street. I was the only car parked on the street because the rest of the homes on the strip were boarded up and vacant. I got out of my whip and pulled my gun out in case it was a set-up. The area was spooking a nigga out. When I walked up the steps to the house, a masked man opened the door and I pointed my gun at him.

"Chill out, nigga. It's me," Tyshawn said. He grabbed me by the neckline of my hoody and pulled me into the house. I almost threw up because of the stench. It smelled of feces, urine, dead bodies, and fish.

"Yo, what da fuck is this?" I asked. I saw a bedroom when I looked up at the hole in the ceiling.

"Follow me," he said. He opened a door by the stairs and I followed him into the basement. The light in the ceiling was dimmed but I could see a man tied up and duct taped to a chair. His chest was covered in blood and his eyes were almost shut. Tyshawn's homeboy, Shag, came over to me and slapped hands with me.

"What's good, nigga? Why you actin' all scared and shit?" Shag asked me.

"Who is dat tied up?" I replied. The nigga in the chair was too big to be Beretta.

"Ammo's bitch-ass. Swan set it up. She called that nigga over to her crib and told him she needed a ride to the hospital. That bitch-ass nigga believed her, too. We were there waitin' on his bitch-ass," Tyshawn said.

"Fuck y'all niggas!" Ammo whispered. Shag took the butt of his gun and smacked Ammo upside the head with it.

"Shut your bitch-ass up, nigga! Y'all muthafuckas think y'all untouchable or sumthin?" Shag asked Ammo.

"Yoo, we aren't supposed to be makin' a move yet! What da fuck is this, nigga? You callin' shots behind my back?" I asked Tyshawn.

"Callin' shots behind your back? Nigga, we planned this!" he gritted.

"Go on ahead and kill me because I ain't gonna fold," Ammo said with blood dripping from his mouth.

"Who is Beretta's connect?" Tyshawn asked Ammo and Ammo chuckled. I grilled Tyshawn because he was making the situation about him and going against my plans.

"This dick, bitch-ass nigga," Ammo said then turned his head towards me.

"Bitch-ass, Poppa. Damn, I got caught slippin' by some baby gangstas. You mad yah sista gettin' her pussy busted in, huh? I bet you wish you was fuckin' her. This nigga is in love with his own sista. I thought Beretta was trippin' when he said it but naw, he was tellin' da truth," Ammo said. I placed the gun to his head and pulled the trigger. The impact caused his neck to snap and his brain matter was dripping down the wall.

"We weren't done with him!" Tyshawn yelled at me.

"Nigga, shut up! You thought dat nigga was gonna rat Beretta out? That's his right-hand man! Y'all niggas askin' about some fuckin' connect when you should've been askin' about his stash!" I said.

"We did that already. This was a waste of time. These niggas ain't gonna fold. I'm tryna get some bread, ya feel me? Kidnappin' niggas and shootin' bitches for free ain't my thing," Shag complained.

"Killin' bitches?" I asked.

"Yeah, I had to merk Swan. Shorty knew too much and she was still fuckin' dat nigga so I didn't trust her. I think dat hoe was pregnant for dat nigga anyway," Tyshawn said.

"Now all we gotta do is make it look like Mike and his niggas did this shit after you sign the deed. Did you get the call back from Rich yet?" Tyshawn asked. Mike wasn't going to put me on the deed until he knew Sid was dead.

"Naw, he didn't hit me up yet," I said.

"What are we gonna do about his body?" I asked.

"Drop it off at Swan's house so they can find his bitch-ass," Tyshawn said. A few niggas came downstairs and I recognized them. They were Tyshawn's cousins.

"They were here all this time?" I asked. I wasn't feeling niggas knowing my business that I didn't fuck with like that. Tyshawn was involving niggas not knowing who was going to rat us out. The nigga was doing too much and I regretted putting him down with my plans.

"Yeah, what you thought? Me and Shag were the only ones who kidnapped this fat nigga?" Tyshawn asked.

"We in this together now, bruh," Shag said.

They wrapped Ammo up in plastic bags then carried his body out the back door in the basement. I followed them out the door and there were two beat up vans parked in the back.

"Nigga, you could've told me to park in the back of the house," I said to Tyshawn.

"Nigga, do it look like enough room back here? Stop actin' paranoid, damn. Nobody knows you around this area, plus this neighborhood has been vacant for two years," he said.

They tossed Ammo's body in the back of the van then slammed the doors.

"We got it from here. I just wanted you to see how serious niggas are about takin' them muthafuckas out," Tyshawn said.

"Good lookin' out," I replied but I still wasn't feeling Tyshawn going behind my back. I watched both vans drive off before I walked around the house to get into my whip. I sat in the driver's seat for a few minutes thinking about the moves I had been wanting to make but couldn't because Beretta was in the way. It dawned on me that I didn't want Beretta dead. I wanted to watch that nigga lose everything he had until there was nothing left!

****

Fifty minutes later, I unlocked the door to my condo. Jasmine had most of our clothes and shoes put up in the closet. I didn't have much yet so it took shorty no time to unpack my shit. I walked into the bedroom and she was hanging her clothes up in the closet. My dick got hard as I watched her ass jiggle in her boy shorts. I wrapped my arms around her waist and she tensed up.

"What are you scared for?" I asked.

"You put your hands on me. I thought you were going to help me, not beat my ass," she said.

"I apologize. Prison made me like this. I have a temper problem and I'm gonna see someone about it soon," I lied.

"How soon?" she asked.

Dumb-ass broad, I thought.

"In a few days. My probation officer is going to help me find someone I can talk to. How about I take you shoppin' tomorrow. I know you want dat Gucci bag we saw the other day with the matchin' boots," I said.

"I guess so," she said dryly.

"Go take a shower. I'll put your clothes away," I replied.

"Okay," she said and walked out of the closet.

All I had to do was spoil her dumb-ass because she was materialistic. But if I had to knock her out a few times to get her in line then that's what I had to do. Shorty was lucky she had some bomb-ass pussy because I would've cut her off after the first time I smashed.

Beretta

Whentmark

When I pulled up to Swan's house, the lights were off and her whip was in the driveway next to Ammo's Benz.

"Damn, the nigga is here," Pistol said, rolling up a blunt.

"Yo, sumthin ain't right," I said in frustration.

"Yo, you need to stop being all superstitious and shit," Pistol said. I got out of my whip and walked up the driveway. I noticed dried up blood on the doorknob when I got to the front door; the door was slightly ajar. I pushed the door open with my foot and the house was pitch-black. I tripped over something when I went further into the house. My body went crashing onto the floor, knocking over something made of glass. I used the light from my cell phone and it was Swan. She was lying on the floor with half of her face blown off. Pistol stood in the doorway.

"Nigga you in here breakin' shit," he said then turned on the light switch by the door.

"Oh, shit!" Pistol called out and hurriedly closed the door. I stood up and had Swan's blood on my clothes. Shorty's body was riddled in bullets.

"Nigga, I told you some shit happened," I spat.

"I'm going to check upstairs," Pistol said and ran up the stairs. I searched the basement of the house. Nobody wanted to find their homeboy dead but I was preparing myself for it. The door to the basement was hanging off the hinges. I saw Ammo's phone on the ground by the door. His phone had blood all over it and the screen was cracked. I picked up his phone and placed it in my pocket.

"FUCK!" I yelled out.

It was almost like a hood thriller movie. Swan was dead and Ammo was missing, possibly dead. I walked back upstairs and Pistol was standing in the middle of the living room with his gun still drawn.

"Yo, this shit ain't addin' up," Pistol said.

"Too bad this dead bitch can't talk," I replied.

"This had to be an inside job. It doesn't look like someone broke in," Pistol said.

"Swan let some niggas in through the basement and they probably waited down there until Ammo came in. They must've took him out the basement door 'cause I found his phone and the door is fucked up. Ammo is a big nigga so it had to be a lot of them to get him through the basement door," I replied.

"You think someone kidnapped him?" Pistol asked, worried.

"Shit looks too personal. Nobody has called asking for ransom money and Swan still got her jewelry on so it wasn't a burglary," I replied.

"We gotta get out of here before somebody comes," Pistol said.

A black van pulled up and the back doors opened while we were leaving out of the crib. A very large trash bag was pushed onto the ground and Ammo's GMBAM chain was tossed on the ground next to the bag. I started bustin' at the van and Pistol followed suit. Glass from the windows in the van shattered onto the sidewalk. A masked man in the passenger seat aimed a gun at Pistol and fired. I pulled out another Beretta and fired back, hitting the masked man in the forehead. He slumped over the passenger door then fell onto the ground. The driver sped off with a flat tire and I ran in the middle of the street and shot at the back of the van until it disappeared around the corner. Pistol was stretched out in the grass with a gunshot wound to his stomach. I helped him up and ran towards my car before the police showed up. He sat in the passenger's seat holding his stomach.

"Go see if that's Ammo in the bag," he winced in pain.

"No, bruh. I can't do it," I replied.

"You got to, bruh. Go see if that's our nigga in the fuckin' bag!" Pistol said. I rushed to the sidewalk and snatched up Ammo's chain. I ripped the bag open and almost threw up. Ammo's forehead was split open like a melon. I got inside my whip and sped off when I heard sirens getting closer.

"Was that him?" Pistol asked.

"Yeah, bruh," I said and clutched the steering wheel.

"Them niggas wanted us to see it," Pistol said.

"We gotta take the bullet out of your stomach before you go to the hospital. If not, they'll link it back to the crime scene," I replied.

"My aunt can take it out. She's a military nurse. Just take me to my crib," Pistol said.

"You sure?" I asked.

"Yeah, I'll be straight," he said but I could hear it in his voice he wasn't straight. I arrived at Pistol's crib ten minutes later doing 100mph. I took a back road because I would've gotten pulled over driving fast through the city. After I parked in front of his house, I got out and ran to the passenger's side door to help him out the whip. He almost fell on the ground but I held him up. Blood was dripping down his leg and he was getting weak. With all my strength, I pulled him up the steps and rang the doorbell. The porch light came on and his aunt, Earlene, opened the door with an attitude. Once she saw Pistol bleeding and losing consciousness, she pulled him into the house.

"What the fuck happened?" she screamed.

"We were robbed," Pistol lied.

SOUL Publications

"I'm calling the police," she said and I stopped her.

"Naw, you can't do that. Get the bullet out of him first because we shot at those niggas back," I replied and she grilled me.

"Get the fuck outta my house, Beretta! It's because of you Pistol is even in this gang-banging shit!" she screamed at me. I felt her pain and even blamed myself. Me and my niggas came up with GMBAM when we were younger. It meant "Getting Money by Any Means." It was something small back then and we were only doing small shit like stealing dirt bikes and hotwiring cars. As we got older, we began doing other shit. I should've stopped it at that point but I couldn't. I became money-hungry and so had my niggas. I didn't influence them, though, because Pistol, Ammo, and Glock had the same mentality as me and that's how we clicked. But even after realizing I didn't play a hand in their lives, I was still to blame. I drove home with tears falling from my eyes, the first time I cried since I could remember. Ammo was my right-hand man. My brother since I was a little nigga was dead with his forehead missing. If only I went with my gut instinct sooner, he might've still been alive.

Kemara

I woke up when I heard glass breaking downstairs. I looked at the clock on the wall and it was past midnight. I called out to Beretta but didn't get an answer. When I heard a loud thud, I grabbed my gun from underneath the mattress and walked out of our bedroom.

"BERETTA!" I called out.

From the top of the stairs, I could see the front door and it was wide open. There was a blood trail coming from the front door, leading to the kitchen. My heart raced as I walked down the stairs. When I pushed the door open to the kitchen, I aimed my gun, ready to shoot at whomever broke into our house. Once I realized who it was, I placed the gun on the kitchen island. Beretta was sitting on the floor, surrounded by expensive broken dishes I paid for. He was drinking out of a Henny bottle like it was water. Tears were falling down his face as his chest heaved.

"Baby, what happened? Are you hurt?" I asked, but he didn't answer. I kneeled next to him and reached out to him.

"You're scaring me. Tell me what happened?" I asked. He wiped his eyes and clutched the bottle in his hand, squeezing it as veins popped out of his forehead. I began

SOUL Publications

crying myself; I didn't know what was going on because I had never seen him like this before.

"Ammo, they killed my nigga, Mara. They killed my fuckin' brother!" he sobbed. I tried to hug him but he pulled away from me.

"Go back to bed. I'm good," he said and took another sip from the bottle.

"Where is Pistol?" I asked.

"He went to the hospital. His blood is still on me," he said. I was so focused on Beretta's mental state that I hadn't realized his clothes were covered in blood.

"Let's get you in the shower," I said and he shook his head.

"GO THE FUCK TO BED!" he yelled at me when he stood up.

"I'm trying to console you!" I yelled back.

"I'm fuckin' good, Mara," he said with his back turned to me.

"You're shaking," I replied.

"I killed him," he said with sorrow in his voice. "I wanted to change my fucked-up ways but that's where I fucked up at. Niggas caught me getting too comfortable! You distracted me, look at me. I'm up here tryna be a family man and shit and my niggas getting merked! I moved betta before I got wit' you. You bad luck, shorty," Beretta said to me.

"Now is not the time to play the blaming game. You're speaking out of anger," I replied.

"I need some space. I came here to get a few things," he said.

"No, you don't have to leave. I can go to Piper's house for a few days," I replied. After I left the kitchen, I went to our bedroom to pack a few things. Beretta was sitting on the couch when I came back downstairs. He was smoking a blunt and I wanted to stay with him but I knew it would've angered him. Niggas like Beretta couldn't deal with vulnerability. Honestly, he didn't feel comfortable with me seeing him in that condition.

"I'll call you when I get to Piper's house," I said.

"Aight, be safe," he said nonchalantly.

"I'm here if you need me," I said.

"Yo, I'm fucking good," he gritted.

Tears fell from my eyes when I left the house. I couldn't deal with seeing Beretta that way, especially since he was happy earlier before he left the house. I was also shedding tears for Ammo. I'd known him as long as I knew Beretta. I argued with Ammo a few times but I loved him, too. Beretta's friends were like annoying older brothers with good hearts.

"Damn," I said aloud as I sobbed. Thickems would have to raise her baby as a single mother. My phone rang and it was Piper calling me.

"I'm on my way there," I said.

"The hood is talkin'. Please don't tell me it's true," Piper cried.

"Ammo is dead," I said, still not believing the shit myself.

"How is Beretta holding up?" she asked as I backed out of the driveway.

"I'm worried about him. I don't think he'll ever be the same," I replied.

"Just hurry here. I'm going to call Thickems," she said and we hung up.

While on my way to Piper's house, I began feeling sick but I didn't stop until I got to her house. My nerves were all over the place. I was worried about Beretta and his squad. Piper came out of the house and grabbed my overnight bag from the back seat.

"Did you talk to Thickems?" I asked.

"No, she isn't answerin'," Piper replied.

SOUL Publications

"Pistol was shot, too. Maybe we can all go to the hospital once we figure out where Thickems is at. I hope she's okay," I said.

"Pistol was shot, too? What the fuck is happenin'?" Piper asked.

"I don't know yet," I said.

I called Beretta when I sat on Piper's couch but he didn't answer. While I was calling him, Piper was calling Thickems but her phone was off.

"Now I'm worried about her. She hasn't been home all day," Piper said.

"Let's go look for her," I replied.

"Where could she be? Her family lives a few hours away from here. I hope she isn't hurt, too," she said.

"I guess we have to wait and see, but in the meantime, I'm going to use the bathroom before we go see about Pistol," I said.

Piper ran up the stairs to grab her shoes and I went to use the bathroom. While sitting on the toilet, I called Beretta's phone again but he turned it off. I was trying to be understanding but it was hard considering he was pushing me away. What he said about me being bad luck was heavily on my mind. It was the same thing Amari's mother said to me after she was murdered. It was my fault her daughter was hit by a stray bullet that was meant for me. I wished me and Beretta fell in love on a clean slate, but realistically we had done too much shit in our lives to do so. After I flushed the toilet and washed my hands, I left out of the bathroom. Piper was waiting for me by the door with her car keys in her hand.

"Thickems called me back while you were in the bathroom. She spent the day with her grandmother in Philly. She hung up on me when I told her about Ammo," Piper said sadly.

"She'll come around when she's ready," I replied.

"This feels like a dream. I mean, Ammo was just here eating a sub on my couch. Damn, Mara, I want to shoot the nigga that killed him," Piper said.

"If I wasn't pregnant, I'd be out combing the streets trying to find out who did it. My man is fucked up behind this and I'm so scared for him. I don't think he'll ever be the same. You should've seen how bad he was shaking and the pain in his voice crushed my spirit. He blames me for it; he said it's my fault he tried changing his life around. This just pushed him further into the streets," I replied.

"At least you have me if he doesn't come back around," she said. We left out of the door to visit Pistol.

****

The waiting area was crowded as we waited to see Pistol. A lot of people didn't like GMBAM niggas but more people loved them because they did a lot for the communities. Although ruthless, they had big hearts when it came to the kids in the neighborhoods. Since Beretta's team started making a lot of money, the kids in the hood had fresh clothes and groceries in their fridge. People were standing outside because the waiting room was too crowded.

"Oh, shit. There go the police," Piper whispered to me.

"They came to question Pistol," I replied.

A pregnant white girl came out of the bathroom with a little girl. She must've been in the waiting area, but it was so crowded, I didn't see her at first. She had on designer clothes and a pair of bad ass stilettos. Her long blonde hair stopped at her hips. Piper rolled her eyes at her and I nudged her.

"Chill out," I whispered.

"That's Glock's baby mother," she whispered back.

"Ohhhh, I see," I replied.

The white girl rolled her eyes at Piper when she caught her staring at her.

"Did that bitch just roll her eyes at me?" Piper asked.

"Would you chill out?" I replied.

"I'm cool, Mara, damn!" Piper spat.

Welcome to the Low Life 2

It's going to be a long night, I thought.

Piper

I t was five o'clock in the morning by the time me and Mara were able to see Pistol. He declined a lot of visitors except for close friends and family. I was uncomfortable because Bridget was in his hospital room with us and for hours she gave me dirty looks. I wanted to snatch her chain from around her neck with Glock's name on it. It was still hard to believe the nigga hid a family from me. It was making me dislike him even more because I had to be around her. Glock's daughter was sleeping in the chair in the corner of the room while we stood around Pistol's hospital bed.

"Why Beretta didn't come to see about a nigga?" Pistol's voice dragged. He was in and out because of the medicine the nurse gave him.

"Beretta isn't doin' too good behind all of this," Mara replied.

"You can come to my house when you leave here and I can look after you. I live in a very safe neighborhood. Glock wouldn't want it any other way," Bridget said and Mara smacked her teeth.

"I can look after him," I spoke up.

"Why? So you can fuck him, too?" Bridget asked me.

"Oh, wait a minute. The fuck is you salty for? Bitch, we're in a hospital and you tryna throw shade over a nigga that was supposed to be loyal to you?" Mara asked her.

"I didn't come here for this ghetto bullshit. I came here because Pistol is my daughter's godfather. You two can leave if it's a problem," Bridget said.

"You're mad at the wrong person," Mara said.

"No, I'm mad at that hoe for fucking my husband and now she's with his friend. What kind of people are you? Is this what you all do? Share men and sleep with married men?" Bridget asked.

"Glock married this bitch?" Mara asked me and I shrugged my shoulders.

"We got married in Vegas a week before he was locked up but he didn't want nobody to know at the time and now I know why!" Bridget said.

"First of all, I'm not Pistol's girlfriend. Your man lied to you to make himself look good. Second of all, I didn't know shit about you until Glock got locked up. So, whateva Glock told you is a muthafuckin lie!" I said.

"So, you weren't pregnant by him? He told me everything!" Bridget yelled.

"Y'all can take all that bullshit out in the hallway," Pistol mumbled in pain.

"That bitch started it," I said.

"I'll come back later when Wanda and Shenaynay leaves," Bridget said. She picked up her daughter and stormed out of the hospital room.

"I'm going to stomp a hole in her Bridget Jones diary-writing ass for that comment," Mara said and Pistol chuckled.

"I told Glock shorty always sayin' some ill shit on the low," Pistol said.

"I'm gonna step out to call Beretta. I'll be in the waiting area if I don't come back," Mara said to me. She kissed Pistol's forehead before she left out of the room. He wiped his forehead off and I giggled.

"Beretta is too jealous for dat shit. Nigga probably look at my forehead and see Mara's DNA on there," he said. I grabbed a chair and pulled it closer to his bed.

"How are you really feelin'? I didn't want to say too much because Glock's bitch was in here," I replied.

"I'm fucked up fa real. My nigga, Ammo, is gone," he said sadly.

"I know, the hood is gonna have a block party for him. You already know he was highly loved around the way," I said and he nodded his head.

"Swan is dead, too," Pistol said.

*Who cares? The bitch had no business stalkin'
Thickems,* I thought.

"Damn, that's messed up," I said and he looked at me.

"I think she set Ammo up to get merked and they
killed her so she wouldn't rat them out. I can't see him
going out like that. Knowing Swan, she probably used her
pregnancy to get Ammo over there. She been on some
sucka shit since she found out about Thickems. Ammo was
like my brother, too. We're all brothers. I can't wait to get
outta this muthafucka," Pistol said. A tear fell from his eye
and I wiped it away.

"You have to lay low until you heal," I said.

"I'll never heal after tonight," Pistol said.

"I'll see you tomorrow. Get some rest," I replied.

I was ready to walk away but he reached out and
grabbed my wrist.

"You owe me for takin' care of yah ass. I'm havin' you
do everything for me over the next few days so I hope you
got a pen and pad ready," he said.

"Seriously?" I smiled.

"Yeah, I got some shit that need to be picked up from
the dry cleaners and all that," he said.

SOUL Publications

"Where is your girlfriend?" I asked.

"I don't pay her bills, I pay yours, so what's the problem, shorty?" he asked.

I need to get away from your fine chocolate ass is what the problem is! Nigga laid up in the hospital and still look better than half the niggas walking around, I thought.

"No, problem. I'll see you tomorrow morning if I don't see you lata," I replied.

"You strippin' tonight, huh?" he asked.

"How else am I supposed to get paid?" I replied.

"Go to school with Mara or sumthin. Damn, Piper, you can't let all of that go to waste. You ain't a little girl anymore and, besides, the streets will turn you out to the point where there is no coming back. It's other ways to work around it," he said.

"I'll quit when you stop hustlin'," I replied.

"Women should always be better than us niggas, so me hustlin' ain't got shit to do witchu," he snapped.

"Get some rest," I said before I left out of his hospital room.

Nigga got me all the way fucked up if he thinks I'm listenin' to him like he's my man or sumthin. It must've

*been the meds the nurse gave him because he was talkin'
crazy,* I thought.

Kemara was in the waiting area using her phone when
I walked down the hall.

"Did you talk to Beretta?" I asked.

"No, his phone is still off. I don't know if I can give him
his space," she said.

"Just do it for a few days. We'll see him at the block
party anyways. It's Beretta we're talkin' about. He might
be combing the streets lookin' for answers," I replied.

"I know and that's what bothers me. What if someone
does sumthin to him? Fuck this, I gotta see where his ass is
at. I'm going back to the house," Mara said.

"Are you sure?" I replied.

"Yeah, he needs me. I should have never left," Mara
said.

Watching Kemara lose her mind over Beretta
reminded me of how much I was missing out on a
relationship. Every guy I had been with treated me like a
piece of ass, especially Glock. Poppa showed me at a very
young age that men weren't shit. He whipped my ass and
gave me an STD. At the rate he was going, he could've
given me something else.

"Okay, let's get outta here. I need to get some rest and figure out what's up with Thickems," I replied.

While we were walking through the parking lot, Lezzi, Pistol's girlfriend, was parking his Cadillac. I knew it was serious between them if he was letting her drive one of his vehicles. Lezzi grilled me when she got out of the car and Kemara smacked her teeth.

"How is he?" Lezzi asked Kemara.

I could tell she was crying in the car because her eyes were puffy. She was wearing scrubs with a badge around her neck. Judging by her badge, she worked at another hospital.

"He's fine, a little drowsy from the medication, but he's still his normal self," Mara said.

"Okay, thank you so much," Lezzi said and smiled at Mara.

She rolled her eyes at me when she walked past.

"These hoes trippin' like you're Pistol's first lady or sumthin," Mara joked.

"That's Glock's fault. Lezzi only likes you because you let her use the bathroom," I replied.

"Whateva, bitch, but let's hurry up so I can get to my car. I need to see where my nigga at," Mara said as she flipped her hair over her shoulders. I unlocked the car doors, and after Mara got in and put on her seat belt, I left the hospital's parking lot.

****

Later on that night, I walked into Fat Cat and it was crowded. Delonte was standing by the bar, talking to the bartender when I walked past him. He called out to me but I wasn't in the mood to talk. My friends were going through a lot of shit and all I wanted to do was get on the stage to escape my life.

"Is everything aight with you? You stormed in here like you're running from someone," Delonte said.

"Yeah, I'm cool. Just dealin' wit' a lot of shit," I replied.

"Come upstairs and have a drink with me. I don't mind lending an ear," he smirked.

Instead of going to the locker room, I went upstairs to Delonte's office, which overlooked the club. I sat in his black leather love seat and he sat across from me. In front of us was a mini bar and he poured me a drink.

"So, what's good?" he asked.

"I lost someone who I've known for years. It's takin' a toll on my friends and I'm going through sumthin else. I thought I knew this one nigga I was talking to but he has a family. He promised me all of this shit after he got locked up but he was lyin' to me the whole time. Niggas ain't shit," I spat as I sipped my drink. Delonte leaned back in his chair and scratched his chin.

"What are you thinkin' about?" I asked.

"A woman like you shouldn't be stressed over a fuck-nigga. You're beautiful and have so much potential to be something better," Delonte said.

"Says the owner of the strip club I work at," I replied, and he chuckled.

"And I highly appreciate it but we both know this isn't the end for you. I can see you doing something wayyy better. You don't want to be like the older strippers who are still hanging onto hope. It doesn't matter how much they change their bodies, niggas still rather see a natural young woman entertain them," he said.

"I'll stop in a few years," I replied.

"Naw, I think you should reach a savings goal so you can move forward from this. At the rate you're going, you should have enough by the end of the year to do something else," Delonte said.

"And if I don't?" I asked.

"I'll let you go," he seriously stated.

"Oh, well, nigga, you betta be giving me more money then," I said and he laughed. I looked around his office and realized he didn't have any pictures of his wife. Matter of fact, Delonte never spoke about his wife.

"Your wife doesn't approve of this place? Is that why she doesn't come here?" I asked.

"My wife is dead. She had a heart attack two years ago," he replied.

"Sorry to hear that," I said.

"But she hated this place when she was alive. Many nights we argued because she thought I was fuckin' the strippers," he said.

"Were you?" I asked.

"I don't mix business with pleasure. Too many club owners have gone down the drain because of that," he said.

"Thank you for the drink. I have to get going now," I replied and stood up. I grabbed my duffel bag and Delonte stood up with me.

"I'll see you around," he replied.

Damn, that was awkward, I thought as I left his office to get ready for my show.

The club was crowded since it was a weekend. A lot of niggas that went to Mikey's were in attendance. When I left Mikey's, I took the clientele with me. The strippers at Fat Cat stayed to themselves unlike Mikey's strippers. I didn't have any issues with anyone which made me go harder on the stage because I knew a bitch wasn't watching and hating. Delonte was standing over the balcony of his office watching me as I bounced my ass on stage. I wasn't one to shy away so I gave him a show. Money flew over my head when I laid on my back, opening my legs so they could get a clear view of my waxed fat pussy. I put my legs behind my head and opened my pussy while playing with my clit. Delonte lustfully eyed me and nodded his head in approval. Before I got on stage, I popped an e-pill and it was in full effect. I told Mara I was going to quit but the pills boosted my ego while I was on stage. After I was finished playing with my pussy, I did a back roll and landed in a split. My ass cheeks took turns bouncing, even the strippers inside the club stopped dancing to watch me.

That's right, hoes! Take notes! I thought as my ass clapped.

"Nobody is leaving out of here with money in their pockets!" the DJ yelled into the microphone.

My show lasted for ten minutes until I got off stage with two buckets filled with money.

"Girrrrrlllllll, you gotta teach me how to dance like that," this white girl named Sugar said. Sugar was attractive and had a lot of ass. Her hair was dyed fire red and tattoos covered her body. She looked to be around my age and was also on the tall side at around five-foot-ten without heels.

"Okay, I'll come in early one day so we can practice, but you really don't need it," I laughed.

"If that's what you think. I got the rhythm but I don't have the sexiness with it. I don't think I can play with my pussy on stage," she said.

"Well, you ain't tryin' to get paid then. Niggas love to see a woman pleasing herself. Try it out," I replied before I walked away.

I went to the locker room to freshen up and change my outfit. I put on a cute pink bob-style wig that matched my pink see-through leotard with the matching heels. I made my way around the club to each VIP section. It was a great night for me. By the time the night was over, I had eight thousand dollars to my name. The pill was starting to wear off and I was getting tired. My feet were hurting and my scalp was sweating from the wig. It was three o'clock in the morning when I finally left the club. Delonte was standing in the parking lot by his apple red Bentley coupe.

"I thought you left an hour ago," I said.

"I stayed back to make sure the place was clean," he said.

"Okay, have a good night," I replied, hitting the alarm button to my car.

"Wait, I need to ask you sumthin.' I hope you don't take this the wrong way, although I might be overstepping my boundaries," he said.

Nigga, if you tell me I can't strip here anymore, it's going to be some shit! I thought.

"What is it?" I asked.

"Can you dance for me?" he replied.

"I thought you don't mix business with pleasure?" I asked.

"It's business if I'm paying you, right?" he replied and I crossed my arms.

"When?" I asked.

"Right now," he said.

"Dancin' for you and that's it?" I asked.

"Of course," he replied.

"I could've danced for you in your office," I said.

"I don't want nobody in our business," he replied.

"So, where are we going?" I asked.

It was late and I was tired but an extra dance damn sure wasn't going to hurt.

SOUL Publications

"My loft," he replied.

"I'll follow you there," I said.

"Cool wit' me," he replied.

Delonte got into his car and I got inside mine. I pulled out of the parking lot following him. He was a mystery—there was something about him that I liked. Maybe it was his persona and the fact he was older and mature. I had dealt with young hood niggas all my life so someone like him would be a change.

Maybe I need an older man to lock my wild ass down, I thought.

****

"This crib is nice but I'm not surprised considerin' the layout of your club," I said, looking around Delonte's home.

"It's aight but it doesn't have that home feeling. I moved here after my wife died. I don't think I will ever get that feeling back," he said.

"Where is your bathroom?" I asked.

"There's one down the hall. Washcloths and towels are under the sink," he said, turning on his stereo system. He called out to me while I was walking down the hall.

"No stripper shit, just your plain and natural self," he said and I playfully gave him the finger.

Once inside the bathroom, I locked the door. It was nicely decorated, the colors were lavender, black, and silver. It was also spacious inside with a double shower and large bath tub. I looked around, searching his cabinets to make sure I didn't see any items that belonged to a woman. Although I was going to get my money regardless if he had one or not, I still wanted a heads up. There was nothing in the cabinets besides soap, washcloths, and towels. I took a fifteen-minute shower, letting my mind drift off to everything that was happening. Through the mist of it all, I couldn't stop thinking about Pistol. The saying, "you always want what you can't have" was very true. Honestly, I think that's what made me like him even more. Curiosity and guilty pleasure was a fucked-up combination. Delonte knocked on the door, bringing me back to reality.

"You aight in there?" he called out.

"Yeah, I'll be out in a minute!" I replied as I dried off.

I went inside my bag and pulled out a jar of coconut and apricot body butter. After I moisturized my body, I ran mousse and water through my short hair to give it a cute and wet look. I also dabbed a little body glitter around my neck and breasts so it could highlight my skin. When I walked out of the bathroom and down the hall, Delonte was sitting on the couch smoking a cigar. His eyes lustfully roamed over my body.

"Damn, you're beautiful," he said.

He pressed the button on his remote to his stereo system and a song by H-town began playing around the living room. My body moved to the rhythm of the music.

Good lovin', body rockin', knockin' boots all night long, yeah...

Makin' love until we tire to the break of dawn...

I turned my back towards him and bent over to grab my ankles so he could see my pussy smile. While bent over, I reached between my legs to part the lips of my pussy while making my ass cheeks bounce.

"FUCK!" Delonte whispered.

I laid on the table in front of him, spreading my legs as I grinded my hips.

"Can I touch you?" he asked, eyeing my fat cat.

I was aroused from the music and the way he was lustfully staring at me. I had given many lap dances, but Delonte's eyes were looking through me, not just at me. I scooted to the edge of the coffee table then placed my legs behind my head. Delonte's thumb brushed across my clit as he bit his bottom lip.

"You got the prettiest pussy I've ever seen," he grumbled.

"Taste it," I dared him.

SOUL Publications

I wasn't shy when it came to sex. Hell, I loved sex. My pussy was dripping from him rubbing my clit. Delonte slid off the couch; he was eye-level with my lips. My legs trembled when he stuck his tongue inside of me. I threw my head back and stared at the ceiling.

"Damn, baby," he groaned as he fingered me.

"Eat that shit, baby," I moaned while he cupped my breasts. His thick tongue parted my lips and pressed against my love button. His head hungrily thrashed around between my legs and I couldn't believe how good his head was. Maybe it was the age difference considering most of the niggas I fucked were around my age.

"OHHHHHHHHH!" I moaned as he pressed his hands against my thighs.

"Cum in my mouth! Yeah, that's it. Make that little pussy squirt," Delonte groaned as he continued eating my pussy like a juicy watermelon. I was dripping down his chin as I fucked his face. My pussy clenched and I dug my nails into his shoulders as I screamed from the mind-blowing orgasm he was giving me. Oral sex made me hornier, so I needed something else to put the fire out. Delonte stood up and wiped off his mouth. The song had gone off and the room was quiet.

"We can't do this," Delonte said, feeling embarrassed.

"It's too late now," I replied, unbuckling his jeans. I didn't give a shit about how he felt. He was going to dick me down until I couldn't walk because my pussy was throbbing uncontrollably.

"Wait, Piper. Chill out for a second and let's talk about this," he said. But it was too late, I had his dick in my hand and he was harder than a brick. He was a nice size, around eight inches. I pushed him down on the couch then went to my bag to get a condom. Delonte was still sitting on the couch with his dick standing at full attention.

"You're wild for this," he chuckled and took off his shirt.

"You shouldn't start what you can't finish," I said.

"Oh, now you talkin' big shit?" he asked. He took the condom from me and opened it. I straddled him after he put the condom on.

"We still going to be cool after this, right?" Delonte asked, but I was already easing his head into my pussy.

"DAMN!" he groaned.

I gripped the back of the couch and propped my knees on his thighs. The way he licked my nipples almost made me cum. I bounced on his dick like I was twerking on stage and he closed his eyes. He gripped my hips and fucked me back. My titty was in his mouth as he hit my G-spot.

"OHHHHHHH!" I screamed.

"Ride that shit!" he groaned as he bounced me. I bucked my hips forward and he called out my name. Delonte picked me up and fucked me in a squatting position. He savagely rammed his dick into me and I screamed from cumming extremely hard. Veins were popping out of his neck like he was turning into the Hulk. Sweat was dripping down our bodies and my hair was soaking wet.

"URRGGHHHHHHHHHH!" Delonte groaned as he slowed his pace. I wrapped my arms around his neck and he went slower—deeper. He licked my lips which caught me by surprised. I thought we were just fucking at first but he began making love to me. His hand wrapped around my neck, gently choking me as he kissed me. No man had ever given my body that much respect. Glock wasn't into kissing or slow stroking. All we did was fuck each other's brains out. Delonte carried me upstairs to his bedroom and laid me down on his bed.

"I'm gonna show you what these lil' niggas can't do," he said. He got on his knees and ate my pussy so good, I was speaking in tongues. He ate me out for over twenty minutes before he changed the condom and entered me again. That time, he was on top of me, licking my neck while digging so deep into me that I couldn't move. I shuttered as each stroke sent a wave through my body.

I'm never fucking a young nigga again! I thought as we both climaxed.

****

Hours later, I woke up in Delonte's bed. He was sleeping peacefully on his stomach with his arm over my body. He opened his eyes when he felt me moving.

"Good morning," he yawned.

I looked at the clock on his bedroom wall and it was three o'clock in the afternoon. My body was aching and my pussy was sore. I blushed when Delonte sat up and stared at me.

"What are your plans for today?" he asked.

"I gotta go see my friend in the hospital," I replied.

"I guess I'll see you at the club then," he said, kissing my shoulder.

"Yeah, you will," I replied.

"Shit got crazy last night but I don't regret any of it," he said and I smirked.

"Me, neither," I replied and he kissed my lips.

"Aight, good," he said and climbed out of the California king-size bed. I eyed his muscled naked body and he caught me staring at him. His dick was sticking straight out at me.

"Come and join me in the shower so I can take care of that for you before you leave," he said. He grabbed me by the ankle and pulled me to the edge of the bed. I giggled when he threw me over his shoulder and headed to the bathroom. As soon as he grabbed a condom out of his medicine cabinet, we went at it again. I was getting fucked by my boss and it felt damn good.

Two hours later...

I knocked on the door to Pistol's hospital room before I walked in. He was sitting up in bed arguing with someone over the phone.

"Nigga, I don't know yet. But chill out before you get into some more shit," Pistol said. I heard Glock's voice come through his cell phone and I rolled my eyes. I was ready to leave out of his room but he called out to me.

"Come here, Piper," Pistol said. I rolled my eyes before I turned around to face him.

"Glock wants to talk to you," he said, reaching his phone out to me. I snatched it from him and he chuckled.

"What do you want?" I asked Glock.

"Yo, don't do me like this. We were friends before anything. I'm losing my mind in here. My nigga is dead and you ain't tryna talk to me. I need you right now," he said.

"How about your wife?" I asked, checking my nails to see if I needed a filling.

"We were in Vegas one night and one thing led to another. We were drunk and I swear that's one thing I regret doin'. I honestly don't think the shit is even legit. I know you hate a nigga right now and I blew my chances witchu, but at least be cordial wit' me," he pleaded.

"You made it seem like I was fucking Pistol!" I yelled into the phone.

"I apologize for that, but at that time I really didn't know how to tell her the truth," Glock said.

"Nigga, I ain't falling for your lonely-ass jail talk. You lied to her because you care about her," I replied.

"Man, whateva. Look, I'll holla at y'all later. I gotta get off da phone," he said. Glock hung up on me with an attitude. Pistol shook his head when I gave him his phone back.

"Y'all niggas wild," he said.

"How are you feelin'?" I asked.

"Better physically. Yo, have you heard from Beretta? Nobody can get in touch wit' dat nigga," Pistol said.

"Mara can't get in touch with him, neither," I said. Pistol stared at my neck and it made me uncomfortable.

"How is work comin' along for you?" he asked.

"Same as usual," I said.

"You be lettin' random niggas suck on you and shit? Damn, I thought you was just strippin', not sellin' pussy," he said.

"And I thought your bitch's name was Lezzi," I replied.

SOUL Publications

"And you wonder why Glock wifed another bitch," Pistol mumbled. I jumped out of my chair, fed up.

"Bitch, I don't have to be here!" I said.

"What are you mad for? I call shit how I see it and right now I see why a nigga ain't wife you up yet," Pistol said.

"You don't know shit. The nigga I was wit' last night thinks highly of me," I said and Pistol shook his head.

"And he's aware of what you do?" he asked.

"Yes, he is, and he has no issues wit' it," I said.

"Whateva, but I need a favor from you. Police is snoopin' around my grandmother's crib because of what happened. I'm crashin' at your crib when they release me in a few days," he said.

"Ewww, where is Lezzi?" I asked.

"Mannnn, dat bitch cursed me out when she came to see me. I'm here laid up from a bullet wound and shorty was accusin' me of some bullshit. I won't be there long. I'll leave as soon as shit dies down. You already know how I feel about hotels. That's the number one place niggas get caught slippin'," he said.

"Aight, whateva," I said and rolled my eyes.

A nurse came in to check on Pistol's wound. I told him I'd see him later before I left his room. Pistol being at my house was going to be hectic and I wasn't sure if it was a good idea but I couldn't turn my back on him. He never asked for anything so him asking if he could crash there meant he probably didn't have another option considering Beretta was on some bullshit with everybody. I prayed Beretta was okay for the sake of Mara.

When I got home, I took off my clothes and got into bed. I was still exhausted from my night with Delonte. I planned on sleeping until it was time for me to go to the club later.

Beretta

Three days later...

"Wake up, baby," a voice called out to me. When I opened my eyes, I was lying across a bed. The night Mara left the crib, I drove over to Ammo's aunt, Lashonda's house so we could discuss Ammo's funeral. Moesha went to the morgue to identify him. She wanted me to go but I stayed back with Ammo's family. I hadn't been home in days. I stayed in the guest room for three days in a drunken daze. Truth is, I never lost someone so close to me before. Ammo was like a blood brother—his beef was my beef and vice versa. It was the hardest shit I had to deal with.

"What's up?" I asked and buried my face into the pillow.

"Today is the block party for Ammo. We have to be there," Moesha said.

"Naw, I can't do it," I replied.

I reached over to the nightstand and grabbed the bottle of vodka. I wasn't a vodka drinker but, shit, anything was good during this time. After I guzzled the warm liquor down, I closed my eyes. Moesha straddled me and grabbed my face so I could look at her.

"We are going to Ammo's block party. You won't be able to live with yourself if you don't. Now, get up so I can drive you to your house," she said.

"I can drive home," I said.

"You're drunk. You have been drunk for the past few days. You haven't eaten anything and you turned your phones off. I understand you're grieving, we all are! But you can't grieve like this. It's going to destroy you," she said. I pushed her off and she went crashing to the floor.

"Yo, you and Mara won't let me fuckin' think in peace! Just leave me the fuck alone, damn! You fuckin' trippin," I said. I crawled out of bed and looked in the mirror on the dresser. I hadn't eaten shit in days or showered. I was seeing Ammo's lifeless body every time I closed my eyes.

"Don't compare me to that young ghetto bitch! I'm trying to be here for you," Moesha cried. Her aunt banged on the door.

"Is everything alright in there?" Lashonda asked from the other side of the door.

"Yes, Aunty. Everything is fine!" Moesha yelled back.

I put my shoes on and searched around for my car keys. I couldn't remember what I did with them.

"Yo, where my keys at?" I asked Moesha.

"I don't know. I can take you home. I have to leave out and grab a few things for the block party," she said sadly. I got a good look at her and realized she looked fucked up, too. Her hair was all over the place and her eyes were swollen from crying. She reached out to me and squeezed me. I lazily wrapped one arm around her waist.

"I'm going to miss him. I should've done more since I was older than him," Moesha cried. When you lose someone close to you, you start blaming yourself, thinking you could've prevented their death. I know it was fucked up that I was consoling another woman, but during that split-second we had something in common. She pulled away from me and I wiped her tears away.

"You ready?" I asked.

"Yeah," she said.

Moesha grabbed her purse and keys and we walked out of the bedroom. A picture of me, Ammo, Pistol, and Glock caught my eye as I walked down the hall. We were around fourteen years old, standing in front of my mother's crib. We had our middle fingers up while holding our dicks. That shit was lame but back then those kinds of pictures meant something to us street niggas.

"I was picking Ammo up from your house that day. He was the one who asked me to take the picture. I value that picture so much," Moesha said from behind me. I took it off the wall and she stared at me.

"I don't care what you say, I'm keepin' this picture. Your family has enough of 'em," I said and she shrugged her shoulders.

"Let's hurry up. I want to catch the grocery store before it gets too crowded," she said. On our way leaving out of the house, Ammo's aunt, Lashonda, was sitting on the couch with a glass of wine in her hand.

"I'll be back, Aunty," Moesha said.

"Okay, and please be safe," she replied.

"Appreciate you for lettin' me crash here. Let me know if you need anything," I said to her.

"You're always welcome here," Lashonda said.

I walked out of the door and Moesha was behind me. She hit the remote to her Audi to unlock the door. I turned my phones on as I sat in the passenger's seat. I had two hundred text messages and mad voicemails. I read the ones from, Kemara first, and to my surprise, she wasn't cursing me out. Shorty really matured over the months because she would've been threatening my life. I wasn't lying about needing to take a break from her. I couldn't give her what she deserved on an emotional level. I'd rather her be happy than dealing with me roaming the streets all night because shit wasn't going to be the same. I also didn't want her stressing while carrying my seed, so time apart for a bit was my only option. The drive to my crib was a silent one, the radio wasn't even on. Thirty-six minutes later, Moesha was pulling up to my house. Kemara's truck and car were in the driveway.

"I'll see you later," Moesha said.

"Appreciate it," I replied.

She reached in to hug me and planted a kiss on the side of my lips which caught me off guard. Suddenly, glass shattered and Moesha ducked down. When I looked up, Mara was standing in front the car, holding a gun with a silencer attached.

"Yo, what the fuck!" I yelled out when I jumped out of the car. Moesha hurriedly backed out of the driveway and sped off.

"You have been gone for almost four fucking days! No calls, no texts, nothing! I jumped out of bed in excitement when I heard the car pull up in the driveway but naw, it was you and that bitch!" Mara screamed.

"Mara, put the gun down!" I gritted and she pointed it at my face.

"You couldn't let me console you? You turned to another bitch?" Mara screamed. I grabbed the gun out of her hand and it went off, shooting air out of one of her tires. We wrestled around in the driveway as I dragged her into the house. I never saw that side of Mara before. I knew shorty was a little crazy but she was trying to kill someone in broad daylight.

"Get the fuck off of me!" Mara yelled and I let her go. She picked up a vase and threw it at me.

"AWWW SHIT!" I yelled out when it slammed into my shoulder.

"Hurt people, hurt people, huh? How can you hurt me like this? You gave me the impression you wanted to be alone but you weren't! I warned you not to fuck wit' me. I'm fuckin' carryin' your child for cryin' out loud!" Kemara screamed as she threw a picture at me.

"You are fuckin' up the house!" I yelled back.

"Nigga, fuck you!" Kemara said and threw another picture at me. She went into the kitchen and came back out with a butcher knife. She charged into me and cut my arm. I choke slammed her into the wall and she dropped the knife.

"Baby, please calm down!" I said, wrapping my arms around her. She pushed me away from her and headed up the stairs. I went into the hall bathroom and cleaned off my arm. The cut wasn't deep but the shit burned like hell. I waited for a few minutes before I walked into our bedroom. Kemara was sitting on the bed with her back towards me. The room was filled with balloons, stuffed animals, and sympathy cards. Shorty really went all out for me to make me feel better and I felt so fucked up behind it. How could I fix myself to tell her I needed space because I wasn't any good to her right now? I knew it was going to get worse because Ammo getting killed was only the beginning to our many problems. I walked around to face her. She was no longer angry—she was sad. Her robe was slightly open, revealing her white lace bra. I reached out to her when I noticed her hand was bleeding. She cut herself when she tried to stab me.

"Don't touch me," she said.

"I didn't fuck dat girl, Mara. I crashed at Ammo's people's crib and she was there. I lost my keys and she brought me home. I promise fuckin' another bitch ain't even on my mind right now," I said.

"I'm loyal to the wrong people," Mara said and wiped her eyes. Mara's pregnancy was beginning to show. She was around twelve weeks and seeing her sitting there carrying my seed brought me out of the state I was in. I kneeled in front of her and she slapped me in the face. She tried to slap me again but I grabbed her hand and kissed it.

"I need you," I pleaded.

When I opened her robe, I kissed her stomach then wrapped my arms around her. Her soft skin smelled fresh out of the shower. I did so much wrong shit in my life, I could never tell when I was doing something right and that's what fucked my head up. I was now living a double life. At home, I had a beautiful shorty who was carrying my seed that I wanted to do everything right for. In the streets, I was a ruthless nigga who didn't care about shit, including my own life.

"Did you sleep with her?" Mara asked.

"You should've asked her instead of shootin' at her," I replied.

"I was shooting at you. Moesha don't owe me shit, but you do. I'm pregnant by you, not her! So, trust me, that bullet had your fuckin' name on it," Mara said and pushed me away from her. She went to the closet and started throwing my clothes on the floor.

"You want your space, you can have all of it!" Mara said, throwing my shit across the room.

"How do you even have enough energy for all of this bullshit, huh? You shot at me, fucked the house up, stabbed me in the arm and now you're kicking me out of my own fuckin' house?" I asked, puzzled.

"A bitch turns into the Energizer bunny when she gets fed up. I'm goin' to keep goin' and goin' until you get the fuck outta my face. You made it clear when you ended up with her. It's not about you fuckin' her! It's the principle of you runnin' to a bitch you have history wit'! A bitch that still wants you! You emotionally cheated on me is what you did. Sugar coat it however you want to but, nigga, not today! You want your fuckin' space and you shall have it! Got me goin' crazy, missin' school and not eatin' because I was worried sick about you! I even missed a prenatal visit. I was here taking on your pain, too, but nope. You were cuddled up with that bitch. I must have 'fool' written across my forehead if you think you gonna come home and feed me bullshit," Mara said.

"Yo, put my shit back!" I yelled at her but she kept throwing my shit. She threw a Timb at me and it hit me in the face. Blood dripped onto my shirt from my nose and that's when I lost it. I slapped the shit out of Mara. Shorty had been putting her hands on me since day one and I had been letting that shit slide. I was trying to tell the bitch I wasn't cheating on her but she was still tripping.

"KEEP YOUR HANDS TO YAH FUCKIN' SELF!" I yelled at her. She laid on the floor, holding her face with tears in her eyes.

"Now do you see why niggas run to other bitches when they're going through some shit? Yo, on God, you're lucky I love you because I was supposed to been had merked you for your fly ass mouth and hand problem. You like seein' this side of me, don't you? You don't respect me when I'm tryin' to be nice to yah ass. This is exactly what I was talkin' about. A nigga starts showin' a passionate side and muthafuckas be trying to test him. I'M NOT DAT FUCKIN' NIGGA, MARA!" I said and pounded my chest. She got up and ran to the bathroom. She locked the door and I banged on it.

"Open the fuckin' door! You don't give a fuck about me! You like seein' me like this, don't you? Why you wanna kick me down after I been knocked down already? You tryna tear me apart, Mara?" I yelled at her. Tears welled up in my eyes as I continued banging on the door but they didn't fall. It wasn't tears from sadness, I was so angry that I wanted to kill the bitch.

Kemara

O n everything, I wanted to be done with Beretta. I had been worried sick about him and it was stressing me out. The nerve of him being with that bitch, Moesha, and not returning my phone calls or texts. I probably overreacted when I shot at him but it happened and it wasn't nothing I could do about it.

"OPEN THE FUCKING DOOR!" Beretta yelled.

I ran to the bathroom after he hit me because I had to vomit. Being pregnant was taking a toll on me because I was easily getting depressed. The door flew off the hinges and pieces of woods went over my head.

"Just leave," I said before I threw up again.

I flushed the toilet after I was finished and went to the sink to look at my face in the mirror. Beretta stood behind me, his handsome face twisted up in a scowl.

"What do you want to do? Hit me again?" I asked.

"I swear if you weren't knocked up, Mara," he seethed.

"Be thankful that I am because I can go all damn day. Nigga, get the fuck outta my face," I said. Beretta stepped over the door and came further into the bathroom. He took his clothes off and stepped into the shower. While inside, I snatched his jeans off the floor and went into his pockets searching for condoms. He was watching me through the glass door, but did I care? I wasn't trying to hide from him. I wanted to know if he was out fucking other women.

"Crazy-ass bitch," he said.

"Your hoe-ass Mama," I spat.

"Yeah, you would know a hoe when you see one," he said.

I snatched the shower door open and he smirked at me.

"Yo, Mara, on some real shit. The hood is gonna be wearin' RIP shirts with your face on it if you put your hands on me while I'm tryna take a shower. Yo, get the fuck gone," he said.

"Lil' dick fucka," I said, walking away.

"But these hoes be on it! Get some act right before I fix dat attitude," Beretta argued. While he was in the shower, I packed a small bag and threw some clothes on. By the time he got out, I was already leaving out the door to go to Silk's apartment. I got to my old hood in no time and sadness overcame me. Ammo's face was spray painted on the side of a building as you drove into the hood. A lot of people were in the street wearing RIP Ammo T-shirts. The parking lots were full so I parked in the grass by the basketball court. I grabbed my bag and got out of my car. Denesha and her friends were standing on the sidewalk when I walked past. I heard them saying something slick about me but, like always, I ignored them.

I walked into Silk's building and the strong smell of weed and other drugs filled the hallway. I knew the smell of crack when I smelled it and a few crackheads lived in Silk's building. Loud music was coming from one of the crackhead's apartments and I chuckled to myself. It seemed like every fiend in the hood listened to the same music: Marvin Gaye, Isley Brothers, Gap Band, Earth Wind and Fire and more. I knocked on Silk's door and he opened it dressed in a jogging suit with a silk scarf around his head. His eyebrows were fiercely arched and his lip gloss was popping as usual.

"Give me some suga," he said and pulled me into the apartment. When he hugged me, he squeezed my ass and playfully licked my neck. I pushed him into the kitchen table and he laughed at me.

"Don't play wit' me," I said.

"Girl, I know that thing is juicy. Pregnant pussy is tighter than fresh ass," he said.

"I swear you need to pick a side and stick to it," I laughed.

SOUL Publications

"What happened to your face?" he asked, grabbing my chin.

"Me and Beretta got into a big fight. This nigga had the muthafuckin' audacity to be stayin' wit' a bitch! Ammo's hoe ass sista dropped him off at home this mornin'. I was happy as hell when I heard that car pull up but when I looked out the window and saw them, I lost it. I grabbed the gun from underneath my mattress and hauled ass outside. That bitch had the nerve to kiss him and he let her, so I fired at his ass. I need to work on my aim," I said, flopping down on the couch.

"Then what happened?" Silk asked and sat down with his legs crossed.

"I put my hands on him then suddenly I found myself on the floor. Honey, I ain't never been hit so hard in my life. That nigga slapped my ass deaf," I said, getting mad all over again.

"Ohhhh, bitch, he was mad. Damn, I'm moist. That fine ass nigga can slap me any day. Hoe, you lucky," Silk said.

"Why am I friends wit' you?" I asked.

"Because I got a big dick and I'm flyer than a crackhead on Easter Sunday," he said, snapping his fingers and jerking his neck. My cell phone rang and it was Beretta calling me.

"Now his fingers work," I said.

"Chile, you better give him your ass to kiss for a few days. But all jokes aside, you can't be out here hittin' niggas. My baby mama slapped me the other day and I almost yanked her head off her neck. I had to remind dat hoe of my female tendencies. One minute, I can be a diva, and then the next minute, I can be a member of GMBAM. She caught me on my diva day 'cause chile I scratched her ass up bad. I was wind-milling on dat hoe," Silk said.

"Then what happened?" I asked.

"The GMBAM came out of me. I snatched her panties off and gave her all eleven inches of my dick. See, I got the best of both worlds," he said.

"Is that why you're dressed like R. Kelly with a RuPaul face on?" I replied.

"Oh, honey, don't do me right now. You know you want this sausage," Silk said.

"Do you still fuck niggas?" I asked.

"Every now and then this ass squirts for a real nigga but I don't do fish niggas. I'm only spreading these tight buns for a hood nigga," Silk said and I shook my head. Beretta called my phone again and I sent him to voicemail. My phone began beeping and I had several text messages from him. He wanted to know if I could come back home so we could talk. The nerve of him! Silk snatched my phone from me and turned it off.

"Sometimes you gotta show a nigga before you tell 'em," Silk said.

SOUL Publications

"I'm not listenin' to you. One minute you think Beretta's behavior is sexy but always lecture me about no-good ass niggas. You ain't no good, neither, shit," I fussed and he grabbed his chest. Piper walked into the apartment dressed in tight jeans, tennis shoes, and a tight-fitting shirt with Ammo's face on it.

"Ummmm, look at my other baby mama," Silk said.

"Don't pay him no mind, Piper. Silk wants all the bitches now," I chuckled. Piper went into her bag and pulled out an Ammo shirt for me.

"I know I'm chubby but am I really this big?" I asked, holding the shirt up.

"I mean, you gained a little weight. You still sexy, though," Piper said and Silk giggled.

"I need new friends," I said with an attitude.

"Come on, Mara. You're pregnant and you have spread a little. It's happy weight. What happened to your face?" Piper asked.

"Beretta was tryna get her to eat the cake," Silk said.

"Oh, hell nawl! We fittin' to jump his ass," Piper said and Silk laughed.

"You know damn well nobody is fittin' to jump Big Daddy," Silk said.

Piper was madder than me after I told her what happened between me and Beretta.

"Don't get pregnant by him again, Mara," Piper said and Silk threw a pillow at her.

"Ain't nobody killin' babies like you. You got dat NICU pussy," Silk said to Piper.

"Shut the fuck up. You just mad 'cause I don't want to pop one out for you," Piper said then they started arguing. Silk said the cruelest shit but we knew he didn't know any better.

"Take care of those corns on your feet, sis!" Piper said to Silk.

"Did anyone talk to Thickems today?" I asked.

"I did earlier for a few minutes. She said she couldn't make it because it was too much on her," Piper said.

"Where is Pistol?" I asked Piper and she rolled her eyes.

"At my house," she said with a fake attitude.

"Now she's actin' brand new because she's fuckin' dat old ass man," Silk snitched.

"Wait, what old man?" I asked.

SOUL Publications

"Please don't shut me out again the next time you're goin' through it wit' Beretta. I hate tellin' Ms. Doubtfire shit. Nigga run his mouth more than an enema runnin' shit outta of his ass," Piper said and I burst into laughter. Silk stood up and pulled his pants down. He turned around then propped his leg up on the couch.

"But I can shake this peach better than you!" he said, bouncing his scrawny ass.

"Ewww, what's that smell?" Piper asked.

"Those dead fetuses in your twat, hoe," Silk said.

"And your daughter gonna be baldheaded like her mama, loose-booty bitch," Piper said. Silk sat on the couch and began laughing.

"She's gonna slay just like both of her mamas," Silk said.

Someone knocked on the door and Silk opened it. My face dropped when my mother walked in with two of her crackhead friends. What bothered me the most was that she was pregnant. Her hair was matted and her church shoes were two sizes too big. Her face was sunken in and more of her teeth were missing. The last time I saw her, she didn't look that bad. My nose burned from the fishy onion smell that was coming off her body. Tears welled up in my eyes but I refused to let them fall. I was honestly tired of crying. For many years, I wished I had a mother but when I hit my teenage years, I gave up on the idea.

Seeing her that way brought back those old feelings again—I wanted a mother.

"Ma, what did you do to yourself?" I asked.

"Can I borrow ten dollas?" she asked, plucking at a scab on her face. When it bled, my stomach began turning.

"You don't need ten dollas! You need to get clean," Piper said.

"Y'all little hoes tryin' to judge me?" my mother asked.

"Who are you pregnant by, Darcel?" Silk asked my mother as he sprayed air freshener around his living room.

"I'm not pregnant," she lied.

"Can I have ten dollas or not, Mara? I saw you pull up in that expensive car and don't think I'on know about you fuckin' Nika's son," my mother said.

"Ma, you look pregnant! You can't be out here gettin' high," I said.

"Let's just go, Darcel. I told you your daughter is on her high horse," one of her crackhead friends said.

"Didn't all of y'all die in the crack house fire with Piper's mother?" Silk asked and Piper slapped his arm.

"I'm just sayin'. I didn't think there were any more crackheads left in da neighborhood after that." Silk shrugged his shoulders.

"Where are you stayin' at, Ma? Do you want me to take you to a rehab or something? It's time you get clean and stop runnin' the streets. Have you ever thought about your kids? What about me and Poppa? Our upbringing doesn't bother you?" I asked.

"Bitch, I didn't come up here for a church service. Do you have ten dollas or not? I'm not leavin' out of this muthafucka until you give it to me. I gave you shelter for nineteen years," she said.

"And for three years, I paid all the bills. I don't owe you anything!" I said. Silk went into his purse on the table and pulled out a twenty-dollar bill.

"Really, Silk?" I asked.

"I want them out of my apartment and I damn sho ain't touching them," Silk spat with an attitude. He handed my mother the twenty and she snatched it from him. Just like that, Darcel and her friends were gone.

"Get over it, Mara. That woman isn't your mother and has neva been a mother to you. You continue raisin' yourself and focus on your own baby, shit. That baby she's pregnant wit' is goin' to be another Poppa," Silk said and Piper agreed.

"I feel like I should do something," I said.

Welcome to the Low Life 2

"You can't help dead people," Silk replied.

I went to Silk's bathroom to shower and get dressed. I applied make-up on my face to hide the bruise Beretta gave me. I also put big loose curls into my weave and made a swoop bang over my eye. The shirt Piper gave me was a little big, so I tied it in a knot. I stood in the mirror behind Silk's door then turned to the side.

"You still got it," I said aloud, admiring my plump backside.

"Ummmm, look at you," Piper said when I came out of the bathroom. Silk tried to smack my ass but I slapped his hand away.

"You need to give Piper some of dat ass 'cause, honeyyyyy, you heavy back there," Silk said.

"I got an ass," Piper said.

"You got a cute handful ass but Mara got that big country booty that jiggles when she walks," Silk said.

"I got more ass than Fushia," Piper laughed.

Silk made mixed drinks for him and Piper. He didn't want me to feel left out so he fixed me a virgin strawberry daiquiri.

"I'm having a glass of red wine next month," I said as we walked out of the apartment.

"Red wine is good for you. Wait a minute, what is Darcel doin'?" Piper asked, pointing.

Across the street in the parking lot, my mother was washing a car and her friends had cardboard signs up with the words, *Ammo's Carwesh* written across it. Hustle Man was walking up and down the street with T-shirts of Ammo. Even Ammo's picture was bootlegged on the shirt.

"Please tell me Hustle Man is not selling some fake pictures of Ammo," I said and Silk laughed. The picture of Ammo was of a white fat man with blond hair.

"Hustle Man! Get your ass over here!" I called out to him. He walked across the street with an over exaggerated pimp walk.

"What's up, Pretty Girl?" he asked.

"You do know GMBAM ain't gonna be happy about you sellin' fake pictures of Ammo. Come on, you can't do this today. Any other day, I'm all for your hustle, but everyone in the hood has a picture of Ammo. You could've gotten one," I said.

"I was in a rush and, besides, not everybody has ten dollas for a T-shirt. I'm sellin' these for two dollas," he said. I reached into my pocket and pulled out a fifty-dollar bill. I gave it to Hustle Man and bought all the shirts from him. Sadly, I saw a few people walk down the street wearing the fake T-shirts. I thought it was disrespectful considering all Ammo had done for the community. One thing about the hood is that after you die, you'll just be one of the many others who didn't make it.

"Appreciate it. I got a few Boost phones on sale for twenty dollas," Hustle Man said.

"Naw, I'm good," I replied and he walked away. I threw the shirts in the trash can and Piper shook her head.

"These niggas about to get their asses beat for wearin' those fake shirts. Wait until the hood gets drunk and wild," Piper said and I agreed.

Flo walked down the street rapping lyrics to Lil Wayne's song, "Man I Miss My Dog" with tears falling down his face. He had a bottle of Grey Goose in his hand with a GMBAM T-shirt on.

"What's up, Pretty Girl? I'm so hurt right now. Ammo was my right-hand man. Me and that nigga got caught doin' a whole bunch of wild shit. I remember dat one time when we got into a big shoot up with the FEDS," Flo said and I rolled my eyes. Everyone knew Flo was a compulsive liar.

"Oh, really? When did this happen?" I asked.

"When we all took a trip down North Carolina to see these bad ass strippers. Ammo loved the strippers. Piper was there, too. You don't remember dat night?" Flo asked Piper.

"Yeah, I caught a few bullets like a G," Piper said and I giggled.

Welcome to the Low Life 2

"So, why was the FEDS shootin' at y'all?" I asked.

Sometimes his stories would brighten up your day although they were fabricated.

"You know how Beretta be trippin' when niggas look at him wrong. We were in VIP wit' big ass Moet bottles to the ceiling. We spent almost three hundred thou' on the bottles. But, anyway, Beretta and this nigga starts arguin' then a big fight broke out. Come to find out, the nigga Beretta was arguin' with was undercover and was there on an assignment. Someone ratted us out, ya feel me? Anyways, Beretta pulls out his burner and starts pistol whippin' the nigga. Glock and Pistol jumped into the fight and that's when they started shootin' at us. Me and Ammo was bustin' back at those niggas, mane," Flo said.

"Oh, yeah, that's right. I gave y'all the keys to my car that night to get away," Piper chimed in.

"Appreciate it. But, look, I gotta bounce. I'm on the run, so I can't stay in one spot too long. Niggas still tryin' to get at me," Flo said then hurriedly bopped off.

"I think Flo is a little behind if you know what I mean. You simply cannot make up shit like that and think it's real," I said.

"His whole family is slow, chile. I'm not sayin' this to be funny, neither," Silk said.

A Navigator pulled up by the bus stop and a few girls hopped out. I recognized the one who got out of the passenger's side; it was Moesha. She slung her weave over her shoulder and strutted down the sidewalk like she was on the runway. Her friends followed her, carrying coolers, and one of them was carrying a small grill.

"There dat bitch go. I'm gonna fight her ass," Piper said.

"That's Ammo's sister, ain't it? I haven't seen that broad in years. She didn't hang out in the hood like dat," Silk said.

"Yeah, that's her," I spat.

"She's phat," Silk said.

"Of course, she is. Beretta likes big asses," I replied.

Carlos ran across the street to me. He was taller than the last time I saw him. He was an adorable little boy but his mother let him roam the streets while she drank and smoked weed with her friends. He lived in my old building on the top floor and had two younger sisters he looked out for.

"What's up, Mara? I haven't seen you in a while," he said.

"I'm okay, how about you? Are you stayin' out of trouble?" I asked and crossed my arms.

"Yeah, I am," he smirked.

"Stop all dat damn lyin'. You got expelled from school for startin' up a fake gang," Silk said.

"Mind yah business, nigga. I'm almost twelve years old and I can do what I want. My mama doesn't care so neither should you. Why are you wearin' make-up anyway?" Carlos asked Silk.

"I might be yo' daddy. Get on before I beat your lil' ass," Silk said and bucked at Carlos. Carlos bucked back at Silk.

"Where are your sisters?" I asked him.

"In da house playin' with their Barbies," he replied.

"Aight, be good and stop tryna be a gang member. You're too young for that," I said and he smacked his teeth.

"I ain't neva too young. Beretta started gang bangin' when he was my age, I heard," he said.

"That's a lie. Who told you that?" I asked.

"Flo," Carlos said.

"I'm gonna kick Flo's ass. Go on in the house or sumthin. It's gonna get rowdy soon," I said and he walked off.

"That lil' fucka is gonna be a handful when he gets older," Silk said and we agreed.

Welcome to the Low Life 2

A black-on-black Mercedes came through the hood and it was Beretta. After he parked and got out, everyone crowded his car, including the bitches that wanted to fuck him.

"Don't you start no bullshit, Mara," Silk said. A few vans pulled up and people got out with equipment for the music. It's crazy how someone's death seemed like a celebration. Beretta walked through the crowd wearing jeans, Timbs, and an RIP Ammo hoodie. The picture on his hoodie was of him, Pistol, and Glock from when they were younger.

"Come here, Mara," Beretta's deep voice called out. I rolled my eyes then waved him off.

"You still trippin'?" he asked when he got closer.

"Don't y'all start dat that shit today," Silk said and I gave him the finger. Beretta snatched my drink out of my hand and dumped it on the sidewalk.

"Yo, you drinkin' wit' my seed?" he asked.

"It was a virgin daiquiri. I'm chillin' though, so we can talk lata?" I said.

"Why you ain't answerin' my calls?" he asked.

"My phone broke," I lied.

"Take mine then. I got another one in da whip," he said, passing me his Blackberry phone.

"I'm good," I said, handing the phone back to him.

"Damn, Mara. What do you want me to do? Keep beggin' you or sumthin?" he asked, frustrated.

"I honestly don't want you to do anything but take all the time you need to yourself," I replied.

"Today is not the day, shorty," he said.

"I'm giving what you want and, honestly, I need a break from you, too. We fought each other earlier like we were enemies. We're supposed to be in love and it just doesn't seem that way right now, so please just leave me alone," I replied.

"Mannnn, I'm not tryin' to hear dat bullshit. I'll see you at home lata because this conversation ain't ova," he said. He wrapped his arms around my waist and kissed my lips. Piper took a picture with her camera phone then her and Silk bust out laughing.

"What's funny?" I asked after Beretta walked away.

"Y'all are crazy. I want a hood love like y'all's one day," Piper said.

"Not with that old man you are messin' wit'. You only got a good five more years outta him," Silk said.

"I fucked him and that was it and he's thirty-five. He might can teach me some things," Piper said and seductively licked her tongue.

"What pills to take for arthritis?" I joked.

"Oh, bitch, hush. You can't take dick anyway. Don't think I forgot how Beretta be makin' you cry," Piper said and Silk spit his drink out.

"The dick dat big?" Silk asked, fanning himself.

"He popped her cherry the first time they did it and she wasn't even a virgin. Matter of fact, the first few times Beretta had Mara spotting. I'on want dat type of dick," Piper said.

"Well, hoe, I do! Shat!" Silk said then downed the rest of his drink.

I sat on the step next to Piper and we clowned around for a few hours. The hood was packed and the music played throughout the parking lot. Beretta was making sure he stayed far away from Moesha. Matter of fact, Beretta stayed on the hood of his car the whole time.

"My nigga ain't gonna be the same after this," I said aloud.

"Yeah, I know. Look at him. He'll bounce back, though, probably just no time soon. If I lost you, I'd feel the same way. Hell, I'm surprised he's even showin' face so soon. I'd be on suicide watch," Piper said.

Denesha and her friends were drunk and high while dancing in the middle of the street. She was trying so hard to get Beretta's attention and it ran me hot. I loved the hood but since I got with Beretta, I hated it!

"I'm going to revert back to my old ways for a day after I drop this baby. I'm cleanin' the streets of these hoes," I seethed and Piper rubbed my back.

"Oh, Lord. Look what the wind blew in," Silk said.

Seeing Poppa and a few of his friends posted up on the sidewalk didn't sit too well with me. The newspaper stated that Ammo and Swan were involved in a deadly love triangle and they suspected more people were involved. I had a gut feeling Poppa knew something. Why else would he come to a block party for Ammo? I couldn't help Poppa if he was involved in Ammo's murder. It was something he would have to deal with on his own. He was creating unnecessary beef because of some childhood jealously he had with GMBAM.

Poppa

We were chilling in the hood scoping out the thirsty bitches. I was with Tyshawn, Shag, and Rich. Rich was just released from prison the day before and like I promised him, I paid him for taking care of Sid. With Sid out the way, I was able to move in on Mike. In a few days, he was going to put me down on the deed to his strip club, then afterwards, I was gonna smoke him. I was going to rob Mike the legal way.

"Yo, I see this little broad I used to talk to before I got locked up. I'm ready go holla at her really quick," Rich said to me before he bopped off.

"Yo, you good?" I asked Shag because he had a fake-ass mean mug on his face.

The nigga Beretta killed at Swan's crib was Shag's little cousin. Beretta and Pistol showing up was unexpected. I had been paranoid since because I was starting to think someone in my camp was snitching. My reason for coming to hood was to find out what the talk was about. I had to make sure my name wasn't linked to that shit. So far, everyone was saying that Swan and some out-of-town nigga set Ammo up.

"Yeah, I'm good. I wanna smoke dat nigga right now for merkin' my cousin," Shag seethed.

"Nigga, everyone in the hood just about is GMBAM. You won't make it out alive, just be patient," I said. Shag was an annoying ass nigga and I didn't want him around me.

"Look at dat nigga. They treat Beretta's bitch-ass like he Jesus or sumthin. Ain't that much genuine love in these streets," Tyshawn said as he smoked a blunt. Denesha walked over to me with her click trailing behind her.

"Heyyyyyy, Popppaaa," Denesha sang.

"What's good witchu?" I asked.

"Nothing, why you don't come through the hood like dat anymore?" she asked.

"This place ain't for me but I only came to show Ammo some love," I said.

"Maybe we can hook up tonight," she said, licking her lips.

"Yeah, maybe we can. Put your number in my phone," I said.

While she was giving me her number, Jasmine was walking past with a girl I had never seen before. Jasmine knew not to put our business out there especially since her brother was across the street talking to Beretta.

Welcome to the Low Life 2

"Heyyyy, Jasmine. Sniper let you out da house?" Denesha asked, handing me my phone.

"I'm grown," Jasmine said with an attitude.

"Well, how grown are you because aren't you still in high school?" Denesha asked and her friends laughed.

"I'm old enough to beat a bitch ass," Jasmine said and Denesha rolled her eyes.

"Let me get goin'. I'll call you lata," Denesha said and walked off with her small click. Jasmine was still standing by me and I turned my back towards her. I wanted to knock shorty's ass out for smothering me. Seconds later, Jasmine stormed away with her friend asking her what happened.

"You got dat little bitch trained," Tyshawn chuckled.

"All day," I replied and slapped hands with him.

"There goes Mara," Tyshawn said.

"Fuck her," I spat.

"Mara on some other shit. Shorty took the dick from me and gave me walkin' papers afterwards," Tyshawn said. Mara cutting him off was all he talked about.

"She knocked up by dat nigga, so you already know she ridin' for him," I said.

"Knocked up? Fuck you talkin' about?" Tyshawn asked.

"She's pregnant is what I'm talkin' about," I said and he was heated.

It was getting dark outside and it was time to light a candle for Ammo's bitch-ass. Mara, Piper, and Silk walked to the middle of the street holding candles. Beretta was on his way to Mara and he had to walk past me to get to her. As he walked past, he bumped into Tyshawn and Tyshawn's beer dropped on the ground.

"Watch where da fuck you goin," Tyshawn spat.

"What's good witchu? Still plottin' on robbin' niggas and shit? Still can't get the cake up I see," Beretta said to us.

"Yo, you trippin'," Shag bitched up. He talked all that shit about GMBAM but was scared. I knew I couldn't trust his bitch-ass.

"Oh, word. Come here, Sniper, check these niggas' pockets," Beretta said. Sniper and a nigga named Machete stepped from behind Beretta and checked our pockets. I wanted to swing on the nigga but we were outnumbered. Machete pulled a stash of money out of Tyshawn's pocket then stuffed it into his. I didn't have much. Sniper took the few hundreds I had in my pocket. The shit was embarrassing and made my blood boil.

"Seriously, Beretta?" Mara asked when she walked over to us.

"We just fuckin' wit' em, chill out. Give these clown ass niggas their money back," Beretta chuckled. Machete dropped my money down by my feet and I picked it up. Sniper threw Tyshawn's money into the crowd. I saw my mother jump off a car into the crowd to catch the flying one-hundred-dollar bills.

Beretta wrapped his arms around Mara and rubbed her stomach.

"I got some active shooters, bruh. Ain't dat right, Mara?" Beretta asked while kissing her cheek. He was taunting Tyshawn and I hoped the nigga wouldn't do anything stupid. I had shit to do and being shot up wasn't one of them.

"You sure 'bout dat because I don't never miss when I bust one off. Nigga, you a step-daddy," Tyshawn said to Beretta. Beretta pulled away from Kemara before he hit Tyshawn in the face. Tyshawn swung and hit Kemara by mistake. All hell broke loose when Beretta slammed him on the ground and stomped him out. People screamed for him to stop as he stomped Tyshawn's face into the ground with his Timb. Shag hit Beretta and Machete stabbed Shag in his stomach. In the hood, cops rarely got called so every man was for himself. They knew not to rat GMBAM niggas out. I hit Beretta to help Tyshawn out who was stretched out cold on the ground. Beretta hit me with a two-piece combo then sent a jab into my stomach. I swung and hit him in the face; he stumbled a little bit and that's when I slammed him into the car. We went blow for blow but nothing I did was stopping the lil' nigga. Even though we were going toe-to-toe, he had the upper-hand because he was a fighter. When Beretta was a teenager, he fought niggas every day and been in plenty of brawls, so my punches meant nothing to him.

"STOP!" Mara yelled when Beretta knocked me into a fence. I grabbed the fence to pull myself up but he kicked me in the face. My bottom tooth went through my lip.

"Yo, chill out!" Sniper said, trying to wrestle Beretta off me but he wouldn't stop. The last blow almost knocked me unconscious so I laid on the ground to cover my head. A minute or so later, Beretta stepped away from me.

"Get da fuck from around here and don't come back. This ain't your hood no more, nigga! Take those niggas with you, too!" Beretta said. A few people helped me up but my vision was still blurry. Blood dripped down my face and Tyshawn was still on the ground. I smiled at Beretta because I still had one up on him. I was the reason his right-hand man was frozen in the morgue. He thought I was a bitch-made nigga but I proved to myself that I could merk a nigga like it was nothing.

Beretta

"**W**hat were you thinkin'?" Mara yelled as I watched niggas carry Tyshawn and his homeboys out the hood. Honestly, I wasn't thinking but those niggas had it coming, especially that Tyshawn nigga. A while back, he bumped into me in the club on some fuck-nigga shit. When that nigga hit Mara in the face, I lost it. I was trying to take his head off until Poppa intervened. I knew he was a lame because he was helping out the nigga that hit his sister. He didn't care about Mara or the fact that she was pregnant. The nigga stood there and watched her fall to the ground.

"Fuck those niggas! Tyshawn was on some sucka shit when I saw him in Mikey's a few months back. A nigga ain't gonna disrespect me and make jokes about me because he fucked my bitch!" I yelled at Mara.

"Let's just go home," Mara said.

"Bruh, you good?" Sniper asked me.

"Yeah, I'm straight," I replied.

"I can merk those niggas right now if you want me to," he said.

"Naw, Poppa is Mara's brother," I replied.

It was a hard decision but I couldn't do my shorty like that after seeing the fear she had in her eyes. I still didn't want her around that nigga because he wasn't any good for her.

"Aight go home and get some rest. I'm ready to pour one out for the big homie," Sniper said before giving me dap. Mara gave Piper the keys to her truck before she got in the driver's seat of my whip. I cracked the top open to the Henny bottle I had on the floor. It was my second bottle. The first one I drank was at the block party. Mara snatched the bottle from me then threw it out of the window.

"So, you're an alcoholic now? Enough drinking!" she said.

"Is that my baby? Just tell me now because I won't be able to deal wit' da shit if it ain't mine," I said.

"I know for a fact it ain't his baby, but I'll give you a blood test if you don't believe me," she said, feeling defeated.

"I think after the funeral I'll be straight. Right now, I can't believe Ammo's gone. I need to see it for myself again," I said. I closed my eyes and dozed off as Mara drove us home.

****

"Wake up, Beretta," Mara shook me. We were in our driveway when I opened my eyes. She got out and unlocked the front door and I deactivated the alarm so it wouldn't go off. Mara walked up the stairs and I went to the hall bathroom to wash my face. I chuckled to myself because Mara did more damage to my face than both of those niggas. My nose was swollen because of the Timb she hit me with and I had scratches on my face from when she slapped me a few times. I rinsed my mouth out before I left out of the bathroom. Mara was coming down the stairs with a backpack.

"Where are you going?" I asked.

"I only came here to bring you home. You said you needed your space earlier, remember?" she asked.

"Yo, let dat shit go," I replied.

"That's so easy for you to say," she said.

"Yo, you shot at me and I ain't trippin' about dat anymore. I told you I didn't fuck the bitch, damn," I replied. Mara walked out of my face and headed towards the front door. I grabbed her back and closed the door and locked it. She tried to walk around me but I trapped her against the wall by the door.

"You ain't leavin'. Can you fix me sumthin to eat? My stomach fucked up. I ain't eat shit in days," I said.

"Only because it's about your health," she said.

SOUL Publications

I sat at the kitchen table while Mara made me something to eat. I ain't realize how hungry I was until I smelled the food.

"Hurry up, Mara," I said.

"I'm almost finished!" she yelled with an attitude.

"Can you make some Kool-Aid?" I asked.

"Aight," she spat.

Twenty-five minutes later, Mara brought me four cheese steak sandwiches with a big bowl of French fries. I devoured the food in five minutes as she sat and watched me from across the table.

"You're gonna choke," she said.

"Shorty, this shit is good. Appreciate you," I replied. I had some fries left so I reached over and put one in her mouth.

"Gave me the fries but couldn't save me a piece of sandwich," she smirked.

"My bad. I'll make you one tomorrow," I said.

I pushed the plates away then washed everything down with the Kool-Aid.

While Mara was at the kitchen washing dishes, I snuck up behind her and kissed her neck. I rubbed her stomach and she giggled.

"Get away from me," she said.

"Let me eat dat pussy, Pretty Girl," I replied and a plate slipped out of her hand into the sink. Kemara acted tough all day but she was shy. Shorty had a lot of layers to her and I loved all of them. I turned her around and unbuttoned her pants. My fingers played inside her thong while I sucked and licked her full pouty lips. She moaned against my lips when I slipped my finger into her pussy.

"I need this," I pleaded.

I kneeled in front of her to pull down her pants and thong. She stepped out of them and her fat glistening pussy was in front of my face. I turned her back around so she could face the sink. I always enjoyed snacking on Mara's pussy from the back so her ass cheeks could smother me. She gripped the edge of the counter when my tongue parted her lips. I pushed her left leg up so I could suck on her clit.

"OHHHHHHHH!" she moaned and I slapped her ass cheeks.

Mara moved her hips, riding my tongue as she accidentally swiped everything off the counter. Her cum dripped down my chin and I sped up the pace. I held her still so I could go deeper and she cried out my name.

"BERETTTTAAAAAA!" she screamed.

While Mara was still gushing on my tongue, I freed myself. I stood up and pushed her forward by the back of her neck. She whimpered when the tip of my dick graced the inside of her tight wet walls. After two strokes, I stopped so I could lick the back of her neck. A nigga was ready to bust after those few pumps but shorty wasn't having it. Mara threw her ass back, rotating her hips while moaning my name.

"SHITTTTTTT!" I groaned, gripping her hips. To keep from sounding like a bitch, I bit my bottom lip. I gave her a few more inches, stuffing my dick inside of her and she gasped. She wanted it rough, so I was going to give it to her. I pulled her hair, clutched her ponytail in my hand, as I rammed my dick into her, repeatedly hitting her gushy spot.

"IT'S TOO MUCH!" she cried out.

"Yo, shut the fuck up!" I grunted.

I hated that complaining shit about not being able to take dick especially when I wanted to fuck some shit up.

"It's tooooo big!" Mara complained.

"You cumming ain't you?" I asked while her legs trembled. Mara squirted on my dick and that shit made me harder. I pulled out of her and turned her around so she could face me. She took her shirt off and I unhooked her bra. Her breasts were round and succulent. I picked her up and sat her on the counter while I sucked her nipples. Her fingers ran through my dreads as she wrapped her legs around me. I pulled her down to the edge of the counter then entered her again. Instead of fucking her like I did moments ago, I made love to her. Her walls gripped the shit out of my dick. I sucked on her neck to keep from moaning out loud. Mara's moans was the sexiest shit I ever heard.

"You feel so good, shorty. Fuck! I swear this shit mine foreva," I groaned. She dug her nails in my back and I reached down to play with her clit. She screamed when I pinned her legs up and went deeper. Her pussy gripped my dick so hard I started telling her how I'd kill her if she fucked another nigga. Crazy thing about it, I wasn't just saying that because her pussy was A-1. I really did love my shorty and would merk a nigga over her. I put that on my unborn seed!

"ARGGHHHHHHH!" I jerked as I exploded inside of her. She wrapped her arms around my neck when I fell into her. I couldn't catch my breath; she drained me.

"We haven't done it like that in a while," she said.

"That's 'cause you keep complaining," I replied.

Her cell phone vibrated. I pulled out of her and snatched her phone off the counter to answer it.

"Yoooo," I answered.

"Ummmm, hi. My name is Emma. Can I speak to Kemara?" the caller asked.

"Naw, you can't. You callin' for somebody or sumthin?" I replied.

"We go to school together," she said.

"Yo, you and this Emma broad double-datin' niggas or sumthin?" I asked Mara. She snatched her phone from me when she slid off the counter.

"We're friends. Females with no-good ass niggas need to stick together," Mara said and walked out the kitchen. I headed upstairs to our bedroom. Ammo's chain was hanging on the mirror of the dresser. It still had blood on it. I took it off the mirror and went into the bathroom to clean it off with jewelry cleaner. An hour passed and blood was still stuck between the diamonds.

"Send it to the jeweler. Let's get ready for bed," Mara said when she stepped out of the shower.

"Naw, I got it," I said.

She took the chain from me. "Get in the shower. I'll do it," she said.

"I want to get away for a few days after the funeral," I replied.

"That'll be good for us," she said then kissed my lips.

Mara was important in my life, no doubt, but I still had an operation that needed more of my time. I wanted to spend as much time with her as I could before I got back to grinding. I had to make sure what happened to Ammo didn't happen to anybody else close to me.

****

The next day...

"You could've crashed at my spot," I said to Pistol.

We were in Piper's crib, sitting in the living room. Pistol had a bandage around his stomach and the nigga was high as a kite. He was taking pain meds and smoking weed. He was heated because he couldn't come to the block party. He was even more pissed off because he heard what went down with me, Poppa, and that clown-ass nigga, Tyshawn.

"Nigga, stop lyin'. You know damn well you ain't havin' anotha nigga in da crib with Mara," he chuckled.

"Come on, bruh. It'll be hard on a nigga, though," I chuckled.

"We still hittin' Mike's bitch-ass up, right?" Pistol asked.

"We? Nigga, you ain't goin'," I replied.

"Yeah, aight. That's what you think," Pistol replied.

"You still fucked up. How are you gonna do this? Anyways, I'm goin' there in a few hours to get my money from his bitch-ass. I'on trust dat nigga at this point, so he gotta go," I replied.

"You stay on dat paranoid shit but on da real, ain't nothin' wrong wit' it. I realized you merk niggas dat you get bad vibes from and could possibly be your downfall. All street niggas need to have dat mentality. It's fucked up but I'd rather be safe than sorry. If Mike gotta go, he gotta go. Do you think he had sumthin to do wit' Ammo?" Pistol asked.

"I'on know, yo, but he's a dead man anyway. We already know what happened to Ammo. Swan was fuckin' wit' a nigga and they set Ammo up. I been told dat nigga to stop fuckin' wit' Swan. He was doin' too much shit to shorty and I knew she was gonna get him back. I wasn't expectin' it to be like this," I said.

"A bitch is every man's downfall," Pistol said, and for some reason that struck a nerve. I know Mara was in love with a nigga but sometimes I thought about how much shit she could use against me. I would never tell my niggas that, though. My business was my business.

Piper came into the house with a grocery bag. She smacked her teeth when she realized I had my shoes on her carpet.

"Why are your shoes on my carpet?" she asked.

"'Cause I ain't take them off. You need help wit' da bags or sumthin?" I asked.

"Naw, I don't trust you bein' nice to me. Where is Mara at anyway? She ain't answerin' da phone," she replied.

"Still sleep from last night," I said.

"Nasty asses. I hope you don't plan on keepin' her pregnant," Piper joked.

"Dat's my pussy. I can nut in dat muthafucka wheneva I want to," I replied and she rolled her eyes.

"The doctor said you can't smoke or drink while takin' those pills," Piper said to Pistol.

"Weed is natural. Did you grab me some Capri Suns and beef jerky?" Pistol asked her.

"Yeah, and your Twinkies," she replied.

"Nigga, you still eat snacks?" I asked Pistol.

"Leave him alone, Beretta. I think it's cute," Piper said. When she went into the kitchen, I shook my head at Pistol.

"You into some shit," I said.

"Yeah, aight. I don't look at her like dat," Pistol said.

"Naw, bruh. It's serious when a shorty starts buyin' your special snacks. She's not gonna be doin' extra grocery shoppin' if she ain't feelin' you. Females hate goin' to the store," I replied.

"How do you know?" He chuckled.

"I've watched Nika do the same shit for all her different niggas. I had to practically beg her dumbass to bring me back some Doritos and I'm her son," I replied. The doorbell rang and Piper rushed to the door. When she opened it, a nigga stepped into the crib. I could tell he wasn't a street nigga and he looked way older than Piper.

"Damn, Baby Girl. I would've straightened up da livin' room if I knew your pops was comin'," Pistol said.

"Ummm, this is Delonte. Delonte, these are my close friends," Piper said. Delonte looked at me and Pistol. He scratched his chin then brushed his hand down his head; me and Pistol was making him uncomfortable.

"What's up," I said and gave him a head nod. He returned the gesture. Pistol, on the other hand, was rolling up another blunt.

"We are goin' out to eat, so I'll be back. Do you need anything before I go?" Piper asked Pistol.

"Naw, I'm good. Enjoy ya self," Pistol replied, not looking up from his blunt. Piper grabbed her purse by the door and stormed out of the house, pulling Delonte with her.

"Damn, nigga. You salty?" I asked.

"Fuck her, bruh. She ain't doin shit but sellin' his old ass some pussy," Pistol said.

SOUL Publications

"He might be the one to calm her down," I said.

"Nigga, he owns the club she strips at. Dat nigga is just smashin' her," he said.

"Aight, bruh. I'll get up wit' you lata. I'm about to head over to Ammo's aunt's crib to drop off his outfit for the funeral tomorrow," I said.

"Dat nigga gonna be stuntin', ain't he? I know you got him, right," he said.

"Yo, he gonna be decked out in Gucci with the shades to match. You know how he felt about Gucci," I replied. I slapped hands with Pistol before I left out of the crib.

****

Ammo's family was seated around the living room when I walked into the house. A few of his cousins flew in from Texas. The house was crowded and kids were running through knocking over plants. Moesha threw her arms around my neck and pressed her body against mine like there was something more between us.

"Do you want something to eat?" Ammo's aunt asked me.

"Naw, I'm good. I gotta hurry up and head home," I replied. I pulled away from Moesha and gave her Ammo's outfit.

SOUL Publications

"Where is his chain?" Moesha asked, looking into the bag.

"You can't bury him in gang shit," I replied and she agreed.

"Well, can I have it?" she asked.

"So you can pawn it?" I asked and she rolled her eyes. Ammo told me stories about how Moesha stole money out of his stash when they were younger. I wouldn't trust her with shit valuable of his other than his vehicles.

"I wouldn't do that," she spat.

Thickems came out of the bathroom in the hallway with red puffy eyes. I wondered if Mara knew she was back in town because she was MIA.

"Hey, Beretta," Thickems said and I hugged her.

"What's good witchu? You need anything?" I asked.

"No, I'm fine. Tell Mara I'll call her lata on tonight," she said before she walked away. Moesha rolled her eyes at Thickems and I thought it was childish.

"Yo, shorty knocked up with your brother's seed. You ain't gotta treat her like dat," I said.

'She's a stripper and I don't know if she's carrying Ammo's child. These little hoes are only looking for a come-up. She's not getting a dime out of Ammo's life insurance. She better pop that pussy on the pole for some pampers and similac," Moesha said.

"She doesn't need your family for shit. I'm gonna look out for her," I replied.

"Don't think I've forgotten how your little girlfriend shot my car window out," she said. I reached into my pocket and peeled off a few hundreds.

"You should stay for dinner," she said as she stuffed the money between her cleavage.

"Naw, my baby mama cookin' for me," I replied and she smacked her teeth.

"Go on ahead. Just know I got what I wanted anyway," she said before she walked away.

I didn't have time for Moesha's mind games. Shorty was losing her damn mind. I said goodbye to everyone before I left. My phone beeped as soon as I got inside my whip. It was picture messages from Moesha. I wanted to snap her neck! Shorty took pictures of me with my dick in her mouth. In one picture, she was sitting on my face like I was eating her out. I cursed out loud when the third picture came through. That broad was fucking me while I was knocked out asleep. She didn't show my face. I guess she didn't want people to see that I was asleep, but you could tell it was me because of my tattoos. I spent days over her aunt's house drunk as shit, not knowing where I was at. That bitch took advantage of me. I knew my dick and I could never get hard while being drunk.

SOUL Publications

Welcome to the Low Life 2

I couldn't have been hard. I would've felt that shit! I thought.

Moesha was looking out the living room window when I looked up at the house. I should've stayed my ass home that night but I damn sure wasn't thinking about how desperate Moesha's ass was. Shorty had never been that devious in the past but then I had to think about what she could gain from me. I was younger and didn't have shit back when I was fucking her. Now I was getting bread and bitches were on my dick. Moesha had a good job and a college education but sometimes you can never take the hood out of a broad. She was still chasing hustlers.

When she waved at me, I pulled off. She called my phone and I answered.

"Yo, you desperate as shit!" I yelled into the phone.

"Don't fuck with me, Z'wan. No other bitch should ever come before me, but don't worry about it. You couldn't stay hard but I did enjoy your lips on my pussy when I sat on your face. It was like old times. I just wanted you to see that I always get what I want," she replied and hung up. I tossed my phone in the back seat after I deleted the pictures.

Moesha will be joining you soon, bro, I thought.

＊＊＊＊＊＊＊＊＊＊＊＊＊

Mara was in the living room dancing to a music video on TV. It was probably something she did on the regular when I wasn't home. She didn't hear me come in, so I stood in the entryway of the living room staring at her. Shorty was dancing like she was a stripper. She was listening to Lil' Wayne's new song, "She Will." Her meaty ass cheeks slipped out of her shorts.

"Damn, Mara," I said and she jumped.

"Fool, I told you about sneakin' up on me like that!" she said.

"Why you don't dance for me like dat?" I asked.

"Because I'm shy, shit," she spat with attitude.

"You weren't shy makin' dat baby, though," I said and she smirked.

"Never when it comes to that," she said. She walked over to me and wrapped her arms around my neck.

"Did you pack? We leavin' right after the funeral," I said.

"Yeah, I packed. Where are we goin'?" she asked.

"It's a surprise," I replied.

"Nika called my phone lookin' for you. She wanted to know if you made up your mind yet about loanin' her the money," Mara said.

"Dat bitch talkin' about a fuckin' restaurant while I'm still dealin' wit' Ammo's death?" I asked and Mara nodded

SOUL Publications

her head. I pulled away from Mara so I could call Nika. She answered on the second ring.

"The fuck you callin' Mara for 'bout some money?" I asked.

"Oh, hold the fuck up, Z'wan!" Nika yelled at me.

"Fuck all dat! Fuck your restaurant! My nigga just got merked and you pressed about me givin' you some money? Get it how you been gettin' it! Go fuck and suck for it," I said and Mara covered her mouth.

"I know damn well you ain't talkin' to me like this," Nika said.

"Like what? You think I should respect you because you gave birth to me? You ain't give a fuck 'bout me and still don't! You didn't even call to see how I was doin' after I told you Ammo was dead! When I got stabbed, you came here for fifteen minutes to make some nasty ass soup then left! It's because of you I got sucked into da streets. Yah niggas had me baggin' up work for them when I was a lil' nigga and you were cool wit' it," I said.

"You had a roof over your head! I did what I had to do so you could have nice shoes and clothes! I did my fuckin' job!" Nika screamed into the phone.

"IT WASN'T ENOUGH!" I yelled back.

"Calm down, Beretta," Mara said.

"Naw, fuck dat! She gotta hear it!" I replied to Mara.

SOUL Publications

"I ain't neva had no discipline, now look at me! I'm a muthafuckin' misfit! Yo, don't call me for shit! I'm takin' care of your daughter so you should be grateful. That should be enough, but you still askin' me for more. I ain't got it. I'm tryna move into a bigger crib and take care of MY own seed when Mara gives birth. This shit ain't about you anymore," I said and she hung up on me.

"She's still your mother," Mara said.

"Yo, not right now. You don't respect your mother, neither, so we ain't fittin' to do this right now," I replied.

"Nika is far from perfect but she's nothing like my mother," Mara said.

"I'm goin' upstairs to take a nap," I replied. I went into the kitchen to grab a bottle of Henny. Mara was ready to say something but I gave her a look, daring her to question me about it. I developed a drinking problem but, shit, a nigga was losing his mind. Henny was my savior at that moment. I decided to chill in the crib for the rest of the night so I hit up Sniper.

"Yoooo," he answered with music blasting in the background.

"Make sure my money is all there before y'all make a move," I said to him about Mike.

"Aight, bet. You ain't comin'?" he asked.

"Naw, I been sippin," I replied.

"Okay, bet. I'll get everyone together and we'll take it from there. Be easy, my nigga, one," he said before hanging up the phone. Mara came into the bedroom and got in bed with me. I ran my fingers through her hair while she was laying on my chest.

"I wish I could fix your problems," she said and I kissed her forehead.

"All I need is you in my life. You ain't gotta worry about nothin' else. I got us," I said.

"I want to help my mother get clean," Mara confessed and I sat up.

"When?" I asked.

"When we get back from our vacation. Her condition is really bothering me. Maybe because she's pregnant and I'd feel bad if something happened to the baby. The guilt would eat me up," Mara said. I wanted to tell her that there was nothing she could do. Truth is, I didn't want my shorty being disappointed after wasting her time just for her mother to relapse.

"Fuck no, Mara. I'd understand if you weren't pregnant but you don't need dat stress right now. Tell your punk-ass brother to do it. You ain't gettin' involved in dat shit and I mean it," I said.

"I hate that you're tryin' to control me," Mara said and sat up on the bed.

"Do what you want after you have my seed but you ain't stressin' yourself out over a fuckin' junky! Do you know how hard it is to talk them into gettin' clean? The shit is just like a job. Focus on school, dat's it," I said.

"Whateva," she said.

It sounded fucked up but I didn't want Mara associated with her family. I didn't trust none of them muthafuckas. And I always went with my gut instinct.

Piper

A few hours later...

Me and Delonte was sitting at a bar, throwing back shots. We had been almost inseparable since the night we had sex. We talked about any and everything. He was a breath of fresh air. I couldn't stop thinking about how Pistol was acting a few hours ago. Thank God Delonte was understanding but I should've been honest with him. I told him Pistol was my cousin. Delonte wasn't judgmental but, shit, I still had some dignity. My phone rang and I excused myself. It was Thickems calling me.

"Hey, girl," I said.

"What's up? I'm calling to tell you that I won't be staying at your place anymore but I really appreciate it. I'm goin' back to the condo I shared with Ammo," Thickems said.

"Anytime, girl. I enjoyed your company," I replied.

"I don't know if I can deal with Ammo's judgmental ass family. His sister has been throwing nothing but shade at me. I'm just leavin' Ammo's aunt's house. Moesha told everyone I was a stripper and that I sold my pussy to niggas inside the strip club. I wanted to beat her ass so bad! But that was after she showed me pictures of her and Beretta. Beretta cheated on Mara with Moesha and I swear I don't know how to tell her. It's too much shit goin' on," Thickems said and I almost dropped my phone.

"Girl, get the fuck outta here!" I screamed and people nearby looked at me like I was crazy.

"She had so many pictures of them in bed. I cursed her dirty-ass out. That's the main reason why she told everyone I was a stripper. I was so mad I thought I was gonna have a miscarriage up in that house," Thickems said.

"I'm beatin' dat hoe's ass on site when I see her! Mark my damn words. You and Mara pregnant, so she's tryna be messy but I ain't wit' child. I'm taggin' bitches for the rest of the year," I replied.

"Naw, don't worry about it. I told her about herself and, besides, she's gonna get hers one day. We both know karma is a muthafucka. But I'm not goin' to keep you on the phone for long. I'm ready to go home and prepare myself for tomorrow. It's gonna be so hard tellin' him goodbye. He drove me insane but I'm goin' to miss it all," she sniffled.

Hearing Thickems break down made me want to kill Moesha. She was already having a difficult time and didn't need Moesha bullying her. It was all good because I wasn't going to let it slide. My friends were my family, especially Mara.

"Is everything, okay?" Delonte asked when I came back to the bar.

"Yeah, everything is aight. I hate to cut this date short but I have to go home and get ready for a funeral tomorrow mornin'," I replied.

"Naw, it's cool," he said and I kissed his cheek.

"Those lips are so soft. I might have to take you into the bathroom or sumthin. What we did a few nights ago has been on my mind all day," Delonte said, licking his lips.

"Do you think what we're doing is wrong considerin' you're like fourteen years older than me?" I asked and he chuckled.

"Naw, you're legal. Plus, you don't act your age. Well, around me that is, because I know your friends see a different side of you," he replied.

"That is true. I'm childish sometimes," I said and giggled.

"Oh, word? You ain't gotta change for me. I want to see all that shit," he said.

Delonte was slowly opening me up to something very different. We talked on the phone a lot and went on little dates during the day, but most importantly he was interested in my mind, not just my body. He paid for our tab then we headed out of the restaurant. He played a rap song by LL Cool J on the way to my house. He rapped the lyrics of, "Around the Way Girl." Delonte told me I reminded him of the girl LL was rapping about.

"What kind of personality did your wife have?" I asked.

"She was pretty much a church girl and somewhat not spontaneous but our opposite personalities matched. It was something about her innocence that drew me in. She didn't want to give me a chance at first because of my hood persona back then. I hung by her job every day at the coffee shop until she gave me a shot. We had been together for thirteen years," he said.

"So, you go from likin' church girls to strippers?" I asked.

"I liked her before I knew she was a church girl. Her snobby attitude was attractive and she was beautiful, which was a plus. I don't specifically have a type. Being able to hold a decent conversation is what catches my eye. I'll be forty in a few years. Big asses and titties ain't enough for me," he said.

The rest of the ride to my crib was a quiet one. I couldn't stop thinking about what Pistol said to me about Delonte. Pistol thought an older man like Delonte only wanted one thing from a girl like me. At times, I thought it was true but then I didn't because there were a lot of beautiful women at Delonte's club; he could've had anyone.

SOUL Publications

"Call me before you go to bed," Delonte said when he pulled up to my house.

"Okay, goodnight," I said and opened the passenger's side door. Delonte called out to me before I closed the door.

"I really like you, and if it makes you feel any better, we can wait for a while before we cross that bridge again," he said.

"I'd like that," I replied and closed the door. I waved at him before I walked away. Delonte didn't pull off until I was safely inside the house. As I was locking the top lock, I heard pots and pans moving around in the kitchen.

Pistol better not be havin' Lezzi cookin' in my muthafuckin kitchen! I thought as I headed that way.

Pistol was standing at the stove flipping steaks in one pan and frying potatoes with red peppers, green peppers, and onions in another pan.

"It's midnight," I said.

"And? Shit, I'm starvin," he said.

He was only wearing basketball shorts and socks. I couldn't help but to stare at his chocolate tatted back while he stood at the stove. His long thick hair was braided into two cornrows. Pistol was so damn fine that it didn't make no sense. I placed my purse on the kitchen island and took some vegetables out the freezer.

"You can't just eat steak and potatoes," I said.

"I don't want those vegetables. There's a reason I left them in there. I forgot to tell you to grab some fresh vegetables instead of those freezer-burnt ones you be buyin'," he said. I snatched the vegetables off the counter and threw them back in the freezer.

"Did you change your bandage?" I asked.

"Yeah. An hour ago," he replied and looked at me.

"What?" I asked.

"You look happy. I guess dat ol' nigga game is A-1," he chuckled.

"No, he's mature unlike y'all cheatin' ass young niggas," I spat and he grilled me.

"Age ain't got shit to do wit' a nigga fuckin' another broad. Niggas of all ages cheat," he said.

"Why are you hating?" I asked and he smirked.

"Neva dat, baby girl. I know a fake nigga when I see one," he replied.

"But couldn't be man enough to tell Glock he was wrong for da shit he did to me," I said.

"What me and him discuss ain't yah business. You don't know what I told dat nigga. Can you grab me a plate?" he asked and I rolled my eyes. I opened up the cabinet and reached for the top shelf but the plates were pushed to the back. After a minute of trying to reach for the plate, Pistol reached over me and grabbed it. His chest was against my back and it gave me butterflies.

"Yo, you stay exaggerating shit. You could've reached dat," he said when he pulled away from me.

"Shut da hell up. You saw me strugglin'," I fussed.

"You could've gotten those thick-ass heels you wear at da strip club to grab the plate," he said.

"You talk about me strippin' like yah gang bangin' ass have a job layin' around here somewhere," I replied.

"Say what you want, shorty. We both know women are judged way more than niggas. We can fuck thousands of bitches and get away wit' it. A woman does the same and is called a, 'hoe.' Yeah, it ain't fair but on da real, it's reality," he said.

"Delonte doesn't feel that way," I said.

"Aight, cool, but promise me one thing," Pistol said, staring at me.

"What?" I asked.

"He takes you around his family when y'all get serious. A nigga will tell you whateva you want to hear just to keep you on his good side. If he can't take you around his family and show you off as his girl then he's just fuckin' you.

Don't argue wit' me, neither, because I know how niggas operate when they don't see a woman as wifey material," Pistol said. I wanted to slap the shit out of him.

"So, you're sayin' I'm not wifey material?" I asked.

"Only you can answer dat," he shrugged.

"Get the fuck outta my house!" I yelled at him.

"Yo, chill da fuck out! I ain't leaving out this muthafucka until I'm ready. I'm tryin' to put you up on game so you won't be out here lookin' stupid and shit. I wouldn't be up here tellin' you this shit if I thought bad about you! Start makin' these niggas work for it. Your pussy shouldn't be served buffet-style is what I'm sayin. If you need help with anything, let me know. It's gotta be sumthin you like doin' besides poppin' pills and shakin' your ass," he said.

"I always fantasized about havin' a small club, sorta like a townhouse. The upstairs can be for jazz music and poetry. The bottom level can be a bar and small restaurant. I want to do sumthin for an older crowd. None of dat hardcore partyin'. Just a small club with good vibes. Sorta like the place in *Love Jones*. I love poetry," I said.

"'To be trusted is a greater compliment than being loved,'" Pistol said.

"George MacDonald," I replied. "'To be yourself in a world that is constantly trying to make you something else is the greatest accomplishment,'" I said.

"Ralph Waldo Emerson. The best quote in poem history. A lot of niggas like me can relate to dat," Pistol said.

"You're the first person I shared my love for poetry wit'," I said and he smirked.

"Yeah, me, too. Dat shit stays between us, though," Pistol chuckled then winked at me.

"Me and Delonte agreed on not havin' sex again until we really get to know each other. I feel good about that," I said.

"He might be aight then. Let me know if you need me to pistol-whip his bitch-ass. I'on trust niggas with bald heads," he chuckled.

"GMBAM doesn't trust nobody," I replied.

"All day, shorty. Now make dat ass useful and pour me sumthin to drink," he said, leaving the kitchen with a plate in his hand.

"You betta not spill grease on my carpet!" I yelled out to him.

"Too late! My bad!" Pistol called out then turned the TV up so he wouldn't hear me curse him out.

I had to bite my bottom lip to keep from doing just that. There was a nasty brown grease stain on my white carpet.

"You know I'm partially handicap," he said and I rolled my eyes at him.

"It's cool 'cause it's comin' out of your pocket," I replied. I sat on the couch next to him and kicked my feet up. Pistol was watching the National Geographic channel and they were talking about a buried city called Pompeii.

"I'm seriously shocked," I replied.

"Beretta got me watchin' this shit. It's interestin' because you learn a lot about history," Pistol said. His phone rang on the coffee table and I saw that it was Lezzi. Pistol turned his phone off like it was nothing.

"That's harsh," I said.

"I'on like dat controllin' shit. Shorty be tryin' to tell me what to do and who I can be around. She'll get some act right once she gets tired of da silent treatment," he said.

"I don't like her," I admitted.

"She already know. Her ass goin' crazy 'cause she know I'm over here. I told shorty I wouldn't have to be here if it wasn't for her naggin' ass mouth," he said. I wanted to ask him about Beretta and Moesha but decided not to because it wouldn't have gotten anywhere. I had to figure out a way to tell Mara but I was scared in a way because Mara wasn't mentally wrapped tight. She was sweet and caring, but became a totally different person when she snapped. I didn't want Mara to lose her mind while she was pregnant. Only if Beretta knew how much Mara loved him. The way she cared for him wasn't healthy. Bored with what Pistol was watching, I fell asleep on the couch.

Poppa

Meanwhile...

When I sat up on the bed, Jasmine was staring at me. My eyes were almost swollen shut and my body ached. Blood from my nose was still on the pillow. It had been a day since we got into it with Beretta. All I could do was take pain pills and sleep it off.

"What da fuck you starin' at me fah?" I asked.

"I think you should go to the hospital," she replied.

"Bitch, so the police can question me? I'll look like a fuckin' snitch," I said and she rolled her eyes. I looked at the time and it was almost time for me to meet Mike. He wanted me to come down to the club so I could sign the papers we were talking about. I had an hour to get dressed. Tyshawn and Shag were in the hospital. Rich's bitch-ass claimed he couldn't help us out because he was still on probation. I wasn't trippin' too much because he merked the nigga, Sid, for me before he came home.

The water from the shower soothed my aching body.

"You gotta drive me to Mikey's because I can't see," I called out to Jasmine.

"Can Rich take you? I'm goin' out with my friends," she said. After I finished with the shower, I snatched a towel off the rack. Jasmine was sitting on the bed texting on her phone. I snatched her phone out of her hand and snapped it in half.

"Seriously, Poppa?" she asked and I backhanded her onto the floor. While she was down, I slapped her.

"Who pays the bills, bitch?" I asked as she held her face.

"You do!" she said.

"Put your shit on and fix yo' fuckin' face! I said you're takin' me to Mikey's! End of discussion," I said.

Jasmine got up off the floor and ran into the bathroom. She slammed the door and I could hear her crying from the other side. I was feeling a little fucked up because of how I was doing shorty but I was trying to make major moves and she wasn't cooperating. I got dressed in a Nike jogging suit with the matching kicks. Jasmine came out of the bathroom ten minutes later with make-up on her face.

"Why do you keep pushin' me?" I asked.

"It won't happen again," she replied with her head down.

"Good, now hurry up," I said, walking out of the bedroom.

I went into the kitchen and took a shot of Absolute Vodka along with a Percocet. Jasmine walked out the bedroom dressed in jeans, a tight shirt, and flat shoes. Through the slits of my eyes, I could see the outline of her hips. I planned on sliding into her tight wet pussy when we came back home.

"What's the matter? Is sumthin wrong with what I have on?" she asked.

"Naw, you look good," I replied.

My cell phone on the counter rang and it was Denesha calling me. I ignored her call. I only wanted to fuck her the night of the block party but those plans were canceled.

"You ready?" I asked.

"Yeah," Jasmine replied with an attitude.

****

When Jasmine pulled up to Mikey's, I told her to stay in the whip and wait for me. I texted Mike and told him I was outside. He told me to come around the back of the club because he was handling business. I bopped across the street then cut through an alley that led to the back door. Skibo was smoking a blunt while waiting for me. I wanted to hurry up and get the shit over with.

"Yo, what's up?" I asked, looking around. It was dark in the alley and I saw a few raccoons rummaging around in the trash cans.

"Nothin', smokin' this good kush. You wanna hit?" he asked, passing the blunt.

"Naw, I'm straight," I said and he shrugged his shoulders.

"You heard what happened to Ammo's bitch-ass? His bitch set him up," Skibo said, making small talk.

"Yeah, you can't trust these bitches," I replied.

"Naw, you can't. I heard what happened to you yesterday in da hood. Beretta fucked you up," Skibo laughed.

"I got my teeth, though, nigga," I spat and he chuckled. He had no room to talk because Beretta pistol-whipped him and knocked some of his teeth out.

"Loosen up, bruh," he said then threw the rest of the blunt on the ground by my shoe.

"Yo, we been out here for a minute," I replied.

Skibo pushed me into the dumpster when I tried to walk around him to get inside the club.

"Yo, what da fuck!" I shouted out and that's when I saw the gun.

"Naw, nigga. Mike decided he don't need you. You gotta be a dumb lil' nigga if you thought Mike was going to put you on the deed. Sid ain't even his real father. His mother was just one of Sid's hoes. You should've done your research, bruh. With Sid out da way, Mike can use da extra money to pay real niggas to knock off GMBAM. You were just a pawn, my nigga. You were used to take care of our dirty work. Do you really think you and your niggas can get rid of GMBAM? It took three of y'all niggas to fight Beretta and all three of y'all ended up gettin' fucked up. You and your lame ass team are a joke. Nothing but a bunch of fruit loop thugs," Skibo teased.

"Y'all niggas set me up!" I said.

"You set yah self up! You thought dat nigga was just gonna make you a partna of his business when niggas like me have been down wit' him since day one?" Skibo asked.

All of a sudden, gunshots rang out from inside the club followed by people screaming. While Skibo was distracted, I hit him in the face and he dropped the gun. We tussled around on the ground, knocking trash cans over looking for the gun. Skibo punched me in the stomach then I elbowed him hard enough to make his head hit the dumpster. I reached for the gun and he yanked me by the jacket. I kicked him off and he charged into me. I let off a shot and the bullet pierced through Skibo's head. The back doorknob wiggled so I ducked and hid behind a few trash cans. There was a war going on and I was caught in the middle of it. Someone ran out of the back door then I heard more footsteps. A shot rang out and I heard something crash into one of the dumpsters.

"Mannnnnn, nooooooo! I just paid y'all Beretta's money!" Mike cried.

"Nigga, Beretta said your time is up so it's up. Machete, take care of this nigga," a voice said. Mike screamed and I winced when a bloody hand fell on the ground and landed in front of me. I kept still and held my breath, hoping they didn't see me. I had a gun but I didn't know how many niggas was in the alley with me. I couldn't chance busting at them because they would've merked me. Suddenly, I smelled something burning. Those crazy niggas set Mike on fire.

"Damn, is dat Skibo?" a voice asked.

"Yeah, dat's him. Somebody caught his ass slippin'. Let's bounce," a voice said then they took off running down the alley. I waited a few seconds before I dashed from behind the trash cans. The fire was spreading. I ran down the alley and that's when I noticed the club was on fire, too. People were standing outside in front of the club crying and hugging each other. A lot of the strippers were ass naked. A few bystanders said ten masked men ran inside the club and started shooting at Mike and his men. I spotted Jasmine sitting in my car and I hauled ass towards her.

"DRIVE!" I yelled out when I got inside the whip.

"What happened?" She panicked as she drove in the opposite direction of the crowd. She asked me questions about what happened but I ignored her. I didn't want to, but I thanked God Beretta and his goons were inside the club because I would've been dead. The amount of pull Beretta had in the streets made me even more furious because he had his own military.

I'm tired of tryin' to compete wit' this nigga! Every time I get close, he comes up on top. It's all good because now we're even. He'll have to think about Ammo's death every day for the rest of his life. Not only dat, I knocked his mama up, I thought to myself. I realized Beretta would have to deal with the shit I caused in his life as long as he lived. The war had been over because I already won. Death didn't really cross my mind until Skibo was ready to merk me. Staring down the barrel of that gun almost made me shit myself. I had never been so scared in my life. At that point, all I wanted to do was stack my money up and forget about starting street beefs. It was time for Jasmine to go to work.

"Tell me what happened! Why are your pants wet?" Jasmine asked while we were at a red light. I looked down and realized I pissed myself when Beretta's niggas chopped Mike's hand off. Ain't no telling what they would've done to me if they saw me.

"I fell on the ground," I lied.

"I saw when all those masked men pulled up to the club. I couldn't move because I was so scared. Please tell me you didn't have anything to do with that," she said.

"Why in da fuck would I go there showin' my face if I was on dat bullshit? Yo, do you ever fuckin' think? I swear you dumb as shit! Check this out, though, next week we are gonna make a move on what we were talkin' about. It's time you bring in some money. You got me fucked up if you think I'm gonna be takin' care of you," I replied then turned the music up. My phone rang and it was Nika.

"Da fuck you want?" I answered the phone.

"Maybe I should hang up and call back after you get that dick outta your mouth," she said.

"Yo, don't fuck wit' me," I replied.

"No, Kamar! Don't you fuck wit' me! I called because I need to meet with you.   Where are you?" she asked.

"On my way home," I replied.

"Meet me in Bowie behind Rips Restaurant in an hour and don't be late," she said.

"And if I don't?" I asked.

"Then you will have to deal wit' all of your consequences," she said and hung up.

"DAMN IT!" I yelled out.

Killing Nika crossed my mind but that was too risky. I didn't know if her and Mara was cool on a level where Nika told Mara about our meetings. Mara would probably rat me out and tell Beretta. The shit was getting way out of hand. I thought Nika was just a dumb money chaser but shorty was conniving. I had to play by her rules or get exposed, which I wasn't ready for.

"I need to go home to shower then leave right back out, so you might wanna stop drivin' so fuckin' slow!" I said and Jasmine rolled her eyes. She heard Nika's voice and knew better than to question me about it. Jasmine thought I was her nigga and I barely knew the bitch like that. I honestly didn't need to know shit about her other than her being loyal to me.

"Aight, dang," she said with an attitude.

Fifty minutes later...

I pulled up to Rips and Nika's truck was parked behind the restaurant where the hotels were. I got out of my car and she got out of her truck dressed in fighting gear. When she clutched her purse tightly to her, I knew she was strapped. I couldn't stop admiring her pretty natural face. The bitch was so sexy I started thinking about knocking her up again.

"Make this shit quick!" I spat and she smirked at me.

She unlocked the door to a hotel room and it was pitch-black. I thought it was a setup. I stood in front of the door while she walked in. Nika turned the light on and the room was empty.

"What happened to all that mouth? Are you scared now?" Nika asked.

"Naw, I'm not. I don't trust money-hungry bitches," I replied. I walked into the room and she closed the door. I had a chance to strangle her but someone was probably watching us. I felt trapped.

"Don't even think about doing anything stupid. You don't know who's watching us," she said.

"Shorty, stop fuckin' talkin' and tell me what you want. It's late as shit and you out here playin' games," I replied.

"My son fucked you up I see," she laughed.

"And I gave his mother a daughter so what da fuck is your point? He ain't beat me the same way I beat dat lil' juicy pussy of yours," I replied.

"You wouldn't be so bad if you weren't a crack baby," she said. I charged into her and she pulled a gun out of her purse. She aimed it at my head and I held my hands up. It was the second time in one night that I had a gun to my head.

"Don't even try it. I have niggas on speed-dial that'll chop your ass up and throw you in the harbor," she said.

"What do you want?" I asked calmly.

"That's better. Now have a seat," she replied. I sat on the bed and she sat in the chair in the corner of the room with her gun still pointing at me.

"I want thirty g's," she blurted out.

SOUL Publications

"I don't have it," I lied. I did have it but that's all I had to my name until Jasmine caught a lick.

"But you can get it for me," she said.

"And how can I do dat?" I asked.

"That's sumthin you have to figure out," she said.

"I just gave you money for Hope and Mara has given you money for Hope, too. I know Beretta is breakin' bread on you, so what's really good witchu?" I asked.

"I have money for Hope but I figure you owe me for emotional distress. Every day I get up and take care of my daughter. Tell me what you do besides be jealous of my son?" she asked.

BITCH! I thought.

"I don't have thirty fuckin' g's lyin' around," I gritted.

"And I don't give a fuck about that. I'm tellin' you that you better come up with it within two weeks," she snapped.

"Aight, damn. When can I see my daughter again?" I asked.

"When you come up wit' da money," she said.

"So now you're blackmailing me?" I asked in disbelief.

"I'm goin' to run this shit until you can't take it anymore. You're gonna be beggin' my son to kill you by the time I'm done wit' you. Niggas like you ain't so smart, even when you think you are. Behind most niggas' downfall is a bitch that's waiting to get paid and that will never change. Trust me when I tell you that," she said.

"I'll get up wit' you in two weeks," I replied and stood up. I was ready to walk out of the door but Nika placed the gun to the back of my head.

"We ain't done," she said and I turned around.

"Sit your ass back down," she said. I sat back down on the bed and eyed her. Nika had lost her damn mind. The bitch was too beautiful to be so fucked up in the head.

"You know in all my years of being on this Earth nobody has ever made me cum as hard as you did. Too bad that beautiful dick belongs to a nigga like you," she replied. My dick got hard at her acknowledging our night together. I hated the broad but I wanted to fuck her at the same time. Nika was a freak and I remembered she let me put it in her ass that night I knocked her up. She pushed me back and went straight to my jeans. She unbuttoned my pants then pulled my dick out. I had to concentrate on the gun so it wouldn't go off. She set the gun on the nightstand daring me to make a move. She made me her bitch so I had to play by her rules until I figured a way out.

I watched her undress. Her round breasts almost made me bust a nut. Nika was older than Jasmine and still had a better body than her. Her nipples and clit were pierced. My dick ached as I watched her walk over to me after she got a condom out of her purse. Pre-cum oozed out the tip of my head. She ripped the condom wrapper then rolled it down my dick. I closed my eyes when she straddled me. Her tight wet pussy gripped my dick as I fought the urge to explode. She slowly bucked her hips forward while rubbing her clit. The bitch was so beautiful I wanted to tell her I'd marry her. We could run off with Hope and be a family. I didn't know why I was having those thoughts because I wasn't that type of nigga but shorty was making me reconsider.

"UMPPPPPHHHH," I grunted. She placed her palms on my chest and lifted up so only the tip of my dick was inside her. She leaned forward so I could suck her nipples and I did. I sucked them so hard I tasted the metal of her nipple ring. She moaned in my ear while speaking some kind of Chinese language. Nika was half Asian so I wasn't shocked. The shocker was how much that shit turned me on. She rode the tip of me and it was crucial. I needed more so I gripped her hips, pushing more of my dick into her. She slapped the shit out of me and it rang my ear.

"This is for my pleasure!" she groaned.

I laid still and let her ride my dick until my eyes watered and I moaned like a bitch. Her pussy was dripping down my nuts and the sounds of her wetness echoed throughout the room. Nika slapped me again then rode me harder.

"STOP!" I groaned.

Welcome to the Low Life 2

She dug her nails into my chest and fucked me harder. The headboard slammed against the wall. The bitch was raping me. My manhood was being tested because pussy wasn't supposed to make a man feel less of a man. I was a pussy-whipped punk but I had to admit the shit was the best thing I ever had in my whole life.

"I'm about to cummmmmm," she screamed. She bounced on my dick and I exploded into the condom. Her pussy gushed on my dick as her legs trembled and sexy moans escaped her lips. I prayed to God my semen broke through the condom to knock her up again. She fell onto my chest and laid there for a minute.

"Wrap your arms around me," she said and I did.

What happened between us seemed so unrealistic that for a second I thought I was still high from the Percocet I took. She sat up after a few minutes then climbed off me. She got dressed then grabbed her gun and purse.

"You have two weeks and don't play wit' me," she said before she left the room.

"FUCK!" I yelled out.

I hurriedly got up and flushed the condom down the toilet. After I fixed myself, I left the hotel room. On my way home, I thought about my life. I had a long way to go to get where I wanted to be. Sadly, I was looking forward to Nika using me. It became a new addiction.

Welcome to the Low Life 2

SOUL Publications

Kemara

I stepped into my black pumps then smoothed out the black pencil skirt I was wearing. Ammo's funeral was an hour away and I was nervous because I didn't know how Beretta was going to take seeing him for the last time. My make-up was done to perfection and my long weave was bone-straight. My stomach felt queasy and I tried not to focus on it because I didn't feel like being stuck in the bathroom all morning. Beretta walked into the bedroom with a bottle of Henny in his hand. He looked so handsome in his black suit. It fit his physique perfectly, and for a split second, Beretta looked like a normal hardworking man. But his diamond chain necklace, watch, iced-out grill, and tattoos told another story.

"That skirt too tight, shorty," Beretta said, eyeing my outfit with an attitude.

"I gained weight. Everything is too tight," I replied and he sat on the bed.

"I'on think I can do this," Beretta said.

"I'm goin' to be there for you," I replied.

Welcome to the Low Life 2

"Appreciate you," he smirked.

"Are you done drinkin' now?" I asked and he gave me the bottle. I went into the bathroom and dumped the rest out into the sink. When I walked back into the bedroom, Beretta was grabbing our luggage for the trip after the funeral. I was glad he decided to get away for a few days. He said he never went on a trip where he could just relax and think. Every time he left the state was to re-up. It was my first real vacation, too, and I couldn't wait to enjoy our time alone. I packed so many skimpy outfits to help take his mind off GMBAM. What happened to Mikey's strip club was all over the news when I woke up that morning. They said it was a robbery gone wrong but the police didn't have any leads yet. I knew Beretta was the mastermind behind it. It was stupid of me to share a life with a gang member, especially since I wanted a new life for myself but love came and conquered. Mikey deserved what happened to him and his club anyway because he raped a few of his strippers and had tried to rape Piper.

I grabbed my purse off the dresser and followed Beretta downstairs.

"I think you should wear some flat shoes," Beretta said when he sat our luggage by the door.

"Nigga, you crazy if you think I'm wearing flats with this bad ass outfit," I replied.

"Yeah, okay. Don't lean on me when your heels start leanin'," he joked. His cell phone rang and he pulled it out of his pocket. He rejected the call and I rolled my eyes at him. Moesha called Beretta six times that morning but Beretta wasn't answering. He thought I didn't know about her calling but I memorized that bitch's number. I couldn't wait to get to the funeral because I wanted to approach her. It wasn't the time or the place for my bullshit but I was going to make it respectable. He said he didn't fuck her and I believed him, therefore Moesha just wanted some attention that she wasn't going to get. I grabbed the keys to Beretta's Mercedes then left out of the house. I popped the trunk to his car so he could put our bags in. He took the keys from me and got into the driver's seat. As soon as I put my seat belt on, his phone rang again. I snatched it from him when he took it out of his pocket and it was Moesha.

"What da fuck do you want?" I asked.

"Oh, hi. This is Ammo's aunt, Lashonda. I was wondering if Z'wan wanted to ride in the limo with us since he's basically like family. There is only room for him, no offense. Is there a way I can speak with him?" she asked with an attitude. I shoved Beretta the phone and crossed my arms. Moesha's hoe ass was being slick. Why couldn't Lashonda call from her phone? Ammo's family had some shit with them but if only they knew I didn't give a fuck who they were to Ammo. Aunts could get slapped, too. I wasn't feeling Ammo's family since Piper told me how they treated Thickems. How could you gang up on a pregnant girl knowing she had a lot to deal with? The whole situation pissed me off but I kept quiet because I didn't want to anger Beretta.

"You good?" Beretta asked when he hung up the phone.

"Yeah, I'm aight. So, what are you gonna do? You ridin' wit' them or what?" I replied.

"What do you think I'm gonna do? Yah ass hold grudges too long. Might fuck around and keep me outta da hospital room when you go into labor. I ain't perfect but I damn sho ain't fallin' for your calmness. Be honest, shorty. You tryna be civil, ain't you?" he asked and I rolled my eyes. He chuckled a little bit as he pulled out of our driveway. I was happy seeing him smile.

"I'm playin' fair today, boo," I replied.

"Yeah, yah ass crazy on da real. I love it, though," Beretta said.

"Niggas really do like dramatic females, huh?" I asked.

"Hell yeah, shit. Dat just mean the pussy real good. Pussy so good, niggas get offended when they see a condom," he said.

"You tipsy?" I asked.

"Yeah," he chuckled.

He held my hand on our way to Ammo's service. When we arrived, cars were everywhere and people were standing outside the church wearing shirts with Ammo's picture on them. Piper pulled up with Pistol riding in the passenger's seat. They looked so good together I couldn't stop staring when they got out of the car. Piper wore a black fitting dress with nude pumps and Pistol wore a black suit. I hated to admit it but we looked like a black mafia. I wore a hat with a veil covering my eyes and the red lipstick I wore gave it an extra pop.

"You're walkin' better," I said to Pistol.

"Yeah, I'm gettin' there, baby girl," he replied.

Two limos pulled up and it was Ammo's family. My stomach turned when Moesha stepped out of the limo wearing a long black dress and her hat was similar to mine.

"Looks like y'all got a lot in common," Piper teased.

"Oh, bitch, hush," I replied.

Moesha looked beautiful for a wedding. She was trying so hard to overdo it. She fell out onto the ground when she saw Beretta. Yet seconds before, she was smiling and waving at folks like she was the mayor of the city.

"NOOOOOOOOOOOOOO! I CAN'T SEE HIM LIKE THAT!" Moesha screamed. Her family fanned her face and someone even gave her a paper bag to breathe in.

"That's the fakest shit I've seen since Hustle Man's Jordans," Piper said.

Silk walked through the crowd wearing a black silk blouse with his chest exposed. His black pants were too tight but he looked good. I giggled when I noticed the gold glitter on his chest, and like always, his eyebrows were perfect and his lip gloss was popping. His hair was cut into a Mohawk. The tip of his hair was dyed honey blond and he had designs on the sides. My jaw dropped when I noticed his baby mama holding their daughter. Silk's daughter was so beautiful; she looked just like him.

"Awwww, can I hold her?" I held my arms out to Fushia. She held the baby closer to her like I had germs.

"Oh no you don't. We talked about this in da car. These are my good girlfriends and have been for a while now so we ain't about to start dat bullshit or you can take your ass home," Silk said.

"Why is she even here?" Piper asked.

"Because my father is the preacher and he's speaking at his service," Fushia snapped. She was a very beautiful girl but I think she had insecurity issues. The way she acted over Silk was sickening. She didn't want him doing anything if it had nothing to do with her.

"I'm about to go over here and holla at Sniper and 'em," Beretta said and Pistol followed him. They didn't want to be around Silk and his drama. I think Silk having a baby mama was too much for most people to deal with.

"Umph, those niggas are fine. Y'all hoes lucky," Silk said, fanning himself.

"Not in front of Jesus's house," Fushia said.

"Oh, he knows how I roll, sweetie. And don't start talkin' about me sinnin', neither, because you got pregnant out of wedlock the last time I checked," Silk replied.

"Whateva, I'm going inside. It's too many people out here for Amber," Fushia said and walked away.

"If dat crazy hoe didn't have good pussy, I swear to God I would be in jail right now for murder. I just want to poison da bitch sometimes," Silk vented.

"Beretta said the same thing on our way over here," I replied.

"I wish you stop playin' and push those panties to the side," Silk said and I playfully smacked him.

A cute light-skinned man walked over to us while we were talking.

"Excuse me, ladies, but can I speak with Silk for a second?" he asked. Me and Piper looked at Silk and he rolled his eyes.

"Not now, Jason. My baby mama is out here and she already knows about us. Matter of fact, I know damn well you didn't follow us here," Silk said, looking around.

"No, I didn't! Ammo is a cousin down the line and I came to support. Look, I don't care about dat bitch you had a baby wit'. We have been messin' around since we were fourteen years old. You owe me an explanation, and if you don't give me da one I want, I'm gonna expose all of your bullshit! I have pictures, texts, and hotel receipts. I bet Little Church Girl won't like dat, now would she? Hurry your ass up because I don't have all day," the stranger said and walked away.

"Let me go see what this nigga wants. This is what happens when you come to church. All your dirty shit comes out. Bless me, Lord," Silk said and dramatically strutted away.

"Why do I have a feelin' Silk isn't coming back?" Piper asked.

"He's gonna use his dick to apologize like the ain't-shit nigga he is," I replied and she agreed.

Ten minutes later, the service began. The line was very long as we waited to go inside and be seated. Beretta squeezed my hand the closer we got to the doors. We heard screaming over the sad funeral music most black churches played when we stepped inside the church. It was cold, and even though we weren't in the front yet, I could feel death. My heart began beating fast as I looked around. Pistol was squeezing the hell out of Piper's hand making her turn red. Ammo's family was already seated in the front rows. Moesha was still falling out and screaming. When it was finally our turn to view Ammo's body, my knees almost gave up on me and Beretta caught me. The person in the casket looked nothing like Ammo but I knew it was him because of his GMBAM tattoo. Ammo had on a hat to cover up the wound on his head. He also had a lot of make-up on his face and his lips were swollen and rubbery looking. His once brown skin was very dark. His face was twisted up—he died painfully. A tear slid out of my eye and Beretta's face was emotionless. I thought he was going to need consoling but he was the one holding me up. I began feeling sick because of my nerves. Maybe it was guilt for all the bodies I'd taken in the past. It was a reflection of my life. The question I used to ask myself popped back into my head.

Who am I? I thought.

I stared at the cross on the wall in the middle of the church and asked God for forgiveness even though we all had a price to pay for our sins.

"Let's sit down, baby," Beretta said, pulling me away from Ammo's casket. When we sat down, I watched Pistol and Piper. Pistol broke down over the casket while Piper rubbed his back.

"Wake up, bruh," Pistol cried.

A few of Ammo's family members went up to the casket to help Pistol calm down. After a few minutes, they escorted him to the back of the church. The church ended up being too crowded, so they closed the doors. The preacher began preaching, and just like I thought, he ended up talking about gang violence. Ammo didn't die from gang violence. He died from fucking with the wrong bitch. Beretta kept fidgeting with the obituary.

"What's the matter?" I asked.

"That muthafucka talkin' bout the wrong shit. It's always gang violence when a black man gets killed in da streets. What he need to talk about is how the church collect niggas' money every Sunday mornin' but don't help with the community. Our gang bangin' asses are the ones who have been goin' hard for the kids these past few years. Fuck all dat," Beretta said and stood up. He walked over to the preacher and whispered something in his ear. Seconds later, the preacher announced that Beretta had something to say.

Baby please don't get up there and curse these folks out, I thought.

I was getting nervous because I didn't know what was to come. Beretta fixed his suit jacket then cleared his throat. I clutched my purse and Ammo's obituary as I closed my eyes.

"I ain't big on speaking in front of a crowd but I'll do anything to make my brother's home going a good one. Despite the accusations of who my brother was in the streets, he was a good dude. He didn't lose his life because of gang banging. He lost his life because he trusted the wrong person. It's easy to preach about the streets and gang violence without knowing the truth. No man wakes up and says, 'I wanna go out here and sell drugs.' Sometimes, lack of parenting can destroy us. I remember a time my next-door neighbor beat my ass with a switch. I was playing ball in the street and it broke her window. I ain't gonna lie, I was a little disrespectful, so that's why she beat me. She took me to my mother and told my mother she beat me. My mother cursed her out and I thought my mother was doing the right thing until the old lady told my mother it takes a village to raise a child. A few weeks later, she died of a heart attack but I'll never forget the woman who gave me my first ass whipping. But, anyways, this is our community church but it doesn't seem that way. Y'all walk past these black boys every day, judging them. Every funeral it's about gang violence but it's never about making the community a better place for the kids. Jonah came to me one day and said we need to do something for the kids in our hood. Many of them are starving and some of them barely have any clothes, so we changed that. I'm far from perfect. I didn't finish high school, got a criminal record, and I do things I ain't proud of, but I would've turned out better if I had someone to show me better when I was younger. It's easy to preach to a dead brother, so how about we focus on the ones who are alive. I don't come to church so I can't sit here and tell the preacher how to do his job, but I can suggest he spread the importance of raising your kids right. Gang banging doesn't start from the streets, it starts from home. But, anyways, I had to clear that up because nobody knew Jonah better than I did. So, I hope everyone can understand who my brother truly was after today," Beretta said.

Everyone clapped for Beretta when he left the podium. There were layers to him. I wanted to slap myself for thinking he was going to act a fool but that's when I realized I didn't know all of his characteristics. I kissed his lips when he sat back down next to me.

"That was amazing, baby," I whispered.

"That nigga mad but he betta take dat up with Jesus," Beretta whispered about the preacher.

"Is there anybody else who want to share something?" the preacher asked while fixing his tie. Beretta squeezed my leg when Flo went up to the podium. He was about to ruin Ammo's image. Someone hurriedly pulled Flo back from the podium and made him have a seat. The service lasted for hours it seemed. Black people's funerals were all day. I was hungry and dizzy by the time Beretta and his friends carried Ammo's casket out to the hearse. I saw Thickems standing next to Piper when I was on my way to the bathroom. She was hysterical and Piper tried to calm her down. I didn't see Thickems come in and figured she was sitting somewhere inside, perhaps in the front with Ammo's family.

"What's the matter?" I asked.

"I didn't get a chance to see him. I was told I couldn't come in because the funeral was crowded when I got here. His aunt told me I could ride with them and that they were goin' to pick me up. I called them and that's when she said they didn't have enough room for me in the limo so I drove here and got here late. I didn't want to cause a scene because the last thing I wanted to do was disrespect his funeral but I can't believe they did this to me," Thickems screamed. She was crying so hard she could barely breathe.

"Oh, hell no!" I yelled out.

"Calm down, Mara," Piper said, rubbing Thickems back but it was too late. I approached Moesha and her family when they stepped out into the hallway.

"Y'all gotta be the grimiest bitches ever! How in the fuck can y'all do that to Thickems knowing she's carrying Ammo's child? Not only are you disrespecting her, but you disrespected Ammo, too!" I yelled and everyone looked at me.

"We don't know if she's carrying his baby and I thought it was gonna be enough room but it wasn't. She'll be aight. Another man will be playing daddy soon," Moesha said. I don't know what came over me but I lost it. I punched her in the face. I was ready to be on her ass until Beretta ran to me. Moesha's aunt reached over Beretta and clocked me in the face. Piper ran over to us and began fighting Ammo's aunt.

"Calm da fuck down!" Beretta yelled at me.

"The funeral is over! It's time for those bitches to be touched!" I screamed. A lot of people intervened to calm us down.

"Everyone, calm down. I know we're all upset right now but this isn't the way," the preacher said while standing in the middle. Beretta dragged me out of the church cursing me out for fighting while carrying his child. When I love, I love hard, and seeing Thickems like that angered my entire soul. She had it worse than anybody so I couldn't understand why Moesha was treating her like that.

"CHILL DA FUCK OUT!" Beretta yelled.

Welcome to the Low Life 2

Pistol was pulling Piper across the street while carrying her heels and purse. I saw Ammo's aunt lying on the ground with a bloody nose.

"I whipped that ass, hoe!" Piper yelled.

"Damn, Mara. You can't even go with me to his burial site now. Yo, I can't believe this shit," Beretta said, pushing me into his car. He got in and slammed the door. I told him to make sure Thickems was alright.

"She's with Piper and Pistol," Beretta said.

"How do you know? I didn't see her with them," I replied.

Beretta called Pistol on speakerphone and he confirmed Thickems was with them.

"Go on ahead to his burial site. I'll sit in the car while you say your last goodbye," I said and he grilled me.

"Yo, I want to slap the shit outta of you right now. If they would've jumped you then what? Do you think I wanna get locked up for fightin' some bitches? People that are like family to me?" he asked.

"Fuck all of them. Don't tell me what to do when it comes to my friends. They are purposely tryin' to make Thickems have a miscarriage. And that Moesha bitch saltier than sardines, ain't she? It's cool, though, because I'm gonna kill her ass. A bullet right through that hoe's head will calm her the fuck down I bet," I vented.

SOUL Publications

"Do what you want after you have my baby. I'm not tryna argue wit' yo ass anymore," Beretta said.

Beretta got out of the car and I stayed in the passenger's seat when we arrived at the burial site. I wanted to get out and snatch Moesha by her weave but I'd started enough shit. Ammo's family tossed roses on his casket as they lowered him into the ground. It was finally over; Ammo was officially gone. Beretta was on his way over to the car but Moesha stopped him. I could tell by their body language they were arguing. Beretta walked away from her and she called out to him but he kept walking. When he opened the door, I heard her tell him that he wasn't innocent and that he didn't love me. I pretended not to hear her. Moesha wanted my man and was doing everything in her power to come between us, but I wasn't having it!

****

A few hours later....

We were in the airport waiting for our flight. Beretta wasn't saying much to me. He was on his phone playing a game and I knew he was doing it to ignore me because he never played games on his phone.

"You really ain't gonna talk to me?" I asked.

"Eventually I will. I'm gonna be stuck wit' yah simple-ass for a week," he said.

"I'm sorry," I said.

"Whateva, shorty. You were out there fighting at a fuckin' church," he gritted and I rolled my eyes.

"I'm a saint and a sinner. You knew that before you got wit' me, so don't be surprised. I'm sorry for disrespectin' Ammo but I'll never regret puttin' hands on Moesha," I said.

"And I won't regret knockin' your fuckin' teeth out if sumthin happens to my baby," he said. I scooted away from him and watched everyone who walked past us until it was time to board our flight to Hawaii. Beretta thought he was gonna be mad at me, but I had a few tricks up my sleeve, and being his naughty girl was one of them.

Part: 5

Zyira

Beretta

July, 2011

It had been four months since Ammo got killed. His death made me grind harder because I wanted to reach at least one mil before it was my time to go. Life was too short, and in order to get what I wanted, I had to invest more time into the streets. I promised Mara I was going to do better and all that shit but the money I started seeing got in the way of those promises. My niggas were packaging up work inside the little rundown house we handled our business in. My phone rang while in the midst of making sure those niggas wasn't cuffing my shit.

"What is it, Mara?" I answered.

"When are you coming home? It's three in the morning," she replied.

"I'm busy, Mara, damn. You need sumthin?" I asked.

"Yeah, I need my fuckin' man in the damn bed lying next to me!" she yelled into the phone.

"And I will be there when I'm done handling my fuckin' business!" I said and hung up.

Mara became too needy and the shit was distracting me. During our getaway to Hawaii, we made love on the beach every night on some romance type shit. I ain't going to lie, the trip made me love her even more because I was able to see how our life together would be with me away from the streets. When we got back home, she was looking for the same romantic shit we did in Hawaii but it was grind time. She wanted me underneath her twenty-four-seven. I won't lie; I had been slacking 'cause me and Mara was only fucking like twice a month. Half the time I was too tired to nut but I made sure I took care of her. Shit drastically changed within a short period of time but it was definitely going to pay off. Pistol came into the house; he had just got back from making a drop.

"We won't be comin' here for a while after tonight," I told everyone. Niggas was getting jammed up for hustling out of the same spot, but I was changing spots like I was changing my draws. Pistol had his own hustle going on; he was selling military-style weapons. That wasn't really my thing but I sometimes pitched in when he had to re-up so I could make a quick flip.

"Yo, go home and I'll take care of this," Pistol said.

"I gotta make sure we get everything outta here tonight. Nigga, you know I'm hands-on," I replied and he chuckled.

"Mara about to merk you," he joked.

SOUL Publications

"Shorty know how to play her part. Shit, our bills ain't the same as they used to be. Mara's ass is expensive and she stay at the spa every fuckin' weekend. I give her half of my money just so she can stay off my back and she still be trippin'," I said.

"That's 'cause she ain't impressed, nigga," Pistol said.

"Yeah, I know, but it doesn't stop her from spendin' it, neither," I chuckled.

"Aye, Beretta! Everything straight," Machete called out. He was letting me know they had everything tucked away in the ice cream trucks. I had five trucks that I used for business but I also used them to sell ice cream, dinners, and other things. I told my lil' niggas they could keep whatever they made from those trucks as long as my work was straight. On average, each truck made five g's a day, sometimes more, depending on what area the trucks were in. I know after the basketball games, everyone be lined up waiting for chicken and fries or a snowball.

"Aight, get up wit' me lata and remember what we talked about. Don't be fuckin' these lil' bitches in my shit, nigga," I said and he smirked.

"What if she got a phat ass, though?" he replied.

"You betta turn yah savage up on shorty in the woods or sumthin but not in my shit," I said.

"Damn, bruh. Cock blockin' like shit," Machete said as he left the house.

"I'm ready to take this shit to Piper so she can count it for me," he said.

"Bruh, what is up wit' you and shorty?" I asked.

"Nothing, damn. A nigga can't have a female friend? Plus, me and Lezzi have been lookin' at this crib together. We have been on good terms lately so I'm ready to take dat move wit' her," he said.

"About time you move outta your grandmother's basement," I replied.

"Nika's grand opening is tomorrow. You goin', right?" he asked.

"Me and Nika ain't really on speakin' terms. Da hoe don't even bring Hope by to see me anymore. I haven't seen Nika since I told her I wasn't givin' her da money for dat restaurant. I wonder what nigga she had to con to get the money. But go on ahead, I'm ready to lock everything up. I'll get up wit' you tomorrow," I said and slapped hands with him. After he left, I punched in the code to the alarm before I walked out of the house. I don't know why I was doing that shit because I had cameras installed. I even had one up in the tree by the house to watch the neighborhood, making sure 5-0 wasn't patrolling the area.

****

Welcome to the Low Life 2

By the time I got home, it was four-thirty in the morning. I had been out for a whole day. Mara was sitting up in bed watching TV when I walked into the bedroom. She was wearing a pajama shirt with a silk scarf tied around her head. Before her stomach got big, she used to come to bed wearing sexy negligees. I kissed her seven-month-old pregnant stomach and she smacked her teeth.

"What's the matter, shorty?" I asked.

"Nothing," she sadly.

"Damn, Mara. You act like somebody died," I replied.

"Something did die. Our fuckin' relationship, now get outta my face," she said then mushed me. Too tired to argue, I went straight to the bathroom to take a shower.

"Always coming in da fuckin' house late at night and makin' a lot of damn noise," Mara fussed. I slammed the toilet seat down after I took a piss. When I opened the shower door, I made sure I slammed that shit as hard as I could. Mara started yelling and screaming at me.

"Grow up!" she said.

"Grow some edges! Fuck outta here," I replied.

"I got edges!" she yelled back.

I took a twenty-minute shower before I stepped out. I grabbed the towel off the rack and walked out of the bathroom. Mara was sleeping peacefully on her side. She was tired but had stayed up waiting for me to come home. I dried off then slid into the bed and wrapped my arm around her. The moment I closed my eyes, Mara got out of bed and took a pillow and the comforter with her.

"Yo, where are you goin'?" I asked.

"Guest bedroom. Sick of layin' next to a dead dick. I'm too sexually frustrated for this bullshit," she said.

"We can do it when I wake up. Bring your ass back to bed," I replied. Mara wobbled out of the bedroom and went into the next room. She slammed the door and I heard her lock it. I shrugged it off and went back to sleep.

****

I woke up to the smell of breakfast. Mara was playing music downstairs and I also heard the vacuum cleaner. That was the shit I looked forward to when waking up. I stepped into a pair of baller shorts and went downstairs. Mara was dancing around and her ass cheeks were spilling out the bottom of her pajama shirt. She turned the vacuum off when she saw me watching her.

"Your breakfast is on the counter," she said.

"Appreciate it. Did you sleep good?" I asked.

"A little bit. So, what are your plans for the day? Plannin' on stayin' out all night?" she asked.

"Yo, why do you wanna argue wit' me? You don't complain when I'm droppin' stacks on you," I said.

"You get a kick out of this, don't you? You want me to depend on you. This was your plan all along. I was financially stable before we got together and now you wanna act up because I'm pregnant and can't do shit," Mara replied.

"You wanna go back to robbin' niggas?" I asked.

"No, I wanna go back to havin' my own shit. Look at me, I'm just a dope boy's baby mama. I want to get a job but nobody will hire me while I'm pregnant and in school. I made a lot of sacrifices for you and it's time for you to do the same for me. I'm not tryin' to change you. I just need you at home a bit more. I'm always in the house by myself," she said.

"I gotta get this work off my back before I make any promises. You know summer time is grind mode. We can lay up and do all dat other shit you wanna do lata. Out of all people, you should understand dat," I replied.

"Cool," was all she said before she walked out the living room.

"I'm doin' this for you and Zyira," I called out.

Mara came up with the name for our daughter when we found out we were having a girl. That same day, I got Zyira and Mara's name tattooed on my neck inside of a crown. I was hoping for a boy but I figured with the life I lived, I didn't need a son following my footsteps.

My burner phone on the kitchen island rang while I was eating breakfast. I was only up for fifteen minutes and work was already calling. Mara sat on the bed and watched me get dressed for the day. It was hot so I only wore jean shorts, a black wife beater and a pair of J's. I tucked my Beretta in the back of my shorts then grabbed my black Louis Vuitton backpack.

"I left some money for you on the kitchen table," I said.

"Are you goin' to your mother's grand openin' lata?" she asked.

"Naw, I'm straight. I'm not steppin' foot inside her business until she lets me see Hope," I replied.

"Hope will be there. I think we should go together," Mara said.

"Yo, I'm not fuckin' goin' to her shit unless she brings Hope to our crib. You really think Nika is gonna bring Hope out wit' her today? Shorty, don't fall for dat bullshit. Hope will be tucked away with a babysitter or sumthin. I know my mother," I replied and she rolled her eyes.

"I give up," she said then walked into the bathroom.

"Oh, hol' up, shorty. Fuck you mean, you give up? What you thinkin' 'bout leavin' me or sumthin?" I asked, standing in the doorway of the bathroom. Mara took her scarf off and let the long loose-curl weave fall down her back.

"You wouldn't notice if I'm gone," she replied.

"Let me get outta here before I slap the taste outta your mouth. Whinin' ass bitch," I mumbled but she heard me.

"I'll get the last laugh. You betta believe that!" she threatened as I left the bedroom. I grabbed my keys to my new white BMW drop top coupe before I left out the door. Mara said the same shit every morning like she was going to do something. I probably did make her less independent but what did she think was going to happen once I started making major moves? She thought she was going to rob niggas and hang out in the hood all day? Fuck all that, she was good where she was at because it was less stress. Everybody was running around and getting into shit and Mara was at home pregnant. The way I saw it, I was keeping her out of trouble and away from her bitch-ass brother. I'd be too distracted while trying to grind if Mara had the freedom she had in the beginning of our relationship. Shorty just had to get over it.

Kemara

A few hours later...

"I love it," Piper said, looking around the two-story condo. It was located in Washington D.C., a few blocks away from the White House. There was something about the area that was relaxing and the scenery was beautiful.

"Bitccchhhhh, this kitchen should be in a restaurant," Piper said, looking at the stainless steal appliances.

"My furniture comes tomorrow. Beretta's ass is so damn simple that he doesn't realize he paid for me to move out. I can sleep peacefully because I won't be expecting him to come home," I said.

"He's gonna kill you," Piper laughed.

"I did it to get his attention. I'm not leavin' him. I'm just showin' his ass he got me fucked up. You should've seen him this mornin'. He thought he had me under control. He didn't even notice half of my clothes and shoes were missin' when he went inside our closet," I said.

"There is a price to pay for bein' a dope boy's girl. It's Beretta we're talkin' about. Hell, you my girl and all, but I'm surprised he's even in a relationship with a baby on da way," she replied.

"All I want is for my man to touch me or sumthin. I'm not askin' for much. The last time we had sex was soooo borin'. It was painful, too. So painful that I couldn't get wet. He was just rammin' his dick into me knowin' damn well he's too big for that," I said and Piper laughed.

"Ugh, I can't believe I'm ready to do this," Piper said.

She went into her purse and pulled out a small box. She handed it to me and I looked at her in confusion.

"What's this?" I asked.

"A bullet. I ordered it the other day and it came in the mail today. I swear this thing will have you squirtin'. All you need to do is rub it on your clit," she replied.

"Is it safe to use while pregnant?" I asked.

"It's safer than Beretta rammin' his dick inside of you like he ain't got no damn sense. Baby Zyira feelin' all of her daddy's dick on her head," Piper said.

"Now you takin' it too far," I chuckled.

"Look, I gotta get goin' to beat the traffic. I would tell you to come with me to the strip club lata but you look like you're ready to pop," she said.

Welcome to the Low Life 2

"It's cool. I'll just watch a movie and eat cucumbers with ranch dressing and chocolate syrup until Nika's restaurant opens," I replied and she gagged.

"Ewww, bitch. Call me if you need sumthin," she said.

Piper kissed my cheek before she headed out of my condo. I looked around the place and asked myself why I was moving out so close to my due date. All I wanted was some type of affection. While imagining how my living room was going to look, my cell phone rang. It was Silk.

"Yeah," I answered.

"I made some lasagna. You want some?" he asked.

"It's a Saturday and you're in the house cookin'?" I replied.

"Yeah, Fushia is in Miami so I got my little girl," Silk said.

"I'll be there in an hour," I replied.

"Beretta is outside. I'm just lettin' you know so you can park in the back of the buildin'. I'on need dat nigga comin' up here startin' shit," Silk said.

"Okay, I'll be there," I replied.

I hadn't broken the news to the rest of my friends about my move to D.C. yet. Thickems isolated herself from me, Piper, and Silk after Ammo's funeral. She called every once in a while but whenever we called her, she didn't answer the phone. I decided to give her space, but I told her to let us know when she has the baby the last time I talked to her.

****

"Why are you standin' on the corner, and pull up your shorts," I said to Carlos when I arrived in the hood.

"Chill out, Mara. I'm grown," he said and the boys he was standing by chuckled.

"Grown? Little boy, you still piss sittin' on the toilet," I said.

Carlos was standing on the corner with a few older boys who were around eighteen. It was summer time so the hood was jam-packed. The hood had gotten worse since Ammo's death. There was a killing every week. It had gotten so bad, people weren't having block parties anymore. A beat-up Buick pulled up to the corner with two crackheads inside. Someone gave Carlos a small dime bag of coke and he took it to the fiends.

"Y'all got little kids servin' muthafuckas now?" I asked the small crew.

"It ain't even like dat, Pretty Girl. Carlos's mother on dat shit now so he tryna take care of his lil' sistas. I mean, we ain't gonna just give him da money. He gotta work for it. Besides, that lil' nigga is twelve now, so he old enough," a boy named Nate said.

"Does Beretta know about this?" I asked.

"What he gotta know for? Carlos old enough to make up his own mind. Look, we gonna take care of him. Don't worry about him," Nate said. Carlos walked back over to us and handed Nate the twenty-dollar bill. Nate went into his pocket and gave Carlos five dollars to keep for himself.

"Be safe out here, Carlos. Go to Silk's house if you need anything and he'll call me," I said.

"I ain't goin' over dat gay nigga's crib," Carlos said and Nate chuckled. He was showing off for the older boys.

"Okay, cool," I said and walked away.

Seeing Carlos standing on the corner was the reality of our society. It made me think back to what Beretta said at Ammo's funeral. You don't just wake up and say, "I'm gonna be a hustla." Sometimes our youth didn't have a choice. I wanted to beat Carlos's mama's ass for putting her kids in a situation like that. When I walked into Silk's building, it smelled of urine and the summer's heat made it stronger. I covered my nose as I banged on his door. He snatched it opened with his daughter in his arms.

"Girl, I was ready to sock your ass for knockin' on my door like dat," he complained.

"You couldn't throw any bleach in the hallway with hot water?" I asked.

Welcome to the Low Life 2

"Bitch, I'm tired of wastin' my bleach for these nasty-ass niggas. All they do is play dice in the building all night long and piss in the hallways," he said.

"You gotta move out," I replied.

He laid his daughter inside her play pen then went into the kitchen to get me a glass of wine.

"I'm not movin' out of here. You know we are finally gettin' renovated so I ain't goin' nowhere. It's gonna be hard finding a cheap apartment with new appliances, carpet, and shit like dat. Ain't nobody ballin' like Beretta right now, shat. What you need to do is hook me up wit' one of those niggas so I can walk around this muthafucka wit' a thong goin' up my ass. I'm about sick and tired of bein' the man of da house. Chillleee, I'm ready to put on my mommy hat so I can find Amber a daddy," he said.

"What about Fushia?" I asked.

"Dat hoe can continue bein' a hoe. I found a nigga's number in her phone and, chile, she was sendin' dat nigga all kinds of pussy pics. Dat hoe ain't neva send me a pussy pic before. She's down in Miami wit' him right now and guess what? The bitch came outta me. I started sendin' her man pics of this ass and told him I'm tighter than her loose pussy ass," Silk said and I spit my wine out.

"Ohhhhhh, noooooooo you didn't do that!" I screamed.

"I sholl da hell did while wearin' her thong, too! He probably down there beatin' her ass because he didn't know her baby daddy like dick, too," Silk said.

"Bitchhhhhhh, see your level of petty behavior cannot be touched," I replied and he got excited. Silk loved when someone praised his erratic behavior. You would've thought I told him he was the best thing walking on Earth.

"I'm crazy, ain't I? Well, you ain't seen nothing yet because I'm ready to put Fushia's ass on child support. I have my daughter four to five days out of the week and I pay for child care, clothes, milk and everything else she needs. Dat hoe ain't supposed to be havin' fun. Hell, hath no fury like a black woman scorned," he said.

"Nigga, shut da fuck up. You're just jealous because she's doin' what you have been doin' to her. Fushia had Amber twenty-four-seven until she realized how much of a hoe you were. She left you with Amber so she can return the favor. I dislike her ass but shorty is givin' you a taste of your own medicine," I said.

"The lasagna is gone," he said and rolled his eyes.

"Fix me a plate, please," I replied.

"What time are we goin' to Nika's restaurant? A lot of people talkin' about it so you know I'm gonna be there. I'm droppin' Amber off to Fushia's parents' house. I'm tryin' to jump into somebody's bed tonight," Silk said.

"It opens in two hours but I need to eat now," I replied.

"Well, go ahead. I'm ready to get dressed. I'm wearin' this cute jean short jumper. Dick gonna be hangin' down my leg," he said and I believed him.

"Where was Beretta at when you saw him because he's not down here anymore?" I replied.

"He was in front my buildin' with Pistol and a few other niggas," Silk said as he fixed my plate. I went to the kitchen table to eat my food while Silk took a shower. Silk could cook his behind off but his food was always spicy. He had a lot of crushed red peppers and jalapenos in his lasagna. It almost made my chest explode. Beretta called my phone and I answered it on the second ring. It had been a while since he called me without me having to call him first.

"Yo, Mara. Take your ass home!" Beretta yelled into the phone.

"What?" I asked.

"I told you I didn't want you in da fuckin' hood. Too much shit has been happenin' down there," he said.

"I'm waitin' for Silk to get outta the shower," I replied. I was trying to hide the stress in my voice.

"Shorty, I'on give a fuck about dat! Get da fuck outta da hood and go home! I'm out here tryin' to make moves and shit. You got me stressin' right now," he said.

"Get off my fuckin' line!" I said and hung up on him.

I turned my cell phone off and threw it back into my purse. Beretta was making me regret a lot of things. Our relationship wasn't shit because he became too controlling.

"Hurry up before Beretta come up here!" I called out to Silk.

Seconds later, there was a loud knock on the door. I sat still at the kitchen table because I knew who it was.

"Open da fuck up, Mara!" Beretta yelled.

Silk's daughter started crying so I picked her up. I kissed her small chubby cheeks while I headed to the door. I opened the door and Beretta was standing in front of me looking calm. His thick tattooed arms never looked so good. He was so fine that I felt star-struck. It made me think back to when I was sixteen years old. Almost five years ago, he took me on my first date. He was the first boy to put his mouth between my legs or even kiss me. Even after all we were going through, he still gave me butterflies. I moved to the side and he stepped inside the apartment.

"You lucky you got the baby in your arms because I was ready to wrap my hand around your throat. I don't think you realize how serious I am about you bein' in da hood," he said.

"And I don't think you realize dat I grew up in this hood and you can't keep me from visiting my friend," I said.

"I'm goin' out of town for a few days to take care of sumthin. Are you tellin' me dat I should have a few of my niggas guarding our home to make sure you don't leave?" he asked.

"Are you serious?" I laughed but he had a straight face.

"Yeah, I'm serious," he replied.

"Okay," I said, playing it cool.

I'm not gonna trip because I'm gonna be sleeping in my new home tomorrow, I thought.

"Aight, call me when you get home," he said then kissed my lips. He walked out of the apartment and I began missing him already. Silk walked into the living room and took his daughter from me.

"What's the matter wit' you?" Silk asked.

"Beretta just left out of here and he looked so good. Damn, it's like he gets finer every day. Maybe because I'm so horny right now and he ain't givin' me no dick. I'm bein' thirsty wit' my own nigga. You would've thought I was a groupie by the way I stare at his ass," I said.

"I'm right here if you need it dat bad," Silk said.

SOUL Publications

"Nigga, don't talk to me like dat because I might end up sliding my thong to the side to let you in. I'm turnin' into a hoe after I have this baby. I'm gonna hit up Fushia so we can be hoes together," I said.

"See, bitch don't get cut. Grab Amber's diaper bag for me so we can roll out. I'm ridin' wit' you today because I'm gettin' drunk," Silk said. I grabbed my purse and we headed out the door.

****

Nika's restaurant was open by the time we dropped Amber off. People were standing outside dressed up like it was a club.

"I know damn well these hoes ain't get dressed up to eat," Silk said.

"That's because they know the hood niggas gonna be here. Every bitch in Annapolis want a GMBAM nigga," I replied. Nika texted me and told me I could park in the alley behind the restaurant so I wouldn't have a far walk. Zyira was going crazy in my stomach and it was tiring me out. All I could think about was getting in bed and sleeping with my favorite pillow—a pillow I used to comfort my body since Beretta was barely coming home. Nika was standing by the back door waiting for me.

"You look so beautiful, Mara. I know Beretta can't keep his hands off you," Nika said when I got out of my truck.

"Thank you," I replied.

Me and Nika wasn't really close but every so often she'd call to check up on me. The issue I had with her was how she treated Beretta. Nika only dealt with people when it was convenient for her. She wouldn't call you if she didn't need you. I wondered where she got the money from but, then again, it was Nika. She probably had the money all along.

"I need to speak wit' you about something. Silk, go inside and grab a table while I talk to Nika," I said.

"Okay, and Nika those heels, huntyyyyyyy!" Silk said, admiring Nika's outfit.

"Thank you. I got them from this boutique by my new house. But I know you got better stuff than them," Nika said.

"I got the perfect handbag that'll match those shoes," Silk said. He gave Nika his phone number before he went inside the restaurant.

"Is everything okay?" Nika asked.

"When are you goin' to tell Beretta about Hope's father?" I asked. Thinking about that piece of information had been on my mind for months. I just wanted Nika to come clean because I didn't want to be responsible for her or Poppa's dirty work.

"I don't think Beretta should ever find out. What's the point of leaking that information? Do you really want the tension between the two of you with a baby in the middle? You're a smart girl and I know you have done a lot of things you're not happy about. Things that you never want to be brought up again. Don't stress yourself over my business," she said.

"It's my business, too, because you and Poppa put me in the middle of it," I replied.

"You mean Poppa put you in the middle of it. Between you and me, Poppa has been great with Hope lately. Beretta doesn't need to fuck that up because at the end of the day Hope needs her father. Beretta's mentality will never allow him to understand," Nika said.

"Poppa is in Hope's life?" I asked and Nika blushed.

"He's supposed to be," she replied.

At that moment, I wondered if Poppa was still scheming or if he really wanted to step up to the plate. Whatever the reason, I prayed Hope didn't get hurt behind it all. I also wanted to know what happened between Nika and Poppa to make her speak so nicely of him. Shit wasn't adding up! I didn't trust Nika anymore.

"Be careful," I replied.

"Poppa told me Beretta was gonna be your lick but you fell in love with him. If I was you, I'd be extra careful, too. I believe you love my son but I know him. Beretta will neva look at you the same if he knew you were gonna set him up. So it looks like our secrets are safe and we can continue on with our lives. Now, come in so I can show you around," she smiled.

Bitch, I definitely don't trust you! Poppa would neva tell you that unless he's fucking you. Wait a minute, it all makes sense now. Nika and Poppa are still fuckin' and they are tryin' to keep it a secret by blackmailing me. That's why she doesn't want Hope to come around anymore, I thought.

I had a feeling someone was going to get hurt behind all this bullshit. The best way to make it go away was if we pretended it never happened. All I wanted to do was be happy in love, but so many signs proved that some shit just wasn't meant to be and I had to learn the hard way.

Nika's restaurant was small and cozy. There were still many people outside waiting to get in. Silk was sitting at a table in the corner of the room going over a menu.

"How long are we gonna be here? It's gettin' late and I'm tired," I said.

"Not long, so sit back and hush. You're only seven months and carryin' on like you're ready to drop," Silk fussed.

"I'll be eight months in a few weeks," I fired back.

"Well, whateva. You have three months to go. The first baby always comes late," Silk said.

Hope's babysitter came over to our table dressed in chef's clothes. I forgot she was the one who Nika hired to cook.

"Hey, Mara. Remember we've met before? I'm Amona," she said.

"Hey, and yes I remember you," I replied.

"Do you two have any questions about the menu? And because you're pregnant, I wanted to come over here to discuss a few things with you. We can make the food on a lighter side for you if you're having indigestion," she said.

"Thanks, but I won't be eating anything," I replied.

Poppa came into the restaurant and I could tell by his jewelry that he was still getting money. Nika knew Beretta wasn't going to be there so she allowed Poppa to strut through her establishment like it belonged to him. Amona was running off with her mouth but I was watching Poppa. Nika pulled him into the kitchen.

"I want the fish, shrimp and grits. You can add extra cheese on it," I heard Silk tell Amona. Amona left our table and went into the kitchen.

"I'm gonna knock some sense into you if you don't stop actin' weird, and was that Poppa's fine ass dat just walked in? Chillleeeeeee, Beretta fucked him up at dat block party but he can still get it," Silk said.

SOUL Publications

"Please don't bring that up. I thought Beretta was gonna kill him," I replied.

It was heartbreaking watching my man beat my brother's ass, but Poppa had it coming because he had no business pushing me on the ground. I hoped the ass whipping he got from Beretta calmed him down and made him realize that Beretta was really about that street life. Poppa lived in the hood and talked a lot of gangsta shit but the truth was he wasn't hardcore. He was a thinker not a doer, which is why he hated Beretta. My mind drifted off into another place as Silk ran his mouth. I wasn't the nosey type but I was very curious about Nika and Poppa. Those two together didn't sit well with me.

Poppa

"**H**ow much is this?" Nika asked, counting the money on her desk.

"Eleven g's," I replied.

"Appreciate it," she said then put the money in her purse.

"Aight, now let's discuss this business movement. I'm givin' you money for Hope plus extra so we can open up dat strip club we were talkin' about," I said.

"We are opening up a club but the buildin' you want is asking for a lot of money. It's not safe to just jump out there like that. We can get a hole in the wall and fix it up. Your impatience is gonna hold you back from a lot of things. It takes a while but we'll get there," Nika said.

For four months, me and Nika had been on good terms. She was even letting me stay at the crib with her out in Jersey with Hope. I thought after I gave her the thirty g's, she was going to cut me off, but it seemed like the shit made her want me even more. Jasmine was catching licks for me like she was born to do it. When I first showed Mara the ropes, she was a little timid but not Jasmine. All I had to do was scope out the nigga for her and she was on it like white on rice. Jasmine was also fucking the niggas and tricking them into believing she was their girl. The only downfall was that the niggas were left alive whereas Mara was robbing them then merking them. We traveled a lot, though, so none of the niggas we hit up were from Maryland. We even spent three weeks in Georgia because Jasmine had some lame ass nigga pussy-whipped while she was milking him. Our little operation was smoother than ever. I was getting money—bands of it. Beretta's GMBAM gang wasn't on my mind anymore. I was so busy traveling, I forgot all about those niggas until I saw Mara when I walked into Nika's restaurant. I wondered if she knew I was still banging Nika.

"Aight, I'll take your word for it. I'll get up wit' you lata before someone snitch on me to your son," I said.

"You can always leave out the back door," she said. Nika walked around the desk and stood in front of me. Her perfume made my dick hard but I wasn't in the mood to fuck her. I was fucking Jasmine all that morning and a nigga was tired. At first, Jasmine was a pest because she was a young-minded ass female, but she was perfect for me after I broke her in. Nika reached for my zipper but I pushed her hand away.

"I'll catch you lata," I said.

"Are you rejecting me?" she asked with an attitude.

"You want me to fuck you after I pulled out of my shorty an hour ago?" I asked.

"That little nappy-headed girl ain't shit but your prostitute. She's fuckin' and robbin' niggas for you like you're her pimp. How old is she anyway?" Nika asked.

"She's twenty but what the hell you questioning her age fah? I'm young enough to be your son," I replied and she rolled her eyes.

"Get outta my office," Nika said.

She was ready to walk away from me but I grabbed her arm and pushed up her skirt. I leaned her over the desk and pulled her thong to the side. I got down on my knees and ate her pussy until she exploded on my chin. Nika always needed sex and was a totally different woman after she got it. I didn't know the bitch could be nice until I started dicking her down on the regular.

"Damn," Nika said as she came down from the orgasm I gave her. She fixed her skirt and I wiped my face off with the back of my hand.

"Now you can go. I'll see you tomorrow night," she said.

"Tomorrow night? I'm gonna be busy," I replied and she raised her eyebrow at me.

"Just because I'm letting you taste the pussy, doesn't mean you can tell me 'no' whenever you feel like it. You need me! I don't need you even though you think I do. It's a lot of niggas out here that wouldn't mind spending a dime on me, baby. You want your strip club, don't you? Who else can make that happen for you? Not your little girlfriend and damn sho' not your mama or your sister. Be at my home tomorrow night," Nika said.

"Man, whateva," I replied.

We had a love-hate situation. I was always thinking about the bitch but I wanted to strangle her when I was around her.

"I'm moving back to Maryland since my business is in Annapolis. I'll be in my new place next week. Amona can't watch Hope anymore because she cooks at the restaurant so you'll be spending more time with her," Nika said.

"That's too hot and you know it. This shit between us is supposed to be on the low and you're about to fuck it up," I replied.

"Get ready because I ain't changing my mind," she said.

I left out of her office and walked down the hall past the kitchen. Mara was coming out of the bathroom as soon as I cut the corner. I hadn't seen her since Ammo's block party. Mara's stomach was out there and her face was round and full. She was wearing a diamond necklace with Beretta's name on it. Her earrings were shaped like guns and the bracelets on her arm were icy. Mara was walking around with over one-hundred g's worth of jewelry on.

"What's up, sis?" I asked.

"I don't know but I'm sure it's Nika's skirt. What kinda of shit are you tryin' to pull? Are still tryin' to take down Beretta? If so, I'm not gonna let that happen. He hasn't done a damn thing to you so you need to let the hate go," Mara said.

"Fuck dat nigga! Do it look like I'm worried about him? I'm eatin' good, shorty. Fuck what you heard," I replied.

"You must still be robbin' niggas because we both know you ain't a hustla," she said.

"Very cute, shorty. I'on give a fuck about what you doin' with your life now, but never forget where you came from. All I see when I look at you is the dingy clothes-wearin' fat bitch I had to take care of. Never forget dat shit," I replied.

"Of course, I won't forget because I'm still the same bitch that'll bust her gun quicker than you'll bust yours, bitch boy. Stay the fuck away from me and I mean it. You're only fuckin' Nika to get close but I'll kill you if I have to. Why do you want to destroy me so bad? What have I ever done to you to make you hate me so much? Your own flesh and blood. I was so loyal to you to the point where I couldn't be loyal to myself. You're supposed to protect me from the world and save me from drowning. Instead, you threw me off the boat so I could sink to the bottom. You wouldn't care if I walked out of here and got hit by a car. Nobody loved you, NOBODY. But I did. You just remember that before you think about sabotaging my relationship and my life," Mara said. I felt something fall from my eye and it was a tear. I wiped it away and rushed out of the restaurant. I got into my brand-new Charger and headed straight home.

****

I smelled food cooking when I walked into the crib. Jasmine took care of home and it made me like her even more. Shorty spoiled me and I spoiled her but sometimes I had to slap her for asking me dumb shit. She didn't know I had a daughter so whenever I stayed with Nika, we ended up beefing. I'd lie to her and tell her I was out chilling with my niggas but she knew I was fucking another woman. One day she found Nika's panties in my whip, but of course I denied the shit. The only reason I couldn't tell Jasmine I was fucking another woman was because I didn't want to mess up our hustle. I had to gain some of her trust so she wouldn't lose focus. I opened up a pot and she was making greens with smoked turkey necks. In the oven was ribs and baked macaroni and cheese. She came into the kitchen while I was fixing my plate but she didn't look too good.

"What's up wit' you?" I asked.

She pulled a pregnancy test from behind her back and I almost dropped my plate on the floor. The test was positive.

"Yo, what the fuck!" I shouted and slammed my plate on the counter.

"Why are you mad?" Jasmine asked.

SOUL Publications

"Yo, I told you to take dat morning-after pill when I went inside you raw that one time. You told me you took the shit and now look at you. We have been on good terms lately and now you want to fuck it up. How are we gonna make moves if you're pregnant? You know what, shorty. It ain't dat big of a deal 'cause you ain't havin' it. So, go on ahead and make an appointment tomorrow mornin'," I said.

"Wait a minute, Kamar! This is a damn child we're talkin' about," she said.

"Bitch, I don't give a fuck! Get rid of it!" I replied.

Nika wasn't going to help me with the strip club if she knew I knocked my bitch up. It was a dirty game but the ball was in Nika's court. A nigga was tired of robbing niggas and being a hustla wasn't my thing. Shittt, I didn't have the patience for bullshit anymore. I wanted legit money and nothing was going to stand in my way.

"You're a heartless punk!" Jasmine said.

I was already in my feelings about the shit Mara said to me, but Jasmine calling me a punk put the icing on the cake. I struck her in the face and she fell into the refrigerator with blood leaking from her nose. She jumped on me and started pounding me with her fists. She was screaming and crying about how I ruined her life and that she was fine before she met me. Tired of shorty's shit, I slammed my fist into her face and she slipped on the floor. I dragged her down the hall to our bedroom so I could beat her ass how I wanted to. She screamed for help and I choked her until her eyes rolled to the back of her head. I let her go before I killed her but it didn't stop me from slapping her. I took all my life's frustrations out on Jasmine until she laid still and cried.

"Look what you made me do! I keep tellin' yah dumb ass to stop fuckin' wit' me!" I yelled at her. Jasmine's shirt was covered in blood and her eye started to swell. I ran to the closet and grabbed a towel, peroxide and band aids. This was the worst I had beaten her. Usually I slapped her a few times or choked her, but this time I almost killed her.

"Get away from me, Poppa," she cried when I wiped the blood off her face.

"Chill da hell out! I'm tryin' to fix your dumb-ass up," I replied. I pressed my weight down on her to clean her face. The blood was gone but she had bruises on her face and around her neck.

"I can't do this anymore," Jasmine sobbed.

"Can't do what?" I asked.

"This! I'm gonna move in with my brother," she said and it angered me.

Jasmine distanced herself from her family after we hooked up. She talked to her brother, Sniper, almost every day, though. He thought she was living with a female friend. The last time they talked, Jasmine cursed him out because he was acting like her father; she hadn't heard from him since.

SOUL Publications

"Go ahead and I'll make sure to give an anonymous tip to the niggas you stole from. We have done too much shit for you to turn your back on me now. Take a nice bath and I'll bring you a glass of wine. While you're in the tub, you better google every damn abortion clinic website in the state of Maryland," I said. She pulled away from me and slowly got up off the floor. Jasmine slammed the bathroom door and locked it. I wasn't worried about Jasmine telling her brother on me because shorty was scared of what I could possibly do to her. Beating her, spoiling her, and fucking her good was a form of manipulation that worked on weak females and I mastered it. My phone beeped and it was Tyshawn hitting me up. I'd been ducking the nigga for about two months. I decided to meet up with him to get it over with. The nigga knew too much shit about me to get on his bad side.

A few hours later...

"What's up witchu?" Tyshawn asked when I sat next to him at a bar.

"Shit, just gettin' this paper," I replied and he nodded his head.

"Let me ask you sumthin. How in da fuck can you start all this bullshit then back out if it? It's because of you dat nigga Ammo is dead. I had niggas hatin' GMBAM because of you and now you're just walkin' around this muthafucka like we ain't have plans," Tyshawn seethed.

"I keep tellin' you to the chill da fuck out. Nika is gonna help me with this club shit. She ain't gonna do it if

Welcome to the Low Life 2

I'm beefin' with GMBAM. Plans change every day, nigga, and you know dat. It's all about the bigger picture, and as far as I can see it, havin' a legit business is better than a street war that we ain't gonna win anyway. The only reason we caught Ammo is because you were fuckin' wit' Swan and she set dat nigga up. What else do we have after dat? It damn sho' ain't Mara because she's pregnant for Beretta. It's time to make legit moves," I said.

"You a pussy-whipped ass nigga is what all of this is about. You ain't switch up until you started fuckin' Nika. She's usin' you, bruh. She ain't shit but an old gold-diggin' bitch. Niggas out here starvin' because of your anti-GMBAM movement and you just said fuck us," he vented.

"It ain't about Nika. It's about Mara and my niece," I said, surprising myself. What Mara said at Nika's restaurant kept playing over and over in my head. That shit fucked me up. *Did I really hate my baby sister?* Truthfully, I didn't have a reason to hate her. All she wanted was to fuck with Beretta. Mara wasn't lying when she said she was the only person who cared about me. I remembered times she used to look at me like I was her hero. That shit made me proud because nobody, not even my mother, gave me that type of admiration.

"Oh, now you love your sista? Nigga, dat's bullshit. It's been four months, bruh. You ignored my calls and text messages. I'm surprised you even came down here to meet up wit' me. But fuck all dat, I know somebody who has connections with GMBAM. Shag's little cousin is fuckin' dat lil' nigga, Machete. She told Shag that Machete be trappin' out of an ice cream truck. All we have to do is hit it up. No other niggas around Maryland is pushing as much weight as those niggas so it's a must we carry this shit out. You either down or you not. But just remember, this shit will still be on your hands," he gritted.

"Do what you gotta do, bruh. Just be careful because GMBAM has grown in the last four months. Almost every nigga in this city has that tattoo on 'em," I replied.

"I'm hittin' dat nigga up then I'm movin' back to Chicago. Let me know if you want in on it," he said then ordered a shot of Jack Daniel's.

"Do what you gotta do," I replied.

"I need my old nigga to come back. Nigga, you been on some sucka shit lately," Tyshawn said.

"I'm tryna move differently," I replied.

"Yo, be honest wit' me. Is Mara carryin' my seed?" Tyshawn asked.

"Nigga, the baby would've been here by now," I said.

"You right, damn. I can't believe she havin' a baby by dat nigga. That's supposed to be my lil' shorty. I didn't understand why you hated dat nigga so much until he started fuckin' Mara. Muthafucka got weight, fancy cars, and a beautiful loyal bitch. How do he do it?" Tyshawn asked.

"I thought merkin' Ammo would've humbled his bitch-ass, but he started grindin' harder. The lil' nigga is just too smart, bruh," I admitted.

"Every man has a downfall. Believe dat," Tyshawn said before he downed his shot.

"Yo, you tryna hit up the strip club tonight?" I asked.

"Cool. My mind just hasn't been the same since dat shit happened in yah old hood. I gotta get dat nigga back for embarrassing me," Tyshawn said.

"I feel you," I replied.

"Finish dat up, bruh. I'm gonna go outside and call my bitch up really quick to see if she's straight," I said.

"You need to leave dat lil' girl alone," Tyshawn chuckled.

"Dat broad feedin' me. She ain't goin' nowhere," I replied and slapped a fifty-dollar bill on the bar.

I rushed out the small country bar where a lot of niggas were line dancing and bull riding. Tyshawn wasn't even hanging around his usual spots anymore. Beretta and his goons had him shook, but I wasn't focused on that nigga anymore. Beefing with him was making my pockets dry. I walked over to my car and unlocked the door. Underneath my seat was a gun with a silencer on it. I placed it underneath my shirt. What I was about to do was going to haunt me for the rest of my life, but I had to do it. I didn't trust nobody anymore, not even my right-hand man, Tyshawn. He wasn't the same nigga and he wasn't thinking clearly. There was no way he was going to rob Beretta and get away with it. I could picture Tyshawn getting jammed up and telling Beretta everything we did to Ammo. Fuck that, me and Tyshawn ended up on different levels in life. Death scared the shit out of me, especially when Skibo was ready to merk me. I couldn't fathom staring down the barrel of a gun again. It robbed me of my manhood and turned me into a bitch that night. I could still smell the burning flesh off Mike's body. Those niggas were too ruthless and I couldn't die like that. There was no use trying to talk Tyshawn out of doing what he was planning to do. Beretta embarrassed him in front of the entire hood and he wanted some type of get back. Tyshawn walked out the bar and lit a Black & Mild.

"Aye, bruh. Jasmine just told me she's around the corner with her home girl. You tryna kick it with them before we go to the strip club? Her friend got a nice lil' fat ass. She's a little chubby, too. Just how you like 'em," I said.

"Damn, nigga. You stay up in some pussy," Tyshawn chuckled.

"How did you get here?" I asked.

"Cab, nigga. You know I'on drive around the city unless I have to," he replied.

"Aight, bet. We can walk there since it's around the corner. I'm not tryna to park my new whip on the strip so someone can side-swipe my shit," I replied.

SOUL Publications

We walked through a cut located by a garage. Around the corner from the country bar was a strip of bars young adults went to on the weekends. The strip was loud and you could hear the music playing from the small clubs. I pulled my gun out from behind me before we stepped out onto the main sidewalk.

"She better be bad, too, nigga. I haven't been to this strip since we were eighteen," Tyshawn said. My stomach bubbled and my heart pounded. Sweat beads formed on my forehead but I had to do it.

"Hold up, I need to take a piss really quick," he said then stood between two dumpsters.

"I love you, bruh. I hope you can forgive me while lookin' down over me," I said.

"Nigga, get off dat sweet shit while I got my dick out," Tyshawn said.

I pulled the trigger and the bullet entered the back of his head. He fell face forward on the ground and I shot him again. I went into his pockets and took his wallet before I walked out of the alley and blended in with the teenagers.

I waited around for two hours before I went back to my car. Tyshawn's body was still lying in the alley. Someone would find him once the crowd died down. It was one o'clock in the morning by the time I made it back home. Jasmine was lying on the couch with an ice pack on her face, watching TV. She said nothing to me when I came in the house and I didn't say anything to her. I took a shower then got into bed.

Nobody loved you, NOBODY. But I did, Mara's voice echoed in my head before I dozed off...

Beretta

Three days later...

I pulled up in my driveway half asleep. I had just got back from a trip to Mexico. I had to meet up with my connect, Chulo, face-to-face. I was copping more weight than before and he thought I was bullshitting until I showed up and presented the numbers. The crazy part about it was I had to go by myself or the deal was off. The nigga was like me; he didn't trust too many muthafuckas. I thought he was going to kill me. Hell, he could've because the Mexican cartel wasn't shit to play with. I kept my game face on and showed those niggas I was about my word. All I had left to do was sit back and wait for the shipment to come in on a fish boat.

I walked into the house at three o'clock in the evening. It fucked me up that I hadn't talked to or seen Mara in a few days. Chulo didn't want any phones around him so I left my phones in my car at the airport. When I turned them on, I had no messages from her. I missed my shorty and knew I had a lot of ass kissing to do. I had a few days of free time and I planned on spending it with Mara.

"Aye, Pretty Girl!" I called out when I stepped into the foyer but didn't get an answer.

"I know her ass ain't leave this house," I said aloud as I walked up the stairs. I pushed the doors open to the master bedroom and she wasn't there. I searched the entire house for Mara. When I went into the garage, both her vehicles were gone.

"I know this muthafucka ain't on no funny shit," I said to myself.

"This number is no longer in service," the operator said when I called Mara's phone.

I ran back upstairs to our bedroom and looked in our closet. Mara's clothes and shoes were gone. I went into the bathroom and her make-up was gone. She even took shit out of the dressers. I called Piper's phone and she answered on the third ring.

"What do you want?" she asked.

"Yo, where da fuck is my shorty at?" I yelled into the phone.

"I don't know. Call and ask her," Piper said.

"She changed her number! Yo, what kind of games is dat bitch playin' while she's carryin' my fuckin' seed? I know you know where she's at!" I said.

"Maybe she's just bein' dramatic. You know Mara can get extra sometimes. Look, I'll call you if I hear anything from her," she said and hung up on me.

I took a shower and changed my clothes. It was impossible to go to sleep knowing Mara moved out of our crib. I left out of the house and headed straight to the hood.

****

"Who is ittttttttttt," Mara's punk-ass friend sang when I knocked on his door. I cringed hearing that nigga's voice. Silk opened the door and the shit angered me. He was wearing a leotard with a pair of tube socks.

"I was doin' yoga and you interrupted me. What do you want?" he nervously asked.

"Where is Mara at, nigga? I know your sugary ass know about her movin' out," I said.

"I know nothing about that. Mara was home the last time I talked to her," he said and rolled his eyes.

"What's her number?" I asked.

"She didn't call wit' the new number yet. Nigga, I'on even know why you're worried about dat girl. You forgot all about her. Had dat girl walkin' around horny and lonely like she's a single mother. Let her be happy where she's at so you continue bein' a fuck-nigga. I told Mara I'd be the father anyway," he said then slammed the door in my face.

"Bitch-ass nigga!" I called out.

As much as that nigga pissed me off, I couldn't see myself putting my hands on a gay man. That shit just wasn't cool. I was thinking about having one of my niggas scare the shit out of him, but I couldn't get mad at him for speaking real shit. I neglected my shorty for four months. I was treating Mara like she was a side-bitch although I wasn't cheating on her.

"What's up, Beretta?" a lil' boy named Carlos said to me when I walked out of Silk's building.

"What's good witchu?" I asked and slapped hands with him.

"Shit, just chillin," he said.

"What da fuck I tell you about dat mouth? You still a little boy. You ain't standin' up pissin' like these older heads out here. And I betta not catch you standin' on da corner. How you get those fresh J's?" I asked and he shrugged his shoulders.

"You lyin' to me, bruh? Where did you get those shits from? What I gotta beat yah lil' ass or sumthin to get it outta you?" I asked.

"Nate gave me da money," he said.

"Nate ain't just gonna give you da money. What did you have to do for it?" I asked.

"What chu mean? I was servin' the fiends," he said and I pulled him to the side. I went inside my pocket and peeled off some bills.

"Take this and go to the corner store for your sisters. Hide the rest of it behind your dresser. Put a hole in your wall if you have to, but you gotta make sure nobody sees you. Don't even tell your sisters you have money 'cause they might tell your mother. I'll look out for you if you look out for me," I said.

"You puttin' me down with GMBAM?" he asked.

"Naw, I'm puttin' my foot up your ass. I want you to be betta than us niggas out here, yah feel me? As long as you do that, I'll break you off with an allowance. I'm gonna beat your lil' ass then cut the allowance off if I catch you out here on the corner. Now, get outta my face and go play," I said and he ran off.

Pistol, Machete, Sniper and a few other niggas were posted up by the basketball court, shooting dice.

"What's good? You look heated about sumthin," Pistol said.

"I can't find Mara. She moved out," I replied.

"DAMMMMNNNNNN!" they said in unison.

SOUL Publications

"I told you shorty was crazy. Mara don't be givin' a fuck sometimes," Pistol chuckled.

"Y'all niggas think it's funny until I get jammed up for merkin' her baby-head ass," I replied.

"Y'all heard what happened to dat nigga, Tyshawn? Someone found him downtown in the alley slumped. He was robbed then shot in da head twice," Machete said.

Mara goes missin' and the nigga she fucked ends up dead. She better not be on some bullshit! Shit ain't addin' up, I thought.

I pulled Pistol to the side so I could holla at him.

"Yo, find out from Piper where Mara's at," I said.

"Piper ain't snitchin' on her home girl," he said.

"Bruh, I don't care how you do it but you gotta help a nigga out. Her friends ain't feelin' me so they ain't tellin' me shit. I came home and thought I was gonna slide into sumthin juicy but shorty straight moved out on me," I replied and Pistol chuckled.

"That's 'cause you been givin' her dead dick, nigga. Everybody knows you wasn't smashin' shorty like dat. Silk told the whole hood. All Mara needs is some dick, bruh, and maybe she'll come back home. You betta eat her ass or sumthin. She's pregnant, too, so I know she's hurtin'," he said.

SOUL Publications

I chilled in the hood for a few hours before I headed back home. The house didn't feel the same. There wasn't a smell of food cooking, sounds of vacuuming or Mara prancing around the living room singing while dusting. If only she understood the importance of her presence at home. I was just grinding so I was going to get right back. Months ago, I wanted to leave her because I knew she wouldn't be able to handle my hustle. I was going to eventually lose her because of my absence, but I couldn't let her go. I went into our bedroom and laid across the bed, thinking of ways to keep Mara in my life. Something popped up in my mind out of nowhere. I didn't know what I was thinking but it damn sure felt right. I called my jeweler on his cell phone and he answered right before I was ready to hang up. I told him I needed to meet with him ASAP.

****

An hour later, the doorbell rang. I opened the door and Mison, the jeweler, was standing in front of me dressed in a black suit with his hair slicked back. Usually he didn't do house calls but I spent so much money with him that he knew I was good for it. He was afraid of getting robbed but he had insurance on his jewelry in case he did.

"Nice crib," he said, looking around.

"Appreciate it. My shorty decorated it; follow me," I said and we went into the kitchen. He sat down at the kitchen island and I grabbed a bottle of Henny off the counter.

SOUL Publications

"Okay, what you got for me?" I asked when I sat across from him.

He opened up his briefcase and pulled out a large velvet box. Inside the box were wedding rings.

"You're twenty-three, right?" he asked.

"Yeah, why?" I replied.

"Are you sure these are the type of rings you want to look at? I have another suitcase in my trunk with promise rings," he said.

"Look, bruh. I called you here to spend money witchu. I don't need a mentor or no shit like dat. I love my shorty and I gotta make sure she doesn't leave me. This right here is going to give me the security I need. Plus, she's carryin' my seed so this is only right. My age is just a number so we ain't gotta ever bring dat up again. Now, how much is this one?" I asked, holding up a platinum ring with large VS2 diamonds.

"Forty-nine thousand," he replied.

"How many karats?" I asked.

"6.5 karats," he replied.

I looked at the other rings, but the diamonds weren't as clear as the first ring I picked out.

"I'm gonna get this one. Box this up while I get da money for you," I said and he smirked.

"She's gonna love it," he said.

I went into the safe in my bedroom and I almost changed my mind. Mara took some money out of my safe. I wasn't tripping because she didn't know shit about my other safe but seeing that she took money made me feel like she wasn't coming back. I grabbed the money for her ring and took it downstairs to Mison.

"It's not too late to change your mind. I can always hold it for you until you think it through," he said.

"Marriage dat bad or sumthin?" I asked.

Mison was a married middle-aged Italian man with kids. He knew shit I didn't know but Mara was a different type of female. She loved hard and her loyalty was genuine. She was a little fucked up around the edges as far as her attitude but I saw past that. She needed me the same way I needed her so I couldn't change my mind.

"No, but I got married at twenty-one and my wife was twenty. We had our first kid when I was twenty-two. Me and her didn't get a chance to enjoy our lives before we tied the knot. Twenty years later, we barely talk. I stepped out a few times and so did she. It doesn't mean we don't love each other. We just jumped right into something without getting to know ourselves. But that is a good ring. Let me know if you decide to return it. It will never lose its value," he said.

"Okay, I'll get up witchu lata. Appreciate you big time," I said and we slapped hands.

"Anytime. Let me know if it's too small or big and I'll get that taken care for you right away," he replied. He grabbed his suitcase off the kitchen island and I walked him to the door. I headed upstairs to the master bedroom after I locked the front door and turned on the alarm.

"Damn, I'm bored," I said aloud. Mara was in the house everyday by herself but I couldn't handle being in the crib for a few hours alone. Baby girl was going through it without me and I did nothing about it. Long story short, I didn't have a life outside the streets and Mara.

Two weeks later....

"Beretta, bruh! Do you hear me talkin' to you?" Pistol asked while I was sitting on his couch.

"Naw, what you say?" I replied.

"What time Machete supposed to be collecting the money from Brasco? Remember him? You gave him two extra bricks and he told you he'd pay you in a week. Well, today is dat day, nigga," Pistol said.

"I'll hit him up in a bit," I replied, rolling up a blunt.

"Nigga, get it together, bruh," Pistol said.

"Get what together? Dat bitch left me and changed her number. Mara on some bullshit. Two fuckin' weeks! I'on even know if she's eatin' right. Mara's blood sugar was up the last few times during her prenatal visit. I thought she was just doin' this for my attention, but shorty really took my money and left. I'm gonna kill dat bitch, on God," I replied.

"Yah love-struck ass," Pistol joked.

"You'd be feelin' the same way if Lezzi left," I replied.

"Shiiddddd, I'on love dat girl. I care about her but that's as far as it goes. We're like roommates in this muthafucka. She doesn't care as long as I pay everything," he said and I shook my head.

"This conversation ain't benefitin' my situation, bruh. I love my girl and she's carryin' my seed. I wanna marry her," I admitted.

"WHOOAAAAAAA! My nigga, you lost your mind? Married? Nigga, we are still young. Da fuck is you talkin' about? Who put you up to this? Glock's lover boy ass?" he asked.

"I always follow my gut and dat's what I'm doin," I said.

"Fuck it then. It ain't like Mara ain't a part of the fam anyway. Piper ain't gonna tell me where Mara at, though," he said.

"I called her doctor yesterday and she told me Mara canceled her prenatal visit. Mara told her that she was no longer living in the area. A bunch of bullshit! She walking around like I was out fuckin' other bitches. I was barely fuckin' her. The reason I wifed shorty was because she understood me. She knows I got business out in da streets. She knew dat shit before we moved in together. That's one selfish ass bitch. All because I was too tired to fuck her. I love her and hate her dumb-ass right now. Some nigga asked me the other day if Mara was pregnant for dat nigga Tyshawn. Yo, dat betta not be the reason she left me. On God, I'll take that life sentence like a G because I'll merk her and everybody in her bloodline. I'on know what to think," I vented.

A nigga was stressing all over again. Just when I took my mind off Ammo's death, Mara goes and pulls some shit on me like I didn't give a fuck about her. That was the exact reason why niggas like me was scared of commitment. It clouded a man's mind. Niggas was probably stealing from me but all I could think about was Mara. She was my weakness. Shorty was addictive, bottom line.

"I hope I neva meet a shorty wit' the same pussy as Mara's 'cause you pussy-whipped like a muthafucka. I've known you since I was a youngin' and not once have I pictured you settlin' down. I saw myself gettin' married before you and I plan on bein' a hoe for da rest of my life," Pistol said.

Welcome to the Low Life 2

Lezzi walked into the crib with a familiar face. After a few seconds, I realized who the shorty was. Lezzi was with the broad Amona. She was my mother's babysitter.

"Oh, hey, Beretta," Amona said.

"Fuck all dat. Where's my lil' sista at?" I asked.

"Wit' your mother. Hope has a new sitter now. I cook at Nika's restaurant," she said.

"Yo, what I tell you about bringin' different people to my crib?" Pistol asked Lezzi.

"She's my cousin! You would've known that if you weren't so busy runnin' the streets. I told you my cousin from New Jersey moved back to Maryland but I guess since my name ain't Piper you don't pay me any mind," Lezzi said.

"Yo, why you always gotta bring her up?" Pistol asked.

"'Cause you're at her house more than you're home," Lezzi said.

"Yo, just get da fuck on before I embarrass you in front of company. I keep tellin' you dat me and Piper are cool and your insecurities can't change dat. She's like family and I grew up around shorty in our old hood," Pistol said.

Amona sat on the couch next to me while Pistol and Lezzi argued about a bunch of bullshit. Those niggas were blowing my high.

"Nika showed me a lot of pictures of you from when you were younger. They are so adorable. I feel like I know you because she talks so much about you," Amona said.

"Oh, word? 'Cause Nika damn sho ain't raise me so I'm curious about what she told you," I replied.

"She said you're difficult to understand and you shut her out a lot. But she also told me some funny stories about you and your friends," Amona said.

"Shorty, Nika told you a bunch of bedtimes stories 'cause she knows shit about me or my niggas," I replied and she felt embarrassed.

"She tries her best," Amona said.

"You a nosey lil' muthafucka, aren't you?" I asked and Lezzi gasped.

"BERETTA!" Lezzi said.

"What? Shorty over here talkin' about some shit Nika done told her. Nika don't know shit about me and neither does this lil' bird," I replied.

"You can't talk to her like how you talk to Mara! Unlike Mara and Piper, she doesn't understand that bullshit ass behavior," Lezzi said.

"Mara ain't a weak female so she can handle whateva I say outta my mouth. Shorty got a serious left hook to put me in my place so that's irrelevant. Amona is curious about this lifestyle so let shorty enjoy the experience," I replied.

"Amona is an educated college graduate is what I'm sayin'. Have some respect when talkin' to a decent female," Lezzi said.

"Y'all bitches are always throwin' education around but be fuckin' the most disrespectful hood nigga alive. Get gone, Lezzi. Me and my nigga was talkin' about some real-life shit, but since we talkin' all sophisticated or whatnot. How about you use your degree and get a real job to pay dat high ass car note. My hood money ain't no good up in this house, baby girl," Pistol said.

"Amona tryna get fucked by a thug," I said and she gasped.

"Oh, wait a minute," Amona said.

"Ain't nothing wrong wit' it, shorty. You ain't da first to want deep back strokes with Jeezy playin' in da background," I joked and Pistol chuckled.

"Ewww, Beretta," Lezzi said.

"Calm down, damn. I'm just fuckin' wit' shorty," I replied and Amona blushed.

"But I was in those guts while listenin' to Lil' Webbie. You ain't gotta put on in front yah cousin," Pistol said to Lezzi.

"Let's go in the kitchen so I can pour you a glass of wine. These niggas ain't shit," Lezzi complained. Amona stood up and smoothed her maxi dress out because it got stuck between her ass cheeks. I already knew what it was, shorty wanted my attention. My eyes landed on her plump ass. Shorty was thick but she wasn't thick like Mara. Mara was chubby with it and I could grip her ass with it spilling out of my hands. Amona walked past me and I caught the scent of her perfume. I had to admit, shorty was bomb.

"Lezzi know her cousin a freak," Pistol said.

Two hours later, I was still at Pistol's crib. Amona cooked steaks with some kind of garlic butter sauce with asparagus and shrimp. We played a game of Uno afterwards and I wasn't too big on card games but I had to keep busy because Mara had me on edge. Lezzi was fixing drinks and she passed me one but I declined.

"You not drinkin?" Lezzi asked.

"Naw, I'm good. Appreciate everything but it's time for me to bounce," I said. I slapped hands with Pistol before I walked out the front door. Amona came out of the house seconds later.

"Wait up," she called out and I turned around.

SOUL Publications

Welcome to the Low Life 2

"I know I shouldn't be telling you this but I know you miss Hope. Nika doesn't want you around Hope because it's not good for her learning. Please don't tell her I told you this because I signed a confidentially paper when I was watching Hope. You don't seem like a bad person to me and I know all about you taking care of Hope so I don't think it's fair," she said.

"What do you mean it's not good for her learnin'?" I asked.

"She's autistic but Nika didn't want you to know. Nika told me you wanted her to get an abortion when she told you she was pregnant. She thinks she's being punished because she wasn't a good mother to you so she can't find the words to tell you about Hope. It's a slap in the face for her. I honestly think what she's doin' is wrong but I work with her and I need my job," Amona said.

"She moved because she didn't want me to know much about Hope's care?" I asked and Amona nodded her head.

"Do me a favor. Bring Hope to me tomorrow mornin'," I said.

"I don't know if I can do that," she said.

I reached into my pocket and peeled off a few hundred-dollar bills.

"Take this," I said.

"I don't want your money," she said and tried to give it back.

"Naw, go ahead. We all got bills, baby girl," I replied and she smiled.

"Okay, I'll see you around ten o'clock in the morning. I have to figure out a way to get Hope," she replied.

"Appreciate it," I said.

Amona got into her Passat and pulled off. I was still standing by my whip not believing the shit about Nika not wanting me around Hope. But I wasn't blind when it came to Nika. She was trying to hurt me because I didn't give her the money for her restaurant. I helped Nika raise Hope for three years until she moved out of Maryland. For a while, I wondered why Hope wasn't as active and didn't talk and Nika's hoe ass hid it all from me. I called Nika and she answered on the third ring.

"What's up, Nika?" I asked, biting the inside of my cheek. It was hard talking to the bitch without wanting to lash out.

"Nothing, just getting Hope out of the tub. What is it, Z'wan? I'm kinda busy," she said. I heard a nigga in the background but I couldn't make out what he was saying.

"Busy suckin' dick?" I asked.

"You are every bit of your father! You have no respect for me!" Nika yelled into the phone.

Welcome to the Low Life 2

"Good, because you don't respect yourself. Tell me why I can't see my fuckin' sista? Four fuckin' months!" I yelled into the phone.

"I don't want Hope around your shit! Your life is dangerous, Z'wan. What if someone tries to do to you what they did to Ammo? As her mother, I can control who I want her around and it damn sure isn't you!" she said.

"But it was cool when you had niggas around me with guns and shit on our dinner table? Or what about dat time I got ahold of one of your nigga's guns and it went off. I could've killed myself but you didn't stop dat nigga from comin' around. You salty because I didn't give you any money! Money that I don't owe yah triflin' ass. I have been takin' care of you since I started gettin' money and all I ask is for you to let me see my sista," I replied.

"Worry about your own daughter so she won't grow up bein' a stick-up bitch like her mother!" Nika cried into the phone. I guess I hurt her feelings but what I said was the truth. My grandparents were alive but they didn't want nothing to do with me because of my mother. The family hated her so much they hated me, too.

I headed home with the radio off so I could clear my mind. Mara's presence would've controlled the anger I was feeling at that moment. Nika was officially cut out from my life; she was no longer my mother. She was just another bitch from the hood with miles on her pussy and bad parenting skills. Often times, I blamed her for the respect I didn't have for women before I got with Mara. A mother was supposed to nurture and love the life that came out of her womb. Sewer rats had more motherly instincts than that bitch.

****

The next day...

Amona rang my doorbell fifteen minutes past ten o'clock. I opened the door for her and she was standing in front of me holding Hope's hand. I picked my sister up and held her close to me. She cracked a smile when I tickled her stomach.

"Z," Hope said.

"She can say a few words but your name might be hard for her to pronounce," Amona said when she stepped into the house. She was wearing tight jeans and a half-top; I think shorty wore it on purpose.

"Is it okay with me being here?" Amona asked.

"Yeah, Mara went to the grocery store," I lied.

We went into the living room and I put Hope down on the floor. Amona pulled a few toys out of her bag for Hope to play with. She walked around the living room, looking at pictures of me and Mara. I sat next to Hope on the floor and played with her.

"How long have you been with Mara?" Amona asked.

"Two years," I said.

"She's a nice young girl. I ran into her at Nika's restaurant a few weeks ago. Pregnancy suits her," she said. Hope placed her Barbie in my hand and I looked at it.

"Naw, baby girl. Yah brotha neva held one of these before," I said. Hope stroked the Barbie's head then gave me a small Barbie comb.

"She wants you to comb her hair," Amona said.

"Mannn, this comb ain't gonna do this Barbie any justice. I think Mara got some grease or sumthin in the closet," I replied and Amona laughed.

"This is too funny. What are you and Mara having?" She asked.

"A girl," I replied.

"Might as well get used to playing with Barbie's now because you can't tell a girl 'no,'" Amona said. Hope crawled onto my nap and rested her head on my shoulders and I hugged her.

"She's very affectionate," Amona said and sat on the couch.

My stomach growled because I didn't eat anything when I woke up. I had to go out to get breakfast since Mara moved out.

SOUL Publications

"Did you eat breakfast? I can hook you something up really quick," Amona said.

"Appreciate it," I replied.

I kept telling myself that Amona being in my crib was innocent but I knew she was feeling me. The reason I brushed it off was because I was focused on Hope. We went into the kitchen and sat at the table with Hope on my lap. Amona was moving around my kitchen like she was familiar with my crib.

"Shorty, how old are you?" I asked.

"Twenty-eight. The same age as Lezzi," she said. I figured she was older by the way she carried herself.

"Oh, so y'all cougars then," I replied.

"How old is Pistol?" she asked.

"A year younger than me. The nigga only twenty-two," I chuckled.

"What makes you think I'm a cougar?" she asked.

"I'on know for sure but sumthin tells me you like younger niggas. Ain't shit wrong wit' it, though," I said and she blushed.

"Have you ever been with an older woman before?" she asked while cracking eggs into a skillet.

"Yeah, plenty of times," I said.

"Were they able to teach you anything?" she asked.

"Yeah. They taught me all bitches are the same," I replied.

"You gotta watch what you say around Hope," she said.

"Hope is asleep. How long you gonna be? I'm starvin," I replied.

"Twenty more minutes," she said.

Amona made me pancakes with sausages and eggs. She put fresh strawberries and blueberries on top of my pancakes with whip cream and syrup. A little whip cream splatted on her breast and she swiped it off with her finger. She placed her finger inside of her mouth and seductively licked it off.

Damn, I thought.

She sat the plate in front of me then took Hope out of my arms. The food was good but it didn't have shit on Mara's breakfast. Mara made my breakfast buffet-style.

"I have to go now. I'm taking Hope to her doctor's appointment unless you want to go, too," Amona said.

"Aight, I'll come," I replied.

SOUL Publications

I spent a few hours with Hope after her doctor's appointment. I bought a lot of toys for her and we went to a park so she could run around. Nika called Amona's phone and asked her where she was at so Amona took me back to my crib. I kissed Hope's forehead goodbye and she smiled at me. She gave me her Barbie doll and Amona laughed.

"She wants you to keep it. Just leave it here for next time," Amona said. I closed the door to the back seat of her car and watched her pull off. Spending time with Hope made me anxious about my daughter. I couldn't wait until Mara gave birth but I wasn't out the dog house yet. I had to find Mara so I could be in my daughter's life.

Piper

Three days later...

"Stop, that tickles!" I said to Delonte as he licked my neck. We were sitting on the couch in my living room watching TV—well, I was because he couldn't keep his hands off me.

"You seen this movie already. Come on, baby. I missed you," he said. Delonte had just gotten back from a family reunion in Arizona. He didn't tell me why he went until after he came back and I felt some type of way about that. It had been almost five months since I started messing around with him and not once had we talked about furthering our relationship or meeting his family.

"I need some," he said and I pulled away from him.

"I said I want to watch da fuckin' movie," I spat and he looked at me like I was crazy. He picked up the remote and turned the TV off.

"I'm not feelin' this type of behavior from you," he said.

Welcome to the Low Life 2

"Why didn't you ask me to go to Arizona wit' you?" I replied.

"It was last-minute. Besides, we had that big event at the club. I thought you wanted to be there considering a lot of heavy hittas were attending," he said.

"We have been datin' for months now. Don't you think there's more to us at this point? We're always together and I practically live at your loft," I replied.

"But everything is perfect the way it is, so why fuck it up? You're still young and I don't want to stop you from enjoying it. I'll be forty in a few years and the shit you wanna do I have no interest in," he said. I was ready to respond until Pistol used the house key to unlock the door. Delonte tensed up because he wasn't too fond of Pistol. Matter of fact, they didn't talk to each other.

"Can I talk to you in da kitchen?" Pistol asked me.

"Ummm, I'm in the middle of sumthin," I replied to ease the tension.

"Da fuck is dat supposed to mean? Dat nigga can wait," Pistol said and walked into the kitchen. Delonte snatched his car keys off the coffee table.

"Wait a minute! Don't go," I said.

"Go on ahead and tend to dat lil' nigga," Delonte said. He slammed the door when he left the house. I rushed into the kitchen and Pistol was looking in my fridge.

"I know damn well you didn't just use your key after seeing Delonte's car in the driveway," I said and he chuckled.

"Shorty, y'all's relationship is faker than Mara and Beretta's break-up," he said.

"What do you want before I get really angry and lay hands on you," I replied.

"Where is Mara at?" he asked.

"I don't know," I said.

"This ain't right. She stole his money then moved out. Beretta wasn't fuckin' another broad so why shorty trippin'?" he asked.

"Why does it matter? He's a cheater because he fucked Moesha a few days before Ammo's funeral," I said.

"I already told you she set him up. You would've told Mara if you believed it yourself. We both know how Beretta was feelin' after Ammo was killed. The last thing on dat nigga's mind was cheatin," he said. Pistol was telling the truth. I didn't tell Mara because I believed Beretta was asleep in the pictures Thickems said she saw.

"Mara just wants to be left alone," I replied.

"He bought shorty a ring," Pistol said.

"Beretta is always buying Mara jewelry. She's not impressed," I replied.

"He bought her a ring, shorty. Da nigga wants to marry her and the only reason I'm tellin' your big mouth ass is so you can get her to come back home. Everything is peaceful in the streets now, but we know how dat nigga gets when he gets on dat tip. He thinkin' Mara left him 'cause dat's not his baby. Give bruh some type of closure or sumthin," Pistol said.

"You're tellin' me Beretta wants to marry Mara?" I asked in disbelief.

"Yeah, but the way shit is goin' he might start hatin' her," he said.

"He can wait another week. I'll help afterwards and that's all I'm offerin'," I replied.

"Okay, cool. Can you go upstairs and grab a few stacks out the safe for me while I fix a sandwich?" he asked.

"Fine!" I spat then headed upstairs.

Ugh, he gets me aroused every time he comes over! Damn it. I bet his ass a freak, too. I can tell by the way he licks his lips, I thought.

Pistol had a safe at my house. For some reason, he didn't trust Lezzi around all of his money. I couldn't understand for the life of me why he was with her when they didn't have shit in common.

"Here you go," I said when I came back into the kitchen. Pistol took the money from me and his fingers brushed over mine. My butterflies were acting up, so I pulled away from him.

"I'm feelin' dat color," he said, talking about my hair.

I cut my hair really short and dyed it midnight blue. The soft curls framed my forehead and it was an easy style to maintain. I was glad he noticed my hair because I styled it like that for Delonte who said he loved when women rocked short haircuts.

"Thanks," I replied.

"Aight, I'll get up with you lata," he said. He went in to kiss my cheek but his lips landed on the corner of my lips. Caught off guard by his own actions, he pulled away from me.

"I didn't mean to do that," he explained.

Tired of the all the tension between us, I kissed his lips. For a few seconds, he stood still not knowing what to do. Suddenly, he wrapped his arms around me and slipped his tongue into my mouth. I thought Delonte was a good kisser but Pistol was better. He grabbed the back of my head and sucked my lips while his tongue explored my mouth. My pussy burst like a bubble. He picked me up then sat me down on the counter. His hands caressed my breasts; I was practically begging for him to put me out of my misery.

"This ain't right," Pistol said and pulled away from me. I fixed my clothes and wiped my lips because he was right, but it felt damn good.

"Go home," I said.

"I don't want to," he admitted.

"But?" I asked.

"Glock ain't gonna be happy about this," he replied.

"Glock isn't here. Besides, this is bigger than Glock. You want me to pretend like we're not attracted to each other?" I asked.

"Who said I was attracted to you?" he replied.

"Oh, you wanna play those type of games?" I asked.

"Yo, I gotta go. You trippin' over bullshit," he said.

He walked out of the kitchen and I followed him to the door. I was pissed off! For months, we'd been around each other so our attraction deepened. He tried to open the door but I stood in front of it. All I needed was one night, a few hours of his time. I wanted Pistol more than I wanted anybody at that point.

"Move, girl," Pistol smirked.

"Move me because you aren't leavin' outta here. Why are you playin' games wit' me?" I asked.

"What games? This can't go any further and we know dat," he said.

"But you know Glock doesn't give a fuck about me like dat. If he did, you wouldn't be here and we wouldn't be standing here talkin' about this," I replied. Pistol pushed me out of the way but I blocked the door again. He picked me up then tossed me on the couch.

"Yah ass crazy," he chuckled then left out of the door.

"Ugh!" I yelled out in frustration. Pistol had me so aroused, even the smell of his cologne drove me insane. I headed upstairs to my bathroom and took off my clothes so I could take a shower. The showerhead was just going to have to do. Delonte had great sex but it was no longer appeasing my appetite. I needed more than physical attraction. I thought Delonte would be able to give it to me but it was obvious I was just an easy lay for him. We'd been seeing each other for months and he knew more about me than I knew about him.

Why does the person I want have to be connected to someone I used to lay with? I thought as I showered.

I closed my eyes and placed the showerhead between my legs. My pussy throbbed as I thought about Pistol's aggressive kiss and the way he touched my breasts. He was just as hungry for me as I was for him. My nipples were hard like pebbles, in need of being sucked and licked. A moan escaped my lips while I was ready to reach my peek. The shower door opened and I jumped. I was scared

SOUL Publications

shitless, but it was Pistol standing in front of me in all his naked glory. My eyes traveled down his tatted chocolate chest to that sexy V-shape, which led to the prettiest chocolate dick I'd ever seen in my life and I had seen a lot of them. He stepped in and closed the shower door.

"What you scared for?" he asked and I rolled my eyes.

"Shut up and do what you came to do," I fired back.

Pistol picked me up and pinned me against the shower's wall. He popped my nipple into his mouth and I wrapped my arms around his neck to pull him closer to me. His tongue touching my skin almost made me have an orgasm. I moaned his name when he licked the side of my neck. Fuck the foreplay, I wanted to feel him.

"We need a condom," he said.

"I'm on birth control," I replied.

I'd been on birth control since I had an abortion over a year ago. I damn sure wasn't ready for any babies until I figured my life out.

"OOOHHHHHHH," I moaned when Pistol's big dick pierced through my slit. His entrance made me explode.

"Damn, shorty. I'm not even all the way in yet," he groaned.

"Shut up, damn," I said, feeling embarrassed.

I must have been talking too much shit because he slid further into me and I almost came again. It wasn't about the size of him or the fact that he made my body feel like it was floating. Our chemistry alone was enough to make me come without penetration, but his stamina was a plus. I tightly wrapped my legs around him as he slowly moved in and out of me. He pulled my lips into his mouth and tongue kissed me.

"Damn, Piper. This shit here, baby girl," Pistol groaned while deep stroking me. He thumbed at my clit and I released again. The dick was so good, I didn't want to move. I just wanted him to do whatever he wanted to do to me. My nails scratched at his shoulders when he sped up. My pussy squeezed him and his body shuttered. He squeezed my ass then roughly slammed into me. That's what I was waiting on—straight pounding with no remorse. Pistol wrapped his hand around my neck and shoved his tongue down my throat as I came for the third time. He carried me out of the shower with his dick still inside me. We were soaking wet, leaving a wet trail on the floor behind us. He dropped me on the bed and turned me over.

"UMMMMMM!" I moaned when he spread my ass cheeks and stuck his finger in my anus. While stroking my ass with his finger, his tongue pulled at my clit. I clutched the sheets on the bed because the sensation was too much. My legs trembled and my pussy gushed as juices ran down my inner thigh. Pistol moaned and groaned while eating me out.

I knew your ass was nasty! I thought.

SOUL Publications

He stood up and gripped my ass cheeks. I buried my face into the bed when he rammed his dick into me and began beating it out the frame. My pussy was so wet, farting noises slipped out which had never happened to me before. Feeling embarrassed, I tried to get away.

"Naw, don't run! That just means I got that thing drippin'," he groaned and palmed my ass tighter.

"JESUS!" I screamed out when he repeatedly hit my spot. He curved his thumb and slid it back in my ass as he pounded my walls. Tears welled up in my eyes and I knew at that moment what Mara was talking about. It wasn't tears of pain, the shit felt too good and my body couldn't take it. I was crying like a baby as he showed no mercy on my pussy.

"I'm about to nut!" Pistol yelled out and I could feel him throbbing inside of me. I gripped the sheets and slammed my ass back on him. My ass cheeks clapped as if I was dancing on stage. I had to show him I wasn't a boring type of chick. He slapped my ass cheeks and I went harder.

"Get dat nut, Pipe. SHIITTTTTTTT!" he groaned.

Pistol moaned as he exploded inside of me and I screamed his name as I exploded on his dick. Seconds later, he fell on top of me and I laid still. I couldn't believe we fucked, but did I feel guilty? Hell no! Folks called it being a hoe and quite frankly I didn't give a fuck. It wasn't my fault I fell for him. Pistol pulled out of me and sat on the edge of the bed.

"I gotta tell Glock about this," he said.

"Why?" I asked.

"Shit doesn't feel right. I'm feelin' you, too, and I tried to curve the feelin' but I couldn't," he said. I sat up and rested my head on his shoulder.

"Glock is comin' home in a few years, but when he does, he's going to be wit' his family. Let's just face facts. He put you in a position to fall for me and wanted you to do things that he neva did for me. He hooked us up and he gotta deal wit' it," I said. Pistol got up and headed to the bathroom to take a shower. We were definitely caught up in a fucked-up place.

****

Pistol stayed in the house with me for two days. I didn't go to the strip club and Delonte was blowing up my phone. Pistol was in the kitchen cooking dinner while I sat at the kitchen table on the phone.

"You need to call Beretta," I told Mara and she sucked her teeth.

"I'm not callin' him until I'm ready. I have been sleepin' good since I moved out. You just don't know how frustrated I was waitin' for him to come home. Now he's lookin' for me? He'll be aight," she said.

"But you know damn well you miss him," I replied.

"I was missin' the nigga when we were livin' together so what's the difference now? Beretta always wants shit to go his way but I can't let it ride. He needs to learn his damn lesson. I'm not a welcome mat. We're not broken up, I just want him to see how it feels to be ignored," she said.

"You want some wine?" Pistol called out.

"Yes. Thanks, baby," I replied.

"Wait a minute, hoe. Pistol cookin' dinner and pourin' you a glass of wine? Did you fuck him?" Mara whispered.

"I meannnnn. You know," I said.

"Was it good?" she laughed.

"Chillleeeeeeee, let's just say I will no longer tease you about cryin'," I whispered back.

"Go ahead and enjoy your dinner. I'm ready to fix myself sumthin to eat," she said then we hung up. Pistol brought me a glass of wine and sat my food in front of me. He made salmon, rice pilaf, and string beans.

"I gotta bounce," he said.

"Wait, you're not stayin' for dinner?" I asked.

"Lezzi keep blowin' my phone up, talkin' about she's ready to throw my shit outside," he said and I rolled my eyes. Pistol had a girlfriend and there was nothing I could do about it.

"Okay," I said.

He kissed my forehead then went upstairs to get dressed. Five minutes later, he was walking out of the door.

Great! I thought.

I wasn't sure how our situation was going to play out, but I hoped it didn't change the friendship we had. I fell in love with him. I'd officially fallen in love.

SOUL Publications

Kemara

I should've stayed my ass home because not being in our house was driving me insane. I pretended like I was okay around my friends but I missed Beretta so much I dreamed about him every night. I crawled out of bed to get some ice cream. I was having problems sleeping. It was five o'clock in the morning when I looked at the time on the microwave. Three weeks had passed since I left home. I was a month away from my due date and could barely walk. My ankles were swollen and I was always exhausted. While I sat at the kitchen island, I stared at my cell phone on the counter. I wanted to call Beretta to tell him I was okay. Tired of being lonely, I picked up the phone. As soon as I picked it up, the doorbell rang. I dropped my phone on the floor because the doorbell scared me. Only Piper knew where I lived so I rushed to the door thinking something happened. When I opened it, butterflies traveled through my body but I kept my game face on. Zyira must've sensed his presence because she started kicking the hell out of me.

"Can I come in?" he asked.

"No, we can talk here," I said.

Welcome to the Low Life 2

"Shorty, I drove for an hour to get here. It's five o'clock in the morning and I'm tired. Matter of fact, fuck all dat," he said and pushed past me. He stepped into my home and looked around.

"How much it cost to decorate this muthafucka?" he asked as I closed the door.

"How did you find me?" I asked.

"Piper told me where you lived. She texted me three sumthin this mornin' wit' yah address. That broad purposely made me wait for it," he said. He looked at the ice cream on the counter and frowned his face up.

"I see you really on some bullshit. I thought the doctor told you to lay off all dat sugar," he said.

"It's sugar-free. You still haven't told me why you're here," I replied.

"I need my family, Mara. I got sick when you left and you know dat shit, too. Three fuckin' weeks. No phone call or text, nothing! Your dirty ass friends ain't make it any betta, neither. So, what's up? You ready to address this shit?" he asked.

"There is nothing to talk about because you know why I left," I replied and headed back to the kitchen. Beretta followed me and wrapped his arms around me. It had been a minute since he touched me. He buried his face in the crook of my neck and kissed me. I closed my eyes savoring his soft lips and the way he caressed my stomach.

SOUL Publications

"You want me to come back home so you can continue to treat me like I don't exist?" I asked and he pulled away from me.

"Mannn, here we go with dat bullshit. Aight, shorty, go ahead and get it off your chest. Hit me, curse me out, do whatever it is you wanna do because I'm done talkin' about the bullshit. You know I wasn't out here stickin' my dick in other bitches so I don't get your attitude. You want me to eat your pussy or sumthin? Fuck you on the counter? What is it? I'm not gonna keep goin' through this shit wit' you. You threw money away by movin', knowin' damn well you can't get rid of me. We are in this for life," he said.

I turned around to face him and he was leaning against the counter, grilling me. He was making me out to be the victim.

"It's not about sex. It's because of how you have been treatin' me. Look at me, I'm swollen and pregnant. You were leavin' me in da house for days and you know how emotional I am right now. It feels good to be held and shit like that at night. You won't get it and it's cool. Just go back home so I can go to sleep," I replied. Beretta took off his shirt and tossed it out of the kitchen and into the hallway. He stepped out of his Air Max's and kicked them across the floor.

"I am home, Pretty Girl. I hope you got some closet space for a nigga. I'm diggin' this crib and the area it's in. I was thinkin' about movin' us further out anyway," he said.

Welcome to the Low Life 2

"Wait a minute. How can you just come in my home and move in?" I asked, trying to hide my excitement.

"Yo, Mara, lose dat fake ass attitude. You missed me, too. But on some real shit, I'm sorry from da bottom of my heart. You won, aight? Now, can you give your man some lovin'? I've been beatin' my dick in the shower for a few weeks now. I was ready to fuck a crackhead dat look like your mama," he said and I mushed him.

"Don't get fucked up in here," I replied.

He pulled me towards him by the bottom of my huge shirt. I was looking a little rough. I had on my favorite Winnie The Pooh pajama shirt with a bonnet on my head. Beretta kissed my lips as he palmed my ass. A moan slipped from between his lips as he stuck his tongue into my mouth. He hadn't kissed me that way since our trip to Hawaii. His dick was poking me in the stomach.

Ten minutes later, we were on the kitchen floor, fucking like wild animals. Beretta stopped a few times because he kept hollering about my water breaking. My water didn't break. He was giving me orgasms back to back which was causing me to continuously squirt. The kitchen floor was slippery from our essence. I laid on my side while he rammed his dick into me in a spooning position. Although he was going fast, he took his time and made sure he reached my spot. He snatched the bonnet off my head and gripped my weave. He bit the back of my neck and moaned from exploding inside of me.

Welcome to the Low Life 2

"I'm tired," I complained. I had got mine off a few times and wanted him to hurry up. He was fucking me like I was a sex toy doll.

Beretta came three times within those ten minutes and I came four. My back was aching and my legs went to sleep. I was a huge lazy mess. He picked the wrong time for make-up sex. Beretta pulled out of me and helped me off the kitchen floor. I felt slight cramping in my lower abdomen.

"I need to sit in the tub," I said.

"The doctor said you can't take baths," Beretta replied.

"Will you shut da hell up about some damn doctor? Maybe I should be a fuckin' doctor so you can listen to everything I say," I snapped.

"Aight, don't come cryin' to me 'bout shit," he replied.

I wobbled up the spiral staircase and down the hall to my bedroom. The spacious tub in my bathroom was sorta like a Jacuzzi. Beretta ran the bath water for me. The cramping was going away which was a good sign because I was getting worried. For the past week, I was getting contractions but the doctor said it was normal. I didn't want Beretta to worry so I didn't tell him about it. He turned the water off after the tub was filled then held my hand so I could step in. He got in and sat behind me.

"Niggas sit in da tub? I feel some type of way about bubbles goin' up my ass. I'on know about this," Beretta complained and I burst out laughing.

"It's relaxin," I said.

"This is some Silk kinda shit," he replied. I handed him the hair band I had on my wrist so he could put my hair up. He usually fussed about it but that time he didn't. He pulled my hair up and wrapped it up in a bun so my weave wouldn't get wet. That's why I fell in love with him. Beretta was really a sweetheart when he wanted to be. It was a long process getting him there but it worked out. Being with him also made me do things I thought I wasn't capable of and giving him a baby was one of them.

"How do you see us in a few years?" Beretta asked.

"You'll freak out if I told you," I replied.

"Come on wit' it. I need to know this," he said.

"I picture us married and livin' a normal life. Raising Zyira better than how me and you were raised. I see you bein' a family man and not runnin' da streets. By then, I'll have my Bachelor's Degree with a good job. It sounds nice but I know you can only offer me two things out of everything I just named. Nobody can ever have the whole package," I said.

"I'm not gonna be sellin' dope for the rest of my life, but I'm not sayin' I'm gonna be legit in a few years, neither," he replied. Beretta was telling me something I been knew. I couldn't change him and I wasn't trying to.

All I needed from him was to be a good man to me and a good father to Zyira. An hour passed and we were still in the tub talking. I caught an attitude when he mentioned Amona bringing Hope to see him. Amona was an extra friendly bitch and that didn't sit well with me. Beretta said Amona brought Hope to see him about six times since I left home. I wanted to slap the shit out of him but I had to control my anger.

"So, that bitch was in my house?" I asked.

"She dropped her off to me for a few hours and that was it. She only stayed the whole time twice but it wasn't dat deep. Do you think I would've told you if it was sumthin? I'm tryna keep shit funky witchu," he said.

"I don't trust dat silly bitch and Nika better not be playing advocate for that hoe, neither. What was Amona's hoe ass wearin' while she was prancin' around in my home?" I asked.

"It's summer time," Beretta replied.

"So, she was wearing booty shorts and short dresses?" I asked.

"I'on know, Mara. I wasn't lookin' at dat girl like dat. Yah ass just crazy and always wanna fight. You got all da ass and titties I need," he said and I rolled my eyes. He helped me wash up before we got out of the tub. The sun was shining through my bedroom window when I walked out of the bathroom. Beretta came out behind me and got into bed. I dropped my towel and slid in with him.

"What time are you leaving?" I asked, disappointing myself.

"I'm stuck in here witchu for a bit. Pistol takin' care of shit for me right now," he replied.

"Humph," I playfully rolled my eyes with a smile on my face. Beretta slid underneath the covers. He spread my legs wide open and ate my pussy out until I begged for him to stop but he wouldn't let up. He gave me head for an hour and let's just say he had to change the sheets when he was finished. I slept like a baby after he put clean sheets on the bed, drooling and all.

****

The next day...

"Ugh, I didn't feel like goin' anywhere," I said when I stepped out of Beretta's BMW. We were in front of an Italian restaurant in Chevy Chase, Maryland. My stomach growled when I smelled the fresh herbs and garlic coming from the restaurant. All I could think about was dipping my breadsticks in seasoned olive oil with extra butter.

"What you thinkin' about?" he asked and grabbed my hand.

"Eatin' breadsticks with a big bowl of pasta Alfredo. This damn child turned me into Pac Man," I replied.

Welcome to the Low Life 2

We were greeted by the hostess when we walked inside the restaurant. Beretta made reservations so we were immediately escorted to the roof top. The setting was romantic. The rooftop only had five tables and a guy was playing a piano. I wore my hair in a high ponytail and my make-up was on point. The summer dress I had on flowed nicely over my body and hid some of my pregnancy. I looked cute but I was so uncomfortable because my ankles were swollen and everything was heavy. The scenery reminded me of a garden room. The waitress set menus in front of us and I almost had a fit because the meals were high as hell and the sides weren't even included. I waited until the waitress left to get our drinks before I said something.

"Babe, I can make this stuff at home for thirty dollars. They want ninety dollars for lasagna?" I asked.

"I know you ain't talkin'. I saw the receipt from the store you ordered your furniture from. Thirty-five g's, shorty? You couldn't go to Value City Furniture?" he asked.

"The furniture is Victorian-style. I wanted my home to look like a place in Paris or sumthin. That's not the same as spending a lot of money on food I can make at home," I said.

"Hush up and enjoy ya self, damn," he said.

The waitress brought over a bottle of wine on ice along with our sodas. It was just me and Beretta sitting in the section. Something was happening but I couldn't put my finger on it. The restaurant wasn't our usual spot to eat. We usually ate at soul food spots or steakhouses. The guy who was playing the piano opened our bottle of wine and poured it into our wine glasses.

"What's goin' on, Beretta?" I asked and he smirked at me.

"I can't spend time wit' my shorty?" he replied.

"You're actin' different," I laughed.

"I'm actin' like a nigga who just finally got some pussy," he said as if it was my fault. I decided to change the subject. We ended up talking about getting rid of some of our old things from the townhouse and selling them online since they were still in good condition. After we ate stuffed mushrooms and calamari appetizers, our entrees came. Beretta had seafood alfredo and I had chicken piccata with garlic butter angel hair pasta. I ate so much I couldn't move.

"I want to go into labor now," I said, rubbing my stomach.

"You sayin' dat shit now but you're gonna be fallin' out everywhere when you do because you can't take pain. I don't want you to get an epidural, though. I heard it ain't natural. We can set it up to where you can give both at home," Beretta.

"Beretta, honey, please don't get on my bad side again. Natural birth at home with no meds? This is my first baby. I'm scared to do all of that. You have lost your damn mind," I said.

Welcome to the Low Life 2

The waitress came over to our table with a slice of lemon cake. The sight of more food made me sick.

"I don't want it. Can I have a box to-go? I'm so full," I said.

"No more to-go boxes, sorry," she said then scurried off.

My eyes zeroed in on the cake and I noticed something sitting in the middle of it. I covered my mouth as I stared at a ring with the biggest diamonds I'd ever seen.

"What's goin' on?" I panicked.

Tears fell from my eyes and Zyira was moving around like she was swimming. Suddenly, I began feeling hot so I used a napkin to fan myself. I was shaking and trembling. Maybe I was overreacting but the mere thought of him asking me to be his wife had me all over the place. Beretta stood up and kneeled in front of me. I closed my eyes and he pinched my leg.

"I have been in love witchu since I was a lil' nigga. Back then I knew I was gonna have you. I wanted you since I was fourteen years old but I fell in love witchu dat night I took you to the movies five years ago. When I came home and noticed you were gone, I lost it. I couldn't eat or sleep. You showed me dat I can't be without you and I think we should make it official. Can you marry a nigga?" Beretta said. He took the ring off the cake and wiped it off before he grabbed my hand.

"Say sumthin, shorty. My knees are hurtin'," he said.

"YES! Oh my gosh," I cried.

Beretta slid the ring on my finger and I jumped up to hug him. I grabbed his face and kissed his lips. He wiped the tears away from my eyes before he kissed my forehead. I held my hand out to admire my ring and it was PHAT!

"I'm posting this on Facebook," I said.

"Da fuck is dat?" he asked.

"It's the new Myspace," I replied.

I usually posted pics of me and my friends but I had to let the world know that I was getting married. I knew there was going to be a lot of talk around our city because we were young but I didn't give a shit. Beretta was my life, he was all mine. You'd think my happy ending would end there, but it didn't. The saying, "when one door closes, another door will open" is true. I had to figure it out the hard way...

Kemara

Three weeks later...

Beretta kept his word and had been coming home every night. He complained about D.C. being too far from Annapolis the first week but he eventually got used to it. Beretta was standing in the mirror in the bathroom combing his beard. He grew out his facial hair and looked older than twenty-three. He could possibly pass for twenty-eight, plus he was weight training. My man had a six-pack and a nice chest to go along with it. The nigga was just beautiful all around.

"Who are you lookin' good for?" I teased as I made up the bed.

"Here we go wit' dat bullshit," he smirked.

He popped his diamond fronts in his mouth after he finished brushing his teeth. I wanted him to stay in the house. I was too needy but I couldn't help it.

"I'll be back in a few hours," he said and grabbed his keys off the dresser. He kissed my lips before heading out the door. Emma called me and I answered on the second ring.

"Heyyyy, pregnant girl. Are you ready for your baby shower?" she asked. My baby shower was in three days and I so wasn't ready for it. I developed a complex with myself because I couldn't dress the way I used to. The only thing I could manage was keeping my hair and nails done.

"I don't know what to wear," I said.

"How about we go shopping. I'm in Annapolis visiting my aunt. Come on out for a few hours. I haven't seen you in forever," she said.

"Okay, but I can't be out too long. Zyira drains me by five o'clock in the evening for some reason," I replied.

"Okay, cool. Call me when you're on your way," she said, then hung up.

I showered and got dressed in a jean boyfriend shirt, a pair of white leggings and silver slide sandals. Instead of make-up, I only opted for eyeliner and lip gloss. It was eleven o'clock in the morning and the traffic in D.C. wasn't bad. I was able to make it to Annapolis in forty-five minutes. It was coming close to the end of summer and fall was approaching. I had the sunroof open and all the windows down, feeling the fresh air. I'd been on cloud nine since Beretta proposed to me. I was at a traffic stop light when I looked over at a bus stop. The lady sitting on the bench nodding off looked familiar. Once she picked up her head, I realized it was my mother, Darcel. It had been months since I'd last seen her. Silk told me she stopped coming to the hood after she lost her apartment. I instantly thought about the baby she was pregnant with and wondered what happened to it. I thought about pulling off but something tugged at my heart. I couldn't help her but I wanted to know about my little sister or brother or even if he or she was alive. I pulled up into the CVS Pharmacy parking lot then got out of my truck. The area was infested with crackheads.

"Ma," I called out to her.

She looked up at me and smiled. She only had five teeth in her mouth and they were rotten. Darcel got down to ninety pounds but her hands were swollen and full of scabs.

"Annapolis finest, Pretty Girl, Mara. It's nice to see you walkin' our streets again. You got wit' dat boy and forgot all about where you came from," she said.

"Where is the baby?" I asked.

"What baby?" she replied.

"The baby you were pregnant with! What happened?" I asked.

"She's at my friend's house," she said, scratching her arm.

"You left your baby with a fuckin' crackhead? You really don't give a shit, do you? When will enough be enough?" I asked.

"I'm sick, Mara," she said and I felt sorry for her. Usually Darcel was a firecracker and always popping slick at the mouth. The woman that sat in front of me didn't have an ounce of life in her body. She was like a zombie— alive but dead.

"What's your daughter's name?" I asked.

"She doesn't have one yet, but she looks exactly like you. Too bad her innocence will be gone once she gets older. You let me down, Mara. You stopped believin' in me. When you were five years old, you were so sweet to me. Poppa turned you sour, angry and bitter," she said.

"I was a child, Ma. I got older and realized how bad of a mother you were to me and still are. You don't love anybody, not even yourself. Just take me to my sister. I have an extra bedroom in my loft. I'll make a room for her and raise her and Zyira like sisters," I replied. It was a big responsibility but there was no way in hell I was going to let my sister turn out like Darcel.

"Your loft, huh? So, you and dat thug livin' like the Jeffersons now?" she asked.

"Get up so we can go get your daughter," I said.

"You're going to pay me for her. You think I'm gonna give her to you for free?" she asked.

"Okay, now get your ass up and let's go," I said.

"There goes the old Mara," she laughed and stood up.

Welcome to the Low Life 2

Darcel got in my truck and she smelled horribly but I was on a mission. I fought the urge to puke as I took an exit to head down Edgewater, Maryland. Edgewater was like another place on its own. It was only ten minutes away from Annapolis but had a southern vibe to it. No real stores, just small, old country markets.

"What are you doin' down here?" I asked, driving down a small dirt road.

"My friend lives back here," she said.

"Why were you at the bus stop in the city?" I asked.

"Counseling," she said.

"But you were noddin' off," I replied.

"I'm fuckin' tired, Mara! I'm tired of everything! I haven't had a hit in a month," she said.

"Good, you don't need it," I said. My cell phone rang and it was Emma calling. I reached into my cup holder to answer the phone.

"Hey, Emma. I'm sorry but we might have to catch the mall another time. I'm takin' care of family issues," I said.

"Okay, cool. I understand. Call me whenever you get free. I wanted to talk to you about something," she said.

"Okay," I replied and hung up.

Welcome to the Low Life 2

Darcel was going through my purse when I hung up the phone.

"Ma, what are you doin? Get your dirty ass hands outta my purse!" I yelled and snatched it from her.

"Just give me the money now!" she screamed.

"Not until I see her! I don't trust you!" I screamed back.

Darcel attacked me and pulled at my weave. I was trying to feel for the gear to put the truck in park but she was blocking it. I yelled for her to stop because she was causing me to cramp.

"My baby! Get the fuck off me!" I yelled and backhanded her. She flew into the passenger's door and hit her head on the window. An eighteen-wheeler was coming towards us, but I swerved off the road. My truck slammed into a tree and the impact caused the steering wheel to smash into my stomach. Darcel wasn't injured because I hit the tree more so on my side. She took my purse, snatched the jewelry around my neck and stole my Rolex. She would've stolen my ring, too, but my arm was stuck between the seat and the door. The pain was unbearable, and when I looked between my legs, I saw blood. I began panicking and told Darcel to get me some help because she had my cell phone.

"Now you need me?" she asked and got out of the truck. I screamed for her to come back because I couldn't move. The contractions were getting worse. I prayed to God, hoping he took me, too, if my daughter died. The guilt was going to haunt me for the rest of my life. I had good intentions with Darcel but ended up getting fucked over in the end. The hood of the truck caught on fire and I tried to break free but I couldn't. I was stuck between the steering wheel and the seat. The smoke was suffocating me and the pain in my stomach caused me to faint...

Beretta

"**W**here is Mara?" Piper asked me when I approached the emergency room. Thickems went into labor and called Piper. Piper called Pistol while me and him were handling business. I tried calling Mara and she wasn't answering the phone which wasn't like her.

"Everything good wit' Thickems?" Pistol asked Piper.

"She's getting an emergency C-section. We can't go back there right now. Where is Mara? She's not answerin' the phone. I've been callin' her for thirty minutes," Piper said.

"Mara gonna make me choke her lil' ass. I hope she didn't leave the house. She hardheaded like a muthafucka. Dat's prolly why her simple-ass ain't answerin' da phone," I said. I called her again but that time her phone was turned off.

Some of Thickems's family members was inside the waiting room along with a few of Ammo's family members. There was tension between the two families. I guess because of how Ammo's family was doing Thickems.

SOUL Publications

The emergency doors in the hospital opened as soon as I sat down in a chair. The nurses were rushing a pregnant woman to the back and blood was everywhere. For some reason, I couldn't take my eyes off the woman lying on the stretcher. My heart was beating faster as I stood up. I recognized the shoes. They were the same shoes Mara bought when we were in Hawaii. I took off running down the hall chasing after the stretcher. They wouldn't let me in the room but I pushed past them.

"MARA!" I called out.

"Sir, you can't be in here! Get out before we call the police!" a nurse yelled at me. Pistol and Piper were arguing with the nurses outside the room. They must've followed me down the hall when I took off running.

"That's my fuckin' wife! Get the fuck off me!" I yelled out.

Mara was in and out of consciousness and I tried to get to her but security came into the room. Seven of them wrestled me out into the hallway. Piper was yelling and screaming and Pistol had to pick her up off the floor. Two police officers came down the hall because I resisted leaving the room.

"Sir, we don't want to lock you up but we will if you don't calm down!" a Hispanic cop told me. I couldn't risk getting locked up not knowing how Mara and the baby was doing. I tried to regain my composure but that shit was hard.

"Aight, I'm cool," I said and the security let me go.

"The victim was found in a ditch on the side of the road. A witness drove by and saw the smoking truck and he pulled her out. She was unresponsive when we got there but the paramedics were able to revive her. Can you give us some information on the victim?" the police officer said and pulled out a pad from his pocket.

"Kemara Lorette," Piper said, wiping her eyes.

"Age?" the officer asked.

"Twenty-one," I replied.

"Her relationship to you?" he asked.

"Fiancée," I said.

"Do you know who she was with before the accident?" he asked.

"No," I said.

"Does she have any family or friends down Edgewater?" he replied.

"Edgewater? Hell no, she doesn't," I said. I wondered what Kemara was doing on that racist side of town. Shorty was always being sneaky about something.

"Here is my card if you find out anything else," he said then walked off. I balled up the card and threw it against the wall.

SOUL Publications

"Who da fuck does Kemara know down there, Piper? I know you fuckin' know!" I yelled at her and she jumped.

"I don't know!" she cried.

"Bitch, stop lyin! You always know what she's up to. You betta get to talkin' before I snap your fuckin' neck," I gritted.

"I swear I don't know. She didn't call me today," Piper screamed.

I went into the bathroom and slammed my fist into the mirror above the sink. What could I do? I was helpless. My shorty and my daughter were possibly about to leave me. Pistol came into the bathroom.

"Chill out, bruh," he said.

"I can't deal wit' this. This too much, man. Mara, though? Yo, why da fuck she never listens to me? Every time I tell her to do sumthin, she does the opposite. Mara thinks I'm tryna control her but I love her too much. I'm tryna keep her safe, but why is it so hard?" I asked Pistol.

"She's gonna pull through," was all he could say. I was emotional and niggas wasn't used to that. I mourned Ammo's death in silence, didn't shed one tear around my niggas, only Mara. But I didn't give two fucks about pride at the moment. I was crying like a baby. A few minutes later, I fixed my clothes and wiped my eyes. Once I stepped out into the hallway, a doctor walked over to me.

He told me Mara was bleeding internally and needed a C-section. Pistol patted my shoulder after the doctor walked away.

"Pray, bruh," he said.

"Niggas like me prayers don't get heard, bruh," I replied.

****

Thickems had the baby and was allowed to have visitors, but everyone's concern was Mara and my daughter. My daughter and Ammo's son were born on the same day. I wondered how he would've felt if he was alive. I could hear his voice in my head joking around. Since his death, I knew shit would never be the same again. I didn't regret Mara coming into my life, but I couldn't ignore how easy my life was before her. The shit I was feeling I wasn't used to. Everything was hitting me back-to-back. Within five months, I had lost a brother, Mara left me, I proposed to her then she got into an accident that could possibly take her life. My mind couldn't wrap around everything and neither could my heart. I was angry, sad, hurt, and confused. Piper was sitting next to Pistol with tears still falling from her eyes. Silk came into the hospital and Piper ran into his arms and broke down crying. We still didn't know Mara's condition and an hour had passed.

"Who was Mara with?" Piper asked Silk.

"She said she was meetin' up with Emma when I texted her earlier. Hustle Man said he saw Mara pick up Darcel from the bus stop in front of CVS," Silk said. I bit the inside of my cheek. I told Mara months ago to stay the fuck away from her mother. I didn't trust her being around Darcel. Mara was walking around the city wearing expensive clothes and jewelry. Mara thought she was untouchable because she wasn't a scared type of female and was capable of merking a nigga, but that didn't mean shit where we lived. She lost all her street smarts but I couldn't blame her for that because I was somewhat responsible.

I stood up when the doctor came back out to the waiting area. The first thing I noticed was his eyes and the sympathy he had. Something bad happened. I could feel it.

"Kemara is stabilized but—um, I don't know how to tell you this," he said.

"My daughter?" I asked.

"We tried everything we could do. The impact to Kemara's stomach affected the baby and caused internal bleeding. The nurses cleaned her up so you can see her. I'm so sorry. I tried to do everything to save her but I couldn't," he said. He told me to follow him through the double doors at the end of the hall. Kemara was in bed with her eyes closed and she had a cast on her left arm.

"Her arm and hip are fractured. She's gonna need physical therapy," the doctor said.

SOUL Publications

Welcome to the Low Life 2

I didn't want to hear shit else that nigga had to say. I was focused on the nurse wrapping my daughter up in a blanket. I saw the top of her head and she had big curls. I sat next to Kemara's hospital bed and the nurse handed my daughter to me. Her eyes were closed and she had dried up blood in her nose. The doctor and the nurse left out of the room so I could spend time with her. Tears fell on her forehead from my eyes and I felt lower than low. I peeled the blanket back off her body so I could remember her small hands and feet. Zyira's skin was almost blue and her mouth was slightly open. I was proud to say I helped Mara create something so beautiful even though she was dead. I kissed her head and held her close to me. I cleaned her nose with the blanket and took a picture of her for Mara. Ten minutes had passed and I was whispering to Zyira, telling her to wake up because I couldn't get over it—I just couldn't. Piper, Silk, and Pistol came into the room minutes later. They took turns holding my daughter.

"She has a lot of hair," Piper said, but I said nothing. Matter of fact, I didn't say shit to anybody until the nurse came back to get Zyira's body. They placed her inside an incubator and took her out of the room. I decided to have her buried with a tombstone.

Piper

Mara woke up hours later but she was still groggy. They gave her a lot of pain medication and she was talking out of her head. We sat with her for hours but Beretta said nothing. His eyes were red and puffy but he still had an emotionless expression plastered on his face—almost as if nothing fazed him, but I knew he was going through it, we all were. Zyira was a beautiful baby and I balled my eyes out because Mara never got a chance to hold her. I was nervous about her finding out her baby was gone and I could only imagine the pain that was going to come along with it. It took her almost twenty minutes to fully open her eyes. She tried to sit up but couldn't. Beretta got up and walked over to her bed. Mara asked him where her baby was and he told her she was gone. She screamed and I winced because it sounded so painful. Two nurses ran into the room and told us to step out in case Mara went into shock. I wanted to do something—anything! But I didn't know what to do or where to start.

"I need to do sumthin!" I said to Pistol as we stood in the hallway.

Beretta came out of the room and told us to go home because Mara was refusing visitors. She didn't want us in her room but I wasn't in my feelings. It was one of those tragedies where you wanted to be alone. Silk went upstairs to see Thickems and her baby. I didn't have the energy to be around Thickems and Ammo's family. I just needed to be home.

****

Me and Pistol went back to my house when we left the hospital. I got into bed and he laid next to me so I could lay on his chest.

"Mara needs a break," I said.

"Yeah, so does Beretta. I'm gonna tell him I'll handle his business for a few months because the nigga hasn't been right since Ammo got killed. I mean, he seems the same but I've known the nigga for years. Beretta ain't the same, period," Pistol said. I was ready to respond but was interrupted by the banging on my front door. I was ready to get out of bed but Pistol told me to lay back down. I ran to the window and saw Lezzi's car in my driveway. Suddenly, I heard yelling and fussing coming from downstairs.

"Bring yo' ass home! You have been layin' up wit' dat hoe ass bitch and I'm tired of your shit!" Lezzi screamed. I hauled ass down the stairs.

"Get the fuck outta my house!" I yelled at her.

Welcome to the Low Life 2

"You think you can just fuck my nigga wheneva you feel like it? Bitch, bring yah triflin' ass outside so I can knock you da fuck out! I'm tired of this shit!" Lezzi said.

"Yo, Lezzi. I swear right now is not the time. My family is goin' through sumthin and Piper needs me over here," Pistol said.

Lezzi slapped Pistol in his face and started fighting him. I lost my patience when my lamp fell on the floor and broke. I reached over Pistol and punched Lezzi in the eye. Pistol tried to break us up but we were fighting each other and him. Lezzi was bigger than me so she used some of her weight. She slammed me into the wall while punching me. I snatched a picture off the wall and cracked it over her head. She screamed for Pistol to help her but I was on her ass. Pistol pulled me off and Lezzi got even madder.

"Is this why you want me to get an abortion? So, you can be with that bitch? FUCK YOU!" Lezzi screamed. Hearing Lezzi talk about being pregnant made me want to fight Pistol myself, but then again, he belonged to her not me.

"Get your sloppy ass bitch and get the fuck outta my house!" I yelled at Pistol.

"Sloppy? Coming from the bitch that's smashing the homies! Did you fuck Beretta, too? All y'all stripper hoes ain't shit but dumb bitches wit' weak ass pussy! Fuck you with your pill poppin' ass. You think I haven't heard shit about you?" Lezzi asked.

Welcome to the Low Life 2

"But yah nigga ate my ass, bitch! How about dat! I exploded on his tongue, too. Let's not forget he got a key to my fuckin' house so you already know what it is. He's here cookin' for me while yah nasty, dry scalp ass is lookin' fuckin' stupid, bitch! You fuckin' MY nigga as far as I'm concerned. I can tell you how many times your calls go unanswered but he neva misses a beat when I call his ass. He picks up, even when he's witchu! So, how 'bout dat whack pussy, bitch! You a side-bitch with a main's chick imagination, hoe!" I said.

I ran into the kitchen and grabbed a knife because I wanted to kill her. Lezzi was gone when I came back out to the living room. Pistol was sitting on the couch rubbing his forehead.

"Get out," I said.

"That bitch ain't pregnant. I use condoms with her. She told me that bullshit last night and I told her she lost her fuckin' mind. Lezzi see everybody else gettin' pregnant and wants us to follow the trend. She's been on my ass since Beretta proposed to Mara," he said.

"Take your black ass home," I replied.

"Man, I ain't leavin'. I already know she gonna fuck up my shit because you told her everything. Damn, Piper, you trippin'," he said.

"She came to my crib and fucked my house up. Her issue should be with you, not me. I'm not fuckin' her, you are," I replied.

"It still ain't none of her business what we do. Dat bitch stresses me out as it is," Pistol said.

"I'm ready to go into the club so you can see yourself out," I said.

"I thought you said you was done strippin' and was lookin' for a job," he said.

"Nobody has called me back yet and what do you care? Go be wit' your housewife type of bitch and let my hoe ass be," I replied.

I stormed past Pistol and headed upstairs to my bedroom. I wanted Lezzi to just disappear, her and Glock. He was still locked up but his existence was getting in the way of me and Pistol. The heart wants what the heart wants. I went into my closet and grabbed a few sets for the night. Me and Delonte weren't on speaking terms but he wouldn't stop me from stripping at his club. I honestly didn't have to strip for a while because I had a few bills saved up. The strip club environment was an escape from reality. Pistol came into my bedroom and grilled me when he realized how serious I was.

"So, you about to go down there and shake your ass because you mad?" he asked.

"Mind yo' business," I said.

"Aight, bet. I'll do that. Here goes your shit back," he said and threw my house key at the wall. Pistol called me all kinds of hoes and bitches as he went down the stairs.

He slammed my front door when he left out of the house. Everything was just falling apart.

****

The strip club was boring. It was crowded but everything just seemed off. I wanted to see how Mara was doing but she didn't want to be bothered. I sat at the bar and ordered a few shots of vodka after I popped an ecstasy pill.

"Can I talk to you for a minute?" Delonte asked when he approached me.

"How important is it?" I asked.

"Come to my office," he replied.

I ordered a third shot then followed him to the upper-level where he sat and watched over the club. He locked the door as soon as we walked in. I sat on his leather couch and crossed my legs. He sat across from me and I rolled my eyes at him.

"What is it?" I asked.

"You haven't been here in days and you damn sure haven't been answerin' my calls. You think you can just pop up without an explanation?" he asked.

"Of course, I can. Who else is bringin' the money in around this muthafucka?" I asked and he chuckled.

Welcome to the Low Life 2

"My club was good before you came here but we can talk about that another time. Why haven't you been answerin' my calls or texts?" he asked.

"I have been busy, and what do you care? You don't think I'm good enough to take around your friends and family. I don't know shit about you other than you being a club owner. I'm over it," I said and crossed my arms. Delonte got up and walked over to me. He sat next to me on the couch and pulled me closer to him.

"How about we work on buildin' a relationship. I have been missin' you and I apologize for not takin' your feelings into consideration. The reason I didn't ask you to go with me out of town is because that nigga Pistol is always around. You said he's your cousin but, come on, baby girl. That nigga ain't related to you," Delonte said.

"He's not related to me but we've known each other for years," I replied.

"Is there sumthin goin' on I should know about?" Delonte asked.

"No, he has a woman. I'm close to everyone from my old hood and nothing will change that," I said.

"Good, because I missed you," he replied.

I took my thong off and opened my legs for Delonte. He knew exactly what I wanted because he got down on the floor and stuck his tongue in my pussy. He was a good pussy eater but Pistol was a better one. I wanted someone I could call my own so I decided to give Delonte a chance. Pistol and Lezzi could go and fuck themselves as far as I was concerned.

****

I went to visit Mara two days later. She was sitting up in bed when I walked into her hospital room. I brought teddy bears and balloons with me. She cracked a smile when she saw me. I placed the things down in the corner of the room and rushed over to hug her.

"I don't want to ask how you're feelin' because I already know, but what's on your mind?" I asked when I sat next to her.

"I don't know, Piper. I still can't believe I'm alive. The impact was enough to kill me and I'm still here. All I keep thinkin' about is karma. I saw faces of everyone I robbed in the past. You know what's crazy?" she asked.

"What?" I asked.

"Beretta told me to stay away from Darcel but I thought I was helpin' the bitch out. She set me up and I didn't see it coming. Zyira would still be alive if I kept driving past the bus stop. Darcel attacked me while I was driving and I ran off the road. I was stuck in my seat, bleeding to death, and she robbed me. Took my necklace, bracelet, and watch. She also took my purse and cell phone. Not once did she feel sympathy for me or her grandchild. I'm gonna dissect that bitch. Don't tell Beretta Darcel was the cause of the accident. He doesn't know the full story and I want it to remain that way because he'll get to her before I can," Mara said.

"Your secret is safe wit' me. Where is Beretta?" I asked.

"He went home to shower. He'll be back later," she replied.

"Did you see a picture of Zyira?" I asked.

"No, I want to forget it happened. It's a distant memory," she said.

I wanted to tell Mara it was okay to grieve but I couldn't form the words. We had a normal conversation and she even laughed a few times. My heart was breaking down for her because Mara was in denial. She wanted to pretend like Zyira didn't exist so the pain could go away. I feared it would backfire.

Kemara

Nine weeks later...

was finally home from rehab. My doctor was surprised at how well I bounced back because of my fractured hip. My left arm was still sore but it was no longer in a cast. I worked hard in rehab because I didn't want to come home all banged up. Beretta placed my luggage by the door. We didn't bring up Zyira, not even once. Pistol offered to take care of business for Beretta, but Beretta declined. He was still in the streets but he made time to visit me. The visiting hours at the rehab worked out in his favor because the hours were from nine in the morning to eight at night. Beretta would stay out all night then come to see me before he went home.

"It's nice and clean in here," I said, looking around my loft.

"Piper is on her way up here to take care of you. I gotta go meet up wit' my connect. I'll be home in a few days. You need anything before I leave?" he asked.

"No, I'm fine. Call me when you get time," I said. I kissed his lips and he told me he loved me before he left back out of the door. I slowly walked upstairs towards our bedroom. Next to our bedroom was our daughter's room. The door was cracked, so I pushed it opened. Beretta's cologne permeated the air and I saw his shoes by the rocking chair. A week before the accident, we decorated her room. Everything was pink, white, and lavender. It didn't take a genius to figure out Beretta spent a lot of time in her room. He acted normal, and so did I, but we were dying on the inside. Zyira's sonogram pictures were lined up on her dresser. From the very first one to the last sonogram photo. Tears fell from my eyes then I went into full sobs. Who was I fooling? How could I forget about my baby? I carried her for eight and a half months. Beretta came into the room and sat on the floor with me. I don't remember falling on the floor. He wrapped his arms around me and caressed my back.

"I knew you was gonna come in here. It's hard goin' to our bedroom without walkin' in here," he said.

"I killed her!"

"Shhhhhh," he said, rocking me. He cupped my face and kissed my tears away. I only cried once over her and that was when I woke up to find out she was dead. One time wasn't enough because I had so much bottled inside of me.

"I'm fine," I said, finally pulling away from him. He helped me off the floor and into our bedroom. I heard Piper's heels coming up the stairs while Beretta helped me into bed. She came into our bedroom and kicked off her heels. She had a bag of food in her hand.

SOUL Publications

"I got us some Chipotle," she sang.

"Don't spill dat shit in my bed. I'm not used to roaches," Beretta said and Piper flicked him off.

"Aight, I'm ready to leave. I'll call you in a few and take care of my shorty. Take her to get her hair, nails, and toes done. Mara walking around here with feet like a goat," Beretta joked. He kissed me again before he left our home.

"At least your hair grew out," Piper said, playing with my ponytail. A bitch named Razor pulled my hair out almost three years ago over Beretta. I hadn't worn my real hair out ever since and it had grown a lot.

"Thickems and the baby will be over here later," Piper said.

"Why?" I asked.

"She wants to see you," Piper replied.

"I don't want to be around a baby right now. It's no hard feelings but I'm not ready," I said.

"I'm textin' her now," Piper said.

"I wonder where Beretta has been sleepin' at," I said.

"Not now, Mara," Piper replied.

"I know how Beretta makes up the bed. This bed hasn't been touched since I last made it up. That was the day I got into the car accident. I didn't want to say anything to him because we've been on good terms lately but that nigga hasn't been sleeping at home. I know he wasn't sleepin' in Zyira's room. He was definitely coming here, though," I said.

"You know your nigga too well," Piper said.

"Of course, I do," I replied.

Me and Piper kicked back and watched TV while eating a bunch of snacks. I had a feeling Beretta was up to something but I shook it off. He said I could trust him and I did.

Beretta

"**G**et away from me! Put me down, Z'wan!" Amona yelled out while I had her over my shoulder.

Me and Amona had been hitting it off for about a month. It was a fucked-up thing to do, but Mara wasn't trying to talk about our daughter. It bothered me how she acted like she was never pregnant. So, I stopped trying to connect with her on that level. So much was going on that I didn't get a chance to fully move out of my townhouse. I had been chilling at my crib with Amona and Hope.

I had to meet my connect in Miami, so I didn't leave Mara to spend time with another broad. It was Amona's birthday so she and Lezzi flew out to Miami to chill with me and Pistol for a few days. I rented a beach house with a large pool in the back. I threw Amona into the pool and she screamed because her hair got wet.

"I'm gonna fuck you up!" Amona yelled at me when she crawled out of the pool. Pistol and Lezzi was arguing about stupid shit.

"Yoooooo, shut the fuck up. I don't want to keep hearin' about a fuckin' abortion. The shit is over and done wit'! I didn't make you do it. I just simply told your simple ass I wasn't ready to be a father," Pistol said.

"Y'all niggas stay arguin' about bullshit," I said.

"He's just mad because Piper got a boyfriend," Lezzi teased.

"Sumthin you don't have," Pistol replied.

I grabbed my cell phone off the table and went into the house. Mara answered on the fourth ring when I called her.

"What's good witchu?" I asked.

"Gettin' my hair done. How is everything?" she asked.

"Good," I replied.

"Ummm, okay. Are you havin' fun?" she asked.

"What do you mean by dat?" I replied.

"Just tryin' to figure out what my fiancé been up to. Don't let me hold you, though. Get back to your unexpected trip and call me wheneva you get free," she said and hung up. I was ready to call her back but Amona came into the house. I eyed her bathing suit that was digging between the lips of her pussy. We hadn't taken it there yet but it was tempting. She caught me looking at her.

"We're still actin' shy I see," she said.

Welcome to the Low Life 2

"My shorty will kill me," I replied.

"You don't take me as the type that's scared of pussy," Amona said. She was a little tipsy and high off the kush I gave her. My dick was hard and my nuts felt heavy. I hadn't had any pussy in a few months. Amona was the opposite of Mara. She was quiet, naïve but mature and had a different vibe to her. There was just something I was attracted to at the time but I still loved my shorty.

"Shorty, go ahead," I chuckled.

I went into the bedroom and Amona followed me. She pulled the doors closed behind her then locked them. She wanted me to fuck her but my mind wasn't into sleeping with another broad. I appreciated shorty's company, though. She rolled up a blunt and passed it to me. While I was smoking, she took off her bathing suit and dropped it on the floor. Her titties were nice and perky and she had nice hips. Her pussy was bald and her body was tattoo free. Temptation was a muthafucka because all I could think about was bending her little cute ass over and giving her the business.

"Yo, go put some clothes on," I said, brushing her off.

"You're not attracted to me?" she asked.

"You know you look good but bein' pretty ain't neva enticed me. Why do you want me to fuck you? I'm not leavin' my shorty so I can't offer you nothin' else but three-minute dick," I said. Amona was tripping if she thought I was going to make love to her like she was my girl.

"Three minutes is all I need. I'll do you one better, let's make it two," she said, spitting game. I grabbed her hand and pulled her down so she could kneel in front of me. I leaned back on the bed and she knew what I wanted. Amona pulled my dick out and held it in her small hand. I blew the smoke in her face as I watched her.

"Da fuck you waitin' for?" I asked, getting agitated. That broad was talking big shit and all I wanted was for her to suck my dick. She put her lips at the tip of my head and worked her lips down to the end of my dick. Amona was sucking my dick like she was a pro. She massaged my nuts as she bobbed up and down my shaft. I clutched her hair and slid further into her mouth. Shorty was giving me straight sloppy toppy. I was in her throat and not once did she gag. Amona's head game was crucial, better than any broad I had been with.

"ARGGGGGHHHH!" I groaned when she wrapped her lips around my dick and jerked me off. I was on the verge of nutting so she took me out of her mouth and sucked on my nuts as she jerked me off. My semen shot on her chin then dripped onto her titties. There was a lot covering Amona's chest. She didn't let up, though. She continued sucking my dick until I got hard again. It almost felt better than pussy. The second time, she swallowed everything I had to give her. Amona left out of my room to take a shower after she drained me with her mouth.

****

The next day, Lezzi and Amona went shopping while me and Pistol went to Chulo's bar. It was Pistol's first time meeting Chulo face-to-face. Chulo had a few Mexican bars in Miami and night clubs. The nigga was everywhere and I had to go to him wherever he was at. He didn't have a specific meet-up spot so nobody could track his moves. Chulo was a small man, probably five-foot-four and weighed one hundred and fifty pounds. He was small, but his reach was far. The waitresses were beautiful and Pistol was flirting with them. Me, on the other hand, I wanted to get straight down to business so I could get back home to Mara.

"Appreciate you for comin' out to my second home. Miami is a beautiful place. Maybe you can get a vacation home here. My real estate agent is the best in this city," Chulo said to me. He offered me a shot of tequila but I turned it down.

"I'm just grindin', ya' feel me?" I asked and he chuckled. When you think of powerful niggas like Chulo, you would think he was one of those snobby bossy ass niggas. But he was good to you if you were good to him.

"Do you feel comfortable with sixty?" Chulo asked.

I'd been copping thirty, so sixty bricks was a lot. That meant I had to lower the price so I wouldn't be sitting on it too long, but even with the lower price, I'd still be getting money. Niggas around my way wasn't copping big weight like that. It was usually the out-of-town niggas who copped three bricks or more from me. I wasn't scared of the hustle but niggas who sat on weight for a long time always get jammed up.

"I ain't gonna lie, niggas ain't fuckin' wit' it like dat right now," I said.

"It's pure. Betta than the last shipment. Wayyy betta. I'll tell you what, I'll give you the extra thirty for six a piece so that way if you lower the price it won't hurt your pockets. Lower prices mean more business. I guarantee you'll be back to see me every few weeks. This is what you've been waitin' for, eh? Remember, you don't move backwards. You move forward until you can pay the government to stay off your back. Money talks, and with a lot of it, you will neva have to speak a word, my friend. Everyone else who cops from me has been coppin' the same amount for a long time. What's the point of having money if you're scared to use it to make more money?" he asked.

"Six a piece?" I asked to confirm. I was adding it up in my head. I was giving Chulo five hundred g's for thirty bricks and the extra thirty would be around one hundred and eighty g's. I was damn near giving him all my money but fuck it. It was an opportunity to make more so I wasn't tripping. I had a little stash tucked away just in case I had to take an "L."

"Aight, bet," I said and he slapped hands with me.

Chulo called out to his waitress and she came over to our table with drinks. Pistol and Chulo were cracking up about something but my mind was focused elsewhere. I was thinking about Mara. I excused myself from the table and walked close to the water on the beach. I pulled out my cell phone and called her.

"Hello," her sweet voice answered. I told Mara a while ago her voice was enough to make my dick hard. She had one of those sultry voices like the women who get paid to have phone sex with niggas.

"What's good witchu?" I asked.

"Just came back from the mall. I'm exhausted and my body aches from walking all day. I thought I was one hundred percent better but I'm not," she said. I was feeling guilty because I had my dick down Amona's throat the day before like I was a single man.

"I was thinkin' we should have a private wedding on the beach somewhere. Just me and you wit' a few of our friends. What do you think about dat, baby girl?" I asked.

"When?" she asked.

"In November," I replied.

"A beach wedding?" she asked in excitement.

"Yeah, we should make dat happen," I replied.

I stayed on the phone with Mara for almost thirty minutes. Amona texted me and told me to meet her at some club she was at but I didn't respond. After I got off the phone, I headed back to Chulo's bar. It was lit and Spanish music was blasting throughout the bar. Pistol was getting a lap dance from some thick Hispanic chick while taking tequila shots. Chulo gave me a bottle of Patrón and a few broads got on the table in front of us. I learned a few Spanish words by the end of the night.

****

"Yo, get the fuck up," I said as I helped Pistol to the house we were staying in. It was six o'clock in the morning, and Pistol was pissy drunk talking out of his head. The party was still going on when we left but we had a plane to catch in a few hours.

"Take me to Piper's house," he slurred.

"Nigga, we in Miami. Yo, I told you to leave that shit alone," I said. Pistol was a heavy smoker but he barely drank alcohol. He was drunk by the third shot of tequila. The door opened and Lezzi stood in the doorway with her arms crossed and a frown on her face. She was ready to attack Pistol but I pushed her back.

"Naw, shorty. Don't even pull dat shit while this nigga is fucked up," I said to her.

"He stood me up! Both of y'all stood us up. We all agreed to meet up at ten o'clock and y'all niggas didn't answer the fuckin' phone. Is that lipstick on his face?" Lezzi asked.

"Yo, I'm good," Pistol said to me and stood up. He stumbled into the house past Lezzi and almost tripped over a rug. He burst out laughing and Lezzi cursed me out.

Welcome to the Low Life 2

"Why did you let him get drunk like this?" Lezzi asked.

"'Cause I felt like it. Da fuck you questioning me for? Shut all dat shit up. All you do is run your fuckin' mouth about nothin'. Pistol a man, shorty, not your son. Da nigga can do what he wants to do," I said.

"Bruh, take me to Piper's crib. Matter of fact, call her and tell her I miss her and to leave dat fuck nigga, Delonte alone before I merk him," Pistol slurred. Lezzi cried about Pistol treating her like shit. Amona came out of the room half-asleep.

"What's goin' on?" Amona asked.

"Pistol talkin' out of his head," I chuckled. I was buzzed myself and the situation didn't have shit to do with me. I headed straight to my room so I could get some sleep. Amona came into my bedroom as soon as I stripped down to my boxers and got into bed.

"I was lookin' forward to spendin' time with you. It was my birthday," she said.

"I had business to take care of, plus I gave you money to shop with," I replied. She left out of the bedroom and came back with the wad of money. She threw it in my face and I got out of bed in case she wanted to fight me.

"I have my own damn money!" she said.

"And you call yourself wantin' me to fuck but you can't keep your feelings under control?" I asked.

"No, I call it being there for me like I was there for you when you were stressed about your dead daughter!" she yelled. I wrapped my hands around her throat and held her against the wall as her feet dangled. Her saying my dead daughter struck a nerve. That shit was still a sensitive subject. I squeezed her neck as she fought to breathe.

"Watch yo' fuckin' mouth about dat! I'll break your fuckin' neck in half," I gritted. I dropped her to the floor and she placed her hand over her chest. She wasn't expecting that from me because she hadn't met that side of me yet. Amona didn't know who she was dealing with.

"I'm sorry. I didn't mean to say it like that," she said after she caught her breath. I brushed her off and got back in bed. She rushed out the bedroom holding her neck. I couldn't wait to get home.

Poppa

Four days later...

I woke up to Nika sucking my dick. I spent so much time at her crib that I barely went home to Jasmine. The pregnancy test Jasmine took was a false one. She went to the doctors to get a sonogram and found out she wasn't pregnant. I was relieved because I was going to slip abortion pills into her drinks until she had a miscarriage. I cared about Jasmine but I damn sure wasn't having more kids. I exploded inside of Nika's mouth and she got up to brush her teeth. I checked my phone and had four missed calls from Jasmine.

"WHAT!" I yelled into the phone.

"Rich is here lookin' for you," she said.

"Tell him I'll be there in a few," I replied and hung up.

I forgot all about the nigga stopping by. Rich was a thorough type of dude, and he also merked Shag a week later after I took out Tyshawn. Those niggas were talking too much about the same GMBAM shit after the plan changed. Rich wanted to get money and stay out of street wars. I wanted the same thing. Nika came out of the bathroom naked. She pulled a cigarette out of her nightstand and I took it from her.

"This ain't it," I said.

"Your name is Poppa but you ain't my daddy. Remember that," she said.

The door opened and a voice called out to Nika. It was her roommate, Amona. The bitch was stuck-up and annoying. Nika grabbed her robe and told Amona to come into the bedroom. I smacked my teeth and Nika told me to behave.

"I put Hope in her room. She was exhausted," Amona said.

"Thank you but I keep tellin' you that Hope has a babysitter and you don't need to help me out anymore," Nika replied.

"I know but y'all became like family so I don't mind," Amona said.

"When are you gonna bring your boo-thing around? It's time I meet him, don't you think?" Nika asked.

"We're just spendin' time together. It's not serious yet, but when it becomes serious, you will know about it," she said. Amona looked at me and rolled her eyes before she walked away from the door.

"I hate dat bitch," I said.

SOUL Publications

"Shut up, Poppa. She's like my little sister. That girl has helped me through a lot. She's the only person I can talk to and I never had that before. I don't trust too many people," she said.

"I don't trust her," I said.

"Who cares? Now, go home to your little bitch since she's been calling all morning," Nika said. It was two o'clock in the afternoon when I left Nika's house. I was hoping to spend time with Hope but that Amona bitch always had her during the day. Hope had a sitter in the evening when Nika's restaurant opened so there was no need for Amona anymore. Something was up with that broad and I was going to figure it out.

****

Rich was sitting on my couch chilling when I walked into my crib. Jasmine was at the table reading some type of textbook; she was wearing some tight ass pajama shorts.

"Yo, go in da fuckin' room and put some clothes on!" I barked. She got up from the table and headed towards the bedroom. She slammed the door and locked it.

"Damn, nigga. You treat shorty like dat?" Rich asked.

"Fuck these hoes, bruh," I replied.

"You a wild nigga. So, what's up? You said you had to holla at me 'bout sumthin," he said.

"Nika takin' too long with this strip club shit. I'm tired of playin' games wit' dat bitch, bruh. She got good pussy but dat shit ain't enough to keep me quiet. She's playin' me. Tyshawn was right about her. Dat hoe only wants to fuck me and have me payin' her dumb ass," I gritted.

"What do you want me to do?" he asked.

"Kidnap Hope," I replied.

"Yoooo, what?" he asked.

"Kidnap my fuckin' daughter, nigga. She'll be safe wit' me but Nika ain't gotta know. Dat bitch Amona takes Hope to the park every mornin' so you can snatch Hope away from her. Do not hurt my daughter, nigga. I'm gonna give you the address so you can follow Amona from her crib. Hope's ransom is two hundred g's. If you gotta kill dat Amona bitch to get Hope, go ahead and do it," I said.

"Aight, I'll follow shorty tomorrow mornin.' You do know this shit will cost, right?" he asked.

"I'll give you half now and half lata but I need this to be done ASAP," I replied.

"It's gonna be a big ass problem if Nika tells her son about the ransom," Rich said.

"Nika ain't gonna tell dat nigga because you're gonna tell her Hope's safety is on the line if she does. Shorty got da money so she's not goin' to put up a fuss," I said.

"Why not just rob da bitch?" Rich asked.

"Naw, she's a street broad. Do you think she'll have dat much money layin' around? She'll have to go to the bank to get it; this will be the only way to make sure she does," I replied and he nodded his head. I called out to Jasmine and told her to grab the envelope in the nightstand. She came out of the bedroom wearing sweatpants. I snatched the envelope from her and handed it to Rich.

"It's all there," I said.

"Okay, bet. I'll get at you tomorrow," Rich said and we slapped hands. Jasmine was down my throat as soon as Rich left out the door.

"Where were you?" Jasmine asked.

"Out takin' care of business," I replied then kissed her lips. Jasmine gained a little weight since we'd been fucking with each other. It was because she stayed in the house a lot and only left out to go to school and when we went out of town. I squeezed her round ass as I picked her up and carried her to the bedroom. Nika had a hold on me but a nigga was about to break free. I had shit to do and I was going to do it my own way.

****

The next morning, I was at the table eating a bowl of Frosted Flakes while Jasmine cooked breakfast. I told her to hurry up because cereal wasn't shit to me but a snack. My cell phone on the table vibrated and it was Rich. I hurriedly answered the phone.

"Yoooo," I answered.

"Bruh, you might wanna put a dent in your plans," he said.

"Da fuck type of shit is dat, nigga? I paid you ten g's yesterday. Fuck you mean?" I asked.

"Amona was at the park wit' dat nigga Beretta. She left and now he got Hope. He just put her in a car seat and drove off with her. But peep this, Amona kissed dat nigga before they went their separate ways. I'm ready to send the picture to you now. I'on know what good it's gonna do but you'll figure it out. Just let me know what you come up wit' and I'm down," he said.

"Aight, good lookin' out," I replied. "FUCK!" I yelled out after I hung up the phone and smacked my bowl of cereal on the floor. Jasmine walked over to me and placed her hand on my shoulder.

"What happened? Is everything okay?" she asked.

"This nigga is always in da fuckin' way! Every time I make a move, this nigga is in the center of it. Now I'm back at square one," I said.

"What do you want me to do?" she asked.

"Nothin.' I just need you to be down for me," I replied. She kissed my forehead and went back into the kitchen. My phone beeped letting me know I got a text message. I opened the picture message and the shit made my blood boil. Beretta and Amona was playing family with my daughter. He had Hope in his arm while Amona kissed his lips. I told Mara a long time ago the nigga wasn't good enough for her. He had a lot of bitches when he was just a corner hustler but now he was big time so I knew the bitches multiplied.

Mara just gotta see for herself since she thinks she has it all figured out. She'll come back cryin' to me because I warned her, I thought.

SOUL Publications

Kemara

I went home to my loft after I had a long day out with Emma. She wanted to tell me she decided to go back to Quanta after being broken up with him for months. We also talked about other things except for Zyira and the accident. I told Emma it was something I couldn't talk about anymore. We went shopping for dresses to wear on the beach for my wedding. I invited her and her boyfriend, Quanta, to the wedding.

When I unlocked the front door, I was greeted by candles and rose petals on the floor. Since Beretta came back from his trip, he'd been up my ass. Piper told me to leave it alone because I told her Beretta was guilty of something. I threw the idea out when I realized how insecure I'd become. Beretta knew not to fuck with my feelings, especially during a time when we needed each other the most. I dropped my purse on the floor and took my heels off before I followed the trail of roses. They led me to the kitchen table where he sat. His eyes were low from the weed he was smoking and a half bottle of Henny was on the table.

"What's the occasion?" I asked.

"Your pussy in my face. Take your clothes off and show me sumthin," he said.

On the table was a bowl of cut up fruit, caramel syrup, and whip cream. I took off my clothes and stood in front of him in a pink bra and thong. He got up from the table and was completely naked. I was aroused, shy, and nervous. It was so unexpected and it was something I probably would've had begged him to do months ago. He had romantic moments but he was far from it. He walked over to me and pulled my thong down my legs. My nipples ached and my clit throbbed. He kissed the incision where I had a C-section but the area was still numb. He squeezed my hips as he worked his way up to my breasts. He unhooked my bra and palmed my breasts in his hands. Beretta's tongue parted my lips and our mouths locked. His strong hands massaged my ass cheeks as my pussy pulsated like a vibrator. His finger slipped between my slit and he played in my wetness. Seconds later, he smeared my wetness on my lips then licked the drippings off. Beretta's foreplay was mind-blowing. He was the type of man that had it all: big dick, a skilled tongue, and bomb ass deep strokes. He pulled me towards the table and told me to lay back.

"Boyyyyy, if this table breaks!" I said. He stuck a strawberry in my mouth to keep me from talking shit. I wasn't sure if the table was sturdy enough for Beretta's antics. He spread my legs; something cold and juicy entered my pussy. I knew it was an orange slice because of the smell. I clamped my legs around his head when he licked and slurped the orange slice in and out of my pussy. He wrapped his arms around my legs to keep me from trembling. I snatched the strawberry out of my mouth because I almost choked.

"Ummmmmmm, muah," he moaned while eating the orange slice. My clit twitched and I grabbed his dreadlocks. The coldness of the fruit mixed with the warmness of his mouth was an intoxicating feeling. He put another slice in me after he ate the last one. My pussy gushed and the orange slice slid out onto the table. It didn't stop him because he curved his tongue into my slit and pulled my clit into his mouth. He massaged my breasts and squeezed my nipples while his head thrashed around between my legs. I gripped his hair and rode his tongue. My pussy slammed into Beretta's face like my life depended on it. He knew I was coming again; he slid two fingers inside my pussy and squeezed his lips around my pearl. He pulled me up afterwards and turned me around. He sat on a chair and lifted my leg on the table. With my breasts smashed against the table and my ass tooted up in the air, I waited for Beretta to make his move. He spread my ass cheeks and I felt something going in my anus. I tensed up and he told me to chill out. The only thing I ever had in my anus was one of Beretta's fingers.

Why did he put a strawberry in my ass? I asked myself.

After the strawberry, he slid an orange slice in my pussy followed by whip cream and caramel syrup. I was ready to tell him it was irritating my holes but he was already eating the strawberry out of my ass. From my ass, he went to my pussy and came back up to my ass again. I gripped the edge of the table and bit my bottom lip to keep from squealing. My eyes were dancing around in my head as he munched away and licked me clean. Beretta slurped on the cum that dripped down my inner thigh. He got up from the chair and pressed the tip of his dick at my entrance. He gripped my ass cheeks and slid in; my pussy took his girth an inch at a time.

"Ohhhhhhh, Mara. Shitttttt," he moaned as he gently stroked my walls. He was balls-deep inside of me. Luckily, I took a pain pill an hour before I came home because there was no way I would've taken all of that in the position he had me in.

"Can I go deeper?" he asked.

"YESSSSS!" I moaned.

Beretta gripped the back of my neck and began fucking me like I hadn't given him none in years. I covered my mouth to keep from sounding like a bear. The table rocked as I held on to it. He snatched the whip cream off the table and squirted it on my back. He leaned forward and ate it off as he hit my spot. He pulled my hair and slowed down his pace. He teased me with the tip of him and I arched my back for more. Beretta went in for the kill by giving me slow, deep grinding strokes. I screamed and went completely limp from the intense orgasms. He moaned loudly as he exploded inside of me. The table all of sudden collapsed and Beretta's heavy body fell on top of mine. We made a mess in the dining room.

"I knew that shit was gonna break. I saw when the leg snapped but I wasn't pullin' out. I'm surprised you didn't feel it," he chuckled.

SOUL Publications

Welcome to the Low Life 2

"It took me a week to find this table. It was the last one in stock," I said. He helped me off the floor and told me to take a shower while he cleaned up the mess. His phone was on the couch vibrating when I walked past. I thought about ignoring it but I couldn't. One thing about me is I didn't have to sneak through Beretta's phone. I went through it in his face.

"Hello," I answered and the caller hung up. It was a blocked number.

"Who was it?" he asked.

"A blocked caller," I replied and he shrugged it off. I tossed his phone back on the couch and headed upstairs to our bedroom. I figured Beretta's dirt would come out eventually because it always does. But sometimes I couldn't bring myself to believe he'd do me like that.

He loved me and wanted me to be his wife, so what was the problem? I asked myself.

****

The next morning, I woke up and Beretta was in the shower. His cell phone vibrated on the nightstand and it was from a private caller again. The person hung up when I answered the phone. He walked out the bathroom with a towel wrapped around his waist. He picked up his phone because he knew I answered it.

"What's up witchu? Is there a reason you keep answerin' my phone?" he asked.

"Yeah, it is. I just felt like answerin' it so I could talk to the person with the blocked number. Is there a reason you askin' me about it? Don't I always answer your phone?" I asked.

"Da fuck you got an attitude for? Yo, I swear you like lookin' for shit. Go ahead and ask me if I'm fuckin' another bitch. I know you want to," he said.

"How is Hope doin'?" I asked.

"Good. She knows how to say a few words. I mean, they ain't clear but it's sumthin," he said.

"And Amona is still bringin' Hope to see you?" I asked.

"Yeah, she drops her off to me for a few hours. You wanna come or sumthin?" he asked.

"I'm not ready to be around kids right now and you know that," I replied.

"You still haven't seen Ammo's son?" he asked.

"Not yet," I replied.

Beretta went into the closet and came back out with a pamphlet. He dropped it on the bed and I picked it up. It was for mothers who experienced the loss of a child or were suffering from post-partum depression.

SOUL Publications

"Your doctor gave it to me when they discharged you, but I was thinkin' we could get through it together. I thought wrong," he said.

"You think I need counseling?" I asked.

"It's just sumthin to think about. Isolating yourself from kids ain't right. What if dat problem neva goes away, then what? We won't be able to have more kids. I think we should go together," he said and I laughed it off.

"I don't need it," I replied.

"Yo, whateva," he said with an attitude.

I waited for Beretta to leave the loft so I could take a pain pill. My last refill was a few weeks ago, but I managed to get stronger Percocets from someone off the streets. It numbed me to the pain I was going through. Taking them made me adapt to everything, including the possibility of Beretta cheating on me. I didn't want to think about that or anything else that would cause me to have a serious breakdown. The way I saw it, the pills were helping me to move on with my life. I called Silk and told him I was on my way to see him.

****

"When are you goin' back to school?" Silk asked.

"I'm takin' online classes until I'm ready to go back. Why is everyone up my ass lately?" I snapped. We were sitting on the step in front his building drinking Bacardi mixed with ginger ale. It was fall and there was a slight breeze though it was still nice out. Fall in Maryland was like early winter with a spring vibe to it.

"Bitcccchhhhhh, don't you start!" Silk said and I rolled my eyes.

Denesha walked past Silk's building with a few of her friends. She moved her hair behind her ear, flashing a pink diamond Rolex on her wrist. Beretta bought me the same Rolex a few years ago. It was a special piece to me.

"Denesha!" I called out to her.

"What!" she yelled back.

I walked off the step and headed closer to her so I could get a good look at her wrist. It was definitely my Rolex.

"Where did you get that watch from?" I asked.

"Why? Do you think you're the only one who is fuckin' a nigga dat got money?" she spat.

"Did you get that watch from Darcel?" I asked.

"Darcel doesn't come around here anymore. And if I got it from her, what's the big fuckin' deal?" Denesha asked. Silk got off the step and pulled me back but I snatched away from him.

"Take that watch off!" I said.

"No, bitch, I'm not. I don't give a fuck if you're Beretta's bitch! This is not your fuckin' watch!" she screamed. I punched Denesha in her face and she fell into the fence. The bitch had it coming! Her friends tried to pull me off but I wouldn't let up on her.

"Y'all hoes must've forgot about how I get down!" I yelled, slamming my fist into her face. Denesha pulled my hair and I slammed her onto the ground. She bit my arm but that didn't stop me from beating the shit out of her while she screamed for help. My fists angrily pounded her face as blood dripped down her neck. Silk wrestled me off her and one of her friends hit me with a glass bottle. I pulled out the pocket knife I kept in my back pocket and charged into her but Silk snatched me by my shirt.

"GET THE FUCK OFF OF ME! BERETTA BOUGHT ME THAT WATCH!" I yelled. Somebody took the watch off Denesha's arm and gave it back to me. The initials engraved on the back of the watch had *P.G.* which stood for "Pretty Girl." Denesha knew it was my watch and she wanted me to see it. That's why her and her friends walked past me. I was tired of bitches fucking with me. Had it been just me and her outside, I would've laid her ass to rest!

"THIS AIN'T OVER!" I screamed as Silk dragged me into his apartment. I rushed to my purse on the table and pulled out my pill bottle. I took a pill and washed it down with straight liquor.

"I love you to the death of me but you need help. That hoe might press charges on you, then what?" Silk asked with his hands on his hip.

"Then I'll kill her after my nigga post my bail. I've been too quiet for these past few years and I'm not rockin' like that anymore. I'll revert back to my old ways if a muthafucka test me again," I vented. Silk threw his arms up in frustration and went into his freezer to get me an ice pack for my hands.

Beretta came to Silk's apartment a half an hour later.

"Let's go home," he said, but I didn't want to. I was buzzed off the liquor and the pill I popped.

"I'll go home later," I said.

"The hood talkin' about Denesha having your watch. How did she get it?" he asked. Silk looked at me and crossed his arms. He knew how she got it but I didn't want Beretta to know because he told me to stay away from my mother.

"Darcel robbed me when I crashed my truck. Are you happy now? My own fuckin' mother robbed me while I was stuck in a smoking truck. She took my jewelry, phone, and purse. Go ahead and blame me! I want to hear you say that I killed my own fuckin' daughter. SAY IT!" I shouted. Beretta walked out of Silk's apartment and slammed the door behind him. I told him I didn't remember that day and what happened to my jewelry so he stopped asking because it was beginning to agitate me. I ran outside after him and stopped him from getting into his car.

"Don't make a scene, Mara," he said.

"Tell me you blame me. Be a fuckin' man about it. Get it off your chest or would you rather fuck another bitch to make it go away? You think I don't know you? I know you betta than I know myself. You thought eatin' my pussy and ass yesterday with fruit was gonna take my mind off of everything?" I asked. Beretta looked around because everyone was looking at us. I was loud enough for the whole hood to hear.

"Yo, you drunk. Stay here and sleep dat shit off," was all he said. He got into his car and sped off, leaving me in the middle of the street. Silk snatched me out of the parking lot by my shirt and pulled me back into his apartment.

"You know I'm gonna give it to you raw, right? Bitcchhhhhhh, you have lost all of your marbles. I talk my best shit all day long but you got a good nigga. You ain't the easiest person to deal wit' at all, so you might wanna check yourself before your actions push him to another woman. This whole not thinkin' about Zyira and the car accident is bullshit. I see it, Piper sees it, and Beretta sees it, too. Go ahead and mourn her death so you can heal before you end up on crack like Darcel. Pills ain't doin' shit but slowly turnin' you into an addict," Silk said.

"The past is in the past and it should stay that way. Thinkin' about old shit ain't neva help anyone and it damn sure can't fix what happened," I said.

"Go in the spare bedroom and sleep it off. This is exactly why I'm done with y'all females. I'm ready to call up my new man right now 'cause, babbyyyy, you lost yah fuckin mind," Silk fussed.

I went into his daughter's bedroom and laid across the full-size bed and closed my eyes...

"Ma, give me my baby," I yelled at her.

Darcel was standing next to a cliff with my baby in her arms. She laughed at me as I begged her for my daughter. I was wearing a wedding dress with blood on the lower half. We were in the woods and my burning truck was a few feet away.

"Why do you want her? You thought you could rob people and kill them without redemption? After all the shit you did for Poppa, you actually thought you'd be able to be happy? It doesn't work like that, Kemara. We all gotta pay for the sins we commit," she said.

"My sins are your sins! You weren't there when I needed you! You let Poppa raise me and you did nothing! I want to change and I asked God for forgiveness. Zyira is innocent, take me instead. Please, take me!" I cried.

"It's too late," she said then jumped off the cliff with my daughter in her hands. I ran to the edge of the cliff and saw darkness...

When I woke up, I had tears falling from my eyes and I was lying on the floor. I had that dream every time I closed

SOUL Publications

my eyes. Silk came into the room and brought me a glass of milk but I pushed it away.

"It'll help you sober up a little," he said.

"I'm fine," I replied. He rolled his eyes.

"It's two o'clock in the afternoon. Piper is on her way over here to see you and don't be on no funny shit. I ought to beat your ass for how you carried on yesterday. Got the hood all in your business. They were talkin' about you at the mailbox this mornin' and I had to check those bitches. I threw mop water on Cockroach Loretta," he said.

"You and Loretta need to fuck already," I teased and he mushed me.

"Don't do me, fish. I'd rather fuck a nigga wit' diarrhea before I fuck dat nasty, boiled oyster-built bitch," Silk said. I got up off the floor and went to my purse on the kitchen table.

"I flushed your pills down the toilet," Silk said when he came down the hallway.

"I was lookin' for my cell phone," I half-way lied.

Beretta didn't call or text me. I knew he was bothered because any other time he would've told me to get in the car so he could take me home.

"Do I have clothes here? I feel nasty," I said.

"Yeah, you have a few things here. And you should feel nasty fightin' Denesha's nasty ass. They said she got dat clapper snapper, hunty. Dat dragon breath, power ranger morphin' time hot pussy. Should I say more?" Silk said.

"Naw, I'm gettin' sick," I replied.

Silk found a few pieces of my clothing. I had a pair of ripped jeans with a cute jean jacket to match it. I remembered the outfit because I wore it on a date with Beretta when I was nineteen years old. I also had a pair of nude stilettos. I showered then styled my hair with a flat iron. Lately, I hadn't been into make-up so I only used eyeliner and lip gloss. My nails were painted black, which was the first time I changed the color. I always wore a French manicure but I remembered blood being on the tip of my nails when I was in that accident, so I didn't want white tips again. My jeans fit perfectly which indicated I was back to my old size. I looked better than before but, spiritually, I wasn't connected to the world. I came out the bathroom when I heard Piper's voice.

"Sexy ass, Mara!" Piper shouted.

"Are y'all hungry? I need to eat sumthin," I said.

"Let me go get cuuute before we go out to eat. Damn, this will be like old times," Silk said excitedly.

Piper asked me about Denesha and I told her everything including what happened between me and Beretta.

SOUL Publications

"Denesha been showin' her ass since you got with Beretta. These hoes jealous of you but you fixed her ass. I wish I was there because I would've jumped on her ass, too," Piper said.

Silk came out of the back room dressed in tight jeans and a collared shirt. He had a metrosexual style to him but it suited his personality. It was both feminine and masculine. He wore a pair of cute brown loafers decorated in gem stones with matching sunglasses.

"Where are we goin'?" Piper asked, applying her lip gloss.

"To Nika's restaurant," I said.

"That food ain't all dat. Bitch, I know you lyin'. That overpriced government cuisine fucked my stomach up," Silk said.

"It was a bad night when we went. It was crowded and I heard it wasn't enough cooks in the kitchen. Let's try it again," I replied.

"You payin', shit. I ain't got dat kind of money," Silk said.

"I'll pay for all of us," I replied.

We rode in Piper's Infiniti truck because my car got towed. I had a feeling Beretta had it towed so I wouldn't drive home drunk. Even when he was mad, he still thought about my well-being. I was feeling sad all over again because I knew I was pushing him away.

****

Nika's restaurant was semi-crowded when we were seated. An old school song by New Edition was playing throughout the small restaurant. Truthfully, I was up to something. I wanted to see if I would run into Amona since she worked at the restaurant. Piper and Silk ordered old bay wings with crab dip to start off with.

"You better eat sumthin," Piper said with a mouthful.

"I will," I replied.

Amona walked into the restaurant at four o'clock wearing black and white striped pants with a chef's coat. I got up from the table and called out to her before she walked into the kitchen. She looked startled to see me.

"Oh, hey, Mara. What can I help you with?" she asked.

"I want to talk to you about something," I replied.

"Can it wait? I'm late for work," she said.

"I think you should hear what I have to say while you're on the clock. You don't want me to catch you outside in the parking lot," I replied.

"I don't get where this is coming from," she said.

"Beretta told me all about you bringin' Hope to see him and I want it to stop," I replied.

SOUL Publications

"Wait, you want me to stop Z'wan from seein' his sister? How would that help him?" she asked.

"How is it helpin' you?" I replied.

"Because Hope loves her brother and Nika doesn't want her around Z'wan. I'm concerned for Hope so I'll do anything to make her happy. Look, Mara, I don't know what this is about but the loss of your child shouldn't be directed towards me at my place of work. I'm trying to figure out what you're insinuating," she said.

"Oh, bitch, please! Reverse psychiatry doesn't work on me. I know what you're doin' and you gotta be the world's first class dumbest bitch to think I'm gonna let it slide. Three-minute dick ain't worth it, boo. I know where you work and I can find out where you live. Don't fuck wit' my intelligence and don't let this hood lingo fool you. Beretta and Nika are goin' through a family feud and, bitch, you ain't related, so stay the fuck out of it," I said.

"Maybe you should stay out of it, too," Amona spat and I flashed her my ring.

"He made everything my business the moment he got down on one knee and asked me to be his wife, but you can come to our wedding next month. Maybe you can catch the bouquet," I said.

"Or maybe you can stop feelin' sorry for yourself and be there for him like a fiancée is supposed to be. Women always tend to throw their relationship status around like it holds value when truthfully you don't value the man you have. If you did, you wouldn't be stalking me at my job and accusing me of fucking him. Get some class, Mara. I'm not stooping to your level. You're what? Nineteen? Twenty? You're a child," she said.

"And you're a dead bitch who will be servin' me my fuckin' food like the peasant hoe you are. Good day, bitch. Oh, and cute bracelet. Beretta bought me one almost similar but mine is bigger and it holds more value. Maybe you can fuck him longer than three minutes to get a matching necklace," I said.

"Are we finished? Unlike you, I have a job," she replied.

"Keep fuckin' wit' me and you won't have any fingers to clock in with. Oh, and I want my steak cooked well, bitch!" I spat before I walked off. Silk and Piper were laughing about something when I approached the table. I told them it was time to go.

"What about the tab?" Piper asked, grabbing her purse.

"We ate for free today. Let's go to the sushi bar," I replied.

I didn't have solid proof that Beretta was fucking with Amona but our confrontation was a dead giveaway that she cared too much about him. That hoe fell right into the trap. Now finding out the actual truth from him was something I wasn't mentally prepared for. I was thinking about my relationship while sitting in the back seat of Piper's truck.

I will wreak havoc if he fucked that bitch and take everything he owns! I thought.

Naw, Mara. Your man won't do you like that. He loves you too much. That Amona bitch just wants what you have but Beretta won't fall for her. At least, that's what I hope, I thought to myself.

Beretta

"**M**ake it quick. I gotta get home," I said to Amona when I walked into her hotel room. She called me screaming into the phone about Mara coming to her job and threatening her.

"She's insane! She came to my fuckin' job and threatened me. On top of that, her friends didn't pay the tab. You need to get her under control," Amona said.

"She's my fiancée. What do you want me to do? Tell her to stay away from the shorty I have been chillin' wit'? How does dat even sound?" I asked.

"She's a ghetto hoodrat is how it sounds! The bitch embarrassed me at work!" Amona screamed.

"You can chill out wit' da the name-callin'," I replied.

"So, you're not gonna be on my side? The bitch needs help! Unlike her, I'm not fuckin' for bags, jewelry, and expensive cars. I have a fuckin' job," Amona ranted.

"Mara is a full-time college student. Her man is takin' care of her so she can focus on her education. But fuck all dat, why are you mad? We did some things we had no business doin'. You weren't thinkin' about Mara when I had my dick down your throat or when I had you bent over in my whip the other day," I replied.

I got caught up the moment I started doing sexual shit with Amona. I had just got finished fucking her when I got a call about Mara fighting Denesha. Being with Amona and Hope gave me the family vibe I would've had with Mara and Zyira. I wasn't trying to hurt Mara on purpose but I couldn't avoid the closure I was getting from Amona and Hope, neither. Mara thought I was doing shit for her because I was guilty of cheating but that wasn't the case. I was going above and beyond so she could see I didn't blame her for Zyira's death even though when it first happened the idea crossed my mind. No matter what I did, Mara was focused on me cheating to the point where I went ahead and did it. Mara was more concerned about who was calling my phone than she was about getting help for her depression. All I wanted was for her to show me she loved our daughter the same way I did. Then I had to think about the fact that I held Zyira and Mara didn't so maybe it was just something she could get over. Amona was crying and fussing at me while I was thinking about Mara.

"I'm goin' home to my shorty," I finally said.

"Go ahead, asshole! You made me fall in love with you and now you want to take her feelings into consideration? You didn't give a fuck about her then but you do now? Just get the fuck out! You ain't shit but a ghetto lowlife bastard!" she yelled and I chuckled.

"Be safe and tell Hope I love her," I said.

SOUL Publications

"You're gonna let her control you when it comes to your own sister? Bet she didn't tell you that Hope is her niece," she replied.

"Da fuck is you talkin' about?" I asked.

"Just like I thought. Nika is fuckin' Mara's brother and Hope is his daughter. She thinks I don't know but I overheard them talkin' one day. He's the one who gave her money for the restaurant and Mara paid Nika to hire me and take care of Hope when we lived in New Jersey. Your bitch ain't so special," she said.

"It still doesn't change nothing. I'm goin' home to my shorty," I replied and left out of her hotel room.

A nigga like me was always up on game. I had known Hope was Mara's niece for a minute. Flo told me a while back that my mother had left the club with Poppa one night. Flo told many lies but I knew he was telling the truth about that. At the time, Poppa was getting money and Nika was a gold digger so it only made sense. That was the reason I wanted her to get an abortion when she told me she was pregnant. I knew my shorty and I knew she didn't want to tell me because she thought I was going to leave her, but Mara was dragged into a situation that had nothing to do with her. The outcome would've been different if I didn't love her, though. Mara had mad skeletons in her closet but her loyalty got her far. Her being loyal to her brother let me know she'd be the same for me so I couldn't get mad at that. But, like always, I had a plan. Someone called me from a private number while I was on my way home.

"Yooo, what's good?" I asked.

"About time you answered. Your girlfriend kept answerin' the phone when I called. Anyways, Poppa planned on havin' Hope kidnapped but Rich saw you with some chick. Look, here, Beretta. I need to merk this nigga ASAP. His dick is good but it ain't dat fuckin' good," she said.

"Chill out, shorty. I'm paying you, ain't I?" I asked and she laughed.

"Yeah you are, but he needs to go. I've been actin' like a little weak bitch long enough. You got me up here cryin' and question' him about shit like I care about him," she said.

"Come on, shorty. You know a nigga feels superior when he thinks he controls shit. Keep actin' like you ain't got a backbone and he might feel comfortable enough to show you more. Niggas confide in bitches they think they can control. All I need to know is if he merked my nigga Ammo," I said.

"He's not gonna admit to dat shit," she said.

"You need to pull the right strings. Oh, and send me a picture of this nigga, Rich," I replied.

"I might can send you his address, too. He was in here a few days ago waitin' for Poppa to come home. The nigga couldn't keep his eyes off my ass so I already know I can get it," she laughed.

"So, you said this nigga tryna own a strip club, right? Do you know which spot he's thinkin' about buying?" I asked.

"Not yet, but I'll know more soon," she said.

"Okay, bet," I replied and hung up.

Jasmine was a set-up chick and worked at different motels to scope out the niggas she wanted to hit up. Poppa was going to be her lick until he started talking shit about GMBAM not knowing she was a member. Sniper, Jasmine's twin brother, was waiting for me to give him the word to smoke Poppa's bitch ass. I wanted to do it myself but I didn't want Mara crying on my shoulder because I pulled the trigger. Niggas thought I was bluffing when I said Annapolis was my city.

****

Mara was sitting on the couch with her laptop on her lap when I came into the crib. She rolled her eyes when I walked into the living room. I took the laptop off her lap and sat it on the coffee table. She was wearing a pink lace baby doll nightgown with feathers on it and her hair was in a ponytail.

"You look good," I complimented her as I stared at her pink glossy lips.

"Thank you for noticing," she said and crossed her arms.

"I'm not used to seein' black polish on your nails," I replied.

"I'm tryin' sumthin new, but I'm assuming you want to talk about sumthin because I was in the middle of typing an essay," she said.

"Yeah, I wanna talk about the shit you said yesterday. You straight trashed me in front of a bunch of muthafuckas about some shit we could've been talked about. Shorty, all this shit is new to me, too, so you can't expect me to see eye-to-eye witchu if we ain't on da same level," I replied.

"I'm goin' to bed," she said. She picked up her laptop and walked upstairs to our bedroom. My phone rang and it was Amona calling me. I declined her call and she texted me. She was apologizing to me but it wasn't about that. I cut shorty off because I couldn't do it anymore. We got caught up in the moment and that was just what it was—a moment.

"Yo, do you want me to sleep in the guest bedroom?" I asked Mara when I went to our bedroom. She was sitting up in bed watching TV.

"No, it ain't that deep. Come get in bed," she said.

Welcome to the Low Life 2

I took my clothes off and got underneath the comforter with her. If I tried to explain to someone how much I loved Mara they'd probably think I was a weak pussy-ass nigga. I pulled her closer to me and wrapped my arms around her.

"Can I see a picture of her?" Mara asked, talking about our daughter. I grabbed my phone off the nightstand and showed her a picture of her. Mara took my phone and sat up in bed.

"Wow, Beretta. She resembles you a lot but I see a little bit of me, too. I wasn't expectin' her to have her looks yet. She's so beautiful and she looks like she's sleeping. I carried her for eight and a half months. Felt her kicking, heard her heartbeats, and then it just ended. I complained about bein' pregnant in the final months because I was big, my ankles were swollen, and I was miserable. But I'd do it all over again if I could," she said. She gave the phone back to me then crawled out of bed. She went into the bathroom and closed the door. Mara was in the bathroom for thirty minutes before she came back out. Her eyes were puffy and red.

"I'm sorry, Z'wan. It's just hard to deal wit' it," she said. Mara pulled the covers back and laid across my lap so I could massage her scalp.

"I'on feel no cornrows underneath here," I said and she giggled.

"This ain't a weave, fool. You know I had inches before that hoe Razor gave me them bald spots. It grew back healthier. I think it was the prenatal pills I was takin'," she said.

"I remember dat night. You started fightin' me, too. Yo, you crazy, fa real. Abusive like a muthafucka. I ain't trippin', though. All I gotta do is choke you a lil' bit and give you some good pipe," I replied and she sat up.

"Oh, you think your dick is that good?" Mara asked and I smirked.

"Shiddddd, I know it's Grade A. You know it, too. I had that thing gushing the other day. A few times I couldn't breathe 'cause dat shit was all up in my nostrils," I replied.

"Why you gotta be so descriptive. Nigga, I know my shit get wet," she bragged.

"Stale pussy ass," I joked and she punched me in the chest.

"You know I love you, right?" she asked.

"Oh, you bein' nice now?" I replied.

"Don't tempt me, Beretta. You know I got different bitches in my head that peer pressure me," she said and I believed her.

"Tell all them hoes to come out so we can have an orgy. I like crazy bitches," I said and Mara burst out laughing. She straddled me and pulled my dick out of my boxers. Mara pushed her thong to the side and slid down my dick.

"Damn, baby," I groaned when she rode me.

Mara wasn't sexually experienced when I first got with her but she was officially a beast with her sex game. The type of sex that would make a nigga drool and scream out crazy animal noises. She rode my dick like slow music was playing in her head and she was catching the beat. She leaned forward and bit my lip only leaving the tip in. There was something about the way she fucked the tip of my dick that made me weak. All the blood I had in my body went to the tip of my shaft and made it extra sensitive. She squeezed the tip of me between her walls and her cream ran down my shaft like milk.

"BITCH!" I groaned and sat up as I blasted off inside of her. I fell back onto the bed after I was finished nutting. I closed my eyes and drifted off to sleep...

SOUL Publications

Kemara

Beretta was lightly snoring when I crawled out of bed. I tip-toed to the closet and silently got dressed in baggy black clothes. I put a fitted cap over my head and grabbed my gun out of the safe. After I had everything I needed, I hauled ass out of the crib. I got into my car in the garage at the bottom of our building and headed to Edgewater, Maryland. I found out from a source where Darcel was staying. To my surprise, the bitch was still in Edgewater. It took me thirty-five minutes to get there because traffic was light. I got her address from a crackhead Darcel used to hang out with and it only cost me five dollars and a cheeseburger.

The house I pulled up to was an eyesore. It sat by itself with tall grass surrounding it. The home had dirty Tweety Bird sheets in the windows and I could hear The Temptations playing from inside of the rundown house. I walked up the dry rotted stairs and knocked on the door. The music was turned off and I heard a baby crying and a guy yelling.

"Take dat baby upstairs and shut it up. It's Greg comin' back wit' our shit! I told you he was comin' back," the man's voice said.

Welcome to the Low Life 2

He opened the door and squinted his eyes at me as he tried peaking underneath my hat. Before he could get a word out I pointed my gun at his head and pulled the trigger. He fell back onto the stairs and a white woman took off running but I shot her in the back of the head. There were five crackheads in the house and I shot and killed all of them. I heard a baby crying and it was coming from upstairs. I stepped over a dead man's body and headed up the stairs. I turned the knob to the door where the baby's cries were coming from. A lamp flew past my head when I opened the door. It was Darcel and she was holding a baby in a dirty blanket covered in shit.

"You're not takin' my damn baby. Someone is gonna buy her," Darcel said. She was wearing men's dress pants with a holey T-shirt and off-brand dirty Timberland boots. Her hair was matted to her head and I could see the bones in her chest.

"Give me the baby," I said.

I was happy to see that the baby looked healthy despite the nasty environment Darcel was living in.

"What in da hell do you want wit' my child? Where is yo baby at?" Darcel asked.

"She's dead and it's your fuckin' fault! You took my baby so you owe me. Give her to me," I said. Darcel opened a window and I had flashbacks of my dream. It was like déjà vu.

"Listen here, you little conniving wench. I'm not givin' you her for free," she said.

SOUL Publications

"You stole my purse and my jewelry! You sold all of it and you still want money from me? I'll leave outta here right now if you just hand her over to me. That's all I ask," I replied.

Darcel dropped the baby out of the window and I pulled the trigger twice. The first bullet went into her chest, the second one into her face, splitting her forehead in half. She fell onto the floor and I ran to the window. The baby was tangled in the sheet as it hung from a pipe on the side of the house. I climbed out the window and grabbed the baby before she fell on the ground. The jump was too high so I went back through the window and stepped over Darcel's body. I left the dirty sheet on the floor and wrapped the baby up in my hoodie. She was in desperate need of a bath. I ran downstairs and out of the house, never looking back.

****

I bathed the baby as soon as I got into the house and she screamed at the top of her lungs. Her cries woke up Beretta and he ran into the bathroom.

"What da fuck!" Beretta shouted.

"Grab me a towel," I said.

"You stole somebody's baby? Mara, you lost yah fuckin' mind bringin' dat baby to our crib. You fittin' to get us locked up," Beretta fussed.

Welcome to the Low Life 2

"She's my sister. She has no records anyway. My mother gave birth to her inside of a crack house so nobody will know where she came from. I doubt if she took her to the doctor's. They would've taken her from Darcel by now," I replied.

"Darcel gave you her baby?" Beretta asked.

"She's dead. I killed her and everyone else in that house. Fuck all of them," I replied. Beretta handed me a towel and I wrapped her up. I went into Zyira's room and dressed her in a pajama set we had bought for Zyira months ago.

"What's her name?" Beretta asked.

"Darcel didn't give her one," I replied.

"How old is she?" Beretta asked.

"Five or six months. I'm not sure when her birthday is, maybe it can be today," I replied.

"Let me get this shit here right. You want to raise your sista as your daughter?" Beretta asked.

"Our daughter. I'm gonna write a list of what she needs so you can run to the store and get her some formula and baby food. She's a little thin," I said. Beretta was still standing in the doorway looking at me like I had lost my mind.

"What is it?" I asked.

SOUL Publications

"Yo, just text me the shit you need. I need to put some clothes on really quick," he finally said.

"Thank you," I replied and he walked away.

I decided to name her Zalia and give her Beretta's last name. It was a reach but love was about sacrifices; he'd just have to understand. She went to sleep after ten minutes of crying. Zalia was a beautiful baby. Darcel was beautiful, too, in her younger years and she made nice-looking kids. Zalia had a golden-brown complexion like Beretta with hazel eyes. Her hair was sandy brown with big curls. I sat in the rocking chair by the crib and waited for Beretta to come back.

SOUL Publications

Beretta

I wanted to tell Mara she had lost her fuckin' mind and that I wasn't raising a child that was no kin to me but I couldn't. Mara had a permanent spot in my life so I had to roll with it. I walked into the house with bags full of shit from the 24-hour Walmart. Mara ran downstairs and took the bags from me. Shit was happening too fast. Mara put the pussy on me and sent me into a deep sleep then I wake up to Mara giving a baby a bath. I followed Mara into the kitchen and sat across from her.

"I need the address of the house you got the baby from," I said and she rambled it off to me. I texted Sniper before I hit his phone up.

"Yoooo, what's good?" he answered.

"You get my message?" I asked.

"Yeah, I'm ready to take care of dat right now. You want me to light some smoke to it, right?" he asked.

"Yeah. Yo, make sure dat shit is down to the ground before you leave," I replied.

"Aight, one," he said.

SOUL Publications

"I didn't have time to do all that," Mara said.

"Crack houses catch on fire all the time, baby girl. Muthafuckas won't even notice it. I just gotta make sure you didn't leave no evidence behind," I replied.

"I named her after you," Mara said.

"Mannnnn, get da fuck outta here! What you do dat for?" I yelled at her.

"She's our daughter," Mara said.

"You can't replace Zyira. You think this will change everything?" I asked.

"I'm not tryin' to replace her but Darcel owes me a fuckin' child and that's just what it is. You ain't gotta like it, but you will accept it if you want me to be a part of your life. Otherwise, you can leave. I'm not askin' you for much. My mind is made up, so what are you gonna do? The door is that way," she said.

"She's not Zyira, Mara!" I yelled louder, so she could understand.

"I KNOW! I might be a little off but I'm not crazy. She's not our biological daughter but me and her share the same blood and I'm raisin' her, which makes me her mother," she said.

It was always something with shorty but I wasn't leaving her.

"What's her name?" I asked.

"Zalia Maria Jones," she said.

"Aight, shorty," I replied.

Mara grabbed a few bottles, pampers, and baby food before she went upstairs.

Two weeks later...

"Where is my fuckin' money?" I asked a nigga named Antwon.

"Some nigga robbed me!" he said with blood dripping down his face. I caught him at his crib in the boondocks. The nigga thought I wouldn't find him because he was hiding on the outskirts of the city. I pulled a combat knife out of my back pocket and placed my knee into his abdomen.

"Yo, Beretta, chill da fuck out! This nigga named Quanta sent some niggas out to my crib and they stole your product. Yo, I swear I'm not lyin' to you," he said. I backed away from him because I had heard that name before. Quanta was a P.G. nigga. P.G, stood for Prince George's County which was near the D.C. area.

Welcome to the Low Life 2

"So, you tellin' me this nigga came to Annapolis and took my shit and you just now tellin' me, muthafucka?" I asked.

"I was tryin' to get it back but I can't find dat nigga. Yo, he gang bangin' and it's a death zone steppin' on his side. MMN don't rock wit' GMBAM niggas, bruh," he said. The gang MMN stood for "Money Makin' Niggas."

"Oh, word?" I asked.

"Word, but I know his bitch goes to Morgan State University. I found dat out earlier. My nigga I was handlin' it," Antwon said.

"Then handle it 'cause da clock is tickin', nigga. If I have to handle it everyone is gonna feel my heat, ya' feel me?" I asked.

"Yeah, bruh," he said.

"And clean up this nasty ass crib, nigga," I said when I stepped on a cockroach. I walked out of his crib and got into my whip. My phone rang and it was Mara calling me.

"What's up, Mara?" I asked.

"I'm callin' to tell you I stepped out for a few. I'm at the mall wit' Emma shoppin' for Zalia," she said and I heard Zalia cooing.

"You got on any jewelry, and which whip are you drivin'?" I asked.

"No jewelry, just my Michael Kors watch and I'm drivin' the Altima," Mara said.

I told Mara she couldn't go places without me looking like a walking lick. She couldn't even drive the new Range Rover I bought her by herself. If it was up to me, I'd keep her in the house, but a happy Mara meant a less complicated life.

"And be in da crib by seven," I said, looking at the time in my whip.

"Ugh, you make me fuckin' sick," she spat.

"Yo, be in da fuckin' crib by seven," I replied.

"How about you go to the grocery store for me then since you puttin' curfews over a bitch's head," she said.

"Text me the shit and it betta not be over fifteen items. I'm tryin' to get in the express line. I ain't got time to be standin' there with a cart full of groceries," I said and she giggled.

"Nigga, get da fuck off my line. Love you," she said and hung up.

Twenty minutes later, I was pulling up at Safeway. I got out of my whip and saw a familiar person putting groceries in the trunk of her Navigator. It was just my luck running into the broad. She smiled at me when she turned around and I noticed her pregnant stomach.

SOUL Publications

"Long time no see. I've been tryin' to call you but you changed your number," she said. I changed my number because Amona kept calling and sending me crazy text messages.

"Call me for what?" I asked.

"What do you think?" she replied.

"Drama and a bunch of games," I said.

"I was callin' to tell you dat we're havin' a son," she said.

"By sittin' on a soft dick? Bitch, you must be gettin' high," I replied and walked away.

"Keep thinkin' that bullshit! I told you I get what I want! I'll see you in court in a few months," she shouted behind me. Moesha must've thought a nigga was stupid. I saw her like nine months ago and her stomach was the size of Mara's when she was five months pregnant with our daughter. I know it didn't mean shit but I wasn't the father. Moesha was full of games and was money-hungry. Shorty wouldn't even look my way if I was still corner hustlin'.

Damn, now I gotta tell Mara about this shit although it ain't my seed. She ain't gonna believe me, especially if Moesha still got those pics, I thought.

Welcome to the Low Life 2

I cheated on Mara with Amona a few times but I didn't fuck Moesha, end of story. Moesha pinning a baby on me was going to send her to a grave and I put that on everything! In another week, Mara was going to be my wife and wasn't shit stopping it...

SOUL Publications

Piper

Present day, August 2017...

"**Y**ou look good, Piper, damn. Why you keep checkin' your make-up like you tryna impress anotha nigga or sumthin?" my fiancé asked me.

"Will you shut up? We're already late. Mara is gonna be pissed off because we were supposed to be there by now. You could've waited until we got back home," I replied. We were an hour late to Mara's wedding anniversary dinner, and even though she didn't get married in August, it was the month she started dating Beretta.

"Call your aunt and see what Jr. is doin'," I said to my fiancé.

"Why does it matter? They in Florida having fun. Besides, we haven't been alone in a minute. Let the boy breathe, damn. I keep tellin' you 'bout tryna spoil him," he said. My fiancé's aunt took our son and Zalia to Disney World so the adults could enjoy a week kids free. Beretta rented a big vacation house in Malibu and all of us were leaving in the morning.

"I'm supposed to spoil him. He's my baby," I laughed.

We drove through the gate to Mara and Beretta's mansion. There were only a few cars in the driveway.

"See, we ain't that late. You rushed my nut for nothin'," my fiancé complained and I rolled my eyes. We got out of the truck and walked up the brick steps to the house. My fiancé grabbed my ass and nibbled on my neck while I rang the doorbell.

"Cut it out," I giggled.

"I can't, shorty. I already told you I wasn't stoppin' until your pregnancy test come back positive," he replied. I was ready to respond but I was cut off by gunshots. My fiancé pulled a gun out from the back of his pants and I used the emergency key Mara gave me. Luckily, I kept it in my purse. My hand trembled in fear as I punched the code in on the door then used the key to unlock it. I was ready to run into the house but my fiancé told me to get back.

"Go get in the truck and don't get out until I tell you to!" my fiancé shouted at me. My hands were shaking when another shot rang out. I panicked and ran to the truck and went underneath the seat to grab the gun my fiancé kept tucked away. I kicked off my heels and ran back into the house. Mara was lying on the floor bleeding with Beretta cradling her. Beretta was wounded, too. I looked around and saw a few bodies in the kitchen on the floor.

"What happened?" I asked.

"The nigga heard the doorbell ring and ran out the back door. I'll find him lata, I gotta get Mara to the hospital," he said. My fiancé stepped over a body and kneeled next to the person who was wearing all black and a white mask. He took the bloody mask off one of the robber's face and I dropped my gun on the floor.

"Yo, what da fuck!" my fiancé yelled out.

"How many were there?" I asked while Beretta helped Mara up. I had to make sure there wasn't more of them in the house.

"Two," he said.

My fiancé helped Beretta carry Mara to the truck so we could get her to a hospital. It was like déjà vu all over again when Mara was pregnant with her first child. I sat in the passenger seat while Beretta cradled Mara in his arms in the back seat. My fiancé sped out of the driveway and side-swiped the gate on our way out. I was shaking badly and my heart was beating out of my chest. It felt like I was having a heart attack.

"Hurry up!" I yelled at my fiancé.

"I am!" he yelled back.

"Who did this to her?" I asked Beretta.

"You know who did it," he said.

"How would I know?" I cried.

"Because she was fuckin' da nigga who did this to her! That nigga has been around my house, my family, and my fuckin' daughter! He was like family and Mara fucked dat nigga!" he said.

"It's your fault she turned to another man! It's always your fault!" I yelled back.

"I didn't do any of the shit Mara accused me of!" Beretta yelled.

"Can you blame her for not believing you? She fuckin' caught you with her own eyes!" I screamed at Beretta.

"You think I'd fuck another bitch in a house I share wit' my wife? I'd neva fuck a bitch Mara is friends wit'!" Beretta said.

"Well, it doesn't matter now because she's dead," I said, referring to the body my fiancé took the mask off of.

All I wanted was for the mishaps to stop in our lives, but the older we get, the harder things were. I had flashbacks of the past years and what led to everything that was happening now. We all played a part in the demise of our friendships and relationships over the years. We weren't perfect, but no human was...

SOUL Publications

Welcome to the Lowlife 3

Coming next...

SOUL Publications

CPSIA information can be obtained
at www.ICGtesting.com
Printed in the USA
LVHW05s1946200618
581394LV00021B/342/P